Sir Joseph Pope

Memoirs of the Right Honourable Sir John Alexander Macdonald

First Prime Minister of the Dominion of Canada

Sir Joseph Pope

Memoirs of the Right Honourable Sir John Alexander Macdonald
First Prime Minister of the Dominion of Canada

ISBN/EAN: 9783337188696

Printed in Europe, USA, Canada, Australia, Japan

Cover: Foto ©Raphael Reischuk / pixelio.de

More available books at **www.hansebooks.com**

MEMOIRS

OF

THE RIGHT HONOURABLE

Sir JOHN ALEXANDER MACDONALD

G.C.B.,

FIRST PRIME MINISTER OF THE DOMINION OF CANADA.

JOSEPH POPE.

IN TWO VOLUMES.

VOL. II.

LONDON:

EDWARD ARNOLD,

Publisher to the India Office.

1894.

CONTENTS OF VOL. II.

CHAPTER XXII.

ADMINISTRATION.

1871-1872.

CHAPTER XXIII.

THE CANADIAN PACIFIC RAILWAY.

1873.

CHAPTER XXIV.

THE RESTORATION.

1878.

CHAPTER XXVIII.

PERSONAL CHARACTERISTICS.

APPENDICES TO VOL. II.

MEMOIRS

OF

SIR JOHN ALEXANDER MACDONALD,

G.C.B.

———◦∙◦———

CHAPTER XVI.

CONSOLIDATION.

1867–1868.

GENERAL ELECTION 1867 — TENURE OF OFFICE OF PRIVY COUNCILLOR — RESIGNATION OF MR. GALT — SESSION OF 1867–68 — SPEAKERSHIPS — INTERCOLONIAL RAILWAY — DEATH OF THE PRESIDENT OF THE PRIVY COUNCIL — ASSASSINATION OF THOMAS D'ARCY MCGEE — SELECTION OF ROUTE FOR INTERCOLONIAL RAILWAY — PROPOSED REDUCTION OF GOVERNOR'S SALARY—THE OPPOSITION LEADERSHIP—ORGANIZATION OF THE PROVINCIAL GOVERNMENT OF ONTARIO—JOHN SANDFIELD MAC-DONALD'S ADMINISTRATION.

SIR JOHN MACDONALD has been more than once known to observe that his greatest triumphs were won before Confederation. I apprehend that, in saying this, he had in his mind the extraordinary difficulties which beset his path in former days, when, from reasons which I have attempted to explain, he frequently found himself in a minority in his own province, and dependent upon his friend, Mr. Cartier, for parliamentary support; when he was compelled to undergo the fatigues and responsibilities pertaining to the position of First Minister, without the prestige and authority which actual possession of

VOL. II.   B

that office alone confers. I think, too, that he desired to impress
upon the minds of the younger generation, to whom the events
of 1854, and even of 1864, had become matters of history, that
his title to fame did not rest solely upon the extension and
consolidation of the Dominion, the inauguration of the National
Policy, or the construction of the Canadian Pacific Railway,
however important those events might be. I shall not undertake to give an opinion as to which portion of his life witnessed
his greatest work, but so much is certain, that after Confederation his pre-eminence was more generally recognized than it
had previously been. From 1867 onward, whatever may have
been his anxieties and responsibilities, he, at any rate, had no
rivals. There can be no truer test of a man's capacity than is
afforded by enlarging his sphere of action. Many, who in the
parish council are looked upon as very oracles of wisdom,
quickly find, on mingling with their fellows, that nature never
intended them for leaders of men. Tried by this standard, Sir
John Macdonald's claim to greatness admits of no dispute. In
the province of Canada, while undoubtedly the controlling mind
of the Liberal-Conservative party, he was continually hampered
by jealousies within the camp. But in the wider arena, we
hear no more of rivalries. Here he is *facile princeps*, and is
everywhere recognized as such. The inclusion of Nova Scotia
and New Brunswick brought a Tupper and a Tilley into the
field, and those who in the past might have been disposed to
question his right to the leadership of the united party, speedily
found that the question was no longer who should be first, but
who should hold second place. As time went on, and the
Confederation flourished and expanded East and West, so likewise grew the loyalty and devotion of his followers to the great
chieftain whom they all acknowledged.

The first elections under the new constitution took place
during the months of August and September. Sir John Macdonald threw himself vigorously into the contest, and personally
conducted a campaign which terminated in an overwhelming
victory for the Government. The result in Ontario was as he
had foretold in his letter to Dr. Tupper. He himself was
returned for Kingston by a large majority.* Mr. George Brown

* The Reform candidate was Dr. Stewart. The election took place on the 26th

was defeated in South Ontario. Altogether the Government carried more than five-sixths of the constituencies. In Quebec the victory was equally decisive, while in New Brunswick the rout of the Opposition was complete. In Nova Scotia alone was the verdict of the people adverse to the Ministry. A violent and unreasoning opposition had arisen in that province, and, led by Joseph Howe, carried all before it. Of nineteen Liberal-Conservative candidates Dr. Tupper alone emerged from the conflict. The remaining eighteen, including Mr. Archibald, Secretary of State for the provinces, suffered defeat, not from any demerit of their own or of the Government they supported, but simply through the resentment of the men whom Dr. Tupper had so signally outgeneralled.*

The satisfaction which Sir John experienced at the result of the elections was naturally heightened by the rejection of his leading opponent. Mr. Brown accepted this defeat as final, and never again sought election to the House of Commons.

Besides Mr. Archibald, Mr. Chapais, the Minister of Agriculture, failed to secure his election. He, however, retained his portfolio, and shortly afterwards was called to the Senate. Mr. Archibald, who appears to have taken his defeat greatly to heart, at once tendered his resignation, not merely of his Cabinet office, but also of his position as Privy Councillor. On this subject Sir John wrote him :—

                                                    "Ottawa, October 12, 1867.

"MY DEAR ARCHIBALD,

            "You will see by my former letter of acceptance of your resignation, that you are still a Privy Councillor.

"When in England, the tenure of the office of Privy Councillor was fully discussed by myself with Lord Carnarvon and Lord Monck, and it was agreed that the tenure should be the

_____

and 27th of August. At the close of the poll the vote stood—Macdonald 735 ; Stewart 142: majority for Macdonald, 593.

* "You will have seen that we have carried everything before us in the two Canadas and New Brunswick. Our majority is, in fact, too large. Nova Scotia, on the other hand, has declared, so far as she can, against Confederation ; but she will be powerless for harm, although that pestilent fellow, Howe, may endeavour to give us some trouble in England " (from Sir John Macdonald to Mr. Charles Bischoff, dated October 17, 1867).

same as that of a Privy Councillor in England—that is to say, that, while it is like other non-judicial offices, during pleasure, yet that in practice it is considered for life. Once a Privy Councillor always a Privy Councillor; the only difference being that a Privy Councillor who is not a member of the Government is not summoned to attend the meetings of Council. Thus Gladstone and Cardwell and the other members of Lord Palmerston's Cabinet, though now leading the Opposition, are still Privy Councillors.

"I had no conversation with the Duke of Buckingham, Lord Carnarvon's successor, on the subject, but left a memorandum with Lord Monck on the point. Lord Monck writes me this morning as follows : ' My own wish would be to treat the Privy Council of Canada, both as to title and tenure, exactly as the Privy Councils of England and Ireland are dealt with. I have stated this view very strongly in conversation, as well as in a formal despatch to the Duke of Buckingham, but up to this time I have had no intimation of his views on the subject. In the mean time, I accept Mr. Archibald's resignation of his office of Secretary of State only, he remaining a member of the Privy Council, unless we shall be prevented by some future rule of the Colonial Office, which I do not expect.'

"It is of some importance that you should retain your office of Privy Councillor, because I believe that my suggestions that the title of Right Honourable should appertain to the office will be adopted, and it is a distinction that your family would naturally desire you should have.

"Yours sincerely,

"JOHN A. MACDONALD."

Mr. Archibald retained his portfolio until the following April, at the personal solicitation of his leader, whose boast it ever was that he always cared for his "wounded birds."

Scarcely were the elections over when Mr. Galt resigned the portfolio of Finance Minister, and left the Government. A certain degree of mystery has always attached to this resignation, which appears to have been determined by mixed motives. It is obvious from Mr. Galt's explanation in Parliament,* that

* See *Commons' Debates*, December 12, 1867.

he dissented, on public grounds, from his colleagues in their refusal to come to the rescue of the Commercial Bank, and his confidential communications with the Prime Minister indicate that, while he might subsequently have been induced to share the responsibility of such a course, his pecuniary losses, consequent upon the failure of that institution, compelled him to devote, at any rate for a season, his undivided energies to his private affairs.

[Confidential.]

"Montreal, November 3, 1867.

" MY DEAR MACDONALD,

" I have had the consultation of which I spoke, and I am confirmed in my decision to withdraw from official life until at least I have had the opportunity of putting my affairs in something like order. I will not dwell upon the subject, as it is excessively painful for me to take any step which may cause embarrassment to my colleagues ; but feeling, as I do, that my matters have been seriously complicated by the C. Bank, I think my plain and paramount duty is to consider first what is due to my family.

" I shall be in Ottawa on Tuesday p.m., and will be most happy to give every assistance in my power to whoever may take my place. As, however, most of the work must stand over till after New Year, I trust my resignation will not interfere with the intended course of public business.

" Pray, be so kind as to give a proper intimation to the press. I shall leave this in your hands.

" Believe me, my dear Macdonald,

" Yours faithfully,

" A. T. GALT.

" The Honourable Sir J. A. Macdonald, K.C.B."

Sir John Macdonald had been connected with the Commercial Bank for many years, as shareholder, director, and solicitor. Naturally he was much interested in its prosperity, but, as he explained to the House of Commons, he had, in this matter, to consider his duty as a Minister, and his obligations to Parliament and the country.

The first session of the first Parliament of the Dominion of Canada met at Ottawa, on the 6th of November. As not infrequently happens, the choice of Speakers was a matter of some embarrassment to the Prime Minister. When, during the formation of the Cabinet in June, Ontario claimed and obtained one more seat than Quebec, the latter with great reluctance

yielded, and only on condition that Lower Canada should have
one chair.   Mr. Cartier and his friends now claimed the fulfilment of this understanding, and put forward Mr. Cauchon for
the Speakership of the Upper House.   That gentleman was
excessively unpopular, and the association of his name with the
high office of Speaker of the Senate called forth many remonstrances.*   Mr. Cauchon was nevertheless appointed, and
approved himself an excellent Speaker.

For the Speakership of the Commons there were several
aspirants, including Messrs. John Rose, James Cockburn,
J. H. Gray, and John Hillyard Cameron.   Mr. Rose represented a Quebec constituency.   As both chairs could not
go to Lower Canada, and as the First Minister was pledged
to appoint a French Canadian, the latter was therefore
out of the running.   Messrs. Gray and Cameron pressed
their claims vigorously, but Mr. Cockburn proved the favourite,
and was unanimously elected Speaker of the House of
Commons.

One of the first measures introduced into Parliament, was
a Bill † respecting the construction of the Intercolonial Railway,
the material tie which was necessary to implement the political
union of the Maritime Provinces with Canada.   It empowered
the Government to raise, by way of loan, the sum of four million
pounds sterling, the interest on three million of which was
guaranteed by the Imperial Government.   During the progress
of this measure through the House of Commons, Sir John
Macdonald took occasion to explain the policy of the Government in regard to it, which, he said, had been arrived at after
mature consideration.   He set forth the reasons which had
influenced himself and his colleagues in the adoption of their
plan, and announced that the road would be built under the
direct supervision of commissioners appointed by Government,
for whose conduct the Administration would hold itself
responsible to Parliament.   The only serious opposition
encountered was an amendment moved by Mr. Dorion, to the
effect that the location of the line should not be adopted

---

* A bundle of telegrams on this subject lies before me. The first reads : " Do
you propose to annihilate the old ladies ? Pork does not suit delicate appetites."
 † 31 Vict. c. 13.

without the previous assent of Parliament. The Ministry opposed this motion, the effect of which, they pointed out, would be to lose the benefit of the Imperial guarantee, which was made conditional upon the Parliament of Canada passing, within two years after the Union, an Act providing that the route should be subject to the approval of the Secretary of State for the Colonies. In view of the delays which had already taken place, it was felt that to impose an additional veto on the Government's choice of route would be fatal to the whole scheme. The amendment was defeated by a vote of eighty-three to thirty-five, and the Bill received the Royal assent on the 21st of December, on which day Parliament adjourned for three months, in order to give the provincial Legislatures an opportunity to meet in the interval. Inasmuch as a goodly proportion of members on both sides of the House had seats in the local Assemblies,* this course was found to be necessary in the public interest.

A few days after the adjournment, occurred the first death in the Dominion Cabinet, that of Mr Fergusson Blair, the President of the Privy Council. Mr. Fergusson Blair was one of the old-time Liberals, who, with Messrs. McDougall and Howland, abandoned George Brown in 1866. He was a member of the Senate and an estimable man.

Parliament reassembled on the 12th of March. On the morning of the 7th of April, the whole Dominion was startled by the astounding intelligence that one of Canada's foremost statesmen had been assassinated in the streets of the capital, within a stone's-throw of the House of Commons.

The story of the cowardly murder of Thomas D'Arcy McGee is well known. An Irishman by birth, Mr. McGee in early life attached himself to the Young Ireland party. He took part in the insurrection of Smith O'Brien, and in consequence was

---

* Of the members of the House of Commons in 1867, Messrs. John Sandfield Macdonald, Edward Blake, John Carling, E. B. Wood, and T. R. Ferguson sat in the Ontario Legislature. So also Messrs. Cartier, Chauveau, Dunkin, Joly, Langevin and others were members of the Quebec Assembly.

Dual representation as regards the House of Commons, was abolished in 1873 (36 Vict., c. 2), but a Senator may still, unless debarred by local legislation, hold a seat in the Legislative Council of any of the provinces. As a matter of fact, two Senators, the Speaker, and the Hon. Mr. de Boucherville, are to-day members of the Legislative Council of the province of Quebec.

obliged to flee the country. After some years spent in the United States he settled in Montreal, where he started a newspaper, and speedily became a great favourite with the Irishmen of that city, by whose influence he was returned to Parliament in the general election of 1857. Mr. McGee's first speech in the House of Assembly drew forth enthusiastic plaudits from friend and foe. When he sat down, Sir John Macdonald, then leading the House, crossed the floor and warmly complimented the young member.

True to the national instinct, Mr. McGee began his political career as an opponent of the Government, and from 1858 till 1862 he acted as an ally of George Brown. He was not included in the Brown-Dorion Administration, but, on the defeat of the Cartier-Macdonald Ministry in 1862, Mr. McGee became President of the Council under John Sandfield Macdonald. I have already related the story of the reorganization of that Government in 1863, and the treatment accorded to the Lower Canada members thereof, of whom Mr. McGee was one. In the summer following his exclusion from office, he formed a political alliance with Mr. John A. Macdonald; together they stumped Upper Canada in the autumn, and to their joint efforts is to be largely ascribed the subsequent defeat of John Sandfield Macdonald.

Mr. McGee appears to have taken to Mr. Macdonald from the first weeks of their association. His letters, written within a short time after the break with his former colleagues, show this, and give one the idea that the writer felt that he never could do enough for his new-found leader and friend.* Before this period he had come to realize the folly of his youthful days. He had learned the lesson that liberty can be loved " not wisely but too well," and that true freedom must ever be regulated by authority. Henceforth he grew more and more Conservative,

---

* Thus he writes as early as November, 1863 :—

" MY DEAR MACDONALD,—I feel satisfied, as far as the Catholics are con-cerned, ―― will not get half a dozen votes. I have arranged for this at Port Hope and here, very quietly. I speak to-morrow night in Whitby, which I would have declined but for our friend Oliver Mowat's sweet sake. Here and at Port Hope every one says: 'If John A. exerts himself, ―― cannot get in.' I need not emphasize the public importance attached to that 'if.' Accept my congratu-lations on being free of the doctors."

a habit of mind which his natural disposition made it easy for him to acquire.*

In 1864 Mr. McGee became a member of the Taché-Macdonald Administration, and remained in that Government until Confederation was accomplished, when, as we have seen, he voluntarily placed his office at the disposal of his leader. In 1865 he visited Ireland, and, while there, made a speech, in which he unsparingly denounced Fenianism, and affectionately besought his countrymen to shun all connection with that odious conspiracy. His patriotic and manly utterances on that occasion incurred for him the relentless hate of those whose actions and methods he had boldly condemned. From that hour he was a marked man.

Mr. McGee was endowed with many and rare gifts, not the least of which was his oratorical power, in respect of which, with the single exception of Joseph Howe, he has never had an equal in Canada. He spoke with great facility and happiness of expression, sometimes rising to a noble and dignified eloquence. In the earlier portion of his career he was, perhaps, too much given to sarcasm, a fault which time remedied. He excelled in repartee and in a species of droll raillery, which was sometimes very effective. Two examples of this occur to me. In the general election of 1857, Mr. Cayley, the Inspector General in Mr. Macdonald's Government, had been defeated. It was said of him that, during his canvass, he distributed a number of Bibles in his constituency. Mr. McGee made great fun of this story in Parliament, and poured ridicule upon Mr. Cayley in this fashion :—

"It was a spectacle rare and refreshing to see the Inspector General, the Chancellor of the Exchequer, the Finance Minister of the Province, voluntarily turn missionary and act the part of a colporteur in the neighbourhood of Lake Huron. I must further remark that the good people of these counties seem to have studied the Sacred Volume presented to them from so high a source to good effect. They appeared to have learned the lesson of retributive justice, for, although they accepted the Gospel, they rejected the missionary." †

---

* "Sir, I will say it in the outset, it is not true. I am as loyal as any Tory of the old or new schools. My native disposition is towards reverence of things old and veneration for the landmarks of the past." (Speech, House of Assembly, August 7, 1858.)

† Speech, House of Assembly, March 3, 1858.

Again, in the course of the debate arising out of the resignation of the Brown-Dorion Government, in August, 1858, and
the return of the Conservatives to power, Mr. Macdonald spoke
thus of Mr. George Brown's eagerness to obtain office :—

"Now some fish are not so easily caught ; they require to be
dallied with and tempted and enticed by skilful angling before
they take the bait ; but the late senior member for Toronto took
it at a bolt." A moment later he changed the metaphor, and
continued : "he was in the clouds"—Mr. McGee was ready :
"looking at the bait ?" he interjected, amid roars of laughter,
in which Mr. Macdonald, who dearly loved a joke, even at his
own expense, was compelled to join.

As time went on Mr. McGee's real character became better
known. Much of the flippancy of his earlier years disappeared,
and he was seen to be a man of high and noble impulses. He
was eminently a peace-maker, and it was fitting that his last
utterance in Parliament should have been what it was. The
debate was on the disaffection then rife in Nova Scotia over
Confederation. Mr. McGee closed an eloquent speech counselling prudence and moderation on both sides in these words :—

"We will compel them to come in and accept this Union. We will compel
them by our fairness, our kindness, our love, to be one with us in this common
and this great national work."

What followed is thus told in the words of a writer of the
day :—

". . . A short time after the debate closed, walking in the lobby, he met
Mr. Macfarlane ; 'Come, Bob,' said he, 'you young rascal, help me on with
my coat.' The member for Perth was ready with as frank and merry reply
to the merry salutation—'Always ready to give you a lift.' They walked
down arm-in-arm from the House, chatting gaily together, for the weary man's
work for the time was done. To-morrow, to-day, he was to go home, where
loving wife and children and warm-hearted friends were waiting with a still
kindlier greeting than was their wont. His birthday was at hand, his portrait
was to be presented to his wife, and kind words said, kindly greetings interchanged. He parted from his friend at the corner : 'Good night, God bless
you,' on both sides. His companion turned away. He crossed the street,
received the salutation : 'Good night,' and replied, 'Good morning—it is
morning now,' and never spoke again. Slowly in the pale moonlight he
walked on to his fate, slowly, but full surely. Stealthily the assassin watched
and crept nigh him. The key is sought for, found ; it is in the lock ; yet, ere

he turns it, there comes a flash, a report, a gurgling of blood welling through his mouth, a ghastly wound, and the door of the unseen world stands suddenly wide open before him. The morning had indeed come." *

Sir John Macdonald had driven home from the House, and was in the act of retiring for the night when a messenger arrived with the dreadful news. He immediately hastened to the spot, and, as he has related, was the first to raise his friend's head from the pavement. Mr. McGee was then quite dead.

This tragic ending of his friend's life, though terrible in its reality, was not to Sir John Macdonald a wholly unexpected occurrence. The head of a government has many sources of information, and, long before the fatal night, certain ominous mutterings had reached the ears of the Prime Minister, who repeatedly warned his friend to be on his guard.† Mr. McGee seems to have paid but little attention to these threats. A circumstance occurred, however, on the day before his death, which may perhaps indicate that he felt some premonition of his approaching fate. On Sunday, the 5th of April, he dined at the house of Mr. James Goodwin, of Ottawa, where he was a welcome and frequent guest. After dinner he lay down on a sofa in the library. A short time afterwards, Mrs. Goodwin, crossing the hall, saw him start suddenly from his sleep, press his hands to his head, and cry out, "Oh, my God, I have had a fearful dream." In reply to a question he said, "I dreamed that I stood on the banks of Niagara, where I saw two young men in a boat being carried down by the current. I shouted to warn them of their danger, whereupon they pulled their oars and rowed up the stream, and I fell over into the boiling abyss." In relating this dream he seemed greatly distressed. A few hours later he was assassinated.

Sir John Macdonald was deeply affected by Mr. McGee's death. The following extracts from letters written by him shortly after the tragic occurrence, show at once his regard for the dead and his solicitude for the living :—

"You will have been shocked by the news of the assassination

---

* Montreal *Gazette*, April 13, 1868.

† The postscript of a letter dated February 25, 1868, apparently the last written by Mr. McGee to his leader, reads as follows: "Many thanks for your hint about my personal safety. I shall not forget it."

of poor McGee. His only crime was that he steadily and affectionately advised his countrymen in Canada to enjoy all the advantages that our equal laws and institutions give to Irishmen and to Roman Catholics. He sternly set his face against the introduction of Fenianism into Canada, and he was, therefore, a doomed man. There is great grief for his loss, and great sympathy with his family." *

"You will have observed that Parker brought up the question of your appointment again, for the patriotic purpose of keeping alive the irritation in Nova Scotia. He was, however, compelled to withdraw his motion. It was on this occasion that poor McGee made his last speech; and a beautiful speech it was! In it he eloquently spoke of your merits, and gave Parker a most deserved castigation. Within an hour afterwards he was a corpse." †

"I can quite understand the shock that poor McGee's death must have caused you. Many thanks for your admirable oration on the occasion. Poor fellow! he was just in the beginning of his usefulness. He had thoroughly reformed in every way, and was giving his genius full play. It was arranged between him and myself that he should retire from political life this summer. He was to have been appointed Commissioner of Patents, with a salary of $3200 a year. This office would have been in a great measure a sinecure; and he intended to live here at headquarters, in the immediate vicinity of our magnificent library, and devote himself to literary pursuits. I have no doubt that, had he been spared, he would have made his mark." [Here follow two or three words illegible in the copy.] "were desirous of giving Mrs. McGee an annuity of $2000; but it was of the first importance that the vote should be unanimous, so we were obliged to consult the Opposition, and we found that, to secure their concurrence, we must fix the annuity at $1200. This, however, with the £1000 settled upon each of the young ladies, is quite sufficient

* From Sir John Macdonald to the Hon. Auberon Herbert, dated Ottawa, April 13, 1868.

† From Sir John Macdonald to the Hon. Charles Tupper, dated Ottawa, April 30, 1868. The "Parker" referred to represented Centre Wellington, Ontario, in the House of Commons.

for their moderate wants. His debts, and the encumbrance upon his house, will amount to some $6000. A spirited subscription is now being raised among his friends which will clear all that off, so that his family may be considered as being comfortably provided for." *

The selection of the Intercolonial Railway route through New Brunswick proved one of the most troublesome questions with which the Canadian Government had been called upon to deal for some years. Concerning the termini of the railway there was no dispute, the Imperial Act providing for the guarantee having fixed one at Rivière du Loup in the province of Quebec, and the other at Truro in Nova Scotia, but as to the best course to be followed between these two points there was much difference of opinion.†

In the British North America Act it is provided that the railway should be commenced within six months after the date of the Union. Ere the Dominion was a week old, instructions had been issued by the General Government to proceed with the surveys necessary to fix the location of the line, the choice of which, at the time of the passing of the Canadian Act, had narrowed down to the northern, or Major Robinson's route, *via* the Bay des Chaleurs (the one eventually adopted); a frontier route by the valley of the St. John River, which, in its course, closely approached the United States' boundary, and a third in a more central direction through New Brunswick. The proximity to the State of Maine, of what was known as the frontier line, caused it to be regarded with disfavour by the Imperial authorities, who intimated plainly that it was one to which their assent would, under no circumstances, be given.‡ Inasmuch as the financial guarantee was contingent upon the approval of the Queen's Government to the route being first obtained, this intimation virtually restricted the

---

* From Sir John Macdonald to the Most Reverend Thomas Connolly, Archbishop of Halifax, dated Ottawa, June 1, 1868.

† No fewer than fifteen different lines and combinations of lines had been projected in various directions through the country. Fleming's " Intercolonial," p. 68.

‡ Despatch from the Duke of Buckingham and Chandos to the Governor General, dated July 22, 1868. Printed in *Sessional Papers* (No. 5), 1869, pp. 7 and 8.

choice of the Ministry to the central and northern lines. The central, which had a powerful advocate in Mr. Tilley, representing the city of St. John, was also regarded with favour by the Minister of Public Works and other Ministers, on the ground of being shorter, more direct, and less costly than the northern line. On the other hand, its comparative proximity to the United States' frontier rendered it obnoxious to the objections of the Imperial authorities, who, for reasons chiefly of a military and strategic character, did not conceal their preference for Major Robinson's line. The northern route was also supported by Sir George Cartier and the Lower Canadians, and strongly championed by Mr. Mitchell, the Minister of Marine and Fisheries, in the interest of northern New Brunswick. Thus each side had its advocate at the Council Board. With the Prime Minister the duty of deciding between the opposing parties finally lay. He himself was perfectly unbiased. " So far as Canada proper is concerned, he writes, " you are aware that we have no sectional interests to serve. We want the shortest and best route. Whichever line will best secure the through traffic and at the same time serve the purposes of New Brunswick locally, is the line we will go for." *

Sir John appears to have spared no pains to obtain the judgment of almost every person, professional and otherwise, whose opinions on this subject were likely to aid him in arriving at a wise decision. Among others, he consulted Mr. Sandford Fleming,† then, as now, a high authority in such matters. Mr. Fleming reported that, having due regard to military and commercial considerations, the northern line was, in his judgment, the one to be adopted. In view of this weighty opinion of the chief engineer, which further inquiry served to confirm, and of the well understood wishes of the Imperial authorities, the Ministry felt that delay in reaching a decision would no longer be warranted. At a meeting of the Cabinet held on the 3rd of July, the Bay des Chaleurs route

* From Sir John Macdonald to the Hon. P. Mitchell, dated Ottawa, June 1, 1867.

† By letter dated February 29, 1868. For Mr. Fleming's reasons, see his work on " The Intercolonial," p. 85.

was finally adopted. This decision, agreeing as it did with the views of those best qualified to judge, was received with much satisfaction by Her Majesty's Government.*

Among the Legislative Acts of the session of 1867–68 was a Bill reducing the salary of the Governor General from $50,000 to $32,000. It was opposed by the members of the Government, and particularly by the First Minister, who deprecated the proposition, which, he argued, would be interpreted in England as indicating that Canada did not realize the position in which she had been placed. He instanced several colonies, inferior to the Dominion in size and importance, which paid their Governors more handsomely than Canada proposed to do under this Bill. He gave as his opinion that £10,000 was required adequately to maintain the dignity of the office, and expressed the fear that any reduction would, by lowering the status of the position, prove detrimental to the interests of Canada. Sir John subsequently expressed himself on the subject thus:—

"The only matter that went wrong during the whole session was a measure to reduce the salary of the Governor General from £10,000 sterling to $32,000. The Government opposed this with all their might, but there was a regular stampede of friends and foes in favour of the reduction, and no arguments could avail. It unluckily so happened that the Governor's salary was the only point in the Union Act that could well be objected to, and it was made a handle of at all the elections. Most of the young members had pledged themselves to vote for a reduction, and they carried out their pledges. There is a great cry for retrenchment just now, which originated principally in the Maritime Provinces. They were unaccustomed to our scale of salaries, and Canadian extravagance has been made a matter of daily discussion in the newspapers. I was a good deal surprised to find that Lord Monck was very unpopular among the members of Parliament. Why, I cannot say. I like him amazingly, and shall be very sorry when he leaves, as he has been a very prudent and efficient administrator of public affairs. Still, he seems not to have the power of making friends, and there is a

* Despatch, July 22, 1868, quoted above.

bitterness of feeling displayed towards him for which I was altogether unprepared.   Some of his unpopularity is attributable
to his being supposed to lean towards the anti-colonial party
in England, and some imprudent expressions of his when he
first came to Canada strengthened that opinion.   Godley, his
private secretary, who is supposed to speak his opinions, was an
out-and-out follower of Bright and Goldwin Smith, and did not
hesitate to state his opinion that the sooner England got rid
of her colonies the better.   With all this, I regret much that
Lord Monck is going away.   He has managed the relations
between Canada and the United States ever since he has been
Governor, and during all the American war, with infinite
discretion.   The slightest mistake on our frontier might have
created a war, in the excited state of feeling that existed in the
United States.   I think that Lord Monck feels the passage of
the Bill a good deal, not that it is of any pecuniary consequence
to him, but because the House refused to postpone the reduction
during his incumbency, and made it commence from the 1st of
July.   The Bill has, of course, been reserved for the Royal
assent.   Lord Monck had no option, inasmuch as Lord Elgin
in 1851 received positive instructions from Earl Grey, when
Colonial Minister, to reserve any Bill affecting the Governor's
salary, and those instructions have never been revoked." *

The Bill passed both Houses (the Lower by a majority of
three to one), but was reserved by the Governor General for the
signification of the Queen's pleasure, which was communicated
by a despatch from the Duke of Buckingham to Lord Monck,
dated 30th of July, 1868.†   This despatch, which reads like
Sir John Macdonald's speech to the House, so clearly had the
latter seized the objections to the measure, stated that Her
Majesty's Government could not invite the services of a statesman possessing the qualities necessary to the proper discharge
of the exalted functions of Governor General, if the income
attached to the office were insufficient to uphold in a becoming
manner the dignity of the Queen's representative.   The proposed salary of £6,500 would reduce Canada, so far as salary

---

* From Sir John Macdonald to the Hon. Charles Tupper, dated Ottawa, May
25, 1868.

† See *Sessional Papers*, 1869, No. 73.

is the standard of recognition, to the third class among colonial governments, and thus restrict Her Majesty's Ministers in their choice of Governors General. For these reasons Her Majesty was advised to withhold her assent to the measure, which accordingly fell to the ground.

Sir John Macdonald's prediction in regard to the effect that such an attempt would have in England was destined to be speedily verified.

In November, Lord Monck relinquished the office of Governor General, which he had held for the previous seven years.* He was succeeded by Sir John Young, who had had a long experience in official life, having successively filled the offices of Lord of the Treasury, Secretary of the Treasury, Chief Secretary for Ireland, Lord High Commissioner of the Ionian Islands, and Governor of New South Wales. In politics he was a Liberal, or more properly a " Peelite," and his appointment, at the hands of the Conservative Administration of Mr. Disraeli, was somewhat unlooked for. It occurred in this wise: The position had, in the first place, been offered to the Earl of Mayo, who accepted it. Very shortly afterwards it became known in England that the Canadian Parliament had cut down the Governor's salary in the manner already explained. When Lord Mayo heard of this he was so annoyed that he immediately threw up the office: not, as he was careful to explain, because of the £3,500, but for the reason that he felt the reduction of the salary lessened the prestige and dignity of the appointment.

Just at this time Sir John Young returned from the Governorship of New South Wales. He intended going back to active political life, and consulted Mr. Gladstone as to his constituency, telling him, at the same time, that there was one feature of his policy that he could not accept—that was the

* Viscount Monck was Governor General of the province of Canada, from the 28th of November, 1861, till the 30th of June, 1866, and of the Dominion of Canada, from the 1st of July, 1867, till the 13th November, 1868. The reason for this prolonged tenure was due to his Lordship's desire to preside over the new Dominion, in the formation of which he had played so prominent a part. Sir John Young was sworn in Administrator of the Government on the 1st of December, 1868, and Governor General on the 2nd of February, 1869. He held that office until the 22nd of June, 1872.

ballot. This qualification was not agreeable to Mr. Gladstone, who at once cooled off towards him. The Duke of Buckingham, then Colonial Secretary, was at that time at his wits' end to find a suitable successor to Lord Monck. He had applied to several men of Cabinet rank in his own party, all of whom had declined for the same reason that had influenced Lord Mayo. In great perplexity he offered the Governorship of Canada to Sir John Young, who accepted it. Speculations upon what might have been, if something had not happened which did actually occur, are seldom profitable; nevertheless it is difficult to avoid the reflection that, had the Parliament of Canada not moved in the matter of the Governor's salary, Lord Mayo would not have gone to India, would not have been assassinated, and Sir John Young would probably never have been a peer.

Apart from the affair of the Governor's salary, the Ministry experienced but little opposition during the first session, in the course of which much useful and necessary legislation was passed. Indeed, a regular Opposition could scarcely be said to exist, the defeat of George Brown having temporarily disorganized the Liberal party. Among those spoken of in the early days of the session as the successor of that great man, was Joseph Howe; but the Nova Scotian refused to identify himself with either Canadian party, or to take any step which might be interpreted to mean that he accepted Confederation. The leadership ultimately devolved upon Mr. Mackenzie, a strong and effective debater, who acceptably fulfilled the duties of that office. With a following, however, of barely one-third of the House, including the Nova Scotia contingent, which obstinately refused to take any part in the working of the constitution beyond endeavouring to destroy it,* and in the absence of any "record" on the part of the Government, Mr. Mackenzie was unable seriously to embarrass the Ministry, who had things

* Apart from the question of Confederation, the Liberals of Nova Scotia and New Brunswick were, in 1867, by no means well affected towards their brethren of Upper Canada, or rather towards George Brown, whom they never forgave for coalescing with the Conservatives in 1864. Previous to that date they were acting as one party throughout the whole of British North America, and the Radical element in the Maritime Provinces regarded Mr. Brown's joining the Conservatives without consulting them as a breach of faith. Under the leadership of Mr. Mackenzie, this feeling ultimately died away.

pretty much their own way. It must not be forgotten, however, that the new constitution had called into existence, besides
the Parliament of Canada, other legislative bodies whose actions
required the careful supervision of the statesman having the
supreme direction of affairs. And particularly was this true of
the Legislature of the province with which Sir John Macdonald
had all his life been associated.

On the formation of the Dominion, Major-General Stisted—
the senior military officer in the province—was appointed
Lieutenant Governor of Ontario pending future arrangements.
The new Governor had recourse to Mr. John Sandfield Macdonald, to whom he entrusted the duty of forming the first
provincial Administration. Mr. John Sandfield Macdonald,
an old-time Liberal, whose name we have frequently met
with in these pages, was one of the few public men of
Upper Canada who opposed Confederation. From the days of
"representation by population" and the "double majority" he
had steadily set his face against any interference with the
constitution of 1841. In 1864 he opposed the coalition of
Messrs. Macdonald and Brown, and fought that Government
until Confederation became an accomplished fact, when he
accepted the situation. Mr. Macdonald, though a Liberal, was
not, in the true sense of the word, a party man. Like some of
his contemporaries, he was too impatient of restraint and too
tenacious of his own opinions to submit to the leadership of
any one. Thus constituted, it is not to be wondered that he
frequently came into collision with Mr. Brown, the most
imperious and self-willed politician Canada has ever known.
Both opposed the several Liberal-Conservative Governments
between 1854 and 1858, and both were members of the famous
two days' Administration of the latter year. The recrimina-
tions which subsequently took place over the formation of that
short-lived Ministry mark the beginning of a divergence between
them, which ever afterwards steadily increased, save for a brief
period in 1863–64, when, under circumstances that we have
considered, the *Globe* supported the Macdonald-Dorion Administration. The 1st of July, 1867, found Mr. John Sandfield
Macdonald still calling himself a Liberal, prepared to accept
the new order of things, and at the same time resolutely opposed

to George Brown.   The Dominion Cabinet had been formed, as regards Ontario, on the basis of a coalition.   It was equally desirable that the first provincial administration should be similarly constituted.   The initiative lay with Sir John Macdonald, who came to the conclusion that John Sandfield Macdonald was just the man to undertake the task.   The position was offered to and accepted by him, and a strong coalition Government speedily formed.   Together the two Premiers fought the general elections of 1867, or "hunted in couples," to use the expressive phrase of the Liberal party, which was scandalized by the alliance between the two Governments, whose functions, they held, were entirely distinct.   The result of the elections was almost as favourable to the local as to the federal Government, and Mr. J. S. Macdonald continued to administer the affairs of Ontario for upwards of four years. The relations between Ottawa and Toronto were, on the whole, friendly, though the local Premier's exalted views of the functions and prerogatives of his Legislature, his intractability and unwillingness to take advice from anybody, added not a little to the weight of Sir John Macdonald's responsibilities.   On the other hand, he expected to have a voice in all matters of federal concern affecting Ontario, and was much dissatisfied when, from any reason, action was taken without reference to him.*

So concerned was Sir John for the successful administration of provincial affairs,† that at one time he seriously thought of entering the local House with a view of keeping an eye on its legislation.   It is not surprising, however, that he found this plan impracticable.‡

During the first part of the year 1868 Sir John Macdonald was far from well, and once more made an effort to relinquish the cares of State.   He seems to have entertained an idea, which twenty years later recurred to him, of resigning office, yet

---

* The appointment of Mr. Howland to the Lieutenant Governorship of Ontario is a case in point.

† See Appendix XVI.

‡ On the death of Sir Henry Smith, the local member for Frontenac, in September, 1868, Sir John thus wrote to Mr. Alexander Campbell : " Do you know (this is strictly *entre nous*) that I have some idea of running (for Frontenac) myself ? I want a check on the powers that be in Toronto, and if I were a member of the Local I could make all things pleasant for Sandfield in the Dominion Parliament. This, however, is merely a crude idea which may never come to anything."

continuing to occupy a seat in Parliament as an independent member. Sir Alexander Campbell, in a letter dated February 28, 1868, tells him that he has filled too large a space in the political world to admit of such a course being practicable, and urges upon him the expediency of his taking the Lieutenant Governorship of Ontario, in which position of dignified retirement he would obtain the ease and rest of which he stood so much in need. But between him and that rest many years of care and toil were yet to intervene.

CHAPTER XVII.

NOVA SCOTIA.

1867–1868.

RESULT OF THE ELECTIONS IN NOVA SCOTIA—MOVEMENT FOR REPEAL OF
THE UNION—JOSEPH HOWE—PROVINCIAL DELEGATION TO ENGLAND—
MISSION OF DR. TUPPER—HIS INTERVIEW WITH MR. HOWE IN LONDON—
MR. TILLEY'S VIEWS—SIR JOHN MACDONALD'S VISIT TO HALIFAX—HIS
REPORT TO THE GOVERNOR GENERAL—POSITION OF MR. HOWE—VIOLENCE
OF THE AGITATION FOR REPEAL—CORRESPONDENCE BETWEEN SIR JOHN
MACDONALD AND MR. HOWE—"BETTER TERMS" TO NOVA SCOTIA—
MR. HOWE ENTERS THE CABINET OF SIR JOHN MACDONALD.

WHILE the great work of consolidation was thus quietly going
forward at the capital, a very different order of things prevailed down by the sea. We have already noticed the disastrous
result that followed the first appeal of the General Government
to the people of Nova Scotia, when out of nineteen members of
the House of Commons eighteen were returned pledged to do
their utmost to detach the province from the Confederation.
The first elections for the provincial Legislature were equally
decisive. Out of thirty-eight members only two were returned
as favourable to the continuance of the union with Canada.
While the Federal members, to whom only it belonged to
discuss the relations subsisting between the province and the
Dominion, were comparatively moderate in tone, being influenced, to some extent, by the national spirit that pervaded
the large assembly in which they found themselves at Ottawa,
the members of the provincial Legislature, whose functions,
according to the constitution, were limited to local affairs, at
once proceeded to consider the burning question of the day,
passed an address to the Queen praying for the repeal of the
Union with Canada, and despatched delegates to England for

the purpose of laying this address at the foot of the Throne, and of explaining and supporting the representations upon which it was based.*

The head and front of the agitation was Joseph Howe, a man of rare intellectual gifts, who for many years had been leader of the Liberal party in Nova Scotia. Between him and Dr. Tupper there had existed, ever since the entrance of the latter into public life, a steady and persistent antagonism. Mr. Howe was not one of the delegates either to Charlottetown or to Quebec in 1864, his duties as Imperial Fisheries Commissioner at that time having necessitated his absence. It may be that had he shared with Dr. Tupper the distinction of being one of the framers of the new constitution he might not have regarded it with such disfavour. It is not improbable also that his misunderstanding with Mr. Hincks about the railway negotiations of 1852, to which I have already referred,† predisposed him to hostility to everything Canadian. Whatever was his motive, he threw himself with amazing energy into the struggle which in 1867 convulsed Nova Scotia.

Mr. Howe was, in many respects, well fitted to lead a popular agitation, possessing, as he did in generous measure, those qualities of head and heart which make a man beloved of his fellows. He had long been a conspicuous figure in Nova Scotia, and was passionately devoted to his native province. In addition to these qualifications he was incomparably the finest public speaker, the greatest natural orator that British North America has ever produced. It is not to be wondered at, therefore, that with such a leader the agitation for repeal in Nova Scotia threatened to assume formidable dimensions.

Impressed with the gravity of the situation, the Canadian Government judged it expedient to despatch a representative to England, not to argue the case for Canada, but for the purpose of affording the Imperial authorities full information as to the grounds on which repeal was asked by Nova Scotia. The Ministry abstained from sending one of their own members, on the ground that such action might be interpreted to imply an

---

* The delegation was composed of Messrs. Joseph Howe, William Annand, J. C. Troop, and H. W. Smith.

† See *ante*, vol. i. p. 109.

admission, on the part of the Dominion, that the possibility of repeal was a subject for discussion. At the same time, it was felt that the mission was one of extreme delicacy and responsibility, and that an injudicious selection might be attended with the gravest consequences.

The Government finally chose Dr. Tupper and the Hon. A. T. Galt to represent them before the Imperial Government. Mr. Galt declined the proffered honour. He disagreed with Sir John Macdonald as to the right mode of dealing with the question of Nova Scotia's recalcitration, holding that it should be met in England with the Federal and Imperial argument, and not treated from a Nova Scotian point of view.

Mr. Galt from the first had manifested much interest in this question. A month before the debate in the House of Commons over Dr. Tupper's appointment,* he wrote thus to the Prime Minister : " At the risk of your telling me that my advice is uncalled for and unwelcome, I am compelled, by my anxiety to see the Confederation succeed, to write you about Nova Scotia." † He then goes on to advise that Parliament should be prorogued, and not meet on the 12th of March, nor until the deputation from the Local Legislature of Nova Scotia had returned from England with their answer.

Sir John differed with Mr. Galt on both these points, but was unable to bring the ex-Finance Minister to adopt his views, although, from the first sentence in the following letter, it would look as if Mr. Galt had agreed to undertake the mission and afterwards changed his mind.‡

---

* March 19, 1868.

. † From the Hon. A. T. Galt to Sir John Macdonald, dated Sherbrooke, February 10, 1868.

‡ This Nova Scotia mission serves to illustrate the different views entertained by certain of Sir John's colleagues on the subject of party loyalty. Sir Alexander Galt, though generally a Conservative, was never a party man. He could not be brought to understand the necessity for sometimes deferring his judgment to that of the recognized leader, without which spirit of subordination all party government becomes impossible. Even in the routine of politics he chafed under the ordinary rules of discipline, and the cry of *non serviam* was ever ready on his lips. This quality did not arise from mere selfishness or jealousy, for Sir Alexander Galt was a man of large and generous mind, but was rather to be ascribed to an inconstancy of purpose which was constitutional with him.

Sir Charles Tupper, on the other hand, is a conspicuous type of another class of statesman. Was it in the interests of the party or for the success of Confederation

"Ottawa, March 23, 1868.

"MY DEAR TUPPER,

"You will see by the papers that Galt regularly sold
Cartier about the mission to England. It has, however, done
no harm except to himself. In order to destroy the argument
that your mission was hostile to Nova Scotia, and an insult to
it, as Blake and Holton declared, I carefully prepared the Order
in Council, a copy of which I enclose you.

"The debate was spirited, but is shockingly reported, in fact
not reported at all. It will serve, however, to show to you
how necessary it is that you should adopt the most conciliatory
tone with your Nova Scotia friends.

"I trust you will be able to arrange matters with Howe, and
I shall look eagerly for a telegram.

"I will write you next mail respecting the fisheries.

"In great haste,
"Yours always,
"JOHN A. MACDONALD.

"The Hon. Chas. Tupper, C.B."

Upon his arrival in London Dr. Tupper lost no time in
entering upon the delicate mission with which he had been
charged. He at once sought out Mr. Howe, with whom he had
an important conference. What passed thereat is thus related
by himself:—

"I called and left a card for Mr. Howe (who was not in) immediately after
my arrival, and saw Annand and Smith, but made no reference to politics.
Last Monday morning Howe came to see me here, and we spent two hours in
the most *intimate* and friendly, I may say unreserved, discussion of the whole
question. He met me by the observation that he could not say he was glad to
see me here, but that he expected me, as he knew that, under the circumstances, I must come. He said that if the Government and Parliament refused
to do anything, he intended to tell the people of Nova Scotia that he was ready
to adopt any course they might decide upon. I told him that I considered it
due to my own character, as a public man, as well as to the best interests of
my country, to obtain the approval of Nova Scotia to the Union : that I had,

that he should not enter the Cabinet? He himself suggests that his place be taken
by another. Were his services required in England? He sails by the next steamer.
Would it promote the great work of conciliation, alike dear to his leader and himself,
that he forego the acceptance of a position of honour and emolument which has just
been offered to him? Without hesitation it is declined.

after careful consideration, decided that it could be done, despite all opposition, and had refused the chairmanship of the Railway Commission, in order to leave myself untrammelled and strengthen my hands for the work; but that I was tired of fighting, and knew that the struggle must be most injurious to all concerned. I told him I expected him to do all in his power to obtain repeal, both with the Government and Parliament; but that, in case he failed, he must see that persisting in a course of antagonism to the Dominion and Imperial Governments would only end in the ruin of himself and his party, and be the cause of immense mischief to the country. I told him if, on the other hand, he went back to Nova Scotia and told them that, before entering upon any further antagonism, they had better give the Union a fair trial, he would find the Government and Parliament of the Dominion not only ready to make any practicable concession to the interests of N.S., but to give the public sentiment of the people, as expressed at the election, the fullest weight. That a seat in the Government and the position declined by myself would afford the means of doing justice to the claims of the Nova Scotia party, and that I would unite my fortunes with theirs and give them the most cordial support. He appeared deeply impressed by my statements, and said a great many civil things, but expressed his fears that, if he took that course, his party would abandon him. I told him that, between us, we could rally to his support three-fourths of the wealth, education, and influence of the country, and that I could assure him that he would thus entitle himself to the most favourable consideration of the Crown. The Duke has entered warmly into my views, and has invited Howe and myself to visit him at Stowe Park next Monday." *

Mr. Howe presented the case for Nova Scotia with all the energy and skill for which he was justly celebrated, but his efforts, though aided by the eloquence of John Bright, proved unavailing. As was generally expected, the Home Government absolutely declined to allow Nova Scotia to dismember the Confederation into which she had voluntarily entered. This determination was communicated in a despatch from the Duke of Buckingham to the Governor General, dated the 4th of June, 1868.† It effectually extinguished the last hope in the minds of those anti-Confederates in Nova Scotia who were amenable to reason. Fortunately for the province, Joseph Howe was in that category. Had he been of the stamp of those men who controlled the local Legislature, there is little doubt that the whole province would have been speedily in a blaze, and the fire thus kindled would not have been easily quenched. Mr. Howe

---

* From the Hon. Charles Tupper to Sir John Macdonald, dated London, April 9, 1868.

† *Journals, House of Assembly, Nova Scotia,* 1868, Appendix 9, p. 2.

realized the responsibility that pressed upon him. Aware that everything had been done that could be done, he shrank from the consequences which he knew full well must result from further persistence in his opposition to the established order. Gradually he came to see the wisdom of a policy of conciliation and of compromise. Meeting with Mr. Tilley soon after his return from England, he invited him to breakfast, and discussed with him the great question of the day. He expressed his strong desire for a peaceable solution of the difficulty, but stated his belief that the acceptance of office by a few leading anti-Confederates, without any previous reconsideration of the terms of Union, would merely result in exposing them to the execration of the whole province without in any way improving the general position.

"He, however, led me to understand," wrote Mr. Tilley, " that an amicable arrangement once effected, a combination or reorganization might be made, and the support of the Antis secured to work out our destiny. The rest of his remarks amounted to this : ' Appoint a Royal Commission, let it decide. If that cannot be done, let a friendly conference be opened between the Dominion Government and the leading Antis in Nova Scotia, including the members of the local Government; the Dominion Government to make some proposal for their consideration ; or, if that would be inconvenient, a friendly talk to see if some agreement cannot be arrived at, with the understanding that by-gones be by-gones, and that they meet as gentlemen anxious to find a solution of the difficulty.' Now, you will observe that this means just this : we will abandon our opposition to Confederation, if some concessions are made. This is an advance in the right direction. The reasonable men want an excuse to enable them to hold back the violent and unreasonable of their own party, and this excuse ought to be given them. He told me that the delegates, the members of the local Government, and a few of their leading friends met yesterday, and had decided upon a call of the members of the General and local Parliaments for the 3rd of August, to decide what course they had better take (the local Legislature meets on the 6th). He said, if any advances were to be made, it was of the utmost importance that steps in that direction should be made previous to their meeting. He thought a visit from you, about that time, would do much good, and we all hope that you will see your way clear to come in this direction about the 1st of the month. They will do nothing until that meeting takes place. I cannot but think that a visit from you, accompanied, perhaps, by Cartier, would be productive of the most beneficial results. He did not indicate what changes they wanted, and I rather suspect that the nature of the concessions is of less importance to them, than the fact that concessions have been made. Our future may greatly depend upon the deliberations of the next three weeks. I cannot urge too strongly the importance of your visiting Halifax before the 3rd of August; all here, who see and understand the state of affairs, agree with me upon this point. I am not an alarmist, but the position can only be understood by visiting Nova Scotia. There is no use in crying peace when there is no peace. We require wise and prudent action at this moment; the most serious results may be produced by the opposite course." *

Mr. Archibald, a keen observer of the situation, also wrote much to the same effect, and concluded his letter thus :—

"From all this the general deduction is, that we have here a ' nodus deo vindice dignus,' that, if you can possibly do it, you should come down here yourself. An hour's conference between you and Mr. Howe, and a mutual interchange of views, would do more to clear the atmosphere than anything else. It would give Howe immense power—if he has the inclination, as I believe he has—to control the storm he has raised. Everybody here, whose judgment is valuable, thinks negotiation the remedy, and you the man. With temper and feeling to deal with, the proposition should not pass through a local channel, and, in any event, the effort to settle the matter would be of incalculable value." †

Messrs. Howe and Tupper returned from England on the same steamer. The latter, on his arrival at Halifax, at once proceeded to Ottawa for the purpose of reporting the result of his mission. He found that Sir John had gone to Toronto. Thither Dr. Tupper followed him, and urged upon his chief the importance of his paying a visit to Nova Scotia and conferring with Mr. Howe in person. This advice, coinciding with that already received from Messrs. Tilley and Archibald, was followed, and towards the close of the month of July, Sir John Macdonald, accompanied by Messrs. Cartier, William McDougall, Tupper, and John Sandfield Macdonald, left Toronto for Halifax. This last gentleman was a great personal friend of Mr. Howe. Like him he had opposed Confederation, but when Confederation became an accomplished fact he accepted the situation, and did his utmost to promote the working of the new constitution.

Immediately on reaching Halifax, Sir John Macdonald communicated with Mr. Howe, suggesting an informal meeting, which Mr. Howe agreed to. ‡

* From the Hon. S. L. Tilley to Sir John Macdonald, dated Windsor, N.S., July 17, 1868.

† From the Hon. A. G. Archibald to Sir John Macdonald, dated Halifax, July 17, 1868.

‡ " Government House, Halifax, Nova Scotia, Saturday, August 1 (1868).

" My dear Mr. Howe,—I have come to Nova Scotia for the purpose of

A record of the negotiations which followed is preserved in a letter which Sir John addressed to the Governor General shortly after his return to Ottawa.

" [Confidential.]

"September 4, 1868.

" MY DEAR LORD MONCK,

"According to your desire, I now send you an account of my visit to Nova Scotia and its results.

"When in Toronto, early last month, I received a letter from my colleague Mr. Tilley, who was then at Halifax, informing me of a confidential conversation he had just had with Mr. Howe, in which, among other things, that gentleman expressed a wish that I should visit Nova Scotia and see some of the leading men personally. As the Nova Scotia Legislature was to meet in a few days, and also a Convention composed of the anti-Union members of the Dominion Parliament and of the local Legislature and also of the provincial Government, both Mr. Tilley and Mr. Howe thought it well that I should be on the spot before any action was taken by the Convention.

"I at once proceeded to Halifax, accompanied by Sir George Cartier, and the day before the meeting of the Convention saw Mr. Howe.

"He told me frankly that, if he saw any course open to him by which he could continue to press for repeal of the Union, with any hope of success, that he would do so, and that he had so stated to all his friends; but that he had not hesitated to declare that he would oppose any attempt at resistance to the law, either active or passive, as well as all attempts at annexation to the U.S.

seeing what can be done in the present state of affairs, and should like of all things to have a quiet talk with you thereanent.

"I shall be ready to meet you at any time or place you may appoint. The General has kindly given me up his office here, and, if it would suit your convenience, we might perhaps meet here after church to-morrow.—Believe me, yours faithfully, JOHN A. MACDONALD.

"The Hon. J. Howe."

"Fairfield, August 1.

"MY DEAR SIR JOHN,—I have just received your note, and will wait upon you at ¼-past 1 to-morrow.—Yours truly, JOSEPH HOWE."

" He stated further, that the feeling of dissatisfaction was as widespread and as strong as ever, and the difficulties were so great that he did not see his way out of them.

" He asked me if I had any course to suggest. I answered that the Duke of Buckingham's despatch to Your Excellency precluded you or your advisers from even contemplating the possibility of Nova Scotia severing itself from the Union, as H.M. Government had declared against the repeal, from Imperial as well as from colonial considerations. That it was open to Nova Scotia to press for such alterations of the Act of Union, short of severance, as it might think expedient, and that the proper place to do so was in the Parliament of the Dominion. That the constitution was now on its trial, and that probably experience might show the necessity of reform in some particulars, but that we were bound to give it a fair trial.

" I added that the despatch invited the attention of Your Lordship and your advisers to the grievances complained of, in matters relating to taxation, commercial regulations, and the fisheries, and that we were quite ready to discuss all such matters. That I knew it was contended that the financial arrangements in the Union Act were unjust in several particulars to Nova Scotia, and that the Government of Canada would be quite ready to remove any proved grievance in that respect.

" I pressed Mr. Howe strongly to give the Government the advantage of his influence and assistance by becoming a member of it, and pointed out to him several instances in which the interests of Nova Scotia were suffering from the want of a due representation at the Council Board.

" He stated that he was not at all prepared to take that step. That in the present excited state of feeling in N.S., he would not be able to take with him the people. That some of the more violent were already suspicious of him, and he would be at once charged with desertion from the cause, and thus his usefulness would be destroyed.

" He informed me that there was already a good deal of jealousy between the members of the Dominion Parliament and those of the provincial Legislature. That the former were generally in favour of a moderate course, but that the majority of the local members were, as yet, in favour of continued agitation. He hoped much, however, from the action of the Convention, and would endeavour to get them to agree to enter into a friendly discussion with Sir George and myself; and he advised me in the mean time to see as many of the leading people as possible.

" This I did, and found that while a large majority were in favour of severance, if possible, yet, with a few exceptions, they were not prepared for any violent or illegal courses. Among the most violent were the members of the provincial Government. They had come into office on the repeal cry, and, as it was generally alleged, felt that their continuance in power depended upon the continuance of the agitation. I found a minority of them, however, moderate men, but quite unable to resist the violent counsels of their colleagues.

" The Government affected to consider that our visit there was an official one, and that we were charged by orders from England to make certain propositions to them. They accordingly, through the Lieutenant Governor, informed me that they were ready to receive any propositions.

" My answer was that we were charged with no such propositions, but that we were there to inquire for ourselves into the state of feeling, and into the alleged grievances; and I stated our desire to enter into a frank discussion on the subject with the Convention or with a committee thereof, which had been appointed to report on the best means of continuing the agitation for repeal. We were subsequently informed that the committee was not prepared to enter into any discussion, but would be ready to hear any statements that we had to make.

" The Convention sat with closed doors, but I ascertained that Mr. Howe, their chairman, pressed for a free discussion, as he had agreed with me he would do, but was unable to carry it. He had even great difficulty in carrying the resolution that I should be allowed to make a statement; indeed I believe it was adopted only on his casting vote.

" Although the resolution was not very conciliatory in its terms, we thought it better to accept it and to meet the Convention. I accordingly went, accompanied by Messrs. Cartier, Kenny, and Mitchell, and we were received with sufficient courtesy.

"At the request of the chairman I addressed them at some length, and Sir George briefly. We took the line suggested privately to us by Mr. Howe as most likely to be effective.

"I shall not weary Your Excellency with the details of our remarks, but we generally stated that, although debarred from entering into the political aspects of the question, we were quite ready to deal with the financial side, and invited the local Government to send its representatives to Ottawa and attempt to arrive at an amicable solution of the commercial and financial questions.

"We stated that, so long as they conscientiously believed that the interests of Nova Scotia would be best served by severance of the Union, they had a perfect right to urge the repeal of the Act by legal and constitutional means, and that we could not complain so long as they confined themselves within those limits. I pointed out that meanwhile Nova Scotia was suffering from her interests being unrepresented in the Government, and from the position taken by her representatives in Parliament, who held aloof from all active concern in the legislation or administration of affairs of the Dominion ; and I referred to the course taken by O'Connell, who, while with his followers pressing for the repeal of the Union between England and Ireland, in Parliament entered actively upon their duties as members of Parliament, and gave a general support to the Government of the day, and had consequently great influence in the administration of Irish affairs and in the protection of Irish interests.

"Mr. Howe, as chairman, then asked a few questions in connection with our statements, and we withdrew, every member of the committee thanking us for our explanations.

"I was glad to see that the Convention adopted the course suggested by us, and, in their resolution which they passed previous to breaking up, agreed that their exertions for the repeal of the Act should be conducted in a legal and constitutional manner.

"Mr. Howe expressed himself afterwards as pleased with the result, and said that our explanations had given considerable satisfaction, even to the violent ; and this was corroborated from other quarters.

" The next thing to be done was to induce the local Legislature to proceed with the public business, and not adjourn again, as they threatened to do on the ground that they would not consent to work the constitution at all. Moderate counsels, I am happy to say, prevailed, and, as you see, the local Legislature, after making a solemn protest to save their position with the country, that their proceeding to legislation must not be considered as an acceptance of the constitutional Act, proceeded to accept it by going on with the work of legislation, and it is hoped that they will rise within a week or two without taking any revolutionary steps. I do not apprehend that there is much danger of this, as it is evident that, although the speeches on the floor of the House are very violent, the leading men are beginning to see the necessity of acquiescence. I shall not, however, be easy on that head until the prorogation.

" I had interviews with nearly all the members of the Dominion Parliament, and was pleased to find that a large majority of them are ready to work in harness; but, in order to do this effectively, they must go, to a very considerable extent, with the people, and only come round by degrees.

" Under these circumstances I agreed that Mr. Howe and his friends would be considered by the Canadian Government as *friends*, and as such would have a fair share of influence in recommending to local appointments in Nova Scotia; but I arranged with Mr. Howe that for the present all the more important appointments that could be kept open without injury to the public service should not be filled up, until the state of public feeling would enable himself and his friends to come to the aid of the Government.

" As rumours were then extensively prevailing that the American Government were about to open negotiations for the renewal of the Reciprocity Treaty, I got Mr. Howe to promise that he would proceed, if asked by the Canadian Government, as one of a delegation to Washington to watch the progress of the question.

" Thus the matter stands at present, and I have great hopes that if no untoward accident occurs and the local Legislature is prorogued quietly, the time is not distant when Mr. Howe will be able to come into the Government. So soon as he feels strong enough to take this step I think all danger will be over, as, although there will doubtless still remain a considerable party for secession, yet his influence is such that those who will continue to support him, together with the Union party (which though in a minority is strong in numbers, and influential from its wealth and intelligence), will form a majority of the people.

"I may mention that Sir George, as Minister of Militia, had a good deal of intercourse with the officers commanding the militia and volunteers, and found that a very good spirit prevailed.

"On the whole my report to Your Lordship is, that our mission was much more satisfactory in its results than we had reason to expect; but we say as little about it as possible, lest it might compromise those gentlemen who are known to have been in consultation with us at Halifax.

"I need scarcely say that my communications with Mr. Howe were entirely confidential, and that I communicate them to you as such.

"So soon as the prorogation takes place I am to address a letter to Mr. Howe, the terms of which will be settled between us, and which, though marked 'private,' he is to use among his friends, with the view of inducing them to come to his support in case he or some leading man of his party should take office.

"I shall conclude my long letter by saying, first, that we received most valuable assistance from General Doyle, with whom we consulted in every step we took; and secondly, that although before our arrival an obscure paper suggested rude treatment, we were received with kindness and courtesy wherever we went, both from union men and anti-Confederates.

"Believe me, my dear Lord Monck,
"Faithfully yours,
"JOHN A. MACDONALD."

Mr. Howe's position was indeed one of great perplexity. The trusted leader of a great party, the beloved of a whole people, the father of a cause, he now stood exposed to the reproaches of those who for years had confided in him, of having deserted and betrayed them. From many quarters inquiries came to him from anxious friends who had read in the newspapers that "Joe Howe" had turned "Confederate." It was as though the people of Ontario had been told that "John A." had become a "Grit." They *could* not believe it. Still, they would like the assurance straight from himself. These letters, some of them strangely pathetic in tone, Mr. Howe answered in a kindly spirit, explaining over and over again the position in which he was placed. Thus he writes :—

"In answer to your letter I may say that, up to this hour, I have accepted nothing and done nothing inconsistent with the general tenor of my life. I am dealing with the difficulties around me with a single eye to the good of my country; but let me add that treason and filibustering expeditions, to tear the province to pieces, are not included in my programme." *

And again :—

"Especially ought I to ponder, who have been largely trusted by the people of Nova Scotia—to whom at this moment they are justified in looking for counsel and advice—who cannot escape from responsibility if I would. I hope to live and die in Nova Scotia, and must be careful of her reputation and my own. In all the struggles of the past, for the elevation and advancement of our country, it has been my boast that no life was lost nor a pane of glass shattered. I owe it to the living that this policy shall not be abandoned. I owe it to the dead, who in honour and sobriety fought by my side, that in the autumnal season of my life I shall not go mad and turn our country into a shambles.

"I have given two years to the battle for a repeal of the British American Act, at what personal sacrifice perhaps only I and my own family know. It has rarely fallen to the lot of any man to confront so formidable a combination. Arrayed against us were the Queen's name, the Houses of Lords and Commons, the Governor General, three Lieutenant Governors, thirty-five delegates, including many of the ablest men in British America, the Canadian press, and, until recently, nearly the entire press of England. How I have borne myself in presence of this vast combination is now a matter of history. My speeches and published papers are before the world, and the honourable men with whom I have been associated, who have shared my labours and my inmost thoughts, know well that I exerted during those two years every faculty with which nature had endowed me, to recover the independence of my native province.

"In this case the battle was to the strong; and when I returned from England twice defeated, I would have been justified, as Lee was, in laying

* From the Hon. Joseph Howe, dated Halifax, October 5, 1868.

down my arms; and had I done so and accepted the situation frankly, my honour would have been as untarnished as that of the unsuccessful soldier is at this day. I have not laid down my arms nor accepted the situation, but I am still labouring in the interests of my country, and utterly regardless of my own, to make the best of a bad business, and to recover what I can out of the wreck that has been made of our provincial organization." *

It was indeed time for loyal men to dissociate themselves from a movement which was rapidly becoming seditious. Threats of appeal to the United States for aid were beginning freely to be heard throughout the province, not only in obscure corners but in the high places of the land, within the walls of the Legislature, nay, in the Councils of the Crown itself. On the 3rd of September, 1868, Mr. Martin I. Wilkins, the Attorney General of the province, was reported to have thus delivered himself in the House of Assembly :—

"I give notice now to England and to Canada, and they will hear my voice, that, if before the next session of this Assembly, redress is not given and the constitution restored to the people, the people will no longer submit. You'll hear no more of constitutional and gentle means after that. We'll not be without a revenue. We'll pass a revenue law. We'll send for the collector of customs at Halifax, and bring him to the Bar of the House and order him to obey our law. This will be done before next session." . . . "If these means won't avail we'll appeal to another nation."

An animated correspondence between the Lieutenant Governor and his Attorney General,† which was afterwards communicated to the press, took place over this outbreak. It serves to show the state of public feeling when a man holding the position of Attorney General of the loyal old province of Nova Scotia would venture so to express himself.

This unseemly episode marks the highest point in the repeal disorder. A few days afterwards, the Legislature was prorogued, and ere it met again the adhesion of Messrs. Howe

---

* From the Hon. Joseph Howe to the *Eastern Chronicle*, dated Fairfield, October 24, 1868.

† See Halifax press, September 7, 1868, and Appendix XVII. The accuracy of the above version of the remarks of the Attorney General was denied by Mr. Wilkins. It is a coincidence that the report of the *Morning Chronicle*, the organ of the disaffected party, substantially agrees with that of the *Reporter* from which I quote. Mr. Wilkins' denial was officially accepted by the Lieutenant Governor, who, however, continued to hold private views on the subject, which he communicated to Sir John Macdonald.

and McLelan to the Union cause had robbed the agitation of its dangerous character.

Upon his return from Halifax Sir John Macdonald addressed himself to the task of completing the good work that had been begun in the mind of Mr. Howe. An interesting correspondence between the two leaders took place,* that illustrates the skill with which Sir John gradually brought his great opponent to realize the wisdom and patriotism of the course he urged, and depicts the process of thought by which Mr. Howe was led to this conclusion.

The details of the readjustment of the financial relations between the Dominion and Nova Scotia, popularly known as the "Better Terms," were discussed and agreed upon in a correspondence which took place during this period between Mr. Rose, the Finance Minister of Canada, and Messrs. Howe and McLelan.†

This having been effected, no further reason for delay existed, and, on the 30th of January, 1869, Joseph Howe entered the Cabinet of Sir John Macdonald as President of the Privy Council.

---

* See Appendix XVIII.

† See *Sessional Papers*, No. 9, vol. ii., 1869. The "Better Terms" were sanctioned by Parliament in the session of 1869 (32 & 33 Vict., c. 2).

CHAPTER XVIII.

THE ACQUISITION OF THE NORTH-WEST.

1857–1870.

GLANCE AT PAST NEGOTIATIONS—NATURE OF HUDSON'S BAY COMPANY'S CLAIM—RUPERT'S LAND—RED RIVER SETTLEMENT—AGREEMENT FOR TRANSFER ARRIVED AT WITH COMPANY—HON. WILLIAM MCDOUGALL APPOINTED LIEUTENANT GOVERNOR—HIS ABORTIVE ATTEMPT TO ENTER THE TERRITORY—REVOLT OF THE HALF-BREEDS—MISSION OF BISHOP TACHÉ—MURDER OF SCOTT—MILITARY EXPEDITION TO FORT GARRY—MANITOBA ACT.

THE framers of the Act uniting Canada, Nova Scotia, and New Brunswick, in making provision for the admittance of Rupert's Land, showed themselves not unmindful of the fact that, adjacent to the new Dominion, there lay a vast extent of British territory, the incorporation of which was essential to the completion of the scheme of Confederation.

The acquisition of this territory had long been contemplated by Canada, though prior to 1867 the question could scarcely be said to have advanced beyond the contemplative stage. In 1857, as we have seen, the Canadian Government sent a representative, in the person of Chief Justice Draper, to England for the purpose of watching the inquiry which took place in that year, before a committee of the House of Commons, into the claims of the Hudson's Bay Company to the North-West. That committee, which included such eminent personages as Lord John Russell, the late Lord Derby, and Mr. Gladstone, reported to the effect that terms should be agreed upon between the Company and the Imperial and Canadian Governments, in order that the territory might be made available for settlement.

On the 22nd of January, 1858,[*] the Colonial Minister addressed a despatch to the Canadian Government, inviting their consideration of certain branches of this important subject, including the question of the boundary between Canada and the Company's possessions. To this despatch both branches of the Legislature replied by an address[†] to Her Majesty, stating that, in their opinion, the only mode of arriving at a satisfactory settlement was by referring the questions of the validity of the Company's charter, and the boundary of Canada on the north and west, to the Judicial Committee of the Privy Council. To this proposition the Hudson's Bay Company would not agree. Subsequent proposals were made during 1858 and 1859 by the Imperial Government to the Company and rejected. For some years thereafter matters remained in abeyance.

In 1863–4 negotiations for ceding to the Crown the territorial claims of the Hudson's Bay Company took place between the Colonial Minister and the Company, which led to the latter offering to accept one million sterling as full payment of all their territorial and trading claims east of the Rocky Mountains. The Hon. George Brown, at that time a member of the Government of Canada, was in England, commissioned to discuss this question. He pointed out to the Colonial Secretary the unreasonableness of such a proposal, at the same time advocating the expediency of securing, without delay, the extinction of the Company's claims. Mr. Brown further contended that the cost of abolishing this huge monopoly should not fall upon the people of Canada, who had neither created nor recognized it, and added that the Canadian Government would be prepared to assume the duty and expense of opening up communication with the country, and establishing a form of Government therein.

In 1865, the delegation which visited England on the subject of Confederation, again brought up the question of the North-West Territory, and urged upon Her Majesty's Ministers the desirableness of negotiating with the Hudson's Bay Company for its acquisition by Canada. In both these instances the efforts of the Canadian Government were unattended by any practical result, and the first day of July, 1867, saw the

---

[*] See Appendix No. 3, *Journals, House of Assembly,* 1858.
[†] See *Journals, House of Assembly,* 1858, pp. 1028–1029.

question in pretty much the same position as it had occupied twenty years before.

It may perhaps conduce to a clearer understanding of this subject briefly to inquire what the pretensions of the Company really were in respect to the North-West, and what was the condition of the country to which they laid claim.

The whole of British North America was divided, for the purposes of the Company, into four departments: the Western, the Northern, the Southern, and the Montreal. Speaking generally, the first-named comprised the country to-day known as British Columbia; the Northern, the territory lying between the Rocky Mountains and the 90th degree of west longitude; the Southern, the region east of the 90th degree, and north of the province of Canada, which latter formed the Montreal department. The Northern, Southern, and Western divisions were so named altogether with reference to the geographical position in which they stood to Hudson's Bay itself. At no time were they all claimed by the Company, which contented itself with asserting the ownership of such territory only as was watered by streams flowing into Hudson's Bay. In the Northern department (with which we are specially concerned) the height of land separating the waters flowing into the Arctic Ocean from those falling into Hudson's Bay begins at Mount Hooker, near the head waters of the Athabasca, and trends north-eastward towards the Melville Peninsula. The whole extent of country lying south of this line, and as far as the United States boundary, and east to the 90th degree of longitude, was styled Rupert's Land, over which the Company asserted rights of proprietorship, exclusive trade, taxation, and government.*

Towards the region lying to the north and west of Rupert's Land, indifferently spoken of as the North-West Territory and the Indian Territory, the Hudson's Bay Company occupied a different relation. Under the provisions of the Imperial Act, 1 and 2 Geo. IV., c. 66, the Company was granted a monopoly of trade with the Indians of that region for twenty-one years. This licence was renewed for a further period of twenty-one

---

* In order to appreciate the magnitude of this claim, it is only necessary to bear in mind that the waters of the Bow River which wash the base of the Rocky Mountains flow ultimately into Hudson's Bay.

years by a Crown grant, dated 30th of May, 1838. After its expiry, in 1859, the Hudson's Bay Company possessed no exclusive privileges in the North-West Territory, nor did they assert any. Traders were free to come and go as they chose, but the remoteness of the country and the difficulty of access rendered this whole region a veritable *terra incognita.* To Canada it was practically inaccessible, and, so long as the Company's claim to the intervening territory held good, entirely useless.

Beyond the fact that the Canadian courts of justice were invested with a general jurisdiction over the whole country *— a jurisdiction which was very rarely exercised—the North-West Territory appears to have been entirely ignored, alike by England and Canada. Without law, government, or administration of any kind, it lay far beyond the reach of those civilizing influences to which it is only now beginning to respond.

A somewhat better condition of things prevailed in Rupert's Land, the affairs of which were administered by the chief officer of the Hudson's Bay Company, styled the Governor, assisted by a Council of sixteen factors, who were practically nominated by himself. In this local Governor and Council was vested the executive power, derived from the Governor and Company in London. Justice was administered by a law officer of the Company, called the Recorder,† as nearly in accordance with the laws of England as circumstances would permit.

Besides these divisions of the North-West Territory and Rupert's Land, there existed a third, or rather a subdivision of the second, namely, the Red River Settlement, which was founded by the Earl of Selkirk in 1811, on lands purchased from the Hudson's Bay Company, which the Company subsequently bought back from Lord Selkirk's heirs. The Red River Settlement, known also as Assiniboia, comprised the country lying within a radius of fifty miles from the confluence of the Assiniboine and Red rivers—that is to say, the site of the present city of Winnipeg, where stood Fort Garry. This little settlement, containing about ten thousand persons, red, white,

---

* By the Imperial Acts, 43 Geo. III., c. 138, and 1 & 2 Geo. IV., c. 66.

† The Recorder exercised jurisdiction over all matters, civil and criminal. The Court of Queen's Bench of Lower Canada had concurrent jurisdiction.

and mixed, was, both ecclesiastically and civilly, the centre of Rupert's Land. Here were the cathedral churches of the Roman Catholic Bishop of St. Boniface, and of the Anglican Bishop of Rupert's Land. Here resided the Governor; for this tiny colony was blessed with Home Rule, possessing, as it did, a Governor of its own,* who held a commission direct from the Company in London, assisted by a local Council, which was composed of ten or twelve of the leading residents, also nominated by the Company. Here, too, the Recorder, or judge, held his court, and here the criminals of the district were confined.

The population of Rupert's Land was made up of Hudson's Bay officials, who were chiefly Scotch, the descendants of Lord Selkirk's hardy companions, and half-breeds, both Scotch and French—the latter a simple, ignorant people, who chafed at times even under the mild, paternal sway of the Hudson's Bay Company, and viewed, with a jealous apprehension, born of complete isolation from their fellow-beings, any step which tended to bring them into communication with the outside world.

Such was the position of affairs in the North-West previous to Confederation.† The exclusive claims of the Company in regard to it were not admitted by Canada, which periodically disputed their validity. At the same time, the question, viewed simply as an extension of our borders, had not come to be regarded as one of practical interest, it being very generally felt that, so long as Upper Canada contained a large proportion of its best lands available for settlement, any acquisition of new territory was not immediately desirable.

Certain far-reaching minds, however, saw in the question something more than the mere multiplication of Canadian farms. They realized the importance to the maintenance of British rule on this continent, of the route to the Pacific

---

* This officer was distinct from the Governor of Rupert's Land. Sometimes, however, as in the case of Sir Francis Johnson, the late Chief Justice of the Province of Quebec, one person was at the same time Governor of Assiniboia and Recorder of Rupert's Land.

† See evidence of Sir George Simpson before a select committee of the House of Commons, *Imp. Parliamentary Papers,* Reports from Committees, 1857, sess. 2, vol. xv. Also see sketch of the North-West of America by Mgr. Taché, Bishop of St. Boniface, 1868; also Appendix No. 17 to *Journals, House of Assembly, Canada,* 1857, vol. xv.

being secured. Thus Sir John Macdonald, writing on the 27th of March, 1865,* says :—

"We have carried the scheme (Confederation) through both Houses by majorities of about 3 to 1. We have voted a million of dollars for permanent defences, and we send a mission to England to 'take stock' of the situation, to ascertain exactly where we are in our relations with the Home Government, and to concert measures in case of war, which, on this side of the water, we think imminent. Should nothing prevent, the mission will sail on the 12th April, and will be composed of Cartier, Galt, Brown, and myself. We shall have every opportunity of talking the subject of the North-West over with you. My own opinions are unchanged. If Canada is to remain a country separate from the United States, it is of great importance to her that they (the United States) should not get behind us by right or by force, and intercept the route to the Pacific."

But not even Sir John Macdonald in 1865 realized the value of that country otherwise than as a highway to the Pacific, for he continues :—

"But in any other point of view, it seems to me that that country is of no present value to Canada. We have unoccupied land enough to absorb the immigration for many years, and the opening up of the Saskatchewan would do to Canada what the prairie lands of Illinois are doing now—drain away our youth and strength."

Yet mark the progressive nature of his mind. Less than three years after he had penned the above lines, we find him writing as follows :—

"The Hudson's Bay question must soon be settled ; the rapid march of events and the increase of population on this continent, will compel England and Canada to come to some arrangement respecting that immense country. We shall ventilate the subject during the ensuing session of Parliament, which commences on the 6th of November, and shall be able to judge what the feeling of Parliament is." †

On the 4th of December, 1867, Mr. McDougall introduced into

---

* To Mr. (now Sir) E. W. Watkin.

† From Sir John Macdonald to Mr. Charles Bischoff, dated Ottawa, October 17, 1867.

the House of Commons a series of resolutions, upon which an address to the Queen was subsequently based, praying Her Majesty to unite Rupert's Land and the North-Western Territory with Canada. In the course of the debate upon these resolutions, Sir John Macdonald thus addressed the House:—

" It is imperative to find a broad country for the expansion of our adventurous youth, who are not satisfied to look here and there for an isolated tract fit for settlement. It has consequently always been a political cry in Western Canada that this country must be obtained; no sentimental cry either, but one eminently practical—a cry expressive both of principle and interest. If this country is to remain British, it is only by being included in the British North American scheme; and, in addition to the necessity which we recognize, with a stronger power in our front and flank, of extending over the whole of the British possessions here, the just and beneficent institutions of Government which we ourselves enjoy, we are also swayed by the interested object of finding fresh lands for the outlet of our adolescent population. There is no use in saying that we have enough land already. The area of the first thirteen states was sufficient to contain the population of the entire Republic, and yet the tendency of the people has been ever and continuously westward. There the reading of the Scripture precept has been: 'Train up a child in the way he should go, and the way he goes is west.' If we are to refrain from action now, we cannot be surprised to find a foreign power established to the west of us. It has been said that England desires to get rid of us. This I deny. It has been said that under the influence of new principles of universal brotherhood, the old doctrines of love of country and nationality are becoming old-fashioned and effete; but such is not the opinion of the Government of England, of the Parliament of England, or of the people of England. It is not the feeling of England that her dominions are too large already ; and we have the pledge of England that, when a shot is fired against us, we shall be defended by the whole might of her Empire. With such assurances what have we to fear ? If the country was offered to us free, should we hesitate to obtain the extension westward we so much require ? Should we be deterred, then, by this

Hudson's Bay bug-bear of a claim which, if well-founded, might be disposed of within moderate limits ? If offered to the United States—the recent purchasers of a tract of ice adjoining—can we doubt that they would consent to pay for it an amount equal to the whole debt of Canada four times over ? It was but the absorbing interest of the late inter-necine war that prevented the country from having been over-run already." |

How well do the above utterances illustrate the leading thought that was ever present in Sir John Macdonald's mind. True it is that, in the interval between 1865 and 1867, he had come to see that the speedy colonization of the North-West would not prove an injury, but, on the contrary, would promote the development of Canada. Further information had imparted new light. But, in 1867, his paramount idea was what it had been in 1865—the idea which ran through all his public utterances, whether made in youth, manhood, or old age. No matter on what subject he spoke, it was always the same thing —the maintenance of British rule, the extension of the British Empire, the advantages of British connection. To fix deep the foundations of England's dominion upon this continent, to cultivate a spirit of loyalty to the Crown and a feeling of oneness with the motherland, to make men realize that they did not cease to be Canadians by being British subjects—nay, that the only way in which they could continue to be Canadians was by remaining British subjects,—these were the objects for which Sir John Macdonald unceasingly strove.

The address went home, and was duly acknowledged in the sense indicated in the following letter from Sir John to Mr. Cartier :—

"[Confidential.]

"Ottawa, February 10, 1868.

"MY DEAR CARTIER,

"I send you a note that I received on Saturday night from Lord Monck, which speaks for itself. I would send you the Duke's letter, only that Lord Monck, as you see, wants it back. It is marked 'private and confidential,' and states that the Hudson's Bay resolutions would be before the Cabinet on the next Tuesday, the letter being dated the 23rd January, and that he hopes to be able to answer during the week. He says it is well that Lord Monck should know that the legal investigation, which has been made by the law officers of the Colonial Office and the law officers of the Crown, has resulted in so decisive a conclusion in favour of the rights and powers of the Hudson's Bay Company, that it will, in his opinion, be found impossible to vest any powers in Canada over the Territory without an Act of Parliament, and, probably, without an arrangement with the Company. He goes on to say that the solution of the difficulty appears to him to be found in the principles laid down in the proposal of the Duke of Newcastle. He says that immediate action by us is required, in order that an Act may be introduced into the Imperial Parliament at the earliest moment.

"Thus you see, my dear Cartier, we are exactly at the point we started from, and the Hudson's Bay question is adding to our Intercolonial difficulties. Will you be good enough to arrange with Langevin and Chapais to be here by the 18th, if possible? . . .

"Yours very faithfully,
"JOHN A. MACDONALD.

"The Hon. George E. Cartier."

It does not appear that all Sir John Macdonald's colleagues privately shared his disappointment at this check to the progress of the negotiations. Thus Mr. Cartier, replying to the above note, writes:—

"Respecting the Hudson's Bay matter, I think that we ought not to be hasty in considering it. I must say that I am not surprised at the intimation of the Duke of Buckingham: I almost expected it. You must recollect that, when we discussed the other day the Intercolonial Railway question, I stated to McDougall that, with regard to the Hudson's Bay question, we might be called upon, in some way or other, to arrange with the Hudson's Bay Company before the Imperial Government would make to us a transfer of the North-West Territory. Now it is evident that we must, at the outset, face the money question, and I think that we ought not to be in too great a hurry." *

* From the Hon. G. E. Cartier to Sir John Macdonald, dated Quebec, February 13, 1868. It may interest those who are in the habit of saying that, after the affair of the honours in 1867, the personal relations which had existed between Messrs.

Mr. Campbell was still more emphatic in advocating delay:—

> "I think the refusal of the Colonial Office to give us the Hudson's Bay Territory is the best thing that could have happened to us. I yielded my opinion to yours at the time, but the probabilities of difficulty and expense in governing such a country were very great, and it seemed to me unwise to undertake them in advance of our being able to deal with the lands and resources of the country. I shall be glad to see a course adopted which will place before the country the amount which the Hudson's Bay Territory is to cost, broadly and squarely, and with our eyes open. We can then decide whether we can take it at that cost or not, but any other means of dealing with the subject will, I think, be unsatisfactory.
>
> "It will be awkward to acknowledge our error and retrace our steps : but we must meet that." *

A few weeks later the official reply was received from the Duke of Buckingham.† By it the Canadian Government was informed that the law officers of the Crown had given it as their opinion that the validity of the Hudson's Bay Company's charter could not be successfully disputed. This had reference only to Rupert's Land, but the Colonial Secretary rightly surmised that, so long as the " North-West Territory " remained separated from the Dominion by the possessions of the Hudson's Bay Company, Canada had no desire to assume any responsibility in regard to it. The Duke further intimated that the transfer of Rupert's Land could only be effected by arrangement with the Company, under the authority of an Act of the Imperial Parliament, which Act was subsequently passed, and received her Majesty's assent on the 31st of July, 1868.‡

On Sir John Macdonald's return from Halifax, he immediately addressed himself to this question. At a meeting of the Cabinet, held on the 17th of September, it was decided to send a delegation to England to negotiate with the Hudson's

---

Macdonald and Cartier were never as before, to know that this letter, written a few months after that occasion, contains no trace of any interruption of their old-time friendship. It is addressed to "My dear Macdonald" and closes in the phraseology invariably employed by Sir George Cartier when addressing Sir John, " Believe me, my dear Macdonald, your devoted friend and colleague, George Et. Cartier."

* From the Hon. A. Campbell to Sir John Macdonald, dated Kingston, February 12, 1868.

† *Journals, House of Commons,* 1867, pp. 367, 368.

‡ Imperial Act, 31 & 32 Vict., c. 105.

Bay Company, through the medium of Her Majesty's Government, for the transfer of the Territories. On the 18th of September, Sir John thus writes to his colleague, Mr. Campbell:—

"I got your telegram stating your desire to go to England, and we had the matter up yesterday. It has been decided, as I telegraphed you this morning, that Cartier, McDougall, and yourself are to go. Cartier was a little unwilling that I should stay behind, and there are a good many reasons why, perhaps, he is right, but the balance of convenience is in favour of my staying. I ought to be here when the new Governor arrives. I must watch the expiring efforts of Fenianism, and I ought to be here in order to aid the progress of the Union cause in Nova Scotia. And, besides all this, I see that it will clearly devolve upon me to get up anything like a show of legislation for next session. For all these reasons, I have made up my mind to stay. It is, however, arranged that, if I receive a telegram across the cable, that I am wanted in England, I am to leave at once. You must sail by the 7th October."

Notwithstanding Mr. Campbell's expressed desire—nay, in view of his telegram, I think one might say of his anxiety—to form one of this delegation, at the last moment he declined to go, much to the annoyance of Sir John, who told him that he "had never been so angry in his life." This action on Mr. Campbell's part had nothing to do with questions of public policy: it simply suited his personal convenience to change his plans, and the student of Canadian politics may not be surprised to learn that personal convenience was ever with Sir Alexander Campbell a potent consideration in his relations with Sir John Macdonald.

Sir George Cartier (who had been created a baronet in August) and Mr. McDougall sailed early in October. Scarcely had they landed in England when Mr. McDougall was attacked by a serious illness, which incapacitated him from attending to business for some weeks. Soon after his recovery, and before any agreement had been reached with the Hudson's Bay Company, the Government of Mr. Disraeli went out of office, and Lord Granville succeeded the Duke of Buckingham as Colonial Secretary. All this involved delay. After much negotiating an arrangement was arrived at, under which the Hudson's Bay

Company agreed, in consideration of the sum of £300,000, to surrender all their interest in the North-West to the Crown, with the reservation of one-twentieth of the fertile belt,* and 45,000 acres adjacent to the trading posts of the company.

While in England, Sir George Cartier was in constant communication with Sir John Macdonald, to whom he wrote long and interesting letters on the subject of Mr. McDougall's illness (which at one time threatened to be fatal), the progress of the negotiations, and the general topics of the day. Sir George was an excellent correspondent, despite the fact that his English was not idiomatic and that he wrote a shocking hand.

The arrangement entered into by Messrs. Cartier and McDougall was accepted by the Canadian Parliament in an address passed on the 1st of June, 1869,† wherein Her Majesty was prayed to unite Rupert's Land with Canada, on the terms therein set forth, and also to unite the North-West Territory on the conditions contained in the address that was passed during the previous session.

The deed of surrender from the Hudson's Bay Company to Her Majesty is dated November 19, 1869. It was understood that the formal transfer would take place on the 1st of December following. In anticipation of this the Canadian Parliament passed an Act, which was assented to on the 22nd of June, providing for the temporary government of Rupert's Land and the North-West Territories, when united with Canada. Under the authority of this Act, the Hon. William McDougall was, on the 28th of September, appointed Lieutenant Governor of the North-West Territories, and the same day left Ottawa for his dreary sovereignty. What followed is well known. The half-breeds of the Red River district, alarmed at the rumours of the transfer of the country to Canada, and fearful that their interests would be sacrificed, forcibly prevented Mr. McDougall's entrance into the Territory, and, under the leadership of Louis Riel, established a provisional Government

* "For the purpose of the last article, the fertile belt is to be bounded as follows: on the south by the United States' boundary; on the west by the Rocky Mountains; on the north by the northern branch of the Saskatchewan River; on the east by Lake Winnipeg, the Lake of the Woods, and the waters connecting them." (Article 6, Deed of Surrender.)

† See *Journals, House of Commons*, 1869, p. 169.

and defied the authorities, until subdued by military force. I do not propose to examine the merits of the controversy which has raged about the figure of Mr. McDougall, further than is necessary to show Sir John Macdonald's course throughout the affair.

For some time previous to the date fixed for the transfer, there had been indications of the approaching change. One party of Canadian surveyors was engaged in building a waggon road eastward from Fort Garry to the Lake of the Woods. Another party was employed in making a pathway from Lake Superior westward to the Lake of the Woods. A telegraph line was in course of erection, and, in the summer of 1869, the surveyors of the department of Public Works, presided over by Mr. McDougall, began to organize a system of surveys in the North-West.

While Canada was thus getting ready to assume her responsibilities, it does not appear that the Hudson's Bay Company took any steps to prepare the settlers for the change of government. Nor did they give any hint to the Dominion authorities of the state of feeling afterwards known to have prevailed at the time, among the half-breeds of the Red River. It seemed, also, as though circumstances conspired against a peaceful transfer being effected. The two most influential men in the North-West were Governor McTavish and Bishop Taché. It so happened that, at the time of Mr. McDougall's visit, the Governor was prostrated by a serious illness, while the Bishop was far away in Rome, attending the Ecumenical Council then meeting in the Eternal City. The absence of the one and the incapacity of the other were the more unfortunate, in that the subordinate officials, both of Church and of State, regarded the change with anything but favour—the Company's officials, because it meant the passing out of their control of a country in which they had come to be considered as lords paramount: the majority of the Catholic clergy, because they were Frenchmen, owing no allegiance to Her Majesty, and inspired by no feeling of regard for Canada.

The ill-feeling was further aggravated by the inconsiderateness shown by the Canadian surveying parties in running their lines through the lands of the half-breeds. These people saw in the proceeding an attempt of the Canadian Government to deprive them of their property, and they resented it accordingly.

It will be seen from the published correspondence that Sir John Macdonald attributed to the lack of conciliation, tact, and prudence shown by Canadian surveyors during the summer of 1869, much of the trouble which afterwards occurred. At the time, however, he knew nothing of it, for it was only after Mr. McDougall had left Ottawa that he learned that Colonel Dennis had observed this discontent on the part of the half-breeds in the preceding summer, and had reported it to his chief, who apparently thought so little of the circumstance that he did not even mention it to his colleagues.

During the winter of 1869-70, Sir John Macdonald wrote long and very full accounts of the Red River difficulty to Sir John Rose, who, a short time before, had retired from the Dominion Government, to become a member in the firm of Morton, Rose, and Co. Mr. Rose was at that time a financial agent of the Government of Canada in London. Between him and Sir John Macdonald there ever existed a warm and sincere attachment, which is reflected in their letters. By means of this correspondence one is enabled to ascertain exactly what Sir John thought and did in relation to the North-West troubles, almost from day to day.

Shortly before Mr. McDougall's appointment, Mr. Howe, Secretary of State for the Provinces, proceeded to Fort Garry, in order to prepare the way for the new Governor, who does not seem to have appreciated the endeavour, for he afterwards charged his late colleague with pursuing a very different course. While at Fort Garry Mr. Howe wrote to Sir John Macdonald a letter which certainly does not strengthen Mr. McDougall's suspicion.

"Winnipeg, Fort Garry, October 16, 1869.

"MY DEAR SIR JOHN,

"I have been here a week, and shall leave for home in three or four days. I shall probably meet McDougall on the way, and will give him the benefit of my observations. For many reasons, which I will explain when we meet, my visit here has been opportune and useful. Any amount of absurd rumours were afloat when I came, and a good deal of strong prejudice had been excited. Some fools wanted to get up addresses, and have me speak at a public meeting.

"This I declined, but by frank and courteous explanations to leading men, who largely represent the resident population, I have cleared the air a good deal, and I have done my best to give McDougall a fair start. All will now depend on his tact, temper, and discretion.

"Believe me, yours ever,

"Joseph Howe."

Mr. McDougall left Ottawa with instructions to proceed to Fort Garry, and make all preliminary arrangements for the organization of the government of the North-West, *on hearing of the transfer of the country to Canada.* Until officially notified to that effect, he was not to assume the functions of Lieutenant Governor, but was to act in every respect as a private individual. When the news of his check reached Ottawa, Sir John Macdonald at once wrote him, counselling patience, prudence, and moderation, as follows:—

"[Private.]

"Ottawa, November 20, 1869.

"My dear McDougall,

"I have yours of the 31st ult., and regret that you have had some little opposition in the commencement of your reign.

"Your despatch was read yesterday in Council, with all its accompanying documents, and we came to the conclusion that it would be inexpedient to give you any instructions. The circumstances will vary from day to day, and we think that we had better leave you to make such arrangements as you think best, having every confidence in your prudence and tact.

"The point which you must never forget is that you are now approaching a foreign country, under the government of the Hudson's Bay Company. You are going there under the assumption that the Company's authorities assent to your entering upon their territory, and will protect you when there. You cannot force your way in. The case is precisely as if a Canadian, going to New York, would find that he would be opposed in entering Buffalo. He ought not to attempt to force his way past them, but should communicate with the United States authorities, leaving them to clear the way for his ingress, and to protect him while within their bounds.

"It occurs to me that you should ascertain, from Governor McTavish, the two leading half-breeds in the Territory, and inform them at once that you will take them into your Council. This man Riel, who appears to be the moving spirit, is a clever fellow, and you should endeavour to retain him as an officer in your future police. If you do this promptly, it will be a most convincing proof that you are not going to leave the half-breeds out of the law.

"Our Lower Canadian colleagues are intensely disgusted at the action of the French priests, as described by you. I hope you will allow no impatience at their factious and irrational conduct to induce you to hold out any but conciliatory language to them. After you are fairly in the saddle, if they attempt to obstruct your administration, you can act summarily with them.

"The course taken by Stoughton Dennis in pressing for strong measures to be taken against parties interfering with his surveys, was exceedingly injudicious. He is a very decent fellow, and a good surveyor and all that, but he has got no head, and is exceedingly fussy. He was in the country simply on sufferance, in anticipation of its future transfer to Canada: on finding any serious dissatisfaction amongst the natives or residents, he should have at once struck work and awaited your arrival. It is, of course, important to have land surveyed for settlement as early as possible, but that is a secondary consideration to your entrance on your duties with the general assent and support of the people. It is, however, difficult at this distance to give you anything like advice, as, long ere this reaches you, circumstances may have altered, so I can only wish you well through with it. . . .

"Believe me, my dear McDougall,

"Yours faithfully,

"JOHN A. MACDONALD."

And again (November 23rd) :—

"I hope no consideration will induce you to leave your post—that is, to return to Canada just now. Such a course would cover yourself and your party with ridicule, which would extend to the whole Dominion. I am in great hopes that, by patience and kindliness, you may be able to subdue the present excitement."

And again (November 27th):—

"You speak of crossing the line and being sworn in the moment that you receive official notice of the transfer of the Territory. Now, it occurs to us that that step cannot well be taken. You ought not to swear that you will perform duties that you are, by the action of the insurgents, prevented from performing. By assuming the government, you relieve the Hudson's Bay authorities from all responsibility in the matter. As things stand, they are responsible for the peace and good government of the country, and ought to be held to that responsibility until they are in a position to give peaceable possession. A proclamation, such as you suggest, calling upon the people, in your capacity as Lieut. Governor, to unite to support the law, and calling upon the insurgents to disperse, would be very well if it were sure to be obeyed. If, however, it were disobeyed, your weakness and inability to enforce the authority of the Dominion would be painfully exhibited, not only to the people of Red River, but to the people and Government of the United States. An assumption of the government by you, of course, puts an end to that of the Hudson's Bay Company's authorities, and Governor McTavish and his Council would be deprived even of the semblance of legal right to interfere. There would then be, if you were not admitted into the country, no legal government existing, and anarchy must follow. In such a case, no matter how the anarchy is produced, it is quite open by the law of nations for the inhabitants to form a government *ex necessitate* for the protection of life and property, and such a government has certain sovereign rights by the *jus gentium*, which might be very convenient for the United States, but exceedingly inconvenient to you. The temptation to an acknowledgment of such a government by the United States would be very great, and ought not to be lightly risked. We have formally notified the Colonial Office by cable of the situation of affairs, and stated the helplessness and inaction of the Hudson's Bay authorities. We have thrown the responsibility on the Imperial Government, and they will

doubtless urge the Hudson's Bay people by cable to take active
and vigorous steps.   Meanwhile, your course has been altogether right.   By staying at Pembina you will be at an easy
distance from the territory, and can, it is hoped, open communication, singly or otherwise, with the insurgent leaders."

December 8th : "As to yourself and your position, you will
find that you will be fully sustained here.   Meanwhile, let me
press upon you to remember the famous axiom of William Pitt,
that the first, second, and third requisites for a statesman are
patience.   Do not let yourself, by any feeling of impatience or
irritation, however natural it may be, show that you have any
distrust of the Hudson's Bay authorities.   I have no doubt of
the good faith of the Company in England, and of Governor
McTavish, but have little doubt that you are correct in the
idea that the subordinate officials dislike excessively being set
aside by new comers.   That feeling is a natural one, and is to
be removed by kindness and confidence, and not by any appearance of suspicion or reserve.   The Montreal *Herald* and the
Globe have got correspondents in Fort Garry, and they both
seem to write very fairly.   The St. Paul *Press* also, edited by
Mr. Whelock, from Nova Scotia, seems to report fairly.   They
all unite in stating that the *origo mali* was the exceedingly
indiscreet and offensive airs put on by Snow and Mair.   You
must bridle those gentlemen, or they will be a continual source
of disquiet to you."

On receipt of the intelligence from Red River, Sir John
Macdonald at once caused Lord Granville to be informed, by
telegraph, of what had taken place, and advised to make no
immediate change in the governing power of the North-West.
He pointed out that, upon the surrender of the Territory by the
Company to the Queen, the responsibility for the peace of the
North-West would devolve upon the Imperial authorities, and
not upon the Government of Canada, which absolutely declined
to accept the transfer in the then disturbed state of the country.
At the same time, Sir John telegraphed Mr. Rose, instructing
him not to pay over the purchase money until the Company
were prepared to give peaceable possession.

This attitude of the Canadian Government was far from
agreeable to the Hudson's Bay Company, which pressed for the

acceptance, by Her Majesty's Government, of the surrender on the 1st of December, the date originally fixed. The Colonial Office was equally desirous to accept it, and turn over to Canada the responsibility of dealing with the difficulties. This Sir John was determined should not be done. " I cannot understand," he writes to Mr. Rose (December 5th), " the desire of the Colonial Office, or of the Company, to saddle the responsibility of the government on Canada just now. It would so completely throw the game into the hands of the insurgents and the Yankee wire-pullers, who are to some extent influencing and directing the movement from St. Paul, that we cannot foresee the consequences. On the other hand, the delay leaves McTavish in power, and all his subordinate officials, with full authority to keep peace in the country and prevent matters going to extremities." And to Mr. McDougall (December 12th): " My previous letter will have told you our action in England. It has stirred up the Hudson's Bay Company, and they have doubtless sent, and will continue to send, urgent messages to everybody under their influence, to act energetically in putting an end to this state of anarchy. From Rose's letters, it is obvious that both the Colonial Office and the Company would like to throw the whole responsibility on Canada, and, if we once accepted it, they would leave us to get out of the trouble the best way we could. By our positively declining to do so, and insisting upon getting peaceable possession, we shall, I have no doubt, secure the active co-operation of both ; and if it be necessary, in the spring, to send a force by Fort William, it will be, I have little doubt, a combined force of regulars and volunteers."

To the remonstrances of the Imperial Government against delay, Sir John Macdonald replied, that while Canada's desire to possess the North-West had in no way abated, it was never contemplated that the transfer was to be a mere interchange of instruments. The Company, he submitted, stood pledged to convey, not only their title, but the Territory itself. That there would be an armed resistance was totally unexpected, at any rate by the Canadian Government. In regard to the difficulty which had arisen, he expressed his opinion that the Company could not be acquitted of blame. They had an old and fully organized Government, to which the people appeared to render ready obedience. Their Governor was advised by a Council, in which some of the principal residents of the settlement had seats. They had every means of information as to the state of feeling existing in the country. They knew, or ought to have known, the light in which the proposed negotiations were viewed by the people under their rule. If they were aware of the feeling of discontent, they ought to have apprised the Imperial and Canadian Governments of its existence. If they were not aware of the disaffection, the responsibility for such wilful blindness, on the part of their officers, should rest with them. For more than a year before the outbreak negotiations had been in progress, and it was, Sir John maintained, the duty of the Company to have prepared the people under their rule for the change, to have explained the precautions taken to protect the interests of the inhabitants, and to have removed any misapprehension that might have existed among them. It does not appear that any steps were taken in that direction. The people were suffered to remain in the belief that they had been sold to Canada, with an utter disregard of their rights. When Governor McTavish visited Canada in June, 1869, he was in frequent communication with the Dominion Government; yet he never intimated that there was a suspicion of discontent existing, nor did he make any suggestions as to the best mode of effecting the transfer with the assent of the inhabitants.

In regard to the statement made by Lord Granville, that throughout the negotiations, it had never been hinted that the Company were to be bound to hand over the Territory in a state of tranquillity, Sir John observed, that the reason why no express stipulation to that effect was made was that it had been assumed by all parties that the Company had both the right and the power to hand over the Territory. It *was* in a state of tranquillity, and no suggestion had been made of the possibility of such tranquillity being disturbed. He added that the resistance did not come from outsiders, but from those born and bred under the Company's rule; and concluded by reiterating his view that the wisest course was to continue the authority of the Company, while steps were being taken to reconcile the people to the change.

"Any hasty attempt by the Canadian Government to force their rule upon the insurgents would probably result in armed resistance and bloodshed. Every other course should be tried before resort is had to force. If life were once lost in an encounter between a Canadian force and the inhabitants, the seeds of hostility to Canada and Canadian rule would be sown, and might produce an ineradicable hatred to the union of the countries, and thus mar the future prosperity of British America. If anything like hostilities should commence, the temptation to the wild Indian tribes, and to the restless adventurers who abound in the United States (many of them with military experience gained in the late civil war), to join the insurgents would be almost irresistible. Already it is said that the Fenian organization looks upon this rising as another means of exhibiting its hatred to England. No one can foresee the end of the complications that might thus be occasioned, not only as between Canada and the North-West, but between the United States and England. From a sincere conviction of the gravity of the situation, and not from any desire to repudiate or postpone the performance of any of their engagements, the Canadian Government have urged a temporary delay of the transfer. This is not a question of money—it may be one of peace or war. It is one in which the present and future prosperity of the British possessions in North America is involved, which prosperity hasty action might permanently prejudice. Even were the £300,000 paid over, the impolicy of putting an end to the only constituted authority existing in the country, and compelling Canada to assert her title by force, would remain. It is better to have a semblance of a government in the country than none at all. While the issue of a proclamation would put an end to the government of the Hudson's Bay Company, it would not substitute the government by Canada therefor. Such a government is physically impossible until the armed resistance is ended, and thus a state of anarchy and confusion would ensue, and a legal status might be given to any government *de facto* formed by the inhabitants for the protection of their lives and property." *

A fortnight after the above was written news reached

* Extract from Minute of Council, December 16th, 1869.

Ottawa that Mr. McDougall had, on the 1st of December, assumed the functions of Lieutenant Governor, and had attempted to effect an entrance into his Government by a *coup de main.* Sir John Macdonald has left on record his opinion of this course, and of the consequences which it entailed, in a letter addressed to Mr. Rose :—

"[Private.]

"Ottawa, December 31, 1869.

"MY DEAR ROSE,

"I have yours of the 13th. McDougall has made a most inglorious *fiasco* at Red River. When he left here he fully understood that he was to go as a private individual to report on the state of affairs at Red River, but to assume no authority until officially notified from here that Rupert's Land was united to Canada. He wrote to that effect to Governor McTavish immediately on his arrival at Pembina, stating that he would take no action until officially notified.

"Notwithstanding this, from mere impatience at his uncomfortable position at Pembina, and before he could possibly have received instructions in answer to his report of being stopped on the way, he chose to assume that, on the 1st of December, the surrender was made by the Company and the Order in Council passed by the Queen, and that the Order in Council was to appoint the day of its issue as the day of the Union. He issued a proclamation under the Great Seal of the new province, formally adding it to the Dominion. He then entered into a series of inglorious intrigues, particulars of which I do not yet know, with the Swamp Indians near Red River, and with the Sioux Indians at Portage la Prairie, and sent the irrepressible Stoughton Dennis, in his capacity of 'Conservator of the Peace,' as he dubbed him, to surprise the Stone Fort. Dennis took possession of the fort, and held it for a little while, and then, as I understand it, after having first summoned all the loyal residents to join him, published a proclamation declaring the inexpediency of their organizing themselves on the rumour that Riel was going to send a deputation to treat with McDougall. What has become of Dennis I do not know, but it is said that he has abandoned

the Stone Fort, and is lurking somewhere. All these movements aroused Riel, who collected his forces, and has a large
band at Fort Garry, estimated variously at from 300 to 700
men.

"By the way, I forgot to mention that Col. Dennis, while
at Fort Garry, consulted the Recorder, Black, as to the advisability of declaring martial law. Did you ever hear such
frenzy?

"Riel, in order to starve McDougall out, took possession
of the Hudson's Bay post, two miles from Pembina, and
McDougall thereupon retreated to St. Paul, where I understand
he will be to-day.

"All this has been done in the direct teeth of instructions,
and he has ingeniously contrived to humiliate himself and
Canada, to arouse the hopes and pretensions of the insurgents,
and to leave them in undisputed possession until next spring.
He has, in fact, done all in his power to prevent the success
of our emissaries, who were to arrive at Pembina on Xmas
Day, and who would, I think, if things had been kept quiet,
have been able to reconcile matters without any difficulty.
As it is now, it is more than doubtful that they will be allowed
access to the Territory or intercourse with the insurgents.

"If my fears should be realized, the only thing left is the
preparation of an expedition in the spring, *viâ* Thunder Bay.
All this I tell you, of course, in confidence.

"McDougall has weakened our case enormously with the
Imperial Government, but we must put the best face possible
on matters. We have undoubted information that the insurgents have been in communication with the Fenian body in
New York, and letters have been interchanged. O'Donoghue,
the young priest, has thrown off the ecclesiastical garb, and
avowed himself a Fenian. The governing body at New York
will send neither men nor money, but have been most liberal
with promises. They have, I believe, sent an agent to stir
them up. It is said that General Spear, one of the U.S.
Generals of the last war, and whom you may remember to
have been in command at St. Albans in '66, is the man who
has gone.

"By the middle of January we may expect to hear from

Donald Smith, the Hudson's Bay man, and from Mr. Thibault; but, as I fear they will be unsuccessful, we must at once address ourselves to preparations for the spring. In this view, we must know what Her Majesty's Government will do, and most likely we shall next week address a despatch to Lord Granville on the subject. Our Council will re-assemble on Monday, the 3rd of January, and I shall endeavour to get the result of our deliberations off by the first Allan steamer afterwards. Campbell has arrived, and is looking well, although using his crutch. His mem. on postal matters, which, I take it, was drawn by you, is a capital paper, and I should think ought to bear good fruit. Personally, I see no objection to your being on the Montreal Bank London committee. I shall bring it up in Council to-day, and telegraph you the result this afternoon.

"Believe me, yours sincerely,

"JOHN A. MACDONALD.

"The Hon. J. Rose, &c., &c."

The "emissaries" referred to by Sir John Macdonald were the Very Reverend Mr. Thibault, Colonel Charles de Salaberry, and Mr. (now Sir) Donald A. Smith, who had been sent up by the Dominion authorities to endeavour to bring the insurgents to reason. Mr. Thibault had spent thirty-seven years in missionary work in the Red River district, and knew intimately every one of the leaders among the half-breeds. Colonel de Salaberry was, as his designation imports, a military man. He was also a member of one of the most distinguished families of the province of Quebec, his father having been the hero of Chateauguay. Mr. Smith was an officer of the Hudson's Bay Company, ostensibly going as such, though provided with a commission from the Canadian Government, to be used if occasion required. His special mission was to endeavour to bring about the dispersion of the half-breeds, and the dissolution of their committee. Dr. Tupper also paid a visit to the Red River at this time, and had a conference with certain of the disaffected leaders.* The vicissitudes experienced by all

* "Dr. Tupper went up to bring back his daughter, Mrs. Cameron, and got into Fort Garry. He was in the country for about two days, and did more good than any one else who has hitherto gone there." (From Sir John Macdonald to the Hon. John Rose, dated Ottawa, January 21, 1870.)

these gentlemen are duly recorded. Suffice it to say here that their efforts at conciliation proved unavailing, and, as a *dernier ressort*, Bishop Taché was summoned from Rome to act the part of peacemaker. The Bishop had spent the best years of his life in the North-West, and, by his devotion to the cause of the half-breeds, had gained an almost unbounded influence over those people. Promptly he responded to the call, and set out for Ottawa, where he arrived on the 9th of February. A week later, he left for the seat of the disaffection, bearing with him a letter of instructions from the Prime Minister.* It is difficult to say what results the Bishop might have been able to accomplish, had he arrived earlier on the scene. Unhappily, five days before he reached Fort Garry, the murder of Thomas Scott made it clear to all men that the time for conciliation was over, and that stronger measures were imperatively called for.

Before, however, the news of the ghastly scene, enacted at Fort Garry on the afternoon of the 4th of March, had reached Ottawa, Sir John Macdonald had pretty well made up his mind that order could be restored in the Territory only by military force.

Thus, on the 11th of March, he writes to Mr. Rose:—

"The propositions adopted at the Red River conference are, most of them, reasonable enough, and can easily be disposed of with their delegates. Things look well enough, were we only assured of Riel's good faith. But the unpleasant suspicion remains that he is only wasting time by sending this delegation, until the approach of summer enables him to get material support from the United States. It is believed by many that he is in the pay of the U.S. We may settle upon the terms of the constitution to be granted to the North-West with the delegates, when they arrive here, and pass an Act for the purpose, but that will not prevent Riel from refusing to ratify the arrangement, if he pleases. Meanwhile, he is in possession of the country, and is consolidating his Government. The foolish and criminal attempt of —— and —— to renew the fight has added greatly to Riel's strength. He has put down two distinct attempts to upset his

* See Appendix XIX.

Government, and American sympathisers will begin to argue that his Government has acquired a legal status, and he will be readily persuaded of that fact himself. —Besides, the longer he remains in power, the more unwilling will he be to resign it, and I have, therefore, no great confidence in his ratifying any arrangements made here with the delegates. Under these circumstances the preparations for the expeditionary force must not be delayed. We shall receive the delegation with all kindness, and, I think, beyond a doubt, make an arrangement with them; but we shall, at the same time, prepare for the expedition to leave by the end of April or beginning of May."

The conclusion of an arrangement with the Imperial Government, respecting this expedition, was attended with a good deal of difficulty. Lord Granville, while agreeing to send troops on condition that Canada first accepted the transfer, laid down in Sir Clinton Murdoch's instructions that the military were not to be employed to force the people to unite with Canada—in other words, writes Sir John to the Governor General, "They are to be of no use. If we accept the country we are committed to its conquest, and must go on; we cannot return the country to Her Majesty or to the Hudson's Bay Company. Again, why should we be called upon to pay for troops that may be ordered not to act when they get into Fort Garry?" *

Eventually an arrangement was arrived at between the two Governments, and, in May, a combined force of regulars and Canadian militia, under the command of Colonel (now Lord) Wolseley, advanced on their bloodless mission to Fort Garry, Riel and his followers decamping on the first sound of the bugles, which told the loyal inhabitants of Red River that the long-looked-for succour was at hand.

On the 2nd of May, Sir John Macdonald introduced a Bill into the House of Commons to provide for the establishment and government of the province of Manitoba. On the 3rd, the fiscal agents of the Canadian Government in London were instructed to pay over the purchase money. On the 20th,

---

* From Sir John Macdonald to His Excellency, Sir John Young, dated Ottawa, Sunday, April 10 (1870).

the Hon. A. G. Archibald, who, in 1869, had been re-elected to Parliament for Colchester, was appointed Lieutenant Governor of the newly erected province, and, on the 23rd of June, an order of the Queen in Council formally transferred Rupert's Land and the North-West Territories to the Dominion of Canada.

The selection of a Lieutenant Governor was a matter of some concern. One error of judgment had been committed in this regard: another might be fatal. On his return to Ottawa in the preceding January, Mr. McDougall had tendered the resignation of his office which the Prime Minister thought it well to accept. Before all hope of a peaceable solution of the difficulty had died away, Sir John Macdonald had some idea of appointing Governor McTavish of the Hudson's Bay Company. A little later, Mr. Donald A. Smith's name occurred to him as a fit man. Subsequently, Colonel Wolseley intimated his willingness to accept the position, but the appointment of a military Governor was not considered expedient. Finally, the Premier's choice fell upon Mr. Archibald.

Sir John's speech in introducing the Manitoba Bill was heard by Sir Stafford Northcote, who thus describes his impressions:—

"After luncheon, I went up to the House of Commons, and was just in time to hear Sir J. Macdonald's speech, introducing the North-West Bill. He seemed feeble and looked ill, but spoke with great skill. He makes no pretensions to oratory, but is clear and dexterous in statement, and gave very ingenious turns to his difficult points." *

Sir Stafford Northcote had arrived just in time. Before the sound of Sir John Macdonald's voice was heard again within the walls of the Canadian Parliament, many months were to elapse, and when he next addressed the House of Commons it was on a subject with which the future Earl of Iddesleigh had much to do.

* Lang's "Life of the Earl of Iddesleigh," vol. i. p. 331.

CHAPTER XIX.

ADMINISTRATION.

1867-1871.

RECONSTRUCTION OF THE CABINET—RETURN OF SIR FRANCIS HINCKS—SIR
ALEXANDER GALT GOES INTO OPPOSITION—BILL FOR THE ESTABLISHMENT
OF THE SUPREME COURT—CHARACTER OF SIR JOHN MACDONALD'S
APPOINTMENTS TO THE BENCH—OFFER OF THE CHANCELLORSHIP OF
ONTARIO TO MR. EDWARD BLAKE—CONDITION OF SIR JOHN MACDONALD'S
PRIVATE AFFAIRS—HIS ILLNESS—TRADE AND FISHERY RELATIONS WITH
THE UNITED STATES—APPOINTMENT OF A JOINT HIGH COMMISSION.

THE Cabinet formed on the 1st of July, 1867, although constructed
with exceptional care, was destined, through the operation of
various causes, to undergo an unusual number of changes in the
first two years and a half of its existence. It behoves us now to
consider the reasons which influenced Sir John Macdonald in
the steps taken by him to maintain the strength of his ministry.
The art of "cabinet making," as he used to call it, so peculiarly
the function of the Prime Minister, was one in which Sir John
Macdonald, by reason of his intimate knowledge of men, and
his far-reaching sagacity, was deeply skilled, and in which he
rarely, if ever, made a false move.

The loss of a colleague, at once so experienced and
accomplished as Mr. Galt, within a few days of the meeting
of Parliament, was no light matter. The old saying, however, which avers that no man is indispensable, received
thereby another illustration, for in Mr. John Rose, Sir
John Macdonald found a Finance Minister in all respects
the equal of the late occupant of that office. Mr. Rose was
eminently fitted to discharge those duties which had been
relinquished by Mr. Galt. In addition to qualifications of a

high order, he was gifted with a courteous and pleasant manner, which rendered him a universal favourite,* while his singularly happy disposition and affectionate nature had long before won for him a high place in the regard of Sir John Macdonald. Circumstances ordained that, for the last twenty years of their lives, the ocean should roll between them, yet a regular and frequent correspondence ever kept their friendship bright. The worst thing I ever heard Sir John Macdonald say of his friend was this : " Rose has a bad habit of economizing all the small words in his telegrams to such a degree, that I am often in great doubt as to his meaning. This always was a peculiarity of his." A few days after the meeting of Parliament, Mr. Rose was sworn of the Privy Council, and appointed Minister of Finance.

Thus far all was well. Succeeding vacancies, however, were destined to be not so easily filled. In considering them, it is necessary to bear in mind the arrangement which governed the selection of the Ontario portion of the Cabinet. When the first Government of the Dominion was formed, although Confederation was adopted with the object of putting an end to the unhappy sectionalism which existed between Upper and Lower Canada before the Union, yet, as it was important that the Administration should receive, at the approaching elections, the support of all men really desiring the success of the new system, it was agreed, so far as Ontario was concerned, that, as in the last Parliament of the province of Canada there had been more Reformers than Conservatives, and as in the proposed Cabinet Ontario would have only five representatives, three of these should be of Liberal antecedents, and two Conservatives. This understanding was merely a temporary arrangement, for, at the time it was entered into, the political complexion of the new Parliament was, of course, unknown, and it was agreed that the future was to take care of itself.

The effect of the elections was to reverse the relative

---

* To this rule apparently there was no exception. Mr. Rose took up his residence in London, in the autumn of 1869. He was scarcely settled, ere the Red River trouble occurred, yet in March, 1870, Lord Granville writes of him to Sir John Macdonald : " The presence of Sir John Rose here has been of great use and comfort to me. It is impossible to have an abler or more pleasant man with whom to transact business."

strength of the Reform and Conservative supporters of the
Government, yet the Cabinet representation was suffered to
remain undisturbed, until the question of filling the vacancy
caused by the death of Mr. Fergusson Blair came to be considered, when strong objections were made by the Conservatives
to the appointment of a Liberal.* It was urged by the former
that the very same reason which led to the selection of
Mr. Fergusson Blair, in July, 1867, called, in 1868, for the
appointment of a Conservative.

The Prime Minister acknowledged the force of this argument
advanced by the main body of his supporters, but, before any
steps were taken in the matter, the appointment of Mr. Howland
to the Lieutenant Governorship of Ontario made another
vacancy in the Liberal section of the Cabinet.

In view of that event, Sir John, a short time before it actually took place, discussed the situation with Messrs. McDougall
and Howland, and explained to them the reasons which rendered
a further continuance of the old arrangement impracticable.
He, however, considered himself bound to maintain the coalition
principle, and expressed his opinion, that while the change in
the relative strength of parties rendered it necessary for three
Conservatives and two Reformers to be in the Cabinet, he
thought the Liberal leaders should have some voice in the
selection of the new Conservative. Messrs. McDougall and
Howland agreed as to the fairness of this proposal, and it was
ultimately settled that Messrs. J. C. Aikins and Alexander
Morris should be asked to join the Administration. Sir John
Macdonald was afterwards accused by Mr. McDougall and
the *Globe* of having broken faith with the Reform section of
the Cabinet in the appointment of Mr. Morris. Sir John, in
his time, was often exposed to accusations as unjust and
unfounded as this one, but seldom has it happened that the
means of refutation, clear, distinct, conclusive, have lain so
ready at hand. It is not merely that his own reasonable
explanation to Parliament of the circumstances bears the stamp

---

* "I find a rumour is prevailing that McKenzie, of Lambton, is a possible
successor to poor Blair, but do not credit it. Nevertheless, I think it only my duty
to advise you that it is causing considerable uneasiness in the Conservative ranks,
and would be most distasteful, etc." (From —— to Sir John Macdonald, dated Ottawa,
March 14, 1868.)

of probability on its very face—Messrs. Howland and Aikins have, over their own signatures, borne public testimony to its absolute correctness.* It is true that Mr. Aikins was unwilling to share with a single Liberal (that Liberal being Mr. McDougall) the responsibility of representing the party in the Cabinet. It is equally true that he consented to do so with Mr. McDougall's successor, and it may be only a coincidence that his objections were finally overcome on the very day that Mr. McDougall ceased to be a member of the Administration.†

Such are the facts in connection with the appointment of Messrs. Morris and Aikins, which, at the time, caused some stir in the political world. It will be seen therefrom how little ground there was for the oft-repeated charge that, by these appointments, Sir John Macdonald in any way compromised his word, or violated any engagement. If he erred at all in his treatment of the Liberal wing of his party, it was, as pointed out by himself, on the side of generosity.

"It is rather hard upon me that I should be pitched into

---

* " In reply to that part of your letter which refers to the proposed arrangements for filling the vacancies in the Government, consequent upon the death of Mr. Blair and my appointment to my present position, I had several conversations with yourself and Mr. McDougall before I left Ottawa, upon the subject, and it was understood that you should fill the two vacancies as soon as satisfactory arrangements could be made for the purpose. After discussing the *personnel*, and having given full consideration to the availability and claims of all the parties, it was decided that it would be satisfactory if one of the places was filled by Mr. Morris, and the other by Mr. Aikins, or some other Reformer of good standing. We considered Mr. Morris a gentleman possessed of high character, experience, and good attainments, and entertaining progressive views of politics, and having been the originator and medium by which the coalition of 1864 was brought into existence, we concluded that he would be acceptable to all who desired to support the present Government." (From Lieut. Governor Howland to Sir John Macdonald, dated Toronto, November 19, 1868.)

" On Mr. McDougall's arrival at Ottawa, I had a further conversation with him, in which he urged me to join the Government without another Reform colleague from Ontario, stating that Sir John found it impossible to assent to that proposition. Mr. McDougall, however, suggested that if I came in at once, the other appointment from Ottawa could stand over for some time, though, when it was made, the vacant seat would be filled as necessity required, and the name of Mr. Morris was mentioned as the person likely to be appointed. I agreed to this course." (Extract from memorandum read by Hon. J. C. Aikins in the Senate, February 17, 1870.)

† Mr. Howland was appointed Lieutenant Governor of Ontario on the 3rd of July, 1868. Mr. McDougall ceased to be Minister of Public Works on the 8th of December, 1869, on which day Mr. Aikins entered the Cabinet as Secretary of State of Canada. Mr. Alexander Morris had been sworn of the Privy Council and appointed Minister of Inland Revenue on the 16th of November previously.

by Mr. McDougall for not taking care of the Reformers, and, at the same time, be grumbled at by my own party for giving everything to that portion of Her Majesty's liege subjects in Ontario. The appointment of yourself, in the first place, and of Mr. McDougall, in the second, was, I think, a sufficient proof of my desire that their claims should be recognized. In order to oblige him and give him a legal adviser, in whom he had confidence, I allowed him to select Albert Richards for the North-West, although that gentleman had always been strongly opposed to myself. I think this appointment caused more dissatisfaction among my Conservative friends than any other." *

The Lieutenant Governorship of Ontario was, in 1868, looked upon as a great prize, worthy, in the estimation of Mr. Alexander Campbell, of the First Minister himself. Sir John did not want it. Neither in regard to Lieutenant Governorships, any more than Chief Justiceships, did he ever think of himself, though, if my surmise be correct, there was at that time another Prime Minister not quite so disinterested. In like manner there were several aspirants to the honour of representing the Governor General in the North-West, yet Sir John Macdonald finally gave both these positions to his Liberal colleagues. It is undoubtedly true that the coalition was destined to become a fusion, but this was no new thing. It had happened in Canada before, and for the same reason. Its cause lay not in the bad faith, or treachery, or deceit of anybody, but in the marvellous gift which Sir John Macdonald possessed of drawing men towards him, and inspiring them with a sense of personal attachment stronger than party ties. Mr. Aikins was a Liberal, and joined Sir John Macdonald's Cabinet as such. So in their day did Messrs. John Ross and Thomas Spence, Sidney Smith and Isaac Buchanan, Fergusson Blair, and others whose names will readily recur to the student of Canadian history. Mr. Aikins was no exception to the general rule. I am not aware whether he still calls himself a Liberal or not, but this I know, that, from the day on which he became a Minister of the Crown, Sir John Macdonald had no more loyal or true-hearted colleague than James Cox Aikins.

* From Sir John Macdonald to Lieutenant Governor Howland, dated Ottawa, February 3, 1870.

But the Prime Minister's difficulties were not yet over. Not long before Mr. McDougall's acceptance of the Lieutenant Governorship of the North-West Territories left the third Ontario Reform seat empty, Mr. Rose, who represented a Quebec constituency, resigned the office of Finance Minister, for reasons which I have already stated. Thus a new minister from both Ontario and Quebec, or rather from a limited section of each province, had to be found. A qualified offer of the portfolio of finance was made to Mr. Galt,* in the month of September, only to be declined, while the fewness of the Ontario Liberals supporting the Administration rendered the choice of a successor to Mr. McDougall a well-nigh impossible task. At this juncture there re-appeared on the scene a Canadian statesman who, for the fifteen years previous, had been representing his Sovereign in a distant part of her dominions. It seems a long time since we bade adieu to Mr. Francis Hincks. In the interval, he had been Governor of Barbados and the Windward Islands, and also of British Guiana. In 1869 he returned to Canada, with a record of honourable service, and the decoration of Knight Commander of the most distinguished order of St. Michael and St. George. Sir Francis Hincks had scarcely touched Canadian soil before Sir John Macdonald realized that he was the very man he was looking for. A financier of unquestioned ability, he would prove a worthy successor to Mr. Rose. A Liberal who for years had led the Upper Canadian Reformers, he was in every way qualified to represent, with Mr. Aikins, that party in the Cabinet. The idea happily conceived was rapidly executed. Sir John met Sir Francis in Montreal, accompanied him by boat to Ottawa, and on the way propounded his scheme, which Sir Francis readily fell in with. On the 9th of October, he was sworn of the Privy Council, and appointed Finance Minister. A few weeks later he was returned for North Renfrew, in spite

---

* The condition being that he should abjure certain recently developed views on the "Independence of Canada." The proposal was made by Sir George Cartier, with the sanction of the Prime Minister. (See the correspondence, *Debates, House of Commons,* February 21, 1870, pp. 126, 127.)

There is reason to believe that Sir John was not at all put out by the refusal of an offer which he authorized primarily to please his French supporters, between whom and Sir Alexander there existed, at that period, an *entente cordiale.*

of the violent opposition of that portion of the Reform party which acknowledged the sovereignty of George Brown.*

Mr. Rose's place as the English representative for Lower Canada was taken by Mr. Christopher Dunkin, who is remembered chiefly as the author of the Local Option law which bore his name.†

The result of these Cabinet changes was on the whole satisfactory, notwithstanding the fact that the appointment of Messrs. Hincks and Morris resulted in the defection of one or two supporters of the Government, including Mr. Galt, respecting whose change of attitude Sir John Macdonald writes:—

"Galt came out, I am glad to say, formally in opposition, and relieved me of the difficulty connected with him. His warm alliance with the Lower Canadian French rendered it necessary for me to put up with a good deal, as you know. But he is now finally dead as a Canadian politician. The correspondence between Cartier and himself, in which he comes out squarely

---

* "The *Globe* is perfectly frantic at Hincks coming into office, and on this point Sandfield Macdonald and George Brown agree. All that the Reform party really wanted was a leader of pluck, around whom to rally, in order to throw off the dictatorship of the *Globe*; and Brown knows right well that it throws him back fully ten years. No step has been left untried to frighten me from appointing him (Hincks), but the game was too clear to admit of a doubt." (From Sir John Macdonald to Alexander Morris, Esq., dated Ottawa, October 10, 1869.) For a fuller explanation of the reasons which influenced Sir John in his selection of Sir Francis Hincks, see Appendix XX.

† 27 & 28 Vict., c. 18. Sir John's first choice was Mr. John Henry Pope, respecting whom he wrote, on the 27th of September, 1869, to Sir George Cartier: "It is necessary that immediate steps should be taken to fill Rose's place. The man for our money is Pope. He is able and energetic and popular with all our friends of British origin, both from Upper and Lower Canada, as well as with your compatriots. . . I suppose Pope will be at Rose's dinner, and you can have a talk with him. I would advise that you should take no refusal."

There is nothing among Sir John's papers to show that this offer was ever made, or, if made, why it was declined. It would appear from the above that the Prime Minister, following the custom of former days, left the selection of the new Quebec minister with Sir George Cartier, who may have had reasons for preferring Mr. Dunkin to Mr. Pope. Mr. R. H. Pope, M.P., however, to whom I have applied, tells me he always understood his father could have had the position at that time, but his business engagements were such as to render it impossible for him to accept. Be this as it may, Sir John Macdonald's desire to have Mr. Pope for a colleague did not fade, for, on the retirement of Mr. Dunkin, two years later, Mr. Pope succeeded him as Minister of Agriculture. Mr. Pope was sworn of the Privy Council on the 25th of October, 1871.

for independence, has rung his death-knell, and I shall take precious good care to keep him where he is. . . . Great attempts have been made to get hold of Sandfield by Galt and Co., but without success. He is sound and true, and for the best of reasons. His only safe policy is to adhere to the present arrangement." *

Occupied with the thousand and one cares that make up the life of a Prime Minister, it is difficult to understand how Sir John Macdonald found time to fulfil those manifold duties of a departmental character which demanded his attention. Yet, as Minister of Justice, he was ever a busy man, and the statute-book of the country bears ample witness to his untiring industry as a law-maker and law-reformer. During the years 1868–1870 he devoted much pains to the preparation of a Bill to establish a Supreme Court for Canada. This measure, which he regarded as being in an especial manner the work of his own hands, was first introduced during the session of 1869, more for the purpose, however, of inviting suggestions and criticisms, than with the object of having it become law. It was again brought forward in 1870, by Sir John, who explained its provisions at some length. Circumstances, however, prevented its reaching a second reading, and not until five years later, under the auspices of another Administration, that which I may call Sir John's pet scheme was enrolled on the statute-book. The Minister of Justice of that day took occasion fittingly to acknowledge the labour and care that had been devoted by Sir John Macdonald in preparing the measure, which it became his duty to submit for the consideration of Parliament.†

The concern which Sir John Macdonald ever evinced for the due administration of justice, and for the character of his appointments to the Bench, has long been proverbial. From the day on which, at the beginning of his official career, he pressed upon Robert Baldwin the Chief Justiceship of

---

* To Sir John Rose, dated Ottawa, February 23, 1870.

† Among the countless suggestions which Sir John received in regard to the framing of this measure, I may refer to one from Mr. Alpheus Todd, the late Librarian of Parliament. Mr. Todd proposed, in view of the proviso for the Governor in Council obtaining the opinion of the Court upon constitutional questions, that, following English precedent, all the members of the Supreme Court should be members of the Privy Council, forming, as it were, a Canadian Judicial Committee.

Upper Canada, he seems to have considered the duty of advising
these appointments as one of the highest and most important
trusts committed to his charge.   An astute politician, he was
by no means indifferent to the influence and power of patronage, and, in the distribution of the favours of the Crown,
thoroughly believed in the wisdom and propriety (other things
being equal) of preferring his political supporters to his political
opponents.   That was his ordinary practice, as it is the rule
of every party leader.   But, when Sir John Macdonald came
to select a man for the judicial office, he knew neither friend
nor foe.   His sole inquiry was, who, by his high character,
legal attainments and experience, is best fitted to uphold the
prestige and dignity of the Bench.   To advocate the appointment of any one on other grounds, whether political or personal,
was to invite a rebuke such as this which, in 1864, he
addressed to a high public functionary who sought a judgeship
for his own son :—

"I am sorry that I cannot recommend J. as judge for
the county of ——.   My relations with yourself and your
family are such that it would give me great pleasure to aid
in helping any man of the name of ——; but J. is not fit
for a judgeship, and I cannot, in conscience, appoint him.
Careful and painstaking as he is, he would be a good administrative officer, and I shall have great pleasure in adopting
the earliest opportunity of giving him an administrative, but
not a judicial, office." *

Not only did he object to having unfit persons recommended
to him for the Bench, but he resented any unsolicited advice
in such matters, even though the suggestion was good in
itself.   I remember very well his displeasure on receiving
a petition, signed by all the barristers of a certain district,
praying for the appointment of one of their number.   "——
would make a good judge," said Sir John, thinking aloud,
as he sometimes did; "but, if those fellows don't withdraw
their requisition, I won't appoint him.   This sort of thing

---

* Four years later, he wrote to another gentleman, who had made a similar
request on behalf of a political friend : "I cannot possibly appoint —— a judge,
and I am rather surprised that you should ask me to do so. If anything turns up
in a non-judicial way, I will do what I properly can for him."

is most unseemly," he added, as he laid the paper down. At the same time, he was much given, especially in regard to the higher judicial offices at Toronto, to consult those who were in a position to furnish him with sound advice. I have shown, in an earlier chapter, how, when he was Attorney General of Upper Canada, he frequently had recourse, on such occasions, to Chancellor Blake, and I cannot find a happier illustration of his manner of making these appointments, after Confederation, than by referring to an incident which the elder Mr. Blake's name and office alike suggest.

In 1868, the retirement of Mr. Draper from the Chief Justiceship of Upper Canada, called for a general reorganization of the Bench. To aid him in effecting the best possible arrangement, Sir John sought the opinion, among others, of Mr. Edward Blake, the eldest son of the late Chancellor, already eminent both in his profession and in politics. Mr. Blake was, at that time, leader of the Opposition in the Ontario Legislature, and one of Sir John's most formidable opponents in the House of Commons. Yet this fact never seems to have weighed for a moment with the latter in considering how best he could · add to the strength of the courts. Thus, he writes to the Chancellor whom he proposed should succeed Mr. Draper, as Chief Justice of Ontario :—

"I am a good deal puzzled about the Court of Chancery. . . . If, however, Blake would take the Chancellorship, I think that, for the good of the Court, I ought to appoint him."

And again :—

"I waited for you at Toronto as long as I could, but I was due here on Saturday. I saw Blake before I left, and had a confidential talk with him. I told him exactly how matters stood—that you expressed a desire to stay where you were, but that I was to see you again on the subject. I said that I had no right to ask whether he would accept the Chancellorship, without offering it to him, but, under the circumstances, would ask him to give me some idea whether he could take it."

To Mr. Blake he subsequently wrote :—

" [Private.]
                    "Ottawa, November 9, 1868.

" My DEAR BLAKE,

    "After I had the pleasure of seeing you in Toronto, I waited a day for Vankoughnet, but, as he did not arrive, I was obliged to return here. I wrote him on the subject of his change in full, and he at last decided to remain where he now is. On public grounds I regret this much, as with your help we could have made a good Court of Equity, and the Common Law Bench would have been strengthened by Vankoughnet's accession to it. However, it cannot be helped. I have done everything in my power to keep up the efficiency of the Bench, but have been thus far thwarted. . . .

             " Yours very faithfully,
                   " JOHN A. MACDONALD."

On the death of Mr. Vankoughnet, in the following year, Sir John at once offered the Chancellorship to Mr. Blake. An intimate friend, to whom he had confided his intention, having expressed a fear that the appointment of so many " Grits " in succession to high office—" Howland, McDougall, Gwynne and now Blake "—would demoralize the Conservative party, was thus answered :—

    " As you are aware, my only object in making judicial appointments is the efficiency of the Bench. . . . I am not insensible to the fact that Blake's politics render his appointment difficult. It is an unfortunate as well as a singular coincidence that the members of the Equity Bar are very nearly all Grits. But what can be done ? Besides, I feel to a certain extent committed to Blake. Had Vankoughnet decided upon accepting the Chief Justiceship last year, Blake would have had the offer of the Chancellorship beyond a doubt. I told him confidentially that I would make him the offer, if the vacancy occurred. I do not think that anything has happened since then to warrant me in changing my course."

    In marked contrast to the success which attended Sir John Macdonald's public administration was the condition of his private affairs. For many years he had been unable to give personal attention to the business of his firm, which from the

ill health and subsequent death of his partner, Mr. A. J. Mac-
donell, became very much involved. The failure of the Commercial Bank, to which the firm was indebted, brought matters
to a crisis. With a view of honourably meeting all his obligations, Sir John transferred to the Merchants Bank of Canada
(which had succeeded to the business of the Commercial Bank)
everything he possessed, and, in the autumn of 1869, I do not
think he was worth one shilling in the world. It is not to
be doubted that the anxiety of mind caused by this unfortunate
condition of affairs aggravated the malady which, a few months
later, threatened his life.

During the session of 1870, Sir John Macdonald's days
were so fully occupied that he had scarcely time to eat. After
a light breakfast, often interrupted by early callers, he would
go to his office—thence to the Council, and thence to the
House of Commons, there to remain with the interval of an
hour for a hasty dinner, often until far into the night. Lady
Macdonald saw that this would not do—that her husband was
killing himself, and that, if she could not lighten the burden
of his work, she could at least insist upon his taking proper
nourishment. Sir John finally consented to allow luncheon
to be sent up to his office every day, and agreed to find time
for it between the rising of Council and the meeting of the
House.

On the afternoon of Friday, the 6th of May, he came out
of the Council Chamber about half-past two, and went to his
office in the same building (the room now occupied by the
Minister of the Interior), where his luncheon was awaiting him.
He had scarcely time to take his seat when Colonel Bernard,
who occupied the adjoining room, heard an unusual noise, and,
on opening the door that connected the two offices, perceived
that Sir John had fallen, and was writhing on the floor.
Doctors were hastily summoned, but when they arrived the
patient was almost pulseless and in a state of collapse. The
disease was pronounced to be biliary calculus. For many days
Sir John lay between life and death in the room where he was
seized, tended by the supreme devotion of a loving wife, who
nursed him with a solicitude to which he has repeatedly
declared he owed his life. Those who ministered round the

sick-bed scarce dared hope, while outside it was generally feared that the disease was mortal, and that Canada would lose her illustrious son. But it was otherwise decreed.

Despite the severity of the attack, and the intense pain with which his whole system was racked, Sir John Macdonald's naturally fine constitution at length triumphed, and, on the morning of the 1st of June, he was able to be transferred in a litter to the Speaker's chambers near by. This removal proved to be in truth what Mr. Blake, in a kind letter of inquiry, styled a "march of recovery." On the 2nd of July he was sufficiently well to leave for Prince Edward Island, where the sea breezes completed the cure. On the 22nd of September he returned to Ottawa, amid the acclaim of a whole people, who welcomed him as one risen from the dead.

The next day, he wrote thus to Mrs. Williamson :—

" Ottawa, September 23, 1870.

" MY DEAR MOLL,

" Agnes and I arrived here yesterday morning from Montreal. The people turned out to meet me in a very gratifying manner. However, you will see all that in the newspapers. I am now in very good health, and *nearly* as strong as before my illness. I hope, by care and regular exercise, I shall soon regain all my strength. I shall not do much work for some months, but act in the Government as consulting physician.

" We found your basket of grapes and letter awaiting our arrival, both very acceptable. Agnes has kept you, and will keep you, posted as to poor little baby. Baby has had a hard time of it, but, if we get her home here safely, I have more hopes of her than I ever have had. The *Pall Mall Gazettes* were sent to me to Prince Edward Island. I have kept them all, however, and will send them on, so that the Professor may read, if his tastes lie that way, the leading articles on the war. They are wonderfully clever and instructive.

" Give my best love to Louisa and the Parson, and believe me, my dear Moll, most affectionately yours,

" JOHN A. MACDONALD."

To read the numerous inquiries which were made concerning

Sir John during these anxious weeks, and the letters addressed to him on his recovery, is to recall another illness destined to have no such happy issue. In 1870, as in 1891, the country seemed to realize that it stood in the presence of a great calamity, from which it shrank back appalled. His Royal Highness Prince Arthur thus gave expression to the general feeling of satisfaction at the prospect of his recovery.

"Spencer Wood, Quebec, July 3, 1870.

"DEAR SIR JOHN,

"I cannot leave this country without wishing you adieu. Although I regret exceedingly not to have seen you before starting, yet it is a great pleasure to me to know that you are so very much better that your complete recovery will only be an affair of a week or two. Your illness has been a very long and tedious one, and I have watched the accounts of your recovery with the keenest interest and the greatest pleasure. May you long be spared to administer the affairs of this vast country, for I know how great is the power and influence you have over it. Canada is a great country, and, under your able administration, I feel sure that it will become one of the most flourishing and powerful countries in the world. I leave this country with great regret, having spent here the pleasantest and most interesting time I may ever have in this life.

"With kindest regards to Lady Macdonald, to whom we ought all to be indebted for the great care she has taken of you during your illness,

"I bid you adieu, and remain ever

"Yours very sincerely,

"ARTHUR."

Among Sir John Macdonald's political opponents there was none more pronounced or constant in his opposition than Mr. L. H. Holton, member for West Montreal. Mr. Holton's Liberalism was of that unyielding type which admits of no compromise. Yet Mr. Holton was one of the first to express his anxiety for the illustrious patient, and his joy at the prospect of his convalescence, in a note which, as every one can see, is no ordinary letter of inquiry.

"Montreal, May 15, 1870.

"MY DEAR MR. BERNARD,

"I rejoice most sincerely to learn from your telegrams and Lady Macdonald's that Sir John continues to make satisfactory progress towards convalescence.

" Although it has been my lot as a public man to be in constant opposition
to him and the party he has led with signal skill and ability, I have always
entertained the highest admiration for his talents, and, in spite of momentary
estrangements resulting from the interchange of hard blows in debate, I have
ever cherished the warmest personal regard for him.   On every ground, therefore, both public and private, do I fervently hope that his life will be spared
and his health and strength restored.

" With kind regards to Lady Macdonald and to Sir John himself, if his
strength admits of such communications,

" Believe me faithfully yours,

" L. H. HOLTON.

" H. Bernard, Esq."

Ten years later Sir John Macdonald, as with broken voice
he moved the adjournment of the House on the occasion of the
sudden death of his friend, showed the world how greatly
Mr. Holton's friendship was appreciated and how warmly it
was returned.

During the convalescence of Sir John Macdonald, Dr. Tupper
entered the Cabinet, taking the place of Mr. Kenny, appointed
Administrator of the Government of Nova Scotia.   The accession of a colleague so able and energetic as Dr. Tupper was
particularly welcome to the Prime Minister, who for several
weeks after his return to Ottawa, did not quite regain his seat
in the saddle.

The session, which opened on the 15th of February, was far
advanced when the illness of the Prime Minister deprived the
House of its leader.   Sir George Cartier promptly stepped into
the breach, and took up the Manitoba Bill, which had dropped
from the hands of his chief.   A few days later this measure
became law.   Under it the province of Manitoba was established, and provided with a system of constitutional government.   To set the machinery in motion was a task which the
unsettled condition of affairs at Red River, and the unfortunate question of race aggravated thereby, rendered extremely
difficult.

Throughout Ontario the cry of vengeance against the
murderers of Scott was strong and deep.   This feeling was
duly taken advantage of by the Opposition, and great was the
pressure upon the Federal Government to bring to justice all
who had taken part in that crime.   On the other hand, the

sympathies of the French Canadians were naturally with the half-breeds, while Her Majesty's Government, which alone had the power to arrest Riel for an offence committed in Rupert's Land before the transfer, made it a condition of Imperial assistance that the Red River settlers should receive considerate treatment at the hands of the Canadian Government. This policy of conciliation and kindness, according as it did with his own views, was carried out by Sir John, who, in the face of an opposition not confined to his political opponents, secured for the half-breeds of the Red River a generosity of treatment which those people appear to have never fully appreciated.

An important event of the year 1870 was the discontinuance of the system of granting licenses to foreign vessels, under which the United States fishermen had obtained access to Canadian waters since the abrogation, in 1866, of the Reciprocity Treaty of 1854. The subject of trade and fishing relations between the United States and Canada is of such complexity and magnitude as to render any satisfactory treatment of it in a few sentences a difficult if not an impossible task, yet it is one with which Sir John Macdonald had much to do, and for that reason cannot be omitted here. I shall, therefore, try to describe very briefly the condition of affairs with respect to this question at the time we are considering. By the Treaty of 1783 the citizens of the United States were acknowledged to possess certain rights of fishing, and were likewise granted certain privileges of fishing in British waters. At the termination of the war in 1812, and during the negotiation of the Treaty of Ghent, it was found impossible to reconcile the conflicting views of Great Britain and the United States regarding the fishery question, and, in consequence, the treaty was silent on the subject. Great Britain maintained that the war had abrogated all the privileges conceded by the Treaty of 1783, while the United States contended that they were entitled to a restoration of all the fishing privileges which they had enjoyed under that treaty. During the years 1815, 1816, and 1817, Great Britain made several seizures of United States fishing vessels, while Mr. Adams, then Minister at the Court of St. James, strongly pressed the American claim on the attention of the Foreign Secretary. At length a compromise was proposed, the basis of which was the concession by Great Britain of the liberty of fishing in certain defined waters, and the right to frequent certain specified coasts for drying and curing fish, and the absolute exclusion of American fishermen from all other waters but those to be specially conceded.

This agreement was made effectual by the Convention between His Majesty the King of Great Britain and the United States of America, signed at London on the 20th of October, 1818. It would be difficult to find language more clear than that employed in this treaty, to exclude United States fishermen from the waters reserved for the sole use of British subjects. Yet for many years before 1854 the Maritime Provinces of British North America had complained to the Imperial Government of the continual invasions of these inshore fisheries (sometimes accompanied, it was alleged, with violence) by United States fishermen and vessels, many of which latter were seized for breach of the provisions of the treaty. Much irritation naturally ensued, and it was at length felt expedient by both Governments to put an end to the unseemly state of things, a conclusion to which the United States were more readily led on perceiving England's resolve to protect the rights of her Canadian subjects.* The result of negotiations between the two powers was the Reciprocity Treaty of 1854, by which not only were our inshore fisheries opened to the Americans, but provision was made for the free interchange of the principal natural products of both countries, including those of the sea. Peace was preserved on our waters, and the volume of international trade steadily increased during the existence of this treaty, and until it was terminated in 1866 by the United States. In consequence of this action of the American Government, Canada was perforce thrown back on the Convention of 1818, and obliged to equip a marine police to enforce the laws and defend her rights. Still, however, desiring to cultivate friendly relations with her great neighbour, and not suddenly

* "Her Majesty's Ministers," wrote the Colonial Secretary, on the 27th of May, 1852, "are desirous to remove all ground of complaint on the part of the Colonies, in consequence of the encroachment of the fishing vessels of the United States upon those waters from which they are excluded by the terms of the Convention of 1818, and they therefore intend to despatch, as soon as possible, a small naval force of steamers, or other small vessels, to enforce the observance of that Convention."

to deprive the American fishermen of their accustomed fishing grounds and means of livelihood, she acquiesced in the proposal of Her Majesty's Government for the temporary issue of annual licenses to fish on payment of a nominal fee. This scheme proved a failure. At first a considerable number of licenses were taken out, but, in 1868, when the fee was increased to a sum which, although still moderate, bore some proportion to the privilege it represented, the number rapidly declined, until, in 1869, only twenty-five licenses were issued. Meanwhile the number of United States fishing-vessels plying their calling within the territorial waters of Canada showed no signs of diminution. In other words, the United States fishermen insisted on forcing themselves into our waters without " leave or license." In consequence of this state of things, the Dominion Government, after consultation with the Imperial authorities, resolved to do away with the license system altogether, and to exclude foreigners from fishing in Canadian waters. This policy was announced by an Order in Council of the 8th of January, 1870, and a small fleet of cruisers was chartered and equipped in defence of the fisheries. Then came the recurrence, in an aggravated form, of all the troubles which had taken place before the Reciprocity Treaty of 1854. There were invasions of our waters, personal conflicts between our fishermen and American crews, destruction of nets, seizure and condemnation of vessels, and intense consequent irritation on both sides.

Throughout the whole of this controversy Canada conducted herself with studied moderation, indulging in no overstrained assertion of any right, and avoiding, so far as . possible, any appearance of harshness, or a desire to push things to extremes. With this object in view, she refrained from making any seizures within bays, or raising the " headland question," which Her Majesty's Government, while sustaining the contention of Canada, wished to be left in abeyance. So also with the assertion of a right on the part of the American vessels to enter our ports for the purpose of trade, under pretence of which they habitually invaded our fishing grounds and fished in our waters. The Canadian Government had the clear words of the Treaty of 1818 in support of their contention, that the United States fishermen were granted admission to our harbours "for the purpose of shelter and of repairing damages therein, of purchasing wood, and of obtaining water, and for no other purpose whatever." They were supported by precedent, for previous to 1854 numerous seizures and detentions of foreign fishing vessels had taken place, for the offence of entering Canadian ports for purposes other than those expressly permitted by the Treaty of 1818.* Yet Canada, while asserting the right to exclude fishing vessels from its harbours and ports, took no measures to enforce it. This policy of conciliation was imposed by Sir John Macdonald, who adhered to it under circumstances of great provocation, partly because of its inherent soundness, and partly because it suited the game of Her Majesty's Government, whose countenance and support he well knew it was essential to retain.

It does not seem as though all Sir John Macdonald's colleagues shared their leader's view of the necessity for this extreme moderation. When, by reason of the Prime Minister's illness, the restraining hand was no longer felt, Canada's despatches took a loftier tone, and a vigorous policy of exclusion was decided on. On Sir John Macdonald's resuming command in October, more moderate counsels again prevailed.†

On more than one occasion the Canadian Government had expressed to the United States its desire to renew the reciprocity arrangement of 1854, but always without success. Besides the fisheries there were other questions at issue between the Dominion and the United States, notably Canada's claim arising out of the armed invasions of this country by American citizens, known as the Fenian raids. The loss and damage to the Dominion, and to many of its law-abiding citizens, occasioned

* See Vice Admiral Seymour's letter of the 12th of July, 1852, to the Administrator of the Government of Nova Scotia; also "Instructions by the Hon. Joseph Howe, Provincial Secretary of Nova Scotia," dated August 28, 1852.

† "We have discussed the subject of the exclusion of American fishermen from Canadian trading ports in Council, and have come to the conclusion, that we will not for the present enforce any such exclusion, the fishing vessels of course being subject to all the regulations and restrictions to which foreign trading vessels are subject in our ports. An Order in Council to this effect will pass as soon as I am able to prepare a report on the matter, which will be in a day or two. Meanwhile, perhaps, it would be well for Your Excellency to write to Sir Edward Thornton to that effect. I told you at Spencer Wood that Council had been going too fast, and that there was a way out of the difficulty." (From Sir John Macdonald to His Excellency the Governor General, dated Ottawa, October 31, 1870.)

by these wanton and unprovoked attacks were very considerable, and the propriety of demanding reparation for them at the
hands of the United States was strongly pressed upon Her
Majesty's Government.

In addition to Canada's grievances, England herself was
engaged about this time in a controversy with the United States,
over the " Alabama claims," which threatened the gravest consequences.   In the amicable settlement of this dispute, Canada
was deeply concerned, for in the event of war between the two
powers this country would inevitably be the battle ground and
chief sufferer.

For many reasons, therefore, Sir John Macdonald welcomed
the announcement, made early in 1871, that an agreement had
been arrived at between Great Britain and the United States,
whereby all matters in dispute between the two Governments
were to be referred to the consideration of a Joint High Commission, to assemble in Washington without delay.

CHAPTER XX.

THE TREATY OF WASHINGTON.

1871.

"WHEN SOME ONE WRITES MY BIOGRAPHY—IF I AM EVER THOUGHT WORTHY OF HAVING SUCH AN INTERESTING DOCUMENT PREPARED—AND WHEN, AS A MATTER OF HISTORY, THE QUESTIONS CONNECTED WITH THIS TREATY ARE UPHELD, IT WILL BE FOUND THAT, UPON THIS, AS WELL AS UPON EVERY OTHER POINT, I DID ALL I COULD TO PROTECT THE RIGHTS AND CLAIMS OF THE DOMINION."—*Speech of Sir John Macdonald in the House of Commons, May 3, 1872.*

I NOW come to the consideration of a subject, in respect of which, more than any other single event of his public life, Sir John Macdonald desired that the part he had taken in it should be made known to the world. Impervious, as a rule, to the attacks of his opponents, he cared little for any accusations they might bring against him. Yet this rule had its exception, for the charge made in the first instance by the *Globe*, and taken up by the Opposition, both in and out of Parliament, that, in the negotiations which led to the Treaty of Washington, he had betrayed the interests of Canada, wounded him deeply. That he had compromised principle for the sake of office; that he had sold a charter; that, overwhelmed with remorse for his crimes, he had committed suicide: these, and a thousand other calumnies equally odious, never seemed to have the slightest effect upon him; but the imputation of having failed in his duty at Washington, he never forgot.

"Take care of those papers," he said to me a few weeks before his death, referring to his correspondence with Dr. Tupper, while in Washington; "they will be of great use some day." At that time I had not studied their contents, nor was it until I carefully read his speech, submitting the treaty to the Canadian Parliament for ratification, in the course of which he uttered the words placed at the head of this chapter, that I realized the obligation laid upon me when he placed these papers in my hands. This duty I must now endeavour to fulfil as best I can.

On the 1st of February, Sir John learned through the Governor General that the suggestion, made in the first instance by Canada, of the appointment of a Joint High Commission to adjust all differences between Great Britain and the United States had been adopted. Lord Lisgar, at the same time, informed him of the desire of Her Majesty's Government that he should form one of that important tribunal, and requested, on behalf of Lord Kimberley, an expression of opinion as to the advisability of asking Sir John Rose to act in a similar capacity.

Respecting the latter suggestion, Sir John Macdonald's answer was at once forthcoming. Though an intimate friend, of whose loyalty to Canada and himself he had no more doubt than of his inherent fitness for the position, Sir John felt bound to inform the Imperial Government that Sir John Rose would not be acceptable to the people as their representative on the Commission. Not only was he not a Canadian by birth, but he had become permanently resident in England. In addition to this disqualification, the chief objection to him lay in the fact that he was partner in an American banking house, which had not the most remote connection with Canada. As regards himself, Sir John Macdonald wrote:—

"I have thought over Lord Kimberley's proposition that I should act on the Joint Commission with the United States on Fishery and other matters. I am a good deal embarrassed by my not being able to communicate with my colleagues on the subject. My first impression was that it would be better for Canada not to be represented on such a Commission. But then we must consider that, if Canada allowed the matter to go by default, and left its interests to be adjudicated upon and settled by a Commission composed exclusively of Americans having an adverse interest, and Englishmen having little or no interest in Canada, the Government here would be very much censured if the result were a sacrifice of the rights of the Dominion. England would at once say that the offer to be represented on the Commission was made to Canada, and that it was declined. Surrounded with difficulties as the matter seems to be, I think that, perhaps, the best answer to be given is this: that I will act on getting the consent of my colleagues, and Lord Kimberley might be requested not to decide the matter until you have an opportunity of writing him on the subject. If the points of agreement and difference between England and Canada on the Fishery question were settled it would all be plain sailing, especially if, as I presume would be the case, any convention would be inoperative until ratified by the respective Governments. I am not aware that there is any difference of opinion, the only divergence, as yet, being as to the extent to which the rights of Canada should be enforced." *

In conformity with the opinion of his colleagues, that Canada should be represented in the negotiations, Sir John, with many misgivings, finally acquiesced in the proposal that he should form one of the Commission. The original proposition was that this Commission should consist of three members on each side. The number was subsequently increased to five, a change which, in the opinion of Sir John Macdonald, obliged him again to take the view of the Cabinet as to whether he should accept, the original consent of his colleagues having been given to his forming one of three. With one voice they said he should adhere to his acceptance. On the 22nd of February he writes to Sir John Rose: "I contemplate my visit to Washington with a good deal of anxiety. If anything goes wrong I shall be made the scape-goat; at all events, so far as Canada is concerned. However, I thought that after all Canada has done for me, I should not shirk the responsibility." Sir John had another reason for hesitation. His acceptance would involve his absence during a session of Parliament, in which event the leadership of the House would fall on Sir George Cartier, who, principally for reasons arising

* From Sir John Macdonald to His Excellency the Governor General, dated Ottawa, February 4, 1871.

out of the lamentable occurrence at Red River in the preceding
year (for which he was in no way responsible, and which he
greatly deplored), had, to some extent, lost the confidence of
the Ontario members. Sir John's forebodings in this respect
proved only too true. Many a time have I heard him say
that, to his absence from Parliament in 1871, he ascribed his
defeat in 1873. For these reasons it was with no very light
heart that he left Ottawa for Washington on the morning of
the 27th of February, accompanied by Lady Macdonald.

The British Commissioners were received with much
hospitality by the President and his Ministers. Sir John
thus describes his meeting with various leading men of the
day:—

"We found Sir Edward Thornton's carriage and one of
his attachés, the Honourable Mr. Trench, awaiting us at the
station. We have comfortable quarters at the Arlington, but
the Commissioners have established a Bachelors' Hall of their
own, which will be gay enough, as Lord de Grey is known to
be hospitable, and has brought his cook with him. In company
with Sir Edward, on Wednesday I called upon Mr. Fish, with
whom I had a short conversation, and subsequently visited
the American Commissioners, viz. General Schenck, Judge
Nelson of the Supreme Court, Judge Hoar of Massachusetts,
and Senator Williams. I also called with Sir Edward on
Charles Sumner. He is very much broken in health, and
looks as if he were not going to last long. He was, however,
full of agreeable conversation, and we talked about a great
many people whom we both knew. I subsequently went with
Thornton to Mrs. Fish's reception, where I met and was introduced to a number of people, and afterwards called upon
Mrs. Colfax, the wife of the Vice-President. All the Commissioners and a number of other swells dined with Mr. Fish
on that day. Of course, I saw Lord de Grey and the other
English Commissioners during the day. This ends Wednesday's
record.

"About mid-day the whole of the British Commissioners
visited the Capitol, General Schenck acting as *cicerone*, and we
were introduced on the floor of both Houses. While in the
Senate we shook hands with most of the Senators, and had

more or less talk with them. They all professed the strongest hopes that the negotiations might result in a permanent treaty. The joke was, that before going into the Senate, General Schenck said he would send for a Senator to conduct us, and he sent for Chandler of Michigan, telling him that the British Lion was waiting for him, and he must come out and confront him. Chandler was very civil, and did the honours with great kindness. In the evening we dined with Lord de Grey, a sort of family party of our own, and went thence to a reception at Lady Thornton's, where we met only the Corps Diplomatique and their wives.

"Before we met we were present at a most interesting ceremony. We went to the House of Representatives and were admitted to the floor—the Diplomatic Gallery, where we have seats of right, having been given up for the nonce to the ladies. Exactly at 12 o'clock Mr. Blaine, the Speaker, delivered a short and very neat valedictory, bidding the 41st Congress good-bye, thanking them for their kindness and support to him, and complimenting them upon the manner in which they had performed their duties. It was altogether very well done. Thereupon they adjourned, and about fifty old members walked out and fifty young ones walked in. The Speaker left the Chair, he having ceased to be Speaker, and the Clerk took possession and called the roll. He then called upon them to elect a Speaker. Blaine was nominated by the Republicans, and a Mr. Morton by the Democrats. Blaine, as it was known he would be, was elected, the vote being 126 to 93, and this vote shows pretty accurately the comparative strength of the parties. So you see that the Democrats have gained considerably on their opponents. The new Speaker, on being conducted to the Chair, made another very neat speech of thanks, and took occasion to refer in very fitting and complimentary terms to the Commission, with an earnest hope that their action would result in permanent peace between the two nations.

"Last night we had another official dinner at Lord de Grey's, where all the Commissioners dined. General Sherman was present. He seems to be a remarkably agreeable person, and is wonderfully popular here. At half-past eleven on Monday, Sir Stafford and I are to be presented to the President, and at noon the Commission will sit. It is intended that we should meet every day at the same hour, so our time will be pretty well occupied.

"When at the House yesterday, I was introduced to Ben Butler. He talked very pleasantly, and told us some very amusing anecdotes apropos of the Parliamentary practice in the House. Among other things, he told us that Saturday is given up to members who desire to make buncombe speeches for their constituents. The Speaker usually makes it a holiday, and appoints somebody else to take his place. Frequently the speakers have an audience of from six to twenty, and sometimes by agreement the speeches are handed in without being read, and appear in the *Congressional Globe*, the American Hansard. This plan, he says, has had its inconveniences. On one occasion a speech turned out to be a violent personal attack upon Sumner. It appears, too, that they have professional penny-a-liners, who write speeches for illiterate members. One of these gentry sold the same speech to two members. It was handed in by both, and appeared twice in the same *Globe*. I think this is gossip enough for one letter." *

On the same day he wrote another letter to Doctor Tupper, from which I make a quotation :—

"Since writing my account of our doings here, I have seen Lord de Grey. He has had an unofficial conversation with a leading statesman here, and thought it of sufficient importance to come down here after church and mention it to me. I now send it on to you, but cannot mention the name of the statesman, as I have but little confidence in the Post Office here.

"This man said that there would doubtless be a good deal of gas talked about the fisheries. That without any question as to the right, the United States must have the inshore fisheries, but were ready to pay for them. Lord de Grey very properly said that he had no instructions on that matter, but would, of course, submit any proposition for the consideration of his Government. He asked if the United States were ready for a renewal of the Reciprocity Treaty on the same terms as before. The man replied that he did not think Congress could be brought to sanction anything of the kind just now, but what

* To the Hon. Charles Tupper, dated Washington, March 5, 1871.

he alluded to was a pecuniary equivalent. There the conversation ended.

" I told Lord de Grey we had not even taken into consideration any other equivalent, but that of enlarged commercial intercourse in the direction of reciprocity, and as nearly approaching the old Reciprocity Treaty as the exigencies of the U.S. revenue would permit. That I did not at all know how a money payment would be received, but my impression was that it would be out of the question for Canada to surrender, for all time to come, her fishery rights for any compensation, however great. That we had no right to injure posterity by depriving Canada, either as a dependency or as a nation, of her fisheries, and in my opinion any surrender must be for a term of years renewable by either party, or, what would be preferable, for an unspecified period, but liable to be terminated by either party. That the fisheries were valuable in themselves, and would, with increasing population, become annually of more value ; but the value of the catch was of less consequence than the means which the exclusive enjoyment of the fisheries gave us of improving our position as a maritime power. That Canada possessed infinitely more valuable fisheries than the United States, with better harbours, and if we pursued the exclusive system vigorously, we might run a winning race with the U.S. as a maritime power. That were our fishing-grounds used in common by our own and American fishermen, the latter would enjoy the same training-school as ourselves, etc., etc.

" I said, however, that I would write in general terms to Ottawa, and get the views of my colleagues on this branch of the question, that is, supposing the Canadian fishing rights admitted to the fullest extent, and reciprocity to the full extent refused, what other equivalent would be a sufficient inducement to Canada to restore the liberty of fishing in our inshore waters ?

" Let me ask you to submit this letter in the strictest confidence to Council, and let me have some general expression of opinion for my guidance, should the question be put to the British Commissioners."

On the 8th of March Sir John instructed his Government to cable the Colonial Office to the effect that Canada considered the inshore fisheries her property, and that they could not be sold without her consent. To this telegram the Colonial Minister replied that Her Majesty's Government never had any intention of selling the inshore fisheries of Canada without her consent.

On the 17th of March, Sir John wrote to Dr. Tupper :—

"It was a most fortunate thought to send a telegram to Lord Kimberley, as on my expression of disinclination to enter upon the question of sale or lease of the fisheries, communication was had with Lord Granville, who authorized the Commission to discuss the question of sale, at the same time expressing a preference for a sale in perpetuity. Upon this I produced Lord Kimberley's answer, which was a floorer. Lord de Grey is now doubtless communicating with Lord Granville as to the apparent discrepancy between his statement and that of Lord Kimberley.".

On the 21st of March he wrote :—

"The result of Lord de Grey's communication with Lord Granville, which I mentioned in my last, was an instruction to proceed with the negotiations for the settlement of the fisheries, but to insert a clause in the treaty that its provisions would be subject to ratification by the Canadian Parliament.

"This instruction, though satisfactory in some respects, places me in an exceedingly embarrassing position. If a majority of my colleagues should at any time conclude to accept terms which I do not approve of, I must, of course, either protest and withdraw, or remain on the Commission and trust to the non-ratification of the treaty by Canada.

"If I take the first course, it will disclose to the Americans the existence of a difference of opinion—a conflict, in fact, between Canada and England. This the Americans are anxious to establish, in order to get up a sort of quarrel between the two, and to strengthen that party in England which desires to get rid of the colonies as a burden.

"If I continue to act on the Commission I shall be attacked for making an unworthy sacrifice of Canada's rights, and may be compelled to vote in Parliament against a treaty which I had a share in making. I must manage matters, however, as best I can, according to circumstances. . . .

" I forgot to say, by the way, that Lord de Grey took occasion to let them know that any fishery treaty must be ratified by the Legislature of Canada. This, Mr. Fish said, might be productive of much delay and inconvenience, and he, or one of them said, they thought they were dealing with the British Empire and not with Canada.

" Lord de Grey replied that he felt bound to give them notice of the fact in the same spirit in which they had given us notice at the commencement of our negotiation, that any treaty that might be settled upon would be subject to the ratification of the Senate. Mr. Fish asked if it would also be subject to ratification by Prince Edward Island and Newfoundland?

" To this Lord de Grey replied that he could not answer them at once, as he was not sufficiently apprised of the constitution of those two islands. I did not choose to enlighten them upon the point, as I think it well to keep the case of Canada separate. If we come to any satisfactory treaty, I shall endeavour to have it limited to the Dominion of Canada, so that if Prince Edward Island and Newfoundland desire the advantages of the treaty they must come into Confederation.

" I do not think there is the least chance of their giving us the coasting trade. I do not believe that they will even agree to free coasting in our inland waters. Having nearly made up my mind that the Americans want everything, and will give us nothing in exchange, one of my chief aims now is to convince the British Commissioners of the unreasonableness of the Yankees. This they are beginning to find out, and are a good deal disappointed.

" I have taken strong grounds with my colleagues, that it would be exceedingly unwise to agree to any terms, which it is not reasonably probable would be accepted by Canada, as, should any treaty be made, and afterwards rejected by our Parliament, the feeling of irritation would be greatly intensified."

On the 22nd of March Sir John telegraphed Dr. Tupper as follows :—

" On Monday we resumed Fishery question, and repeated

our desire to obtain Reciprocity Treaty in principle as an equivalent. Americans stated that was impossible, but offered one million dollars for the fisheries in perpetuity. We could not agree to this. To-day discussion continued. We offered to take free fish, salt, coal, lumber, and coasting trade. They refused the coasting trade at once. We then offered to leave out the coasting trade, and take instead a sum of money to be settled hereafter. After long consideration they offered free coal and salt, and free admission into their market of mackerel, herring, and cod; also to allow lumber free from 1st July, 1876. And they desired mutual free fishing in the lakes and the St. Lawrence above St. Regis, but not in the streams falling into them. They admit that coal and salt must be free in December next. We think they may be induced to consent to make all fish free, and perhaps to free lumber at an early date. They refuse any additional money payment. All this was to be for a term of years to be agreed upon, and on two years' notice afterwards. I do not think it likely they will offer better terms. Please send me decision of Council." *

On the 29th of March he wrote Doctor Tupper:—

"My long telegram of the 22nd will have informed you of the state of fishery matters up to that time. You may imagine that my position was exceedingly embarrassing. In our separate caucuses my colleagues were continually pressing me to yield—in fact, I had no backer, and I was obliged to stand out, and, I am afraid, to make myself extremely disagreeable to them.

"In order, however, to show that I would go as far as possible, I consented that we should offer to accept free coal, salt, fish, lumber, and the coasting trade, in exchange for the fisheries. I had ascertained, almost beyond a doubt, that the coasting trade would be refused. If, however, it had been accepted, I think the bargain would not have been a bad one, as we would very soon have absorbed all the coasting trade on

---

* This was answered on the 24th. "Council considers terms offered in your telegram of the 22nd are so inadequate to the value of the fisheries of Canada, that no Government could carry a proposal so obnoxious to the people through our Parliament. Although very anxious to settle this question, such a solution would only make matters worse, as great irritation must follow the certain rejection, by the Parliament of Canada, of the terms proposed."

the lakes and that portion of the Atlantic which they would have given us: probably to the 36th or 39th parallel.

"I always held that even with coasting trade the equivalent was insufficient, and that it must be supplemented in some way. The offer was, however, as I anticipated, declined without a moment's consideration. Mr. Fish said, and said truly, that, with our advantages of cheap ships and cheap labour, we would get possession of the whole of the coasting trade, and drive them from their own waters.

"They then made the counter proposition mentioned in my telegram, offering free coal and salt, and free mackerel, herring, and cod. Also to allow lumber free from the 1st July, 1876, and claiming mutual free fishing in the lakes and the St. Lawrence.

"On the 23rd the question of the navigation of the St. Lawrence and canals was taken up. The Americans said that they considered that the free navigation of Lakes Michigan and Champlain, the use of the Sault Ste. Marie Canal and of the canal at the St. Clair Flats, would be an equivalent for the St. Lawrence, and the use of our canals on equal terms with our own people.

"A long discussion followed, in which I, with Mr. Fish, took the principal part. I argued that the navigation of the St. Lawrence, in its natural state, should be considered as an equivalent for Lake Michigan. That we had the same right to navigate Lake Champlain as we had Lake Ontario, neither more nor less. That by the Ashburton Treaty we had the same right to use all the channels through the St. Clair Flats as the Americans, and if they (the Americans) chose to improve any one of those channels by artificial means, they could not deprive us of the right to use them, though they might have a fair claim to a contribution to the cost of construction. That the only thing that remained was the Sault Ste. Marie Canal of one mile, against our Welland and St. Lawrence canals of seventy miles.

"Mr. Fish, in the course of the discussion, expressed his desire that our canals should be deepened to fourteen feet, and spoke of our agreeing to do so. I asked what consideration would be given us by the United States for such an obligation.

He said that the American shipping would use our canals much more than our own would, and that a fair toll might be agreed upon, not discriminating, however, which would be sufficient to maintain the canals in good repair and form a sinking fund to pay off the debt. That that would be a fair contribution from the United States towards the construction.

"I replied that we had no present intention of putting on a discriminating toll, but we should, unless fully compensated, reserve the right of dealing with that subject as we thought best. That, if the canals were enlarged, it would be for our interest to draw as much trade as possible through them into our waters, and the United States might fairly leave the question of tolls to our judgment. That there was no more reason why Canada should not make a profit out of her canals than the State of New York out of hers. That, with respect to the Sault· Ste. Marie Canal, the report of the Canal Commissioners, which I had just received, enabled me to state that Canada could construct one for $550,000, and that, probably, we should think it better to go to that expense, at all events, so as to have a connected water route by lake, river, and canal in our country.

"I made no allusion to the stoppage of the *Chicora*, it might have led to an annoying discussion, and would have answered no good purpose. After a great deal of desultory talk we adjourned without coming to any conclusion.

"The British Commissioners had a meeting after the adjournment, and I found they were in favour of ceding the fisheries for ten years, with two years' notice—that is to say, for twelve years certain—in exchange for coal, salt, fish, and lumber; hence my great desire to get your answer to my telegram of the 22nd. It arrived on the morning of the 24th, but there was no meeting of the Conference on that day.

"On the 25th I thought it better to see Lord de Grey alone before our usual meeting at 11 a.m. I placed in his hands my message of the 22nd and your answer, thus giving him distinct notice of the opinion of the Canadian Government. I proceeded to state my own objections as a Commissioner, and that I could not concur in the proposition, and I desired he should consider this as a formal statement of non-concurrence on my part. He consented to my putting it in writing.

" I suggested the expediency, in order to induce the Americans to grant more liberal terms, of his stating to them when we met that it was not likely the present offer would be accepted by Canada. He said that might lead to an argument which would disclose the existence of a divergence of opinion between Canada and England, which would be certain to make the Americans hold more firmly to their point. I therefore left that to his better judgment.

" I then placed in his hands your answer to my telegram of the 24th, and thought it as well to show him your private one, stating that Council might agree to the four articles free, with a substantial money consideration; and I took the opportunity of hinting that that compensation must come from either the United States or England. To the last suggestion he made no reply, but smiled. I did this to lay the foundation of a demand on England for full compensation for any sacrifices she might call upon us to make.

" We proceeded to the Conference, when Lord de Grey stated that, with respect to the navigation of the rivers and lakes, our views of the comparative value of what we had respectively to offer were at such variance that we thought it better to leave things as they were. That the present arrangements were perfectly satisfactory, and we believed it would be in the interest of both nations that no change should be made. That, however, we did not desire to be understood as closing the door against the consideration of further propositions on the subject, should they be inclined to make any.

" He then proceeded to state that the British Commissioners thought the offers made on both subjects, viz. navigation and fisheries, were quite inadequate. That he desired them to understand that this was not merely a formal statement, but the full and honest conviction of us all. That, however, in order to prove the earnest desire of the British Government to settle all cases of possible conflict or irritation, he wished to state, having special reference to his position in the British

Government, that he was ready to recommend the granting of the fisheries for a term of years with notice, in exchange for the four free articles.

" The U.S. Commissioners took time to consider, and then replied that they would allow lumber free from the 1st of July, 1875; but, in consequence of existing contracts, they could not go any further. That, if we did not give them mutual free fishing in the lakes and the St. Lawrence, they must specify the fish that were to be admitted free, and they also desired to change the 36th parallel in the second article of the Reciprocity Treaty to the 39th parallel.

" After consultation, Lord de Grey replied that he was not at the moment able to give an answer as to the lake fishing, and we adjourned until Monday the 27th.

" On Sunday I prepared and sent a letter * to Lord de Grey, stating the substance of our conversation on the previous morning. I was quite prepared for the effect of my letter, as it showed itself at our next meeting on Monday morning. It was formally read, and His Lordship proceeded at considerable length to object to its terms, admitting it had been agreed that I might reduce our conversation to writing as a safeguard for myself.

" He objected to its form being of such an official character as to compel him to put it on record. In stating, as it did, that I objected to the proposal being made, it led to the inference that no previous attempts had been made to get better terms, and he recapitulated the many offers that had been made, and the stout battle which had been fought for them. He objected to my unqualified statement that the Canadian Parliament would reject the treaty, and also to the statement which I had made as firmly, that I could not justify or defend it in Parliament. Under these circumstances the continuance of the discussion with the U.S. Commissioners would be a farce. It would be uncandid in us to go on with the negotiations, when officially informed that they must result in nothing. That he felt strongly that it was his duty at once to inform the U.S. Commissioners that negotiations

* This letter and the memorandum which was eventually substituted for it form Appendix XXI.

as to the fisheries were at an end, and this might lead to disastrous results as to the negotiations generally.

"He was followed by the other Commissioners *seriatim*, who all made speeches *at* me. Montague Bernard objected only to the time of my making the objection, the proper time being, in his opinion, at the conclusion of the negotiations.

"I replied at length, stating that I was not wedded to the form of the communication, but what I desired was to place my position on a more firm basis than a mere recollection of the conversation would leave it. That if my letter was considered too formal, I would substitute for it a memorandum to the same effect, for reference hereafter. That as to the time of my making the objection, it must be remembered that it was arranged on the 22nd that I should telegraph to the Canadian Government the exact position of affairs and get their answer. That so soon as the answer arrived I, of course, placed it in Lord de Grey's hands, and followed it up by my own statement in accordance with it. That the reason why I did not enter, in my letter, into a detail of all the previous negotiations was, that I had not done so in my conversation, and my letter was merely to be a re-statement of that conversation, when, of course, no reference was made to such negotiations. That with respect to the positive assertion that Canada would not ratify such a treaty, I was bound in candour to give them my best opinion, and I was confirmed in its accuracy by the telegram received and submitted by me. That I had not stated in my letter that I would not justify or defend any such treaty, but that it would be difficult for me to do so. That I then felt the difficulty, and did not see how it could be surmounted. That *possibly* it might be, but when the time came I must be free to act according to my conscience, and as the interests of my country required. That, however, I would so modify my expressions with respect to the anticipated action of the Canadian Legislature as to remove the obstacle which Lord de Grey saw in the way of continuing negotiations.

"My reason for taking this line was, that it was evidently Lord de Grey's aim to make me and Canada responsible for a breach of the negotiations generally, in case things went wrong. I was resolved not to let any blame be attached to

Canada in that respect, and thus strengthen the hands of the party in England who consider Canada a burden to be got rid of and an obstacle to friendly relations with the United States.

"Having had this preliminary shindy, we proceeded to the conference room. Lord de Grey, repeating that he considered the question of navigation at an end, proceeded to say that he had discussed the question of lake fishing, and we thought matters should remain as at present for reasons that I could better explain.

"I explained that the fishing in the St. Lawrence, between the point where the parallel of 45 strikes the St. Lawrence and Kingston, was of no commercial value and required no treaty. That the seizure of the fishing party at Cornwall was a mere indiscretion of a person there, and it had been at once disavowed by the Canadian Government, and the property seized had been restored, and we would take care that such things should not happen again.

"That we could not agree to free fishing in the lakes, as we did not allow free fishing to our own people, but had introduced a system of licenses and leases, with very stringent regulations as to a close season, as to the protection of other lessees and licensees, and also as to the artificial stocking and breeding of our rivers and lake shores. That the United States had no lake fisheries to offer, as their fisheries had been destroyed from the refusal of the several States to protect them. That we had hitherto allowed Americans to take out and pay for licenses on the same terms as our own people. That if we put in a clause for free fishing they would come over and, disregarding our regulations, would insist on free fishing under the treaty; and therefore, for the sake of peace, which had hitherto never been disturbed, I thought it better that the matter should remain as at present.

"Lord de Grey then pressed that the right of fishing to the 36th parallel should be retained, and all the other language that was used in the Reciprocity Treaty; and he hoped that they would reconsider the question of the time for the admission of free lumber.

"Mr. Fish replied, that the treaty had been so unpopular in

the United States that they wished to alter its terms; to which we answered, that, on account of its popularity in Canada, we wished to preserve it as much as possible.

" He (Mr. Fish) said the reason why they desired the limit to be the 39th parallel was, that no Canadian fishing vessels had ever fished, or would ever fish, between the two parallels, and the retention of the most southerly one would cause great expense to both Governments in providing for the marking of the mouths of the rivers by a commission, similar to the one under the old treaty.

" That they would grant free fish, except fish preserved in oil, and the fish of the lakes and their tributaries. That they would grant also fish oil, and they would make a still further concession as to lumber, which would become free after the 1st of July, 1874, but that this was their ultimatum. That any earlier period would ruin their saw-millers and excite immense opposition to the treaty, besides interfering with contracts, etc.

" There were several withdrawals for the purpose of consultation during these discussions, and I took occasion to have it clearly understood that, as I took objection to the acceptance of the equivalent proposed by Lord de Grey, I was, of course, still more opposed to any further restrictions, and they must understand that all such restrictions would make the treaty, if possible, more unpalatable to Canada.

" Mr. Fish said he presumed, in case an arrangement took place, that the fisheries would be thrown open to the fishermen for the present season. Lord de Grey replied that this depended on the state of the law, but if the treaty were ratified, he would say for the British Government, that every endeavour would be made to meet their views in this particular. Lord de Grey then asked when our coal, salt, and fish would be admitted free. Mr. Fish replied, that, if the treaty were ratified by the Senate, they would be admitted free from the 1st of July next. We then adjourned, it being understood that Lord de Grey would recommend his Government to accept these terms. I forgot to say that, in one of our consultations, we discussed the question of our authority to make our waters free during the present season.

" I said the Government of Canada could, of course, if it

thought proper, order its officers not to seize; but I apprehended that any Canadian fisherman might lay an information before a justice for breach of the law, in which case the Canadian Government had no power to interfere, but might remit the penalties after conviction.

"It was then suggested, I think by Lord Tenterden, that the principal statute respecting the fisheries was the Imperial Act, 59 George III., c. 38, which could be repealed in England.

"I at once said that I disputed this power. That the Act might be repealed by the Imperial Parliament, if they chose to do so; but it was now a portion of the law of Canada, and, although repealed as to England, might still be held to be in force in the Dominion.

"This, however, is a serious question. On looking at our Acts, I find that our own Colonial statutes are very defective if deprived of the Imperial Act as their basis. I cannot suppose, however, that England would take the extreme step of repealing the Act without our consent, or of refusing to sanction an Act of ours to the same effect. Thus the case now stands.

"A confidential cable was sent by Lord de Grey, stating the terms, and at the same time stating that I did not concur in the settlement, on the ground that the compensation was inadequate, and that I doubted whether the Canadian Parliament would ratify the arrangement, although the rest thought the settlement reasonable.

"I now consider that I have merely a watching brief. I will stay to see that a clause is inserted in the treaty providing that the article relating to the fisheries shall not take effect until ratified by the Canadian Parliament.

"I shall watch the San Juan case and the Fenian claims. I am now, as you know, looking into the practice as to the mode of expressing my non-concurrence in the treaty. Of that I am resolved there shall be no doubt in the public mind.

"I think you will see from these details that my position has not been a pleasant one. We are, however, masters of the position, if we play our game with skill and firmness.

"My colleagues are very anxious that I should agree to mix up the question of navigation and of the fisheries together, with an attempt to get free wool and animals as the equivalent for the use of our canals. This I absolutely declined, and we can hereafter, if so disposed, use our power over our canals so as to force reciprocity. They have now literally nothing to give us in exchange for free transit but free trade.

"I imagine that the Americans will begin a series of propositions on the navigation matter, but I will listen to no offer short of reciprocity."

On the 1st of April Sir John wrote Doctor Tupper :—

"On Thursday morning I had another scrimmage with my colleagues. The night before, Lord de Grey had seen Mr. Fish informally on the Alabama matter, and, in the course of their conversation, Mr. Fish stated that he apprehended considerable difficulty in carrying the treaty in the Senate if some concession were not made as to the canals. That, personally, he was satisfied with things as they are, but the West attached an exaggerated importance to an arrangement for free navigation.

"This statement was, of course, made to frighten Lord de Grey into his terms by exciting his fears of losing the treaty. Mr. Fish stated, as I have to-day telegraphed you, that he was willing to allow the St. Lawrence to stand against Lake Michigan and Lake Champlain, and the Sault Ste. Marie and St. Clair Flats canals against the Welland and St. Lawrence. That he desired the bonding system to be made a permanent arrangement, instead of being at the discretion of both Governments, and he would give the right to our vessels to carry from American to American ports on the lakes, in bond, where land transport intervened, and, in that respect, make a breach in their coasting laws, on our granting the same privilege to them, in the manner my telegram will have informed you.

"That, as part of the arrangement, however, he would ask that the export duty should be taken off lumber at St. John, New Brunswick, and that no export duty should be charged upon the products of either of the countries when shipped from the other.

"I stated that this relaxation of the coasting trade would be of considerable advantage to us, but not in any way an equivalent for our canals. That we desired to keep the control

of them until we had free trade in exchange for free transit.
As to the export duties, I said I feared it would be found
that they were under the control of the New Brunswick
legislature under the British North America Act, 1867.

"My colleagues all argued strongly that we would never put
on discriminating tolls, and that, therefore, there was no object
in keeping the power and using it like the crack of a whip
over the Americans. That they believed that, so long as it
was kept as a threat, the Americans would not grant us free
trade. That this coasting transhipment was a substantial
boon, and so on. I said the canals were the property of the
provinces of Canada exclusively, and we had a right to do as
we liked with our own. That Canada stood with respect to
the empire in that respect, exactly as the State of New York
did with regard to the General Government.

"In 1854 the United States promised to endeavour to get
us the use of the New York canals. That they would have
failed if they had tried; and we submitted, as a matter of
course, knowing that New York had every right to refuse
if it chose. That we claimed the same right. That, while
English statesmen might say that we were injuring ourselves,
that our course was contrary to the present Liberal principles
of trade and the rules of political economy, our answer was,
this was for us to consider.

"Lord de Grey hinted that the instructions specially
enjoined them to deal with the navigation of the St. Lawrence.

"My answer was that, with respect to this question, it
certainly was a matter of Imperial as well as colonial concern.
That I presumed England would not abandon the exclusive
right to the river, inasmuch as the Americans did not claim
it; but, if she did, we could not help it. That, as to the
canals, I protested against any interference.

"I stated that England had no more right to give transit
through our canals than she would have to give the people
of France, by treaty, free transit over the London and North-
Western Railway. The matter ended in my agreeing to write
you in full on Friday morning, and point out to you that the
Commissioners thought it of great importance to the Empire
and to Canada that there should be lasting peace between

England and the United States. That this could only be kept by the removal of all difficulties, and, if by any accident the negotiations were broken off, things would be worse between the two nations than ever.

"I agreed, also, to inform you of Mr. Fish's statement that the non-mention of the canals in the treaty might induce the Western Senators to vote against it. Instead of writing you, however, I thought it better to telegraph you at length, so that I might have an answer more speedily, and I hope that this answer will be a full and statesmanlike document, giving the reasons for not agreeing to the proposition. Your previous answers have been simply statements of your conclusions.

"After this conversation we went to the conference room, where Mr. Fish made the formal proposal. The answer was, that it would be taken into consideration.

"After discussing the Alabama matter a little, which has got into a snarl, we adjourned until Monday. I hope we shall get an answer from England on the Alabama question before we meet again. It has been unfortunate for me that we were not able to settle this question first. Had we come to a satisfactory arrangement on the subject, Canadian matters would, I think, have gone much more easily. As it was, we were forced to discuss the fisheries, as we had nothing else to do.

"The transhipment question is a matter of very considerable importance to us, and has been pressed upon me by letters from Mr. Merritt as representing the Welland Railway, but it can be fairly placed against a similar privilege granted to the United States.

"If any of you have suggestions to make to me, now is the time to make them, as I hope to have a little cessation of Canadian discussion for a week or so, during which we shall discuss the Alabama and San Juan matters.

"I must say that I am greatly disappointed at the course taken by the British Commissioners. They seem to have only one thing on their minds—that is, to go home to England with a treaty in their pockets, settling everything, no matter at what cost to Canada. I was at first a good deal encouraged, because both Northcote and Bernard stood by me against any permanent cession of the fisheries, but the four have since gone together against me. It is, therefore, exceedingly unfortunate that Sir Stafford is on the Commission, as his party in England will feel themselves a good deal fettered in Parliament by his action, and will be unable to defend the position which Canada will certainly take. The effect which must be produced on the public mind in Canada by a declaration from both parties in the Imperial Parliament against our course, will greatly prejudice the idea of British connection, as British protection will have proved itself a farce. I do not like to look at the consequences, but we are so clearly in the right, that we must throw the responsibility on England."

On the 5th of April Sir John wrote :—

"My telegram of this morning will have informed you that the Home Government has backed me in a satisfactory manner, and given me rather a victory over my colleagues. We telegraphed the provisional arrangement made, to England, and stated that I did not concur, on the ground of the inadequacy of the compensation, though the rest thought it was a fair arrangement. They replied, asking for my reasons and the views of the others. We sent home a copy of the memorandum which I sent you, and my colleagues added that they thought the arrangement a good one, considering the political necessity of allaying all causes of irritation between Canada and the United States, and they were the best terms that could be got. A return cable came to us—a good deal, I think, to the annoyance of Lord de Grey—stating that ' the Government thought Sir John Macdonald's propositions were quite reasonable, and that there should be a substantial money payment and an immediate repeal of the duty on lumber.' It was added, however, that ' we would not be too strict as to the date of the repeal of the lumber duty.'

"On this my colleagues asked me if I had any proposition to make. I said the propositions I had made had all been refused by the U.S. Commissioners, and I despaired of anything coming of the negotiations. I said, however, I would think the matter over, and see whether I had any proposition to make. But, on consideration, I thought it better to send you the telegram of this morning, and I told my colleagues to-day that, as it was a commercial question altogether, and I was not a commercial man, I felt bound to consult the Canadian Council, which contained men of commercial ability, who would understand much better than myself the money value of a concession for twelve years.

"Lord de Grey frankly admitted he never thought the equivalent, in a commercial sense, a just one ; but the political consideration weighed with him.

"My uniform reply to an observation of this kind has been that, while I admitted the importance to Canada, as well as to England, of friendly relations with the United States, I could not suppose that those relations were endangered by the maintenance of an undisputed right. That no civilized nation could take umbrage at the assertion of such a right; and the only complaint that really had any force in it was, that our officers had carried out the law too strictly. I denied that there was good ground for such a charge, but said that in the future we would take still more pains to prevent even the semblance of harshness, or over-eagerness to capture.

"I will do all that I can to keep back the settlement of the Fishery questions until the others are adjusted; and then, if we fail to come to an agreement on the fisheries and free navigation, I will suggest that the Joint Commission should report in favour of a minor Commission, to meet here next winter to settle Canadian questions. Such a Commission to consist, on our side, of two Canadians and Sir Edward Thornton. This arrangement, as it will hold out hopes of a satisfactory settlement to the Western members, will carry the treaty through the Senate, and, at the same time, give Canada a far better chance than she has just now, where her pecuniary interests are considered as altogether secondary to the present Imperial necessities. I have not mentioned this plan to any one yet, and shall not do so until the right time.

"I may say that acquaintance with Sir Edward Thornton has raised him a good deal in my opinion. He is not a strong man, but he is a straightforward, painstaking person, who desires to do his duty, and who, with two Canadians at his elbow instead of an English Cabinet Minister and a Foreign

Office man like Lord Tenterden, would do good service for the Dominion."

On the 16th of April :—

"Since I last wrote you Fishery matters have not been going on satisfactorily, as my telegrams will have informed you. Lord de Grey had a meeting with Mr. Fish, and told him that his Government thought the terms offered not an adequate compensation, and that he (Mr. Fish) must increase his bid. In other words, he must supplement the proposition by a money payment.

"At the time of this conversation I had not received your telegram stating that you would take $150,000 per annum, and $50,000 additional until lumber was free.

"Mr. Fish stated that there would be great difficulty in making a tariff arrangement with a money consideration, and he thought the best way would be to confine it to a money payment alone. He said further, he had ascertained that there would be more difficulty in carrying the tariff proposition than he had anticipated, especially as to salt and lumber, and he hinted that he considered the proposition as rejected by the British Commissioners. Lord de Grey parried this as well as he could, and there, as I understand, the conversation ended.

"When the British Commissioners met we were informed of this conversation, and I gave Lord de Grey a copy of your telegram. He said you could not be serious in asking so much. We certainly would not get it, and he was rather glad he had not had the message at the time of the interview, as he felt he would not have been able to press so large a sum. We had a rather warm discussion on the subject, in which, as usual, I stood alone. Since then, Lord de Grey and Mr. Fish have had another meeting, in which the latter repeated that he felt there would be so much difficulty in carrying any tariff arrangement, that he was pleased it had not been accepted.

"He then proposed a money consideration, the amount to be left to an impartial arbitrator. Lord de Grey, I understand, stated (though he was not very clear in his account of the conversation), that a purely money consideration had been objected to by Canada before, and he did not think there was any chance of such an arrangement being accepted.

"They then had some conversation as to free fish, and a sum of money to be settled by arbitration. Mr. Fish spoke of the difficulty of commingling the two subjects of the tariff and a money consideration, but did not positively refuse to consider the matter. In this, or another conversation about the same time, Mr. Fish said if the Alabama and Fishery matters were settled satisfactorily, the United States would leave the San Juan affair to arbitration also, but not otherwise.

"There the matter stood until yesterday morning, and, in the mean time, we turned our attention to the settlement of the terms of the article connected with the Alabama claims, which may now be considered as finally arranged.

"At first I was puzzled by Mr. Fish's evident eagerness to get out of a tariff proposal, when I looked back and remembered that at our first meeting he had offered a million of dollars for a perpetual sale, together with free fish, coal, salt, and firewood, or, at all events, an important reduction of the duties on those articles, and that he had, after frequent discussions, extended the offer to lumber; but now I am almost convinced that his reason is the unfortunate repeal of the coal and salt duties in the Canadian Legislature. The Bill for the repeal of the duties on coal and salt had passed the House of Representatives and stood in the Senate, and although the latter body had passed a resolution not to take up any other matters during the present session but the Southern question, Trumbull, who had charge of the Bill, had good hopes of getting it through. So much so that he sent for my friend Greenough, who is at the head of the Gas Company at ———, and interested in getting Nova Scotia coal free, to come here and lobby for the measure. Greenough at first thought he might succeed, but went home without doing anything; and Mr. Trumbull has since made no effort, although he told me himself that he intended to bring the matter up on every opportunity. Mr. Fish says that there is more objection to salt than to anything else both in Michigan and New York. I can quite understand that the United States salt-makers would have preferred our market being open to them to the keeping up the Canadian duty on the small production in Western Canada, and so perhaps with the coal owners with reference to coal. The moment, however, that our market was opened for those articles, by the Act of our Legislature, they had evidently put the screws to Mr. Fish and the members of the Senate to keep up the duty on the same articles of our production. However that may be, I must go on with my story.

"Yesterday morning the British Commissioners had a caucus, at which Lord de Grey stated that the time had arrived when we must come to some practical conclusion as to Mr. Fish's offer. He said he considered that the tariff proposition was closed, and would not be reopened by Mr. Fish. That the question now was a reference to arbitration for a money arrangement, to which he thought it likely free fish might be added. I said the previous offer had been made in Conference, and had not been formally withdrawn, but, of course, the United States Commissioners could at any time, before final arrangements were made, alter the terms. That I was satisfied that the present proposition would not be acceptable to Canada in any sense. That the fisheries were our own property, and we should be the judges of what their value was to us. That we would fix our own price, and if the buyer would not pay the price, then we would keep our property.

"I stated that the origin of the present High Commission had been in consequence of our proposal made by despatch, and through Mr. Campbell, and such proposition had been assented to by the Colonial Secretary. Sir Edward Thornton's first letter was in accordance with the promise of Her Majesty's Government to open negotiations with the United States. This letter stated the desirability of ascertaining, in a friendly way, the extent of the respective rights of Canada and the United States in the fisheries, and this in fact was to be the basis of the whole Commission. That what Canada desired was, if she could not get a satisfactory equivalent for her fisheries, that she should be allowed to remain in exclusive possession of them, leaving the questions as to ports and headlands, the only matters in dispute, for adjustment by the Commission. That we had the promise of England that our fisheries would not be given away without our consent, and that the B. N. A. Act of 1867 handed over to our Government and Legislature the exclusive right of dealing with the fisheries, and Canada would insist upon her position. We had a very warm discussion, which resulted in nothing, and then we went to the Conference, where we settled an article for a Commission to settle general claims on both sides (this article having no connection with the fisheries). Lord de Grey, at this, or a previous meeting, mentioned the Fenian claims, and the American Commissioners objected on the ground which I feared they would take, viz. that the correspondence only speaks of the mutual claims of British subjects and American citizens, and that the Fenian claims would be claims by the Governments of England and Canada. Lord de Grey strongly resisted this, and it stands over for further consideration. His Lordship is of opinion, however, in which I must say I concur, that it will be difficult to bring in the Government claims under the language of the correspondence. Of this, however, more hereafter.

"After the Conference rose for the day we met again in caucus. Lord de Grey stated that the time had come to communicate the state of matters to H.M. Government, and read a telegram which he had prepared on the subject. I objected to its terms in several respects, and inserted, in my own words, my position. My language was to the following effect: 'Sir John Macdonald objects to any arrangement based on a money consideration only, or with free fish added, and adheres to the proposition that Canadian coal, salt, fish, and lumber should be admitted free into the United States, to be supplemented by a money payment. If this cannot be obtained he would desire that an arrangement should be made as to the headland question and as to the admission of American vessels into Canadian ports for trading purposes, leaving Canada in exclusive possession of the inshore fisheries.'

" The telegram went on to say that the rest of the Commissioners were satisfied that my first proposition would not be accepted by the United States, nor did they think the second would ; but, at all events, they were of the opinion that the second proposition was inadvisable and objectionable. And if the Fishery question were not settled there would be a great chance of the whole of the negotiations being broken off, etc.

" I did not approve of the tone of the message, but of course could not help myself. I have no objection, however, though I did not say so at the time, to the latter part of the communication.   It informs H.M. Government that, unless Canada is settled with satisfactorily for the fisheries, they will lose the chance of settling the Alabama and other questions.   They will thus see the gravity of the position, and, I think, make us some offer to induce us to assent. We shall probably get the answer to-morrow morning.

" The discussion took an unpleasant turn, and Lord de Grey commenced to lecture me on my duty as a Commissioner, and I was obliged to tell him very shortly that I believed I knew what my duty was, and I would endeavour to perform it.

" I agreed to send the message which you received and answered yesterday. I sent a copy of both to Lord de Grey this morning, with a request that he would communicate them to H.M. Government by cable, which he has done.

" I have on several occasions stated that, if we did not get adequate compensation from the United States, and it was necessary for England's purposes that we should give a lease of the fisheries, England must compensate us.   To this I have had no satisfactory response.

" To-day, after church, Lord de Grey came down to see me, and we had a long and interesting conversation, in which he thought it as well to take quite a different tone. He said he had come as an individual, and as an old friend, to talk over the matter with me.   This we did at great length, and, at his request, I will forward what I recollect of the conversation to Canada.   I shall address the letter to Cartier, who, they know, has been acting as my *locum tenens*, as I may have occasion to use it hereafter.

" Thus the matter stands, and you will see that it is pretty well mixed.   That we shall come to some solution of it, I have little doubt, but I find it absolutely necessary to hold my position with great firmness.

" Sir Stafford Northcote has disappointed me altogether.   I think he feels now, that he has put himself in a false position by coming here, and Lord de Grey knows he has done so, for twice he (Lord de Grey) has told me that Northcote, although bound not (*sic*) to support the Acts of the Imperial Government in the House of Commons, is bound to support his own acts. That his political friends in the Opposition would, of course, support him, and so Canada would have no friends.

"With regard to the Fenian claims, Lord de Grey and I had a talk on our way home from the Conference, and after the Americans had taken the objection. He evidently felt that the English Government and Thornton had made a mistake in the language of the correspondence. He said he would sound his Government as to their willingness to pay Canada a sum of money to get rid of the question. I availed myself of the opportunity of speaking about a guarantee for railways, as being a preferable mode of aiding Canada in any money arrangement with England, for any purpose that might be made. That it did not involve an advance of money but a mere pledge of credit, and if the guarantee was for a Pacific Railway it would be for a matter of Imperial interest, as the railway would give the shortest course across the Continent for British commerce with China and the North Pacific generally.

"To-day he informed me, and authorized me to convey it to Council, but in strictest confidence, that H.M. Government, if all other matters were settled, and if it were not to be drawn into a precedent, would agree to pay to Canada a sum of money for the Fenian claims, if the United States did not. If, however, other matters were not settled, this understanding was to go for nothing.

"He informed me that this undertaking had been conveyed in answer to a cable message which he had sent according to his promise to me. He stated, however, that he had not proposed a guarantee at all, as he had discussed the matter with Sir Stafford Northcote, and they both agreed that there was no likelihood of Mr. Gladstone or the present House of Commons assenting to a guarantee for any purpose. So we now know exactly where Sir Stafford Northcote is to be found."

On the same day, he wrote to Sir George Cartier:—

"Lord de Grey came to see me to-day, as he said, for the purpose of having a frank and full discussion on the present state of the Fishery negotiations.

"He said the situation was now one of the greatest gravity,

involving consequences of the most serious character, and affecting equally England and the United States and Canada. In the first place, he would ask me whether I had communicated to my Canadian colleagues the fact that Her Majesty's Government had in their instructions mingled the principal subjects of reference, viz. the Alabama claims, the Fisheries and San Juan, so that the Commissioners could not agree upon the settlement of the one without the others—the object of Her Majesty's Government being to remove at once all causes of difference between the two nations; or, whether, in my communications with you, I had not discussed the Fisheries from a commercial point of view only.

"I answered that I had not conveyed to you the nature of those instructions, as I did not feel myself at liberty to disclose them to any one.

"In reply, he said he would assume the responsibility of enabling me to do so.

"He proceeded to say that failure in the settlement of the fishery question would involve the complete rupture of the negotiations, and would leave matters in a much worse position than we found them. That no one could foresee what the consequences might be. That, in case of a failure, the United States Commissioners would tell their story to the Senate, and the British Commissioners must do the same thing in Parliament. That it would then appear that two propositions had been made to Canada (both, in his opinion, reasonable), one for the free admission of the four articles, so often named in my communications, and the other for submission to impartial arbitration of the question as to the amount of a money consideration for free fishing during ten years. That Sir Stafford Northcote, though in Opposition and not at all bound to support the Government, would, of course, define and defend his own position, and would look to his friends to support him, and so Canada would have no friends in the British Parliament. That I knew as well as he did that there was a large anti-colonial party in England, not confined to the Liberal party, many of whom would rejoice at the action of Canada as proving the colonies to be a danger and a burden. That the arrangement would be only for ten years, and at the end of that period Canada's rights would be the same as they are now. That, in the mean time, a satisfactory treaty would have been obtained, settling the various questions in dispute, and Canada would during that period have time to consolidate the new Dominion and develop her young resources.

" He desired that the Canadian Government, whose message of yesterday I had communicated to him, and which he had sent to England at my request by cable, should be fully informed of the gravity of the situation, and he warned it of the responsibility which would fall upon it by the rejection of a reasonable compromise.

" He wished to call particular attention to the fact that Canada was more interested in the avoidance of unfriendly relations with the United States than any other portion of the British Empire, and would suffer most if those relations became hostile.

" This, I fear, is but a meagre statement of His Lordship's views, and I cannot pretend to convey to you, as I should wish, the force and earnestness of his manner and argument.

" On the other side, I stated I was fully alive to the gravity of the position, and desired to treat the matter as one that might involve serious consequences. That Canada, however, was not responsible for the commingling of the various subjects of difference between the nations, and she was, in my opinion, prejudiced by it. That Canada had, by written despatch and by the mission of Mr. Campbell, urged on H.M. Government the propriety of having the geographical limits of Canadian fishing grounds settled with the United States. That this application was assented to and Sir Edward Thornton instructed to open the matter to the Government here. That no other subject was contemplated by Canada, and probably the proposition would have been made long ago by Sir Edward, had not the question of the right of American fishermen to trade in our ports been raised, and it was felt that until the British and Canadian Governments understood each other on this point, he had better defer making any communication on the subject. That the message to Lord Lisgar from the Colonial Secretary, asking me to be on the Commission, did not state that there was to be any necessary connection or interweaving of the different subjects. That Canada was not fairly dealt with in so mingling them without her knowledge or consent, as they were all separate and distinct in their nature, and, if I had been aware that it was the intention of H.M. Government so to intermingle them, it would have been a matter of grave consideration with me and my colleagues, whose consent of course I had to obtain, as to whether I should accept a seat on the Commission or not. That, on a reference to the correspondence between Sir Edward Thornton and Mr. Fish, it would be seen that the opening letter of Sir Edward Thornton confined itself to a proposal for settling the extent of the rights of British subjects and American citizens in the fisheries, and made no allusion to the Alabama, San Juan, or any other matters ; and the proposition to enlarge the scope of the Commission came from the U.S. Government.

"Here Lord de Grey interposed the statement that, as a matter of fact, the proposition about the Alabama did not originate with the United States, although the correspondence indicated that it did so.

"I said, of course I quite understood the arrangement had been a verbal one, and the letters were subsequently prepared in the manner that it was thought would put it in the most advantageous form for both Governments, but the fact was that we in Canada did not know anything of the correspondence until it was published in the Washington papers. That we were, of course, pleased to see a prospect of having all disputed matters settled, and would have no objection that they should be settled at the same time and by the same Commission, but, neither from the correspondence nor in any other way were we informed that the settlement of any one of the questions would depend upon the settlement of the others. That the consequence now was that Canada was called upon against her will to enter into an arrangement, which she considers in the highest degree unsatisfactory to her people, in order to secure the settlement of other matters in which England is more immediately interested. That the right to the inshore fisheries which she was now called upon to sacrifice was not a matter of difference between the two countries. Canada's property was undisputed. That Canada did not wish to sell her fishery rights or to lease them, but what she desired was a fair commercial equivalent by a tariff arrangement. That the U.S. Government could not object, or raise any question if we declined to sell or lease, and the present attitude of the American Commissioners was simply an attempt to bully us into a surrender of our rights by speaking of probable collisions involving the shedding of blood and consequent irritation, etc. That, however, the United States Government as a civilized Government of a civilized nation could not countenance any of their citizens in such lawless proceedings, and any hostile action of the Government was not to be apprehended as an appreciable danger. That it was intolerable that these New England fishermen should say they were resolved to fish in our waters right or wrong, and if not allowed would force on a war between the two nations; and we ought not to sacrifice our property by reason of such threats. That, as there was an anti-colonial party in England, so was there an annexation party in Canada; and if we were told that England was afraid or unwilling to protect us in the enjoyment of our undoubted rights, not from fear of the American Government or the American people, but from fear of the Gloucester fishermen, that party would gain great strength in Canada and perhaps imperil the connection with the mother country. That in case such connection was severed, the consequence, in my opinion, would be annexation to the United States. That our maintenance as an independent nation was not to be thought of; we must be either English or American: and if protection was denied us by England, we might as well go while we had some property left us, with which we could make an arrangement with the United States. That the postponement of the difficulty for ten years would not mend matters much. That if we were unable to keep our fisheries now, how could we hope to do so ten years hence, when the fishing interests of the United States, and the number of men and the capital employed, would have largely increased.

"Here Lord de Grey interposed a remark that then, at any rate, the fisheries would be the question to be settled, and it would not be intermingled with the Alabama and such like claims.

"To this, of course, I gave due weight. I added that with respect to the first proposition, said to have been rejected by

Canada, the reasonableness of our claims to some additional money equivalent had been acknowledged by H.M. Government, and, as to the second proposition, which was in effect to lease for a money equivalent only, or with such equivalent as the chief element, Canada had objected from the beginning. That for the sake of reciprocal free trade we would go far, but we preferred keeping our fisheries as a growing industry and a nursery for our seamen to any amount of money. I said personally I would go as far, or perhaps further than most men to maintain the connection with the mother country, and to establish amicable relations between the two nations on a permanent basis, and to gain those objects I would be prepared to make any personal sacrifice of position or popularity, if my doing so would serve the purpose. That supposing I should agree to the last proposition, and sign the treaty, the moment it was laid before the Senate it would be published in every paper in Canada, and I believed that from one end of the country to the other the indignation of the people would be roused, more especially in Nova Scotia and the Maritime Provinces, and, even before I could get back to Canada to explain my position, the treaty would be condemned finally and irretrievably by the public voice. That in such case the danger of collision in May next, when the American fishing vessels began to fish in our waters, would be enormously increased. That with the treaty ratified by England and the United States, the fishermen would disregard the fact of its not having been ratified by the Canadian Parliament; in fact, this danger would be so great that, although our Parliament had just been prorogued, it would be necessary to call it together again to deal with the subject, and there could be no doubt what the mode of dealing would be—it must be a summary rejection. That, therefore, I considered that all the dangers and hazards which Lord de Grey apprehended if no arrangement about the fisheries were now made (in which fear I did not concur), would be a matter of certainty if a treaty were made on such conditions as were certain to be rejected.

" I think this is the substance of my reply.

" I have undertaken to convey to you, which I do in this imperfect and hurried manner (for I have not time to revise

my letter), the considerations which Lord de Grey pressed upon
me. I invite your earnest and immediate consideration of
them, and your reply by telegraph as soon after the receipt of
this letter as possible.

"Before leaving, Lord de Grey said he was in a position to
inform me (though in the strictest confidence, and I convey it
to you in the same manner), that H.M. Government would, if
all other matters were settled and it were not to be considered
as a precedent, consent to pay Canada a sum of money in
settlement of the Fenian claims, if the United States refused to
do so.

"P.S. Lord de Grey said he had been much surprised to
learn from me that we did not apprehend any danger from
leaving the fishery matters unsettled. That he believed it was
the general impression in England, and especially of the
Government, that the danger was great and pressing, and Lord
Granville had informed him that if this question alone were
settled the mission would not be a failure. I replied that this
apprehension must be of very recent growth. That Lord
Clarendon could not have felt it when he corresponded with
Mr. Adams in '65. That no such fear was conveyed to us in
the three years during which the license system existed, or
in 1870 when the principle of exclusion was adopted, and the
instructions to British and Canadian officers settled between
the two Governments, nor when Mr. Campbell was in direct
communication with Lord Kimberley, and the apprehension
could only have been caused by the President's message of last
December. As to this I stated that no great importance
ought to be attached to it—that it was understood to have
been prepared by General Butler, and it was known that
Mr. Fish had not seen it until it was in print. That it was
written to attain an object, and that I was sorry to find that
this object had been attained and England had been frightened
by it into coercing Canada."

CHAPTER XXI.

THE TREATY OF WASHINGTON,—*continued.*

1871.

" WHEN SOME ONE WRITES MY BIOGRAPHY—IF I AM EVER THOUGHT WORTHY
OF HAVING SUCH AN INTERESTING DOCUMENT PREPARED—AND WHEN, AS
A MATTER OF HISTORY, THE QUESTIONS CONNECTED WITH THIS TREATY
ARE UPHELD, IT WILL BE FOUND THAT UPON THIS, AS WELL AS UPON
EVERY OTHER POINT, I DID ALL I COULD TO PROTECT THE RIGHTS AND
CLAIMS OF THE DOMINION."—*Speech of Sir John Macdonald in the House
of Commons, May 3,* 1872.

" [Private and confidential.]

" The Arlington, Washington, April 18, 1871.

" MY DEAR TUPPER,

" To continue the narrative of events. Yesterday
(Monday) morning I went to a caucus at Lord de Grey's. He
stated that no answer to our cable telegram to England could
be expected that day. That we had, in fact, no business to go
on with at the Conference, as the Alabama matter and the
question of claims had been arranged, and Mr. Fish had intimated that, if other matters were settled, the United States
would leave the San Juan matter to arbitration. Congress was
to adjourn in a day or two, and if we told the U.S. Commissioners that we were not prepared to go on, it would cause
great annoyance and irritation among them, especially in the
case of Mr. Fish, who wished to be able to inform the Senate
when they might expect to be summoned back here to confirm
the treaty in executive session. He therefore thought we had
better go on provisionally with the details of the article on the
fisheries, and for this purpose assume that H.M. Government
had given its assent to the principle of arbitration, but the
U.S. Commissioners should be distinctly informed that if Her
Majesty did not assent to the proposal our labours in this

respect would go for nothing. The others expressed their concurrence in his view.

" I stated that I greatly doubted the expediency of taking any steps, even of a provisional nature, until we received the expected instructions from England. We should only be committing ourselves by so doing, and be rendering it more difficult to get back to the point at which we then were, and the Americans would be exceedingly disappointed if, after going into and settling the details, the proposition was rejected altogether. However, I said that as a majority of them had so decided, it was necessary for me to consider my own position, and what I should do to keep myself right.

" I stated again the position I had taken, namely, that I did not believe that Canada would ratify the arrangement, and my belief had been strengthened by your telegram which had gone home to England. That if I went to the Conference and sat silent, the U.S. Commissioners would naturally suppose that I assented to the proposition, and might afterwards, I feared, charge me with want of candour. It seemed to me, therefore, on the first impression, that I ought either to absent myself from the Conference, or, when present, state that I did not believe the arrangement would be satisfactory to Canada, and that I doubted its sanction by her Parliament.

" Lord de Grey was taken aback by this, and said it was a very grave statement to make, involving serious responsibility, and, after such a formal statement, he thought that he and his English colleagues should together consider what should be done.

" They accordingly withdrew, and, after an absence of a considerable time, returned. Lord de Grey then stated that, although they felt that any delay would be most unfortunate by causing great annoyance and irritation among the U.S. Commissioners, the U.S. Government, and the Senate, and might be productive of evil consequences to the whole negotiation, yet, in the face of my statement that I would absent myself, or, when at Conference, make a formal protest against the proposal, they had come to the conclusion that the only course left them was to postpone everything until formal instructions from England were received.

" I, of course, could not allow them to place me in such a

position as to enable them hereafter to throw the responsibility
of failure on my shoulders entirely, and I therefore replied that
I did not inform them that I would make any protest of the
kind. What I desired was to protect myself from any subsequent charge of want of candour towards the U.S. Commissioners. Hitherto we had acted on each side as a unit through
our respective spokesmen, but I presumed we did not any of
us lose our individuality. This being in the nature of a mixed
Commission, I presumed that we might divide in opinion, having
British and Americans voting one way, against British and
Americans voting the other way. However, I was new to the
conduct of matters in diplomacy, and therefore would be glad
to have the opinion of my colleagues. They replied *seriatim.*
Lord de Grey said we were not a mixed Commission, but held
the position of plenipotentiaries, and he thought that, as such,
we must act as a unit.

"Sir Stafford Northcote concurred, and stated that whatever
his own opinions at any time might be, he felt that as a Commissioner and plenipotentiary he was an agent of the Imperial
Government, and, as such, was bound to carry out the instructions received from them, although he might disapprove of the
policy of those instructions, but that he would take good care
to put himself right with the Government on any point of
difference. Sir Edward Thornton and Mr. Bernard spoke in
the same strain.

"I replied that I was certainly not strictly correct in calling
it a mixed Commission, that it was a Joint Commission, and I
recognized the fact of our being empowered as plenipotentiaries.
I repeated that all I desired was to protect myself from any
future charge of disingenuousness from any quarter, and stated
that if they thought my presence would not be held as committing me finally to the arrangement, of course I would submit
to their better judgment, and would not absent myself from the
Conference, reserving to myself, however, full liberty to express
my dissent at such time and in such way as I thought
expedient.

"They again retired for consultation, and on their return
stated they had come to the conclusion that on the whole it
was better to proceed.

" We then went to the Conference, and Lord de Grey stated formally that, taking up the Fishery matters where he had left them, he desired to say that H.M. Government, with which he had communicated, had come to the conclusion that the offer of free coal, salt, fish, and lumber, the latter to be free at a future date, was not an adequate equivalent for the fishery privileges. That it was understood that the duties on coal and salt would be removed at the next meeting of Congress under any circumstances, and therefore they could not be fairly considered as any portion of an equivalent. That the proposed arrangement being for ten years, the postponement of the removal of the duty on lumber for three years rendered it of no present advantage, and. so there only remained, practically, the proposal of free fish, which was altogether insufficient of itself. That H.M. Government thought that, in addition to those four articles, there should be an additional payment of money, the amount to be settled in some way.

" Mr. Fish replied that the American Government were not prepared to make any additional money grant whatever, and wished it to be understood that the United States Government formally withdrew their offer. All this, of course, was simply the official statement in Conference of what had previously occurred at the informal meetings between Lord de Grey and Mr. Fish. It seems to be the practice of conferences that only results are talked of in them, all matters being settled out of conference and only the arranged conclusions stated there.

" Mr. Fish proceeded to say that, the ground being cleared, the United States Government were now prepared to revert to the proposal of a purely money consideration, and, as it appeared there was an irreconcilable difference of opinion between the two Governments as to the value of the fisheries, he proposed that it should be left to an impartial arbitration, one arbitrator to be chosen by each Government, and the third selected by the Minister of some friendly power.

" Lord de Grey said that he presumed this proposition was for a term of years.

" Mr. Fish replied that he wished to press upon the British Commissioners the expediency of settling the question by arbitration for all time.

"Lord de Grey said he could not hold out the most distant hopes that such a proposition would be entertained by England; it must be for a term of years. Mr. Fish then said ten years was too short a period; it would soon pass, and would involve the necessity of a new arbitration or settlement at the end; and he named twenty-five years, or one generation. Lord de Grey said it was a matter for consideration, but, if the Americans thought ten years too short, he thought twenty-five years too long; that point, however, must stand over for the present. He then proceeded to state that, in any arrangement whatever, they must include free fish. . . .

"I am now satisfied that the repeal of the coal and salt duties in Canada has been the cause of the change of feeling here. The moment the coal and salt owners found that our market was open to them, they put the screws on their representatives at Washington. The present Government here is as weak as water, and they have not the pluck to resist in the slightest degree the pressure from their friends in the Senate. The coal and salt owners, with the usual blind cupidity of monopolists, calculate on the supply of our market for the present season, and trust to the chances of the future in still further postponing free coal and salt in the next session. In this I do not believe they have the slightest chance of success, but it is clear that they will not throw away the chance, however small. The absurd attempts of the U.S. Commissioners to depreciate the value of our fisheries would be ridiculous if they were not so annoying. They found our English friends so squeezable in nature that their audacity has grown beyond all bounds.

"We got a cable last night informing us that we should receive full instructions after a meeting of the Cabinet, which is to take place to-day, but I do not suppose that we shall receive those instructions until after the Conference rises.

"I hope you will receive my letters to-morrow morning at latest, and that I shall receive your answer in the course of the day. It is useless to speculate on what the English Cabinet may say. They are in this position: they have formally and officially told us, first, that they will not dispose of the fisheries without our consent; second, that our right to the inshore fisheries is beyond dispute, and should not be ceded without adequate compensation ; third, that they agree with me that the offer of free coal, salt, fish, and lumber is not an adequate consideration, and should be supplemented by a money payment. And they have been informed that I adhere to this proposition, and, if it cannot be carried out, Canada desires to retain her inshore fisheries, and to have the headlands question adjusted in some way according to the original arrangement made through Campbell. Added to all this, they have the formal statement of the Canadian Government that our Parliament would not ratify any treaty of the nature now proposed.

"Whenever the answers from London and Ottawa are received, I shall be able to write you exactly how, in my opinion, matters will end.

" Believe me, yours faithfully

"JOHN A. MACDONALD."

On the 21st of April he wrote to Dr. Tupper :—

" On Tuesday morning, the 19th, before going to Conference, I read to Lord de Grey that portion of my letter to Cartier which related the substance of his conversation with me on Sunday. He said it was perfectly correct, and he had nothing to add to or take from it.

" I afterwards showed the whole letter to Sir Stafford Northcote, so that he might understand the position I took. I was anxious for him to see the remark of Lord de Grey that we should have no friends in the Imperial Parliament, as he (Northcote) would be obliged to support the Government. He read it with great attention, and said he was obliged, but made no other remark. . . .

" I omitted to state that, in our discussions on Tuesday as to the articles of reference, the Americans pressed that the reference should be so worded as to convey the idea that the arbitration should ascertain whether any compensation more than free fish was just. We replied that it did not lie in their mouths to put the statement in any such hypothetical way. They had already offered us free fish, coal, salt, and lumber, and, therefore, could not now say that free fish alone was a sufficient equivalent.

"Judge Hoar (who, you may remember, stated the day before, that their previous offer had so enormously exceeded the value of the fisheries that it would hazard the passing of the treaty in the Senate) now said: 'Oh, we did not offer you much more than free fish, because you are going to get coal and salt whether or no next session, and you will get lumber before the expiration of the three years.' Hoar is considered the honest man of the American Commission, so you may fancy what the others are like." *

On the 23rd of April Sir George Cartier telegraphed :—

"We are sensible of the gravity of the position and alive to the deep interest which Canada has in the settlement of all disputes between Great Britain and the United States. The Queen's Government having formally pledged herself that our fisheries should not be disposed of without our consent, to force us now into a disposal of them for a sum, to be fixed by arbitration, and free fish, would be a breach of faith, and an indignity never before offered to a great British possession. The people of Canada were ready to exchange' the right of fishing for reciprocal trade rights to be agreed upon ; but, if these cannot be obtained, she prefers to retain her fisheries, and she protests against the course which, against her will, is being pursued with reference to her interests and property. We were never informed that the fisheries would be inextricably mixed up with the Alabama question, and could not have apprehended that an attempt would be made to coerce us into an unwilling disposal of them to obtain results, however

---

* It should be borne in mind that these letters were written in moments of irritation, when there is always a tendency to exaggerate. I do not believe that Sir John Macdonald meant this and other not wholly complimentary allusions to his American colleagues to be taken literally. Rather do I think that the estimate of them, which he expressed a few months after his return from Washington, more accurately represents his real sentiments. Writing to his friend Mr. (now Senator) Gowan, under date of June 27, 1871, he says: "While you have been enjoying yourself, I have been among the great men at Washington. While the standard of excellence there is far lower than the English one, I am glad to say that the statesmen of the United States have risen greatly in my estimation since I have had personal intercourse with them. Socially, my sojourn was pleasant enough, but the embarrassments and difficulties of my position were at times almost beyond endurance."

important, on other points in dispute. Our Parliament would never consent to a treaty on the basis now proposed [and, if persisted in, you should withdraw from the Commission].* We concur fully in the statement and arguments which you have used to Lord de Grey, as given in your letter to me."

On the 27th of April Sir John wrote Dr. Tupper :—

" It was very unfortunate that the telegram, in answer to my letter to Cartier, did not arrive in time. Had I received it on Thursday, or even on Friday morning, it would probably have produced such an effect on Lord de Grey as to have induced him to send a copy of it by cable to England, which would, I am almost certain, have made the Home Government pause before taking the final step that they did. As it was, however, we got instructions from England on Friday afternoon, to agree to a settlement of the inshore fisheries on the terms of free fish and a money compensation, the amount to be decided by an impartial arbitration. The arrangement, however, to be subject to ratification by Canada.

" As the United States Government had become impatient, and as the Senate had also become very restive at the delay, no time was lost in acting upon the instructions.

" The articles as agreed upon are substantially as follows . . .

" Such are the articles. My first impulse, I confess, on the arrival of the cable message from England, authorizing the reference of the value of the fisheries to arbitration, was to hand in my resignation of my position as ' Commissioner, procurator, and plenipotentiary ' to Lord de Grey for transmission to Earl Granville ; and I stated so to the former, and to my other colleagues.

" After thinking over it for a night, however, I refrained from doing so, reserving to myself the right of ulterior action. It was fortunate that I did so, else the Articles would have been much worse than they are. The lease of the fisheries would have been for twenty-five years instead of for ten with notice. Fish oil would have been excluded, and only the fish proved to have been caught in the inshore fisheries admitted.

" These alterations, it may perhaps be said, are of no consequence, as Canada is certain to reject the treaty *in toto.*

* The words within brackets were subsequently withdrawn.

I felt, however, that I ought not to throw away any chance for Canada, and it is quite on the cards that England, in her desire to settle all matters with the United States, may be forced to offer a substantial compensation to Canada as an inducement to our Parliament to consent to the arrangement. With that possibility before me, I felt it my duty to remove as many objections as I could. Had I not been present, the article about the St. Lawrence would have been settled in a manner altogether disadvantageous to us. The U.S. Commissioners pressed most persistently from the beginning for the free navigation of the river and canals. They returned again and again to it, and used the argument which has an overpowering effect on my colleagues, that without such grant the Western Senators would never vote for the Alabama settlement. They (the British Commissioners) were just as urgent with me to assent, but, of course, I refused to do so. The instructions from England, however, were positive to consent to the free navigation of the St. Lawrence, the Government holding apparently that, by international law, as now understood, the Americans had really a right to its navigation to the mouth, and the two secretaries of the Commission had settled a clause for that purpose.

" I protested most loudly against the concession. I had to admit that the river up to Montreal was already open to American commerce, as it was to the trade of any other friendly nation, and that it was specially so by the Commercial Convention existing between the two nations; and that, as the river was not navigable from Montreal up to the point where the United States owned the southern bank, we were, in fact, giving them no practical advantage. But I argued that England had finally refused the right in 1828—and the fact that the Americans had no right to it was recognized by the Reciprocity Treaty—and now it was too late for them to urge it, and we were not getting anything for it, etc.

" The reply was that England had finally made up her mind on the point, and would yield to the request as a reasonable and proper one.

" I then objected to the words of the clause, which gives the right of navigation ascending and descending, and argued

that, as it was known no vessels could ascend the river by its
natural channel, the grant of such navigation would give the
Americans the opportunity of arguing that the treaty conferred the right to use our canals, as being the only mode by
which the river could be ascended at the time the treaty was
made. Professor Bernard had to admit that it was a point
capable of argument. The trouble was, however, how to prevent the argument being raised, and, as Mr. Fish was specially
anxious that some hope should be held out in the treaty of
getting the use of the canals, in order to please the Western
Senators, I suggested that both objects might be accomplished
by putting in an article similar to that in the Reciprocity
Treaty regarding the State canals. By looking back to item
No. 10 you will see that the Queen engages to urge the Government of Canada to secure to the U.S. citizens the use of the
Welland, St. Lawrence, and other canals, and the United States
agrees to do the same thing with respect to its State canals.
This article shows expressly that the canals are not a portion
of the St. Lawrence, but are within the sole control of Canada.

" In the same article you will observe that the free use of
the canal over the St. Clair flats is secured for ever to Canada.

" Then it happened that Donald A. Smith mentioned to
Sir Stafford Northcote and myself that it was of great importance to the North-West to secure the free navigation of the
three rivers mentioned in item 8. He says that the use of
the Yukon is absolutely indispensable. That already American
vessels from San Francisco carry goods *via* the Yukon into
our country at rates much cheaper than they can be conveyed
by any other route. The Stikine River, he says, goes through
a gold country, and its navigation is also of importance. The
Porcupine is a branch of the Yukon. As the Americans contended for the general principle, they were obliged to consent
with respect to these three rivers.

" The Americans have positively refused to grant the free
navigation of Lake Michigan in perpetuity. They alleged that
it stood in quite a different position from the St. Lawrence;
that Canada owned no portion of the land on its shores; that
it was closed by a narrow strait, and was altogether American;
and that, without any express provision, it was open to

Canadian shipping (Chicago being as much a port of entry as New York), and would not be closed so long as the countries were at amity.

"The right of transit in bond is also secured.

"You will observe that item No. 11 provides for goods arriving at New York, Boston, Portland, and other ports that may from time to time be named by the President. I asked Mr. Fish, as Sir Francis Hincks suggested in his telegram to me, that Baltimore, Philadelphia, and New Orleans should be expressly stated. He said he would prefer to keep the article as it was, because it contained the exact language of the Act of Congress authorizing the bonding system, but there would be no difficulty at any time in getting a Treasury Order for any port in the United States. The right conferred by this article will probably be for ten years, like the fisheries. I suppose you would prefer it should be for all time to come. Let me know the opinion of Council on this point by telegraph, as soon as possible after the receipt of this letter.

"By Article No. 12 Her Majesty agrees to urge the legislature of New Brunswick to take off the export duty on lumber. I fancy I see the legislature granting the request ! This is a part of Fish's buncombe to get the votes of the Senators from Maine to the treaty as a whole.

"Article 13, as to the transhipment, will be made subject to Canadian legislation. It will, I fear, be settled in such a manner as not to be acceptable to our Parliament, and therefore the Welland Railway will not get what it wants. I am obliged to deal very gingerly with this matter. The American Commissioners seem to hold that the carrying in bond from one American port to another, even by different British vessels, is a breach of their coasting laws, and therefore a cargo cannot be carried, say from Chicago to Collingwood, in a British vessel in bond, thence over the railway to Toronto, and from there in another British vessel to Oswego. This I cannot believe to be the law, if tested in the courts here, but there are three judges on the American Commission, and they hold to that doctrine."

On April 29 :—

"The rights of Canada being substantially preserved by

reserving to her the veto power as to the fisheries, I am sincerely desirous that a treaty should be made, as it is of the greatest importance that the Alabama and San Juan matters should be settled, especially the former. The expectations by the American people of a settlement of these matters have been strung to a very high pitch, and the disappointment, in case the negotiations end in nothing, will be very great. If this attempt to settle the Alabama question should fail, no peaceable solution of it is possible, and the war cloud will hang over England and Canada. Lord de Grey has told me several times . . .

" In all this I am satisfied that Lord de Grey is quite sincere, and of course I appreciate the weight of the argument, as well as the consideration that Canada would be a greater sufferer in case of hostile action than England possibly could be. With a treaty therefore once made, Canada has the game in her own hands. All fear of war will have been averted, and between now and next February, when Parliament meets, our Government will have plenty of time to consider the whole position. The American fishermen having been excluded from our waters for two seasons, their clamour will be very great, and the importance of finally settling the question will be increased in the minds of the two Governments of Great Britain and the United States. Canada may then be in a position to say that she must get pecuniary compensation from England, and liberal tariff arrangements with the United States. I need not, however, dilate on this subject, which we can talk over at leisure when I arrive at Ottawa.

" I took a fitting opportunity of giving Lord de Grey Cartier's telegram in answer to my letter. I omitted that portion of it which said that I should withdraw from the Commission. The reason that I did so was, that my Commission is that of an ambassador, acting directly as an officer of the Imperial Government, over which Commission of course the Canadian Government have no control. I took occasion, however, to let him know that such was the opinion of my colleagues.

" Lord de Grey thought it necessary, after considering the tenor of Cartier's message, to write me a letter, of which I enclose a copy.* I also enclose a copy of my reply.

* For these letters, see Appendix XXII.

"I may mention that whenever I have hinted at severing myself from the Commission, I have met with an unanimous protest from my colleagues. They say that my doing so would probably prevent the treaty being confirmed by the Senate; that it would at once be held by the New England Senators that my withdrawal must be accepted as an unequivocal statement that Canada will not ratify the treaty, and they say that if all the questions are not settled they may as well all be left open, as the omission of one subject would greatly imperil the settlement of the others.

" My colleagues say this would be a most serious responsibility for me to take and for the Canadian Government to advise; the blame of the failure would fall altogether on Canada, and the irritation and annoyance in England against us would be intense.

" They also say that, like other ambassadors, we are bound by instructions, and it would be a complete justification of our action that we have carried out the positive orders of the Government which we represent.

" Sir Stafford Northcote says he will take that line in the Imperial Parliament, although he does not acquiesce in the policy of some of the instructions from England. I listened to all this, but uniformly stated that I held myself free to take such ultimate action as I might think advisable.

" As I said before, I shall continue to watch events, lest in my absence they might play the devil with our interests. I cannot divest myself of the apprehension that if I were away, either from ignorance or from carelessness, some stipulation might be introduced into the treaty which, though contravening England's engagements with us, or even our rights secured by the Act of Union, would still be binding between Great Britain and the United States.

" The Americans would, of course, hold England to any treaty stipulation, and say it was no affair of theirs if in making that treaty they had trampled on the rights of Canada.

" You may think it surprising that the U.S. Commissioners attach so much importance to the fishery articles when they are dependent altogether on their subsequent confirmation by our Parliament. We cannot, however, make them believe or understand that the Imperial Government has no dispensing power, as a paramount authority, which would override any action of the Canadians. When Lord de Grey tells them that England is not a despotic power, and cannot control the Canadian Parliament when it acts within its legitimate jurisdiction, they pooh-pooh it altogether. In fact they think that, when the treaty is once made, the ultimate ratification of it by the Canadian Parliament is a mere matter of form. They began to hint that Her Majesty might order the Canadian Parliament to be summoned at once to deal with the question, and were at first incredulous; but they now understand that the treaty cannot be submitted to our Legislature until its next session in February. This, I think, is enough for to-day.

" Yours sincerely,
" JOHN A. MACDONALD.

" P.S.—I have strongly advised Lord de Grey (and he promised to take my advice) to urge H.M. Government to lose no time in having the referees chosen in the Alabama matter, and to get the decision, if possible, before the Canadian Parliament meets. If they once make their award, the subsequent proceedings will be merely the appointment of a minor commission to take evidence as to the amount of the claims. I advised the same course with respect to San Juan. My reason for doing so is, that whenever the Americans find that Canada has rejected the fishery articles, they will endeavour to impede or obstruct proceedings on the other matters. It is of great consequence, therefore, that the references should be gone on with and brought to a substantial completion before our Parliament meets. I stated to him that such, in my opinion, were the advantages both to England and Canada of having these two great questions out of the way before we took up the fishery question, that I had little doubt the Canadian Government would, if England desired it, postpone the meeting of Parliament in the spring to the very latest moment possible, which would be in April next.

" J. A. M.D."

The concluding letter of this correspondence is addressed to Sir George Cartier.

"[Private and confidential.]

"The Arlington, Washington, May 6, 1871.

"MY DEAR CARTIER,

"As Tupper is away, I address this to you.

"The Commission did not take the course generally taken by such bodies in having a protocol of the proceedings of each meeting. In order that the discussion might be more unrestrained, it was agreed that the protocols should be merely of a formal character, except the last one, which would contain a condensed statement of all the proceedings. This has been prepared, and is a fair enough statement of what did occur. It will be signed to-day, and, as soon as I get a copy of it, I will send it to you confidentially.

"The language put into the mouths of the British Commissioners is strictly correct, but I cannot say so much for the statements of our American colleagues. They have inserted certain statements as having been made by them, which, in fact, never were made, but which they think it of importance should appear to have been made, in order that they may have an effect on the Senate. My English colleagues were a good deal surprised at the proposition, but, as the statements did not prejudice England, we left them at liberty to lie as much as they liked. I will give you some amusing instances of this when we meet. As our labours had substantially come to an end on Wednesday last, I took occasion to have an *éclaircissement* with Lord de Grey.

"I told him that, while I had, as in duty bound, done all that I could to prevent serious mistakes being made with respect to Canadian questions, and to make the treaty as little distasteful as possible to the people of Canada, yet I must repeat my opinion that the arrangements with respect to the fisheries were decidedly injurious to Canada, whose interests had been sacrificed, or made altogether of secondary consideration, for the sake of getting a settlement of the Alabama and San Juan matters; I concurred entirely in the opinion expressed by the Canadian Government in your telegram, which stated that the Canadian Parliament would not sanction the arrangement, and I said the time had come when I must decide what course I should take. It was quite true that Canada would still retain, in a great measure, the control of the Fishery question by the clause which stated that the fishery articles should only take effect when the necessary legislation was had by the Dominion Parliament, but this had been done in a manner least beneficial to Canada, as, in the case of her refusal to ratify the treaty, it would be patent to the people of the United States that Canada and England had a different policy on the question, and that we could not expect any real support or backing from the mother country. In fact, I went over all the arguments which I have already conveyed to you in my letters, over and over again.

"I went on to say that I must consider what course I would take; it would be difficult, if not impossible, to make the people of Canada understand that I had not concurred in the articles, if I signed the treaty: the easiest and most simple manner in which I could protect myself from attack would be to decline, or, rather, omit, to sign the treaty, which would be a sufficient indication of my non-concurrence: this course was so plainly my interest to take, that I was afraid lest a sense of my own interest might induce me to take a step which might prejudice the sanction of the treaty by the President and the Senate; in fact, it was a struggle between interest and duty.

"He replied that, in the first place, he considered it was the duty of us all, as plenipotentiaries acting on behalf of the Imperial Government, to carry out the positive instructions sent to us, whatever our individual opinions might be; that I was sufficiently protected by the fact that, on the two occasions when I differed from my colleagues, the questions were submitted to H.M. Government, and, after such submission, the articles were settled by direct orders from home; that the protocol sufficiently showed that we acted under direct instructions. He further stated, and pledged his honour for the sincerity of his statement, that he believed my refusal to sign would involve the certain rejection of the treaty. He said that, in fact, he had not the shadow of a doubt on the subject, and he put the question to me as to what my feelings would be if the negotiations fell through. It would thus be shown to the world that the Alabama question was incapable of a peaceable solution, and he stated that, sooner or later, whenever England happened to be in trouble elsewhere, a solution would have to be found in a war with the United States.

"I may say that, before having this final conversation with Earl de Grey, Sir Stafford Northcote breakfasted with me, in order that we might have a *tête-à-tête* conversation on the subject. I appealed to him as being a member of the same party with myself, and as having a great interest, through his Hudson's Bay relations, in the future well-being of the Dominion. We talked over the whole position with the most unreserved frankness, and his opinion is identical with that of Lord de Grey.

"But to return to my conversation with the latter.

"I replied, after having heard all he had to say, that I, of course, felt deeply the gravity of the position and the weight of his arguments. I said that, if I were unable to protect myself in some degree, I should have to suffer the consequences of the attacks which would certainly be made against me, and that in so doing I should consider myself as making a personal sacrifice for the good of my country.

"I stated, however, that I should expect from him, as the head of the British Commission, a letter,* the contents of which I might use, stating that, although I did not concur in the treaty arrangements respecting Canada, and thought them prejudicial to her interests, yet that he, on his own behalf and that of his colleagues, must urge upon me the necessity of my being a signatory to the treaty; first, as we had positive orders from Her Majesty, whose commission we hold, that it should be signed by all; and, second, because my declining to do so would, in his opinion, insure the defeat of the treaty in the Senate, even if it were signed by the President.

"I further said, it must be understood that I was at liberty to address an official letter to Lord Granville, under whom we act, stating the grounds of my non-concurrence, and pointing out the sacrifices which Canada had been called upon to make. To this he assented, and I said I would show him the draft of my letter before it was sent.

* See Appendix XXIII.

"I went on to say it must also be distinctly understood that no act of mine as Commissioner must be held to prevent my taking such course as I might deem proper on the subject as a member of the Government and Parliament of Canada, and I desired that he should, at the proper time, so inform Mr. Fish, as the head of the American Commission, and the U.S. Cabinet.

"He informed me, he had already stated to Mr. Fish that I objected to the main terms of the treaty as regards the fisheries, and it would be very difficult to carry it through the Canadian Parliament, and he continued, 'Although, of course, there were no individual expressions of opinion in our conferences, yet you know that all the American Commissioners are aware of your opposition.'

"To this of course I assented (as I had, in fact, told Mr. Fish myself in a conversation on the subject, that I did not believe that Canada would be satisfied with the arrangement as proposed).

"I said, further, that although my Commission was from Her Majesty, yet I knew I was appointed in consequence of my connection with the Canadian Government, and as representing Canadian interests, and therefore I should feel it my duty to make a report on the subject to Lord Lisgar as Governor General. To this he also assented.

"I pointed out the expediency of the Fenian matter being taken up without delay, and settled by H.M. Government, as the protocol would show that Canada had been thrown over in consequence of a blunder of Sir Edward Thornton. I pressed him, therefore, to take the matter up and have it finally settled the moment he returned to England. This he promised to do. He thanked me very much for the course I was going to take. He felt the great embarrassment of my position, and stated that H.M. Government would do all that they could to back me up. He said that before he left here we should settle the line which he is to take in the House of Lords on the discussion arising from the treaty.

"In addition to the letter which I shall send to Lord Granville, and which will be such as can be published, I shall prepare a letter to him marked 'secret,' pointing out the sacrifices which

Canada has been called upon to make. I shall do this because, if the manner in which Canada has been treated by England were fully known to the Canadian people, I am afraid it would raise an annexation storm that could not easily be allayed. This ends the history of my mission here. On Monday the treaty will be signed, and on Wednesday transmitted to the Senate."

For the sake of brevity I have omitted from this correspondence a good deal bearing upon the purely Imperial questions to which it relates, and also some paragraphs of minor importance, but no portion of it relating to Canadian interests has been withheld. The whole forms a remarkable chapter in the history of diplomacy, a " revelation," as a subsequent Governor General once appropriately styled it. Whatever opinion one may form of the course Sir John should have taken, in regard to the Treaty of Washington, no one, I think, can deny that his letters amply sustained his contention, that throughout the whole course of the negotiations he did his very utmost for Canada.

When it was all over, he wrote to Sir John Rose a long account of the negotiations. After detailing the circumstances with which we are already familiar, he went on to say :—

" I at first thought of declining to sign the treaty. That would have been the easiest and most popular course for me to pursue *quoad* Canada and my position there, and *entre-nous* my colleagues at Ottawa pressed me so to do. But my declining to sign might have involved such terrible consequences that I finally made up my mind to make the sacrifice of much of my popularity and position in Canada, rather than run the risk of a total failure of the treaty.

" It was known here that I was not in favour of accepting the American offer, and, had I refused to sign, it would have been accepted as a conclusive evidence that Canada would reject the proposition. The treaty would therefore have gone to the Senate with the Fishery question left, in fact, an open one, and this would have insured its rejection by that body. If the treaty were lost in the Senate, matters would be worse than ever. The hopeful expectation of the people of the United

States would be changed to a feeling of great irritation ; and, in fact, the conviction would force itself upon everybody's mind, that there was no chance of a peaceable solution of the difficulties between the two countries, and that the only solution would be war, whenever the United States thought they might profitably undertake it. Lord de Grey, on behalf of myself and my other colleagues on the Commission, wrote me a strong letter to the effect that the absence of my name would greatly endanger the acceptance of the treaty. I therefore could no longer hesitate taking the course that I did, and I am quite prepared for the storm of attack which will doubtless greet my return to Canada. I think that I should have been unworthy of the position, and untrue to myself if, from any selfish timidity, I had refused to face the storm. Our Parliament will not meet until February next, and between now and then I must endeavour to lead the Canadian mind in the right direction. You are well out of the scrape." *

Sir John Macdonald was not mistaken as to the nature of the reception awaiting him at home. Incited by the *Globe*, *i.e.* by his old friend George Brown, who greeted him with a storm of obloquy, the whole Opposition press broke out in violent denunciation of the treaty, and of the "traitor" who had sacrificed Canada to his own ambition. As he has often said, he was Judas Iscariot and Benedict Arnold rolled into one. Sir John met these reproaches with silence. For a whole year he said not a word on the subject, but waited patiently for the effect of time. " How eagerly was I watched during these twelve months ! If the Government should come out in favour of the treaty then it was to be taken as a betrayal of the people of Canada. If the Government should come out against the treaty, then the First Minister was to be charged with opposing the interests of the Empire. Whichever course we might take, they were lying in wait with some mode of attack. But ' silence is golden,' Mr. Speaker, and I kept silence. I believe the sober second thought of this country accords with the sober second thought of the Government, and we come down here and ask the people of Canada, through their representatives, to accept this treaty, to accept it with all its imperfections, to

* To Sir John Rose, dated Washington, May 11, 1871.

accept it for the sake of peace, and for the sake of the great Empire of which we form a part." *

This "sober second thought" was in great measure induced by the unexpected reception of the fishery articles by the Nova Scotia fishermen, who, as a whole, proved favourable to their adoption. In Sir John's opinion, at the time, they were the weak spot in the treaty. As to everything else, he considered, speaking generally, that the treaty was a fair one, but in regard to the fisheries, Canada's interests had been subordinated to Imperial necessities. When, therefore, he found that, contrary to his expectations, the fishery articles were acceptable to the people of the Maritime Provinces, and to the commercial portion of the country, neither he nor his Government felt that they would be justified in opposing its ratification, because of its unpopularity with the farmers of Ontario and Quebec, whom it did not immediately concern.

The Treaty of Washington was duly ratified by Canada, and was brought into operation by proclamation, on July 1, 1873. While it failed to restore the provisions of the Treaty of 1854, for reciprocal free trade (except in fish), at least it kept the peace, and there was tranquillity along our shores for twelve years, until, in July, 1885, it was terminated, not by Great Britain or Canada, but again by the United States.

* Speech in Parliament, May 3, 1872.

CHAPTER XXII.

ADMINISTRATION.

1871–1872.

A FEW weeks after Sir John Macdonald's departure for
Washington, the Ontario Legislature was dissolved. The
general election took place on the 14th of March, and resulted
unfavourably for the Government, whose majority was largely
reduced. Several causes contributed to this result, among them
the absence of the Premier of the Dominion, and the provincial
leader's illness. The election was brought on prematurely, in
the judgment of Sir John Macdonald, who wished to have it
delayed until his return, but John Sandfield Macdonald would
take no counsel from any one upon the point. Never a good
tactician, his petulance increased with years. The feeling
excited in Ontario against the Dominion Government by the
murder of Scott at Fort Garry, re-acted upon the provincial
Administration. Sandfield Macdonald's thrifty, some called it
penurious, administration of affairs had raised up many enemies
against him, thereby illustrating the paradox, that, however
much the Canadian taxpayer may favour a policy of strict
economy in the abstract, he likes nothing so little as its
application. The Opposition, led by Messrs. Edward Blake and
Alexander Mackenzie, carried on the campaign with much

vigour, and at the general election were reinforced by some strong men, among whom was the late Adam Crooks. Elated with their success at the polls, they made every effort to improve it, and in the matter of election petitions secured a decided advantage over the Government, by protesting more seats than their opponents.

On his return to Canada Sir John Macdonald did his utmost to retrieve the errors that had been committed, but, whether owing to his feeble health, or to his constitutional obstinacy, the Ontario leader could not be persuaded to take advice. He would not believe that he, who had been such a faithful steward of the people of Ontario, could run any danger of defeat at the hands of their representatives. Sir John Macdonald, with longer experience of parliamentary majorities and greater knowledge of human nature, was not so sanguine. In June he wrote : " I hope nothing will happen to Sandfield or his government. I am vain enough to think that, if I were in his place just now, and had his cards, I could carry him through the first three weeks of the session (wherein alone there is any danger) triumphantly. I am not so sure that he will be able to manage it himself."

The materials for writing, in detail, the inner history of the downfall of John Sandfield Macdonald's administration exist, but the time for doing so has not yet arrived. Suffice it to say, that, despite the earnest remonstrances of Sir John Macdonald, who repeatedly predicted what would happen, at a time when eight of his supporters were unseated by the courts, the Ontario Premier called his Legislature together, and was beaten on the address by a majority of one vote.* The Government then attempted to adjourn for a fortnight, but were defeated by a substantial majority, whereupon they resigned, and Mr. Edward Blake was called upon to form a new administration. A few days after this event, Sir John thus addressed a member of the defeated Government :—

"I need scarcely say that I look upon the defeat of Sandfield's administration as a most unfortunate event, of which one cannot see the result. There is no use in ' crying over spilt milk,' but it is vexatious to see how Sandfield threw away his

* December 15, 1871.

chances. He has handed over the surplus, which he had not the pluck to use, to his opponents ; and although I pressed him on my return from Washington to make a President of the Council and a Minister of Education, which he half promised to do, yet he took no steps towards doing so. With those two offices, and that of Solicitor General and the Speakership, he had the game in his own hands. You see that, as I prophesied would be the case, the first act of the new Government was to increase the Cabinet." *

While upon the subject of provincial affairs, we may profitably devote a few minutes to consider the efforts made by Sir John to "round off the Dominion" by the admission of the outlying colonies. In doing so, we shall have to depart somewhat from the chronological order of events.

The importance to Canada of the colony of British Columbia was so apparent, that, from the beginning of the new Dominion's existence, steps were taken with a view to its acquisition, but the Imperial Government declined to sanction the negotiations until the intervening territory had been taken over by Canada. In 1849, the Island of Vancouver had been granted to the Hudson's Bay Company,† whose trading posts at Victoria and other places along the Pacific coast contained, prior to the discovery of gold in 1856, almost the whole white population of the colony. In 1859, when the Hudson's Bay Company's charter had expired, and with it their license of exclusive trade, Vancouver Island was erected into a Crown colony, but was reunited to the mainland in 1866. In British Columbia, as elsewhere, the officers of the Hudson's Bay Company used all their influence to thwart the designs of the Canadian Government. The Governor of the colony also was unfriendly, but in this, as in nearly every other case, the controlling mind at Ottawa saw and overcame every obstacle. In 1869, Sir John thus wrote to the Governor General :—

" [Private.]

"I enclose a letter from a newspaper man in British Columbia to Mr. Tilley, giving, I fancy, an accurate account of affairs in that colony. It corroborates the statements of

---

* To the Hon. John Carling, dated Ottawa, December 23, 1871.
† Under stipulations that they should colonize it. This the company failed to do.

Mr. Carrall, whose letter I enclosed you some time ago. It is quite clear that no time should be lost by Lord Granville in putting the screws on at Vancouver Island, and the first thing to be done will be to recall Governor Seymour, if his time is not out. Now that the Hudson's Bay Company has succumbed, and it is their interest to make things pleasant with the Canadian Government, they will, I have no doubt, instruct their people to change their anti-Confederate tone. We shall then have to fight only the Yankee adventurers, and the annexation party proper, which there will be no difficulty in doing, if we have a good man at the helm.

"It has been hinted to me that Mr. Musgrave, whose time is out in Newfoundland, would have no objection to transfer his labours to British Columbia. Such an appointment would be very agreeable to the members of your Government, and to the country generally. Mr. Musgrave has acted with great prudence, discretion and loyalty to the cause of Confederation. He has made himself personally very popular in Newfoundland, and I have no doubt would do so on the Pacific as well, if he had the chance. Almost everything, I may say, depends upon the choice of the Governor, as we found to our cost in New Brunswick, where we were thwarted and for a time defeated by the Lieutenant Governor, Mr. Gordon, Lord Aberdeen's son, who took strong grounds at first against us. All his subsequent endeavours on the other side, after receiving instructions from the Colonial Office, were fruitless, as his private opinion was known to every one; hence the necessity for his removal to Trinidad, and the substitution of General Doyle."

In June, the death of Governor Seymour gave to the Imperial Government an opportunity of showing their appreciation of Sir John Macdonald's judgment. Mr. Musgrave was immediately transferred from Newfoundland to British Columbia.[*] Through his influence, aided by the efforts of the Hon. (now

---

[*] Within a week. Governor Seymour died on board H.M.S. *Sparrowhawk*, at Bella Coola, on the 10th of June, 1869. Seven days later Lord Granville notified Mr. Musgrave of his appointment in a despatch in which this sentence occurs: "I shall probably have occasion to address you on the question, now in agitation, of the incorporation of British Columbia with the Dominion of Canada." This he did in a despatch dated August 14, 1869 (see British Columbia *Gazette*, October 31, 1869).

Sir) Joseph Trutch,* and other friends of the union, an agreement was entered into, the principal condition of it being the construction by Canada of the Canadian Pacific Railway. In the autumn of 1870, the people of British Columbia approved this arrangement, at a general election. On the 20th of the following January it was ratified by the Legislature, and on the 20th of July the waters of the Pacific Ocean marked the western limit of the Dominion.

In the autumn of 1868 negotiations were renewed between Canada and Newfoundland, and in the following May a delegation visited Ottawa for the purpose of arranging the terms of union. A few months later the Government of the "ancient colony" submitted the arrangements they had made with Canada to the people at the polls, and were defeated. The acquisition of Newfoundland was a matter of little importance, *per se*, and, as is shown by the following extract from a letter written by Sir John to the Governor General, soon after the news arrived of the defeat of the confederate party in that island, Canada viewed the result of the election with equanimity.

"[Private.]

"The result of the general election is unfortunate in so far as it postpones the completion of the Imperial policy to unite all the British North American possessions under one Government. The acquisition of the island itself is of no importance to Canada, and the terms offered by us and acceded to by the Government of the island were so liberal, that, in a pecuniary point of view, we made a bad bargain. We can wait, therefore, with all patience for the inevitable reaction that must take place in a year or two. It would never do to adopt Colonel Hill's suggestion of adding Newfoundland to the Dominion by an Act of the Imperial Parliament. There can be no doubt of the power to do so, but the exercise of it would seem to me to be very unadvisable. We have had an infinity of trouble with Nova Scotia, although both the Government and the Legislature agreed to the union, because the question was not submitted to the electors. We have, at a large cost, settled that difficulty.

* Sir John Macdonald considered Sir Joseph Trutch a man of high honour and integrity, whose advice was always dictated by a regard for the public interest.

The case would be much worse in Newfoundland, where there was a dissolution, and an appeal to the people for the express purpose of getting their deliberate opinion for or against the union. They have decided for the present against it, and I think we should accept their decision.

"Canada is more directly interested in the immediate acquisition of Prince Edward Island, from its proximity to Nova Scotia and New Brunswick, and the extent of its fisheries. Neither the Imperial Government nor Canada can carry out satisfactorily any policy in the matter of the fisheries under present circumstances, and most unpleasant complications with the American fishermen may ensue. It will, besides, become a rendezvous for smugglers, and, in fact, be as great a nuisance to us as the Isle of Man was in days of old to England, before its purchase from the Duke of Athol. We must endeavour to get Her Majesty's Government to help us as much as possible in our attempts to conciliate the islanders, of which I am glad to say there is now good hope." *

In no colony had the anti-confederate feeling developed greater strength than in Prince Edward Island. In 1865 the Legislature emphatically declined a union "which it believes would prove politically, commercially, and financially disastrous to the rights and interests of its people." This declaration was renewed in 1866, the House of Assembly expressing its conviction that no terms could be offered by Canada to the island which would be acceptable to the latter. At that time, confederation could scarcely be said to have had any friends in the colony, there being in fact only ninety-four persons in the whole island who could be induced to sign an address of thanks to the seven members of the Legislature who had supported the scheme. Such was the state of affairs when the conference took place at the Westminster Palace Hotel, in December, 1866. At this meeting Prince Edward Island was unrepresented, but Mr. James C. Pope, the leader of the Island Government, happened to be in London at the time. Mr. Pope was then a pronounced anti-confederate, and among those who voted for the "no terms" resolution in the local Assembly. To him the proposal was made that, in addition to the terms offered at the

* To His Excellency the Governor General, dated Ottawa, December 8, 1869.

Quebec Conference, the Dominion should allow the island the sum of $800,000 to extinguish proprietary rights which had long been a fruitful source of discontent. Mr. Pope returned home favourably impressed with this offer, but, before the question could be submitted to the Legislature, the general election occurred, and his Government was defeated on other issues.

In 1869 a proposition known as the "better terms" was made by Canada, only to be rejected by the administration of the day, and no further action was taken until 1872. Meanwhile the Island Government had entered into extensive contracts for railway construction, and had issued bonds for a large amount, which were negotiated through a local bank. This institution experienced great difficulty in floating the bonds, and was obliged to seek the assistance of Messrs. Morton, Rose, and Co. of London. The president of the bank, though not himself a politician, was closely connected with leading members of the Island Government. It was manifestly to the advantage of the bank that these bonds should appreciate. Nothing was so calculated to bring about this result, as their assumption by Canada, which could be secured only by Prince Edward Island entering the union. It was under such circumstances that Sir John Rose received a letter from the Island banker in which this passage occurs:—

"Since I last wrote to you, I have had several interviews with the members of our Government on the subject of our railway bonds and Government finances generally, and, from what I see and know, I am quite sure, although no development has as yet taken place, that the way is open for our joining the Dominion of Canada on fair terms, and that, as soon as the matter can be brought about without prominent advances on our part. It will require, no doubt, some delicate movement at first to open the matter, but the time has come when it can and will be done. Of course I have no authority, official or otherwise, for saying this, but still I know it. . . . I am writing now in strict confidence and entirely private, and without the knowledge even of any member of the Government, but I should be glad if some of your Canadian friends would open negotiations with some persons here who have influence with the Government, if not members of the Government, unofficially. I have no doubt it would lead to a more formal negotiation." *

Sir John Rose, as was his duty, immediately acquainted the leader of the Canadian Government with the turn matters had

* From —— to Sir John Rose, dated ——, November 16, 1872.

taken. Ere his letter arrived, Sir John Macdonald had learned, through another source, that the Government of Prince Edward Island were not indisposed to a renewal of the negotiations. Replying to Sir John Rose, he wrote :—

" I have this moment received yours enclosing ——'s letter. The matter stands thus : Governor Robinson of Prince Edward Island has written privately, and as if off his own bat, to Lord Dufferin, saying that he thought that he could bring round his Government to consider the subject of Union, if Canada were still inclined in that direction. He wrote beyond a doubt at the instigation of his Council, and, as we know from experience the style of these men, we replied guardedly. Lord Dufferin answered that, after what had occurred, Canada did not propose to initiate a renewal of negotiations. She would, however, carefully consider any proposition made by Prince Edward Island. He added that Canada had no desire to recede from the offer of better terms made by Tilley in '69. Since then, Robinson telegraphed in cypher to know whether he was to understand that the island railway debt would be taken into consideration. The answer was, that the railway debt was a proper subject for negotiation, and that any proposition with regard to it would be carefully considered here." *

A few months later, the Island Government despatched a delegation to Ottawa, for the purpose of arranging the terms of union. Negotiations were eventually successful, and on the 1st of July, 1873, Prince Edward Island joined its lot with Canada.

The meeting of Parliament, in the spring of 1872, was delayed almost until the last possible day, in accordance with a hint from England. Serious differences of interpretation and opinion had occurred between Great Britain and the United States, in the matter of the reference of the Alabama claims to the Geneva tribunal. The Imperial Government objected to the proposal of the United States to submit what was known as the " indirect claims " for damages, to arbitration. At one time it looked as though the proceedings would be broken off, in which case it was by no means improbable that the United States would declare the whole treaty at an end, thus relieving the

* To Sir John Rose, dated Ottawa, December 13, 1872.

Canadian Government of a most embarrassing question. On the other hand, if it were decided that the Alabama question alone was to be remitted to the domain of politics, and that the rest of the treaty should hold, the difficulties of the Canadian Government would be greatly multiplied. The chief argument relied upon by Sir John Macdonald was, that although Canada was making a sacrifice in accepting the treaty, she was doing so for the sake of securing to the Empire at large the entire and permanent removal of all sources of friction between the two countries. Until the middle of April, the Canadian Government were absolutely in the dark as to what was going to happen. At length the difficulty was adjusted, and Sir John was enabled to determine his policy. Parliament met on the 11th of April, and, on the 17th, Sir John wrote thus to Sir John Rose:—

" Thanks for your several letters about the treaty. Your telegram of Saturday was satisfactory. I have little doubt now that there will be a pacific solution of the difficulty. Meanwhile, after very many months of labour and anxiety, I have screwed my colleagues to the sticking-point. We have finally agreed to go to Parliament this session, for an act to bring the fishery articles into force."

This measure was introduced by Sir John Macdonald, in a speech which took the house by storm. The second reading was carried by a vote of 121 to 55, and the measure passed the subsequent stages by majorities equally large.

The last reference to the Washington Treaty with which I shall trouble the reader is as follows :—

" Thanks for your various letters about this important treaty. Never was there such a bungled matter from beginning to end. You may tell Lord Granville from me, confidentially, that if he wants his business done at Washington correctly at any time he must send me alone. But seriously, the whole thing was badly managed, first at Washington, and still worse in England. I suppose that the treaty will come to something in the end, but instead of removing heart-burnings, it has laid the foundation of new suspicions, and all without the slightest necessity." *

* From Sir John Macdonald to Sir John Rose, dated Ottawa, June 18, 1872.

During this session there was passed an Act providing for the grant of a subsidy in money and land to the company to whom should be entrusted the construction of the Canadian Pacific Railway, of which more hereafter.   Prorogation took place on the 14th of June, after a most successful session, in the course of which the Government did not experience a single check of any kind.

A few days later the Governor General, who, in 1870, had been created a Peer of the United Kingdom under the title of Baron Lisgar of Lisgar, and of Bailieborough Castle in the county of Cavan, bade farewell to Canada.   In Sir John Macdonald's opinion, Lord Lisgar was an ideal Governor, the ablest of all those under whom he served.   Sir John Young was a man of great sagacity, of large experience and sound judgment.   His single desire was to promote the best interests of the Dominion of Canada, and to his wise and prudent counsels Sir John Macdonald was greatly indebted.

Lord Lisgar was succeeded by that astute and versatile diplomatist who at the present time represents Her Majesty in Paris.   Lord Dufferin assumed the reins of government on the 25th of June.   Almost his first act was to issue a proclamation dissolving Parliament.   The general election followed immediately.   In anticipation of this contest, Sir John had, some time before the session, undertaken a political tour in Western Canada.

"I find the country in a sound state," he wrote on his return to Ottawa in February, "the only rock ahead being that infernal Scott murder case, about which the Orangemen have quite lost their heads."

At that time, however, the treaty had not been ratified, and in July the outlook was less promising than it had been six months before.

Sir John Macdonald entered on the campaign of 1872 with just two anxieties.   He was doubtful of Ontario, and he was apprehensive lest his physical strength should fail him.   As regards the Dominion as a whole, he felt reasonably sure of success ; but the result in Ontario, for a variety of reasons, was very problematical.   Upper Canada had always been Liberal, save in 1867, and in 1867 the victory was not that of a

Conservative, but of a distinctly coalition ministry. In 1872 the original leaders of the Liberal wing of the coalition had all disappeared, and many of the rank and file had fallen back to their old positions in the Liberal party. The bringing in of Sir Francis Hincks, although it secured to Canada the best available Finance Minister, could not be said to have fulfilled Sir John's expectations, for, while it offended some Conservatives who felt they had been passed over, it failed to hold all the Liberals who had followed McDougall and Howland.

"Hincks," wrote Sir John, "is as suggestive as ever in finance matters, but his rashness (always, as you know, the defect of his character) seems to increase with his years, and, strange to say, he is quite a stranger to the popular opinion of Canada as it is. His Canada is the Canada of 1850. For all that, he is a worthy good fellow, and has been successful in finance." *

Another of Sir John's colleagues proved anything but a source of strength in Ontario. In February, 1872, Mr. Howe, the Secretary of State for the Provinces, in the course of a lecture delivered before the Young Men's Christian Association at Ottawa, gave expression to views strangely out of place on the lips of a Minister of the Crown. In forcible language he criticized the withdrawal of the regular troops from the Dominion, "the desire of England to throw off her colonies, the buying of her own peace at the sacrifice of Canada's interests, the comedy of errors into which she had blundered," and demanded that the Imperial policy with respect to the colonies be at once proclaimed "in order that we may know just where we stand." †

The *Globe* not unnaturally seized upon these public utterances of a Cabinet Minister, and used the circumstance with some effect. The affair made quite a commotion in the Conservative ranks, and great pressure was brought to bear upon the Prime Minister to call for Mr. Howe's resignation. Sir John Macdonald fully recognized the gravity of Mr. Howe's indiscretion, but, for fear of the result in Nova Scotia, which, even then, was but a slumbering volcano, he thought it well,

---

* To Sir John Rose, dated Ottawa, January 19, 1872.

† For the full text of the objectionable passage in Mr. Howe's lecture, see Appendix XXIV.

though much against his will, to accept his colleague's dis-claimers and excuses.

The substitution of a hostile for a friendly administration in Toronto was another important factor to be reckoned with, but the chief sources of danger lay in the unpopularity of the Washington Treaty, and especially of the settlement of the Fenian claims by an Imperial guarantee, and in the feeling excited among the Orangemen by the murder of Scott, which latter, being purely a matter of sentiment, was most difficult to contend against. Added to all this, the influence of the Roman Catholic Hierarchy—or, at any rate, of the Archbishop of Toronto—was directed against the Government. A few days before the issue of the writs, Sir John proceeded to Toronto, and undertook the direction of the campaign, leaving his own con-stituency in the hands of his colleague, Mr. Campbell. His absence from Kingston, although absolutely necessary in the general interest, was resented by certain of his supporters, who were duped by the silly cry raised by his opponents, that Sir John was neglecting his old friends. Mr. John Carruthers, a wealthy and influential Liberal, was brought out against him, and a desperate effort made to capture the constituency. So hard was the fight, that Sir John was obliged abruptly to suspend his western tour, and visit Kingston in person. He arrived there on the 22nd of July, and immediately laid siege to the town. His presence infused new life into his supporters, who were roused to enthusiasm by the very sight of the chief-tain who had so often led them to victory. Nor were they disappointed on this occasion, for when the poll closed on the 1st of August, Sir John Macdonald was elected by a substantial majority.*

His own seat having been secured, Sir John returned to the west, where he remained until the elections were over, which was not before the end of August. The current in Ontario set strongly against the Ministry, and it required all the leader's efforts to avert disaster. He has thus summarized the result of his labours:—

"The Government have carried the elections swimmingly in all the provinces but Ontario. Strange to say, Nova Scotia,

---

* The vote stood Macdonald 735, Carruthers 604. Majority for Macdonald, 131.

which five years ago returned only one Union candidate, Tupper himself, now returns twenty, being all but one of its representation. In New Brunswick, out of sixteen, we can safely calculate on thirteen. In Quebec we have lost two or three members, but still we can count forty-three out of sixty-five. In Ontario, of eighty-eight members, we can, I think, count forty-two. The Opposition can reckon on forty, and there are six Independents, who will likely go with the winning side. However, at present we reckon them against us. British Columbia and Manitoba return ten members together, and they are all Ministerialists. I had to fight a stern and up-hill battle in Ontario, and had I not taken regularly to the stump, a thing that I have never done before, we should have been completely routed. The chief ground of attack on the Government was the Washington Treaty, and our submitting to Gladstone's resolve not to press the Fenian claims. Added to this, of course, were all the sins of omission and commission that gather round an administration of so many years' duration as ours.

" I never worked so hard before, and never shall do so again ; but I felt it to be necessary this time. I did not want a verdict against the treaty from the country, and besides, I sincerely believe that the advent of the Opposition, as it is now constituted, to power would greatly damage the future of Confederation. That Opposition has much deteriorated since you left Canada. Poor Sandfield is gone, Brown is out of public life, or, rather, out of Parliament ; Blake, who is a gentleman by birth and education, has broken down in health ; Dorion has all but retired from public life, and was elected against his will and in his absence ; and the rest, with one or two exceptions, are a very inferior lot." *

If Sir John's estimate was not too sanguine (and he was not given to exaggeration), there must have been a considerable falling off from the ranks of his followers between October and the meeting of Parliament, in April. This is not unlikely, for, apart from the numerical reduction of his supporters, it was generally felt that the Government had received a severe check. The failure to carry Ontario—the largest and wealthiest province—had, as it must always have, an unfavourable effect

* To the Viscount Monck, dated Ottawa, October 11, 1872.

on the outlying portions of the Dominion, and the impression thus produced was heightened by the defeat of two leading members of the Government, the Finance Minister and the Minister of Militia. The former, desiring to represent a western constituency, offered himself to the electors of South Brant, only to suffer a humiliating defeat at their hands. Sir Francis was subsequently returned for Vancouver, but his public career was at an end. Shortly before the meeting of Parliament in 1873, he resigned his office and his seat in the Cabinet. Sir Francis had had this step in contemplation for some time. He strongly resented Mr. Howe's speech to the Young Men's Christian Association, to which I have alluded, and it was only at the urgent solicitation of his leader that he consented to remain a colleague of the Secretary of State for the Provinces.* His defeat in Brant, no doubt, revived and confirmed his resolve to retire from public life.† In his letter of resignation,‡ Sir Francis thus takes leave of Sir John Macdonald :—

"You and I can afford to treat with contempt the gossip of newspaper correspondents, but this is a suitable occasion for me to state that, during the term of our political connection, you have invariably treated me with the greatest consideration and confidence, and that I continue to believe that the integrity of our great Dominion depends much upon the success of your Administration."

Upon the retirement of Sir Francis Hincks, Mr. Tilley

---

* "You will have seen the *Globe*. Rely on it, your friends throughout Ontario will take the same view as it takes of Mr. Howe's lecture. If Mr. Howe refused yesterday to suppress the pamphlet, it seems to me that your course is clear, and that you should insist on his resignation. You have given him the option. I own that I deeply regret that extreme consideration for Mr. Howe should have led me to write to you yesterday, consenting to remain a member of the Government with him under any circumstances. I believe that we have all blundered, but our motives have been good, and we may hope will be appreciated. Still I shall, even though the pamphlet be suppressed, reserve to myself the right to condemn on all occasions the language used." (From Sir Francis Hincks to Sir John Macdonald, dated Ottawa, March 2, 1872.)

† "Hincks is about to withdraw from the Government, which I greatly regret. No inducement could make him remain until the end of the session. Though he does not admit it, I fancy that the real cause of his reluctance is that he dislikes the idea of being taunted by the Opposition with being unable to get a seat in Ontario and sitting as a Minister for such an out-of-the-way place as Vancouver Island." (From Sir John Macdonald to Sir John Rose, dated Ottawa, February 13, 1873.)

‡ Dated February 10, 1873.

succeeded to the office of Finance Minister. Dr. Tupper, who was then Minister of Inland Revenue, became Minister of Customs. Mr. John O'Connor, M.P. for Essex, who entered the Cabinet in succession to Mr. Morris, appointed Lieutenant Governor of Manitoba, had previously accepted the Presidency of the Privy Council. In January, 1873, Mr. Chapais gave place to Mr. Theodore Robitaille, M.P. for Bonaventure. In the following June, Mr. T. N. Gibbs, M.P. for the South Riding of Ontario, became Secretary of State for the Provinces, which office had been vacated by the Hon. Joseph Howe, appointed Lieutenant Governor of Nova Scotia. On the 1st of July, the Act abolishing the department of the Secretary of State for the Provinces, and creating in its stead the department of the Interior, was brought into effect. On the 13th of August, Mr. Hugh McDonald, M.P. for Antigonish, was appointed Minister of Militia and Defence ; Mr. Campbell was transferred to the new department of the Interior ; Mr. O'Connor became Postmaster General, and Mr. Gibbs Minister of Inland Revenue.*

The defeat of Sir George Cartier in Montreal East, though not unexpected by Sir John, was no less a blow to the Government. For some time previous to the election Sir George had shown unmistakable signs of failing health. In the summer of 1872 alarming symptoms began to develop themselves. He was thus ill-fitted to fight a battle in which everything was against him. East Montreal was not *rouge*, and almost any strong local man could have held it for the Administration. Sir George, however, had quarrelled with the Roman Catholic Bishop on personal grounds, and the whole influence of the latter was thrown against him. Because of his professional connection with the Grand Trunk Railway Company, he was supposed to be adverse to the rival road then being constructed on the north bank of the St. Lawrence, from Montreal to Quebec. It was understood that the terminus of this railway was to be in Montreal East, and, in consequence, every one who

---

* John O'Connor was sworn of the Privy Council on the 2nd of July, 1872 ; Theodore Robitaille on the 30th of January, 1873 ; Thomas Nicholson Gibbs on the 14th of June, 1873 ; and Hugh McDonald on the 13th of August, 1873. The last-named was appointed a member of the Privy Council and its President on the 14th of June, 1873 ; but he was not sworn nor did he sign the roll until the 13th of August following, and it does not appear that he ever exercised the functions of President.

expected to profit by its construction voted against him. The British element, which in former years went as one man for him, was dissatisfied, and the volunteers, on account of some petty detail of administration, were all against him. Sir John Macdonald, who plainly foresaw the consequences of his attempting to carry Montreal East, begged him to give up the idea, and take a safe constituency, but all to no purpose :—

"I should not regret his defeat at all," writes Sir John to Lord Lisgar,* "as he brought it on himself by sheer obstinacy, were it not that I fear it will greatly affect his health. I am sorry to say that he is in a very bad way. His legs are swollen to an enormous extent. It has all the appearance of confirmed dropsy. But, still worse, Dr. Grant tells me confidentially that his ailment is what is commonly known as "Bright's disease," which is generally considered as incurable. I do not anticipate that he will live a year, and, with all his faults or, rather, with all his little eccentricities, he will not leave so good a Frenchman behind him—certainly not one who can fill his place in public life. I cannot tell you how I sorrow at this. We have acted together since 1854, and never had a serious difference."

A few days after his defeat in Montreal, Sir George was elected for Provencher, in Manitoba, but he never took his seat in Parliament. Early in October he left for England, to place himself under medical treatment, which was powerless to save him. His letters from England to Sir John indicate that he had no adequate notion of the grave nature of his malady.† He was always improving, always full of hope and courage. One letter would relate his interview, had the day before, with the Colonial Secretary, on a matter of importance to the Dominion. Another would be filled with speculations as to what was going on in Canada, and with expressions of regret at his enforced absence. Then he would tell with evident pleasure of his social doings— how he dined here and there, and discussed affairs with so and so. All this time he was dying, yet, while Sir John Macdonald feared the worst, his letters to Sir George showed no trace of

---

* September 2nd, 1872.

† For extracts from Sir George Cartier's letters of this period, also an account from Sir John Rose of the former's death, see Appendix XXV.

the anxiety which he felt on his friend's behalf. With all that kindliness of heart and delicacy of feeling which pre-eminently distinguished him, he cheered his friend by every mail with letters which not only conveyed the impression to Sir George that his sanguine reports of himself were confirmed by others, but made it appear that in all his weakness and pain he was doing good work for Canada. Thus :—

" I am glad to learn, not only from yourself but also from other sources, that you are doing so well. Cyril Graham writes me that you are holding your own well."

And again :—

" I read your letter of the 23rd Nov. in Council yesterday. I need not say that all your colleagues were delighted with the good progress you are making. Go on and prosper. You seem to have converted Lord Kimberley, as the Governor General had a cable from him that the Tea and Coffee Bill will not be disallowed. If you secure the transference of the fortification guarantee, your mission will have been successful on every point. Do not hurry too much about coming out."

From the date of his arrival in England Sir George wrote to Sir John once a week and sometimes oftener. To the very last he kept up this correspondence. Sir George Cartier was in truth a man of marvellous courage. Three days before his end, when the very shadow of death lay on him, his indomitable spirit sought once again the old familiar intercourse with his leader and friend. Calling for materials, he feebly endeavoured to write a letter. But ere his trembling fingers had finished tracing the oft-repeated line, "My dear Macdonald," weakness compelled him to desist, and obliged him to have recourse to an amanuensis in the person of his daughter, who wrote this letter at her father's dictation.

" London, 47, Welbeck St. West, May 17, 1873.

" My DEAR MACDONALD,

      " I am ill in bed since a few days, suffering from rheumatic pains in my chest. I am so weak, I cannot hold a pen, and I use Josephine to write for me. I hope to get rid of my pain in a few days, and always purpose to sail on the 29th of May. Allan communicated to me your last about Grand Trunk, and other matters. You did well in writing him thus. I have not as yet got a reply from Lord Kimberley about the extension of the railway

building time, but I expect it from day to day. Very likely he is waiting for
the opinion of the Law Officers on the subject. With regard to my disease,
Dr. Johnson says, I am progressing as well as possible. But the cold
weather and the cold wind we are having here since several weeks, do not
work favourably for me. I presume you have prorogued, or you are on the
eve of doing so. My kind remembrances to our colleagues, and the same
from us all to Lady Macdonald. And, my dear Macdonald, believe me, as
always,

" Your very sincerely,

" G. E. CARTIER.

" P.

" Josephine Cartier."

Five days later Miss Cartier wrote again :—

" 47, Welbeck Street West, London, May 22, 1873.

"DEAR SIR JOHN MACDONALD,

"I wrote to you by the last Cunard mail, under my poor father's
dictation. By that letter, which has now reached its destination, you probably
perceived that he was labouring under the delusion that he suffered just then
rheumatic pains, brought on by the damp climate here, and that if he could
return promptly to Canada a cure would be effected. In fact, his yearning
after Canada was preying so upon his mind, that, although in his presence we
humoured this fancy, we inwardly shuddered that he might make use of all
his energy to carry this out.

" Truly it is a solace now to think, that, if Providence had ordained he
should be taken away from us so soon, it were better his last moments were not
accompanied by the horrors and agonies of a death at sea. He died on
Tuesday morning, at six o'clock, and during Sunday bade us to read, even
to minute details, the contents of the Canadian newspapers, as if to surmise
upon the doings of that country he beloved, before undertaking his final
journey up above. His last words almost were, to congratulate himself on
the good tidings from Prince Edward Island.

" Since a week only, had my poor father been confined to his bed. Life
was ebbing away quietly, and none of us could perceive it. On Sunday
night, however, this evil work became conspicuous, and several doctors were
called in. All agreed, on Monday night, that another consultation would take
place on Tuesday morning, at nine o'clock, as danger was imminent. That
night he slept, which was unusual of late, and towards dawn, mamma, who
had been by his bedside all night, left the room for a few minutes, with some
of the attendants. On her returning, a change had occurred, she gave the
alarm. Doctors, clergymen were called, and all was over in twenty minutes.
He rallied strength and told us himself : ' I am dying.'

" The body being embalmed cannot sail before the 29th inst. Thomas,
his devoted attendant, is unable to accompany it; in fact the shock was so
great, that we are all prostrated. All friends in England show us a deep and

most heart-felt sympathy; but mamma, my sister, and myself intend leaving London after the funeral service, to recover a little before sailing for Canada. Thomas sails on the first week of June. From him you can learn more than I can write to-day.

"Pray accept our united kind regards to you, dear Sir John, and to Lady Macdonald, and also to all the members of the Canadian Cabinet, whom four days ago my poor father still called so fondly "his colleagues," and believe me,

"Your most sincere little friend,

"JOSEPHINE CARTIER.

"P.S.—The inclosed is a photograph, taken some very short time ago. Would you kindly give it over to Notman, or some other photographer at Ottawa ; all of whom might like to reproduce it. Mamma has a larger card, which she intends to be given to Lady Macdonald and yourself.—J. C."

In January, 1872, Sir John Macdonald received from the King of Spain the Grand Cross of the Order of Isabel la Catolica, in acknowledgment of his action, as Minister of Justice, in taking steps to frustrate an attempt made by a few hotheads in Montreal, during the summer of 1871, to procure the enrolment of volunteers for a filibustering expedition against Cuba. Sir John consulted the Governor General, who had been similarly honoured, as to what course he should pursue with reference to this Order, which, as a British subject, he was in the ordinary course of things debarred from accepting. "As for myself," replied Lord Lisgar, "of course, in my position, I cannot take it, but were I in your place, I should accept it and say nothing about it." Sir John took this advice, but he never applied for the requisite permission, and consequently never wore the decoration.*

In the following June, the Prime Minister received an intimation that another and more highly prized honour awaited him—that, in recognition of his distinguished services to the Empire, his Sovereign purposed to summon him to her Privy

---

* This affair of the Spanish Order affords an illustration of the kind thought which Sir John Macdonald ever had for his subordinates. After acknowledging to the Consul General of Spain his sense of the honour proposed to be conferred upon him, he wrote a private note, chiefly to say :—

"I hope you will permit me also to mention that the Canadian official who had the most to do with the promptness of the action of the Government here, was the Deputy Minister of Justice, Lieutenant Colonel Bernard, who had charge of the whole affair, and, as the superior officer of the commissioner of police, gave the necessary instructions to him." The hint was taken, and the next mail from Madrid brought Colonel Bernard the insignia of Knight Commander of the Order.

Council. Sir John, while deeply sensible of this mark of Royal favour, desired it to be made quite clear that the honour was for Imperial, and not for colonial service; and to this end he suggested that the offer should come through Lord Granville, the Foreign Minister, rather than through the Colonial Secretary.

" I thought it best," wrote he to the Governor General,* " to allude in one of my speeches to the Privy Councillorship, as the thing had got abroad—I fancy from some letter of Sir John Rose to a friend—and all kinds of stories had been circulated about it. I shall be glad to be gazetted at any time, but the appointment should, I think, come from Lord Granville. I was obliged to hold the ground that, as one of the Joint High Commission, I was an Imperial servant (and not a colonial representative), and as an Imperial officer bound to obey instructions from England. Even those Canadians who approve of my course, including my colleagues in the Ministry, hold that, in signing the treaty, I, for the sake of the Empire, assented to the sacrifice of the special interests of Canada. This point is of some importance to me, and I enclose you Lord Granville's official letter of thanks, showing that he takes the same view."

In this year, also, Sir John Macdonald received still another recognition—this time of service distinctively colonial. In a previous chapter I have spoken of the unsatisfactory condition of his private affairs. When, in 1870, he was supposed to be on his death-bed, the true state of his bank account became known to some of his friends, in whom the information evoked a feeling akin to remorse. They realized that he, who had given his time, his energies, and all his splendid talents to the service of the State, had done so at the sacrifice, not only of his material interests, but, in the event of his death, of the future well-being of his family. It was felt that while no recompense could requite his services to Canada, provision should at least be made for those whom he might leave behind. The idea of a testimonial was taken up by certain of his friends at Toronto, and elsewhere, and, on the 6th of April, the sum of $67,500 was vested in trustees duly appointed to administer the fund.

* September 2nd, 1872.

CHAPTER XXIII.

THE CANADIAN PACIFIC RAILWAY.

1873.

THE idea of reaching the east from the west has exercised for many centuries a fascination over the minds of men. To it, in great measure, is due the discovery of the New World. It stimulated the zeal and fired the imagination of the early explorers of North America. Cartier, Champlain, La Salle, all dreamed of a north-west passage to the Indies, and a new road for commerce to the riches of China and Japan. In the last century we have the gallant La Vérendrye and the intrepid Mackenzie, the latter the first white man to penetrate the Rocky Mountains, and to view from their slopes the waters of the Pacific Ocean. Then follows a long line of enthusiasts, who advocated one form or another of communication with the western coast. But these were men born before their time, and it was not until the invention of railways had revolutionized the world, that schemes hitherto regarded as visionary became theories, premature it might be, but not wholly chimerical in the judgment of practical men.

In 1851, application was made to the Legislature of the province of Canada for a charter to construct a railway through

British North America to the Pacific Ocean. The railway committee to whom the petition was referred "reluctantly" reported against the project, on the ground that, until the claims of the Indian tribes and of the Hudson's Bay Company to the intervening territory were adjusted, such application was premature. At the same time, they recorded their impression that the scheme ought not to be regarded as visionary or impracticable, and ventured to indulge the hope that it might one day be undertaken by Great Britain and the United States.[*]

The union of the provinces, followed by the acquisition of the North-West, marks a further stage in the development of the idea which animated the early explorers of this continent. That which was beyond the resources of a single province was but legitimate enterprise to a great Dominion—nay, in the judgment of the head of the Government, it had become a political necessity. For years, indeed, it had been advocated in academic fashion by those who spoke only for themselves, and upon whom the responsibility of action did not rest. But Sir John Macdonald was the first statesman who realized the necessity for the railway, and formed the resolution to build it. Even before the transfer of the Territories had taken place, his resolution was formed.

"Many thanks for your letter of the 26th, giving me an account of your conversation with ——. It is quite evident to me, not only from this conversation, but from advices from Washington, that the United States Government are resolved to do all they can, short of war, to get possession of the western territory, and we must take immediate and vigorous steps to counteract them. One of the first things to be done is to show unmistakably our resolve to build the Pacific Railway."[†]

The admission of British Columbia into the Union furnished

---

[*] App., U.U., *Journals, Leg. Ass.*, 1851, vol. x.

On the 15th of May, 1851, Joseph Howe uttered this prediction at Halifax : " I am neither a prophet nor the son of a prophet, yet I venture to predict that in five years we shall make the journey hence to Quebec and Montreal and St. John by rail ; and I believe that many in this room will live to hear the whistle of the steam-engine in the passes of the Rocky Mountains, and to make the journey from Halifax to the Pacific in five or six days " (*Speeches and Letters, Hon. Joseph Howe*, vol. ii. p. 61).

[†] From Sir John Macdonald to C. J. Brydges, Esq., dated Ottawa, January 28, 1870.

an additional reason for the construction of the Pacific Railway. Without such a bond that province, lying three thousand miles from the seat of Government, separated by an almost unbroken wilderness and gigantic ranges of mountains, might as well have been on the other side of the globe. Both the Dominion and the province realized the necessity, not merely for the undertaking, but for its speedy accomplishment. Accordingly, in the terms of union, we find Canada pledging herself to construct a railway to the Pacific Ocean within ten years.[*]

It is not my intention to trace here the progress of events connected with the carrying out of this vast undertaking— that remarkable chapter in the history of Canada has yet to be written; to me it falls merely to relate the story of what is commonly called the " Pacific scandal," or, more properly speaking, to arrange in the form of a narrative that which Sir John Macdonald has written upon the subject.

The agreement entered into with British Columbia encountered much adverse criticism at the hands of the Parliamentary Opposition, who viewed it as an obligation that would press with undue severity upon the people of Canada. They argued that, in contracting to build the road in ten years,[†] the Government had committed Canada to an undertaking greatly beyond its resources, in fact, to a physical impossibility. This cry was not without its effect in the general election of 1872, and, when Parliament met in March, 1873, there was an uneasy feeling, even among the supporters of the Ministry, that the Government had made an imprudent bargain, which would be found exceedingly difficult of fulfilment. It was under these circumstances that, at an early

[*] " The Government of the Dominion undertake to secure the commencement simultaneously, within two years from the date of Union, of the construction of a railway from the Pacific towards the Rocky Mountains, and from such point as may be selected, east of the Rocky Mountains, towards the Pacific, to connect the seaboard of British Columbia with the railway system of Canada ; and further, to secure the completion of such railway within ten years from the date of the Union."

[†] As a matter of fact it was built in less than six. The contract with the Canadian Pacific Railway Company was signed on the 21st of October, 1880, and on the 24th of July, 1886, Sir John Macdonald himself arrived at Port Moody in the car in which he had left Ottawa a few days before. At the date of the signing of the contract the only portions of the main line built were : 152 miles from Fort William westward, track laid but not completed ; 112 miles, Keewatin to Selkirk, track laid ready for operation.

period of the session, Mr. Huntingdon, member for the County of Shefford, gave verbal notice that he would, on the House going into committee of supply, bring up the subject of the Canadian Pacific Railway charter. The Ministers in the House understood from this notice that the railway policy of the Government was to be attacked, and the motion was stated in the Ottawa correspondence of the Toronto *Globe*, the chief newspaper organ of the Opposition, to involve a vote of want of confidence. When, on a subsequent day, the Minister of Finance rose to make his budget speech, Mr. Huntingdon asked whether he proposed to do so with the Speaker in the chair, or in committee of the whole. Mr. Tilley replied that he intended to address the Speaker. Mr. Huntingdon then stated that, as the speech would probably take up some time and cause debate, he would postpone his motion till another day. He did not, however, then state the tenor or effect of his motion.

On the 2nd of April he rose in his place and made a statement * to the effect that the Government, in consideration of large sums of money supplied for election purposes, had corruptly granted to Sir Hugh Allan and his associates the charter for building the Canadian Pacific Railway, ending by a motion for the appointment of a committee of seven members to inquire into the truth of his charges.

It was then first perceived that his design was not to attack the railway policy of the Government, but to make a personal charge against the integrity of the Ministers. The motion was not accompanied with any proof or statement of particulars or details. The House was called upon by Mr. Huntingdon to adopt a resolution, which had been announced to be a censure of the Government, on his naked and unsupported assertion. The Minister of Justice, as leader of the House, felt that there was only one answer to it, and that was to leave the House to deal with the statement and charge without reply. A vote was taken without debate, and the motion negatived by 107 to 76.

* For the text of this resolution, see Appendix XXVI.

The best collection of documents relating to this whole affair is to be found in Lord Dufferin's despatches to the Colonial Secretary, *Journals, House of Commons*, 1873, vol. vii. pp. 5-119.

The motion, as one involving a want of confidence in the Government, was thus finally disposed of. But the Ministers had no desire to remain under the imputation, and, on the next day, Sir John Macdonald gave notice that he would, on the following Tuesday, ask the House to appoint a special committee of five, to be selected by the House, for the purpose of considering the subjects mentioned in the motion of the member for Shefford; that the committee should be chosen by the House and not named by the mover; and that, if need be, they should have special power given them to sit in recess, or that a Royal Commission should be issued to them for the purpose of giving them such power.

On Tuesday, the 8th of April, the following resolution was carried on the motion of Sir John Macdonald :—

"That a select committee of five members (of which committee the mover shall not be one) be appointed by this House to inquire into, and report upon, the several matters contained and stated in a resolution moved on Wednesday, the 2nd day of April instant, by the Hon. Mr. Huntingdon, member for the county of Shefford, relating to the Canadian Pacific Railway, with power to send for persons, papers and records, to report from time to time, and to report the evidence from time to time, and, if need be, to sit after the prorogation of Parliament."

The members to compose the committee were then named by the House, as follows : Hon. Mr. Blanchet, Mr. Blake, and Hon. Messrs. Dorion (Napierville), McDonald (Pictou), and Cameron (Cardwell). Of this committee, Messrs. Blanchet, McDonald of Pictou, and Cameron of Cardwell usually supported the Administration ; while Messrs. Blake and Dorion were leaders of the Opposition. In the debate which took place on this motion, Mr. Mackenzie, the leader of the Opposition, expressed himself in favour of the committee having power to take evidence on oath. He doubted whether it was consistent with Parliamentary practice that the committee should sit after prorogation, and suggested that a Bill should be introduced conferring that power, and also giving the power to the committee to swear witnesses. Messrs. Blake and Dorion concurred in this opinion.

Mr. Joly, also a prominent member of the Opposition, stated that he thought it was so essential that the witnesses should be examined under oath, that he would take upon himself the responsibility of moving that the following words be added to the motion: "and empowering them to examine witnesses under oath;" but did not press his motion, as it was explained to him that it appeared to be the unanimous wish of the House that the witnesses should be examined upon oath. Sir John Macdonald expressed a doubt whether the House had power to pass an Act giving the power to a special committee to administer oaths. He stated that, in his opinion, the evidence ought to be taken under oath, and added that if the House could not confer the power, it could be conferred upon the members of the committee by issuing a Royal Commission to them under the Act 31 Vict., c. 38. He hoped the committee would sit at once, and report the best and most expedient mode of securing that object, either by Bill or by Commission.

On the 17th of April, Mr. Cameron, the chairman, reported the opinion of the committee that it was advisable that a Bill should be introduced empowering the committee to examine on oath witnesses brought before them. A Bill was introduced accordingly on the 18th of April, passed the House of Commons on the 21st, the Senate on the 29th, and received the Royal assent on the third of May. On the same day Mr. Cameron moved "that it be an instruction to the select committee that the witnesses brought before it should be examined upon oath." This was unanimously agreed to. On the 5th of May the committee reported, among other things, that in view of the absence of Sir George Cartier and the Hon. J. J. C. Abbott, two members of the House of Commons of Canada, and of the impossibility of the investigation with which the committee was charged being either carried on or completed in a proper or satisfactory manner without an opportunity being afforded them of being present and hearing the testimony adduced before the committee, it was advisable that the committee should adjourn until Wednesday, the second day of July, if Parliament should then be in session. From the proceedings of the committee, it appeared that this resolution was carried by three to two.

On the 6th of May the recommendation of the committee

was concurred in by a vote of one hundred and seven to seventy-six.   It then having been ascertained and admitted by all parties that the committee could not sit after prorogation, and that the House could not confer that power upon it, it was arranged that the House, after disposing of the business of the session, should adjourn to a period beyond the 2nd of July, the day appointed for the meeting of the committee, giving sufficient time for the committee to complete their report on the inquiry entrusted to them.

The day of re-assembling was finally fixed as the 13th of August; but it was distinctly stated by Sir John Macdonald that the meeting on that day would be merely a formal one, that no business would be transacted beyond the reception of the report of the committee ; that the members need not return, and that none would be required save the Speakers of both Houses in the chair, and the members of committee, who were to make their report, which would be read and published and would go before the country with the evidence.

Mr. Holton, a member of the Opposition, said that to do any business there must be a quorum; to which Sir John Macdonald replied that if a quorum were necessary a sufficient number of members could be collected in the vicinity of Ottawa for the purpose, a quorum being the Speaker and nineteen members.   On this distinct understanding that the meeting was to be purely formal, and no business transacted but the reception of the report, and that Parliament would then be prorogued, the House agreed to the adjournment.

So little was it within the contemplation of any member that Parliament would meet again in midsummer for any business, that Mr. Blake, at an early period of the discussion on this subject, stated that, as it seemed to him that no committee appointed by the House could live after the prorogation of Parliament, the correct course would be to introduce a short Bill authorizing select committees in special cases to sit during the recess.

Meanwhile His Excellency the Governor General had transmitted the Bill enabling special committees to take evidence on oath to Her Majesty's Government for consideration, and, as His Excellency afterwards stated, expressed his own views in

favour of the competence of Parliament to pass it, and entered
at length into the reasons which induced him to come to that
opinion. His Excellency was also pleased to state that Sir
John Macdonald, while expressing his opinion that the Act was
ultra vires, hoped, although in a matter of this kind he was not
in a position to press his advice, that his Excellency would see
his way to assent to the Bill, and not to reserve it for the
signification of Her Majesty's pleasure.

The Bill was disallowed on the advice of the law officers of
the Crown in England, on the ground that it was not competent
for the Parliament of the Dominion to pass such a measure;
and the disallowance was at once made known by proclamation.

It was argued at the time, in some of the public prints,
that the disallowance might have been withheld until after the
committee had taken the evidence and completed its labours.
To have done so would, however, have been obviously a breach
of duty on the part of the Governor General. The Act was
disallowed, not on the ground that it was an unwise and inexpedient Act, but because it was absolutely void and illegal.
All proceedings under it would have been illegal without any
disallowance, and had His Excellency postponed the proclamation he would have deliberately sanctioned the administering of
illegal oaths, giving countenance and effect to an Act which he
had been advised was altogether void. He would, besides, have
been deliberately thwarting the intention of Parliament, which
was that the witnesses in the inquiry should give their testimony under the obligation of a legal oath, and with the
liability of being indicted for perjury in case of wilful false
swearing. No witness could have been convicted of perjury,
no matter how gross, under the Act in question. It was,
therefore, the clear duty of His Excellency, without delay, to
make the decision of Her Majesty authoritatively known by
proclamation.

When the committee met on the 2nd of July in Montreal,
they had the proclamation of disallowance before them, and
they came to the conclusion that they could not depart from
the instruction given them by the House of Commons to take
the evidence under oath. In order to enable the committee to
proceed without delay, Sir John Macdonald repeated the offer

of the Government to issue a Royal Commission under the Act. 31 Vict., c. 38, and addressed a letter to the chairman of the committee to that effect. It was understood that Messrs. Cameron (the chairman), Blanchet, and McDonald would have accepted the commission had the committee unanimously agreed to do so, but not otherwise. Messrs. Dorion and Blake having refused to act on the Commission, the offer was rejected. The committee having refused, the Commission had nothing left but to adjourn until the 13th of August.

While all progress in the inquiry was frustrated by the course taken by Messrs. Dorion and Blake, an attempt was made to excite and prejudice the public mind on the subject by the publication, in the Montreal *Herald* of the 4th of July, of a number of letters and telegrams written by Sir Hugh Allan to Messrs. McMullen and Smith of Chicago, and some persons unknown, in the United States, on the subject of the Canadian Pacific Railway.

Now, Mr. Huntingdon, in his place in Parliament after the committee was granted, on two several occasions attempted to read some papers of which this correspondence formed a part, but the Speaker decided, and the House acquiesced in his decision, that such a course was irregular and unfair, that it was out of order, and that "upon the point of order, as well as on the strong justice of the case, he ruled that the honourable member should not be allowed to proceed."

The publication of this correspondence induced Sir Hugh Allan to make a statement on oath, which was published in the Montreal *Gazette* of July 5th, and in which he substantially denied the truth of the charges made by Mr. Huntingdon, or of any corrupt bargain, or, indeed, of any bargain having been made between him and the Government or any member of it. On the publication of these papers it seemed to be the general impression that Sir Hugh Allan's affidavit had sufficiently met the case as presented by the correspondence published in the *Herald*. So matters rested until the 18th of July, when a letter appeared in the Montreal *Herald*, from Mr. G. W. McMullen of Chicago, the person above referred to. This communication contained some very grave charges against members of the Administration, and certain documents were attached to it, to which were appended the names of Sir George Cartier and Sir John A. Macdonald. Mr. McMullen's letter was a tissue of abominable misrepresentation, and the appended papers, which had been purloined, were ingeniously misused in order to support the allegations in the letter. This publication was made, like the previous one, to prejudice the public mind, and, from the gravity of the statements, naturally caused great public excitement.

The Opposition press made strong appeals to the public, and urged the reassembling of Parliament on the 13th of August, to take immediate action on the Pacific Railway matter. The members of the Opposition were strongly pressed to be in their places in Parliament and to proceed with the inquiry. Now, it so happened that the main strength of the Opposition came from Ontario and Quebec, and they could, at a few hours' notice, be assembled at Ottawa. On the other hand, all the members from British Columbia were supporters of the Government, as were a large majority of the members from the province of Nova Scotia, and a considerable number from New Brunswick. The Opposition evidently hoped to be able, if they succeeded in securing a breach of the arrangement under which the House was adjourned to the 13th of August, and if business were proceeded with, to obtain a majority by surprise, and to carry a vote of want of confidence. It would have been physically impossible for the Ministerial supporters to have reassembled in full strength on the day of adjournment. The British Columbia members were far away on the shores of the Pacific, some were in Europe, and some in the United States; and besides this, several members would have found it impossible to attend in midsummer, the height of the business season; and thus the Opposition, by a breach of faith with the House, would have been enabled to convert their minority into a majority.

On reference to the journals it will be found that the opinion of the House was clearly expressed when the chairman of the committee moved that the select committee should have leave to sit although the House was not sitting at the time the committee met.

Mr. Dorion moved, in amendment, " that inasmuch as the committee will have no power either to force the attendance

of witnesses or to compel them when in attendance to give
testimony without the action of this House, it is essential to the
proper conduct of the investigation that it should be prosecuted
under circumstances that will admit of the prompt exercise of
the authority of the House.   It is therefore necessary that the
House should sit on the day to which the committee has leave
to adjourn."

On reference to the debates it will be found that Mr. Dorion
stated that he would add, that "there was nothing to prevent
the House meeting on the 2nd of July and sitting for ten or
fifteen days, or until the inquiry should have been gone
through."

Mr. Thompson, a British Columbia member, protested
against the proposition that the members from the distant
provinces, who were anxious to get to their homes, should
return to Ottawa on the 2nd of July, and Mr. Dorion's motion
was lost, the "yeas" being 66 and the "nays" 101.

There can be no doubt, therefore, that the will of the House
of Commons was that its members should not reassemble in
July or August for the transaction of business.   The consequence was, that, notwithstanding almost every Opposition
member from Ontario and Quebec was in his place, and although
a number of Ministerial supporters, who would not otherwise
have been in attendance, came when they heard of the efforts
made by the Opposition to collect their forces, there were
upwards of sixty members absent, every one of whom would
have had a right to complain of being prevented from performing
his duties as a member of the Legislature by the breach of the
understanding.   Supposing the House had proceeded to deal
with the matter, they could only have done so either by
rescinding the resolution which appointed the committee, and
taking the matter into their own hands, or by rescinding the
instruction to the committee to take the evidence on oath.
Now both those resolutions, to refer the matter to a select
committee, and that such committee should swear the witnesses,
were unanimously adopted in a full House, and could not, without great unfairness and injustice have been rescinded without
giving the absent members an opportunity of voting upon
them.

It was argued in the newspapers that there might have been an adjournment for a period long enough to enable the members to assemble, instead of a prorogation. But the very act of the House in discussing the question of adjournment and voting upon it would have been a breach of the understanding. Each member had a right, under that understanding, to be present at every discussion and vote of the House; and no discussion or vote could properly be had in his absence. Besides, the Government had no power to make the House adjourn, while it had the power to carry out the agreement by prorogation. Neither His Excellency nor his advisers could foresee what would be the result of a discussion if it were entered upon. It might, and from the course taken by the Opposition members and the tone of the Opposition press, probably would have ended, not in an adjournment, but in a surprise vote of want of confidence.

Had such a vote been given, the Governor General would have been placed in a position into which no one had a right to force him. The statement that the meeting on the 13th of August would be only a formal one, and that Parliament would be prorogued on that day, was made by the First Minister with His Excellency's sanction. If, therefore, he had disregarded the vote of want of confidence, he would have been brought into apparent collision with the representatives of the people. If he had yielded to the vote and dismissed his Ministers, he would have been liable to be charged, not only by his Ministers, but by every absent member, with having dealt unfairly by them. The purpose of giving sufficient time for the assemblage of all the members could as well be effected by prorogation as by adjournment, the only difference, and that a substantial one, being that by a prorogation the promise to Parliament would be kept, while by an adjournment it would be violated. Indeed, so thoroughly was it understood that the members need not return on the 13th of August, that by the Act of that session, c. 31, which increased the amount of salary or indemnity to be paid to members for their attendance in Parliament, it was specially enacted as follows:—

"The said amendments shall apply to the present session of Parliament; and if in the said present session either House should adjourn for a longer period than thirty days, such adjournment shall, for the purposes of the said Act as hereby amended, be equivalent to a prorogation."

This provision was made so that the members need not wait until the 13th of August, the day of actual prorogation, for the payment of their salaries and travelling expenses to their several homes, but that the 23rd of May, on which day the Governor General assented to all the measures of the session, and on which the House adjourned until the 13th of August, was, for all but the one purpose of receiving the report of the committee, substantially a prorogation.*

Parliament, then, having met to receive the report of a committee which had done nothing, was immediately prorogued, despite the vigorous remonstrances of the Opposition, who had assembled in full force in anticipation of carrying a surprise vote of want of confidence against the Ministry, in the absence of many of its supporters.

To find a parallel to the scenes enacted on that memorable 13th of August, it is necessary to go back nearly twenty years in the history of Canada, to that day of June, 1854, when Lord Elgin came to the rescue of his Ministers by an abrupt prorogation. I speak, of course, merely of the *coup d'œil* presented to a spectator, not of the causes which produced the excitement, for, beyond the shouts of " privilege " which resounded throughout the chamber, and the angry protests of an incensed Opposition, the two occasions had little in common. What a commentary on the shortness of life and the mutability of human affairs does this retrospect afford! Of the members of the Assembly in 1854, only three—Sir John Macdonald, Sir Francis Hincks, and Mr. John Young—sat in the Parliament of 1873. Messrs. MacNab, Cartier, William Lyon Mackenzie, John Sandfield Macdonald, and many less conspicuous figures had passed away. Of the Opposition leaders in 1873, all were new men; Mackenzie, Blake, Dorion, Huntingdon, not one of them was in public life on the day when George Brown poured

* The foregoing account of the proceedings consequent upon Mr. Huntingdon's motion is taken almost word for word from a memorandum on the subject prepared by Sir John Macdonald. A few verbal changes necessary to the present use of the paper have been made, and so much of it (*e.g.* the text of Mr. Huntingdon's motion) as is already public property has been omitted; but the statement of facts, as well as the comments and opinions expressed thereon, are in Sir John's own words.

out the vials of his wrath on the Hincks Administration, and John A. Macdonald stood forth " for the liberties of the people of Canada." Nor are the changes wrought by time less remarkable when we consider its effect upon the mutual relations of those who remained. In 1854, Francis Hincks occupied the position of First Minister, while foremost in the ranks of the Opposition, its rising hope, was the member for Kingston. In 1873, Sir John Macdonald, as the absolute chief of a great party, which had held power almost continuously during the interval we are considering, had no more loyal and devoted follower than the Prime Minister of twenty years before.

On the day following the prorogation, a Royal Commission was issued under the great seal, authorizing and empowering three judges * to investigate into and report the evidence bearing upon the charges made by Mr. Huntingdon. It began its sittings on the 18th of August, and examined thirty-six witnesses, including Sir John Macdonald and several members of his Government—Sir Hugh Allan, Messrs. Macpherson and Abbott. Mr. Huntingdon, who was duly summoned to appear, and was requested to furnish a list of such witnesses as he might wish to examine, declined to attend, or to facilitate the inquiry in any way, holding that such action on his part would be inconsistent with his duty as a member of Parliament, and a breach of the privileges of the House. Sir John Macdonald gave his evidence on the 17th of September, a date full of significance to him in after years. A few days later he addressed this statement to the Governor General :—

"Ottawa, October 9, 1873.

" My dear Lord Dufferin,

"The evidence in the Pacific Railway investigation is now being printed, and will shortly be ready. In addition to this, I understand a gentleman in Montreal is preparing a condensed statement of the case and evidence for circulation. The public in Canada will thus be fully informed of the case as it has been presented before the Commission. I think it, however, due to your Excellency to send you a statement myself of the facts.

* The Hon. Charles Dewey Day, the Hon. Antoine Polette, and James Robert Gowan, Esq.

" In 1870 the Governments of Canada and British Columbia entered into a provisional arrangement for union, one of the conditions being the construction of a railway from Canada proper to the Pacific.

" In the session of 1871, when I was at Washington attending as one of the Treaty Commissioners, the terms of union were submitted to the Canadian Parliament for approval, and concurred in after a strenuous resistance from the Parliamentary Opposition. They contended that the railway was a work altogether beyond the resources of Canada, and rang the changes on the burden of taxation that would be thrown by it on the people. The Administration, however, were obliged to carry the measure, or to abandon all hope of the union with British Columbia, and they did carry it. Such, however, was the feeling aroused in the country by representations of the enormous cost of the road, that the Ministerial supporters became alarmed, and, when a suggestion was made by the Opposition that the road should not be built by the Government, but by a railway company of capitalists, aided by subsidies in land and money, it was received with such favour in the House that the Government thought themselves obliged to yield to it.

" Sir George Cartier, who led the House in my absence, in order to carry the Union, was obliged to promise that he would submit a resolution that the road should be built through the agency of an incorporated company, as I have mentioned. I think it probable that, had I been present, I would have persuaded the House to accept the Union without this condition.

" I do not think I am wrong in believing that the Opposition pressed this suggestion for the purpose of preventing the construction of the railway. They did not believe that a body of capitalists could be found ready to undertake the work, and, when Sir George Cartier brought forward his resolution that the road should be built by an incorporated company, Mr. Dorion moved an amendment that the words 'and in no other way' should be added. This amendment, however, was not carried.

" This was the only action taken in the session of 1871, it being understood that the Government should, in the session of 1872, be prepared to submit a scheme, and that meanwhile the preliminary surveys should be undertaken by it.

" No steps were taken by the Government in the matter, except by commencing the surveys, until the autumn of 1871. It being a matter, however, of exceeding interest, the subject was much discussed by the press, especially as to the extent of the aid in land and money that would be required from the Government.

" Reference was made to the grants to the several Pacific Railway Companies by the United States, and public opinion seemed to settle down that a money grant of at least from twenty-five to thirty millions of dollars would be necessary, together with a grant of at least fifty millions of acres of land.

" About this time, Mr. Waddington, an English gentleman, formerly of British Columbia, who had spent a great deal of money in that country in railway surveys, waited on me, saying that he had asked several American gentlemen of means to come to Ottawa and make a proposition to the Government for the construction of the railway.

" I told him that the movement was premature, as the Government would enter into no arrangement until authorized by Parliament to do so. He pressed that I should see them, and Sir Francis Hincks and I met them, we two being the only Ministers then in town.

" I told them that we were glad to see that our railway attracted the attention of foreign capitalists, but that with respect to this particular enterprise, we were unable to entertain any propositions until a scheme was laid before our Parliament, and sanctioned by it. They were a good deal disappointed, but showed us a list of American capitalists, who, if satisfactory arrangements could be made, would undertake the work.

" This offer aroused the attention of the Government to the expediency of interesting Canadian capitalists in the enterprise, and we accordingly individually spoke to our leading men in Montreal, Toronto, and elsewhere, stating that it would be too bad to allow the Americans to carry off a work of such importance, and urging them to attempt to get up a Canadian company.

" Sir Francis Hincks, when in Montreal, spoke to Sir Hugh Allan, he being believed to be the richest and one of the most enterprising men in the Dominion, and he at the same time mentioned the names of the Americans who had offered to undertake the work.

" In the same way I spoke to the Honourable D. L. Macpherson of Toronto, a gentleman who had made a fortune by railway contracts.

" Both these gentlemen set to work, Sir Hugh Allan communicating with the Americans, and Mr. Macpherson with leading men in the Dominion, the hope of the Government being that these two gentlemen, with the strength that they would each gather round them, would coalesce and form a Pacific Railway Company.

" The application of the Americans was not made a secret of in any way ; on the contrary, it was used as a means of inspiriting Canadians to undertake the enterprise.

" The discussion of the subject in the press developed great sectional jealousies between the two provinces of Ontario and Quebec, and especially between their commercial centres, Montreal and Toronto.

" Toronto was afraid that the road would be built in a direct line from Manitoba towards Montreal, and run so far north of Toronto as to take all the western trade past it to the rival city. It was known that Sir Hugh Allan had made some arrangements with the Americans, and the cry was raised at Toronto, in order to weaken the Montreal combination, that these Americans were not actuated by a legitimate desire to get a profitable contract, but that they wished to get control of our Canadian line in order to make it subsidiary to the American railway interests. This opinion was strengthened by the fact that the list of American names submitted by Mr. Waddington and his party included the names of several gentlemen largely interested in the railway system of the United States.

" The public feeling had grown to such an extent against the connection of American capitalists with the undertaking that, by the time Parliament met in 1872, it was quite clear that they must be excluded.

" Sir Hugh Allan and Mr. Macpherson came to Parliament each with a railway Bill of his own. The Government did not desire to evince any preference for one company over the other. They therefore announced that they would not oppose the incorporation of any bodies of capitalists, for the purpose of building the railway, and accordingly Sir Hugh Allan's company, called, " The Canada Pacific Railway Company," and Mr. Macpherson's company, called " The Interoceanic Company," received Acts of incorporation.

" The Government brought in a measure of their own providing for a subsidy of thirty millions of dollars and a grant of fifty millions of acres of land to be given to the company to whom the building of the road might be entrusted.   This proposition was not considered as at all excessive, and was accepted as a reasonable one by Parliament, Mr. Macpherson in his place in the Senate declaring that he did not think it sufficiently liberal.

" The Government measure further provided that the privilege of building the road might be given to either of the incorporated companies, or to an amalgamated company composed of the two; or, if the Government thought it more advantageous, they were empowered to grant a Royal charter to another and distinct company.

" So soon as Parliament was prorogued the Government endeavoured to procure the amalgamation of the two incorporated companies.   It was felt to be impossible to give the work to either to the exclusion of the other.   To have done so would have aroused against the measure, and against the Government, the hostility of the province whose company was excluded.

" Sir Hugh Allan always expressed his desire for amalgamation, but the Interoceanic and Mr. Macpherson objected. Mr. Macpherson professed to dread the influence of the Americans through Sir Hugh Allan, and, although the latter had pledged himself to the Government and to Parliament that all connection with the Americans had been severed by him, such assurance was not satisfactory to Mr. Macpherson.   It afterwards proved that Mr. Macpherson's suspicions were not without foundation, as the private correspondence published between Sir Hugh Allan and his American friends showed that he was still keeping up a connection with them, in the hope that he would be able to overcome the feeling against them. The real and principal reason, however, for Mr. Macpherson's objection was a rivalry as to who should be the president of the company, both being desirous of connecting themselves in that position with the great work. Had Mr. Macpherson been sure of obtaining the position of president, it is certain that the amalgamation would have taken place, and that both he and Sir Hugh Allan would have been members of the same board.

" The general elections were to commence in July, and I was naturally very anxious to go to the country with a completed scheme. I spared no effort, therefore, to effect an amalgamation, and on several occasions had nearly succeeded.

" As to the presidency, my own opinion was that it was really of little consequence who should be the figure-head, but that, as between the two, Sir Hugh Allan, from his infinitely greater wealth, and from the fact of his having been the first to take up the subject, as well as his having largely connected himself with other railway lines which would be auxiliary to and in effect connect the Pacific Railway with the Atlantic Ocean, should have the preference.

" The feeling in the province of Quebec on the subject had become intense. Sir Hugh Allan had put himself at the head of several railway enterprises, and was selected by the voice of the whole province as their representative man. He was especially and pecuniarily interested in all these lines of railway from his position as a ship-owner.

" The Montreal Ocean Steamship Company, in which he has the chief interest, had practically the control of the Canadian freight and passenger trade to Europe.

" An opposition steamship line was announced as being about to be formed under the auspices of the Grand Trunk Railway of Canada, which railway, as you know, is the great artery of trade and transport through the two Canadas to the sea. Sir Hugh Allan felt that his steamship line would get no fair play from the Grand Trunk Railway Company, but that all its efforts would be directed to sending the current of freight and passengers by the new line. He therefore took up warmly the Northern Colonization Road, which is intended to connect Montreal with Ottawa. He encouraged the North Shore Railway, which is the one to connect Montreal and Quebec, and he also became party to a project for building a railway from Ottawa to Toronto by an interior route, thus establishing a rival line to the Grand Trunk Railway from Toronto to Quebec.

"His connection with these lines made him, as I have said, the representative man in Lower Canada, and his support was of great consequence to Sir George Cartier and the French Canadian wing of the Government.

"A coolness had arisen between them, as Sir George was believed, justly or unjustly, not to favour the Northern Coloni- zation Road. He had, from its inception, been intimately connected, professionally and otherwise, with the Grand Trunk Railway, and was charged by his countrymen with throwing cold water on all rival schemes. Sir George, however, finally agreed to give his influence and countenance to the Northern Colonization Railway, and the other roads with which Sir Hugh Allan had, as I have mentioned, connected himself.

"These roads, it must be remembered, did not form portion of the Pacific Railway scheme, and the Canadian Government had no connection with them. The Northern Colonization Railway was incorporated by an Act of the Legislature of the province of Quebec, and Sir Hugh Allan was naturally anxious to obtain the powerful support and influence of Sir George, with the Government and Legislature of that province, in order to obtain aid in money and lands.

"This being understood between them, Sir Hugh gave his strong support, as he had done previously for many years, to Sir George Cartier and his friends at the general election.

"While this matter was being arranged at Montreal, I was at Toronto pressing the amalgamation, with good hope of success, and Mr. Abbott came up from Montreal, as agent for Sir Hugh Allan, to negotiate the details. Mr. Macpherson and he nearly came to terms, the only question really in difference between them being the presidency.

"Such being the case, I considered that the amalgamation would be carried out, but, as the elections were then going on, it was felt to be impossible to enter into the details until they were finished.

"And now as to the expenditure of money at the elections. In Canada, as in England, elections cannot be conducted without expenditure of money.   There are legitimate expenses which must be incurred by those candidates who are resolved in no way to infringe the law; and the legal expenditure in the rural constituencies, which are of large area, with bad roads and a sparse and scattered population, is necessarily large.

" In addition to strictly legal disbursements, there is a cause of expense which, though against the letter of the law, has by all parties been considered necessary, and the law is in this particular a dead letter—that is, the conveyance of voters to the polls.   By universal consent this seems to have been considered so necessary, that never in my experience of twenty years has the hiring of carriages for that purpose been pressed before a committee on controverted elections.   At every general election in Canada, therefore, political parties have always created funds for the purpose of assisting their candidates.   At this particular election we had every reason to expect a stern contest, especially in the province of Ontario.

" The leaders of our Parliamentary Opposition had got possession of the Government of that province, and, we knew, would use all their power and influence against the Ministerial candidates for the Dominion Parliament.

" The Treaty of Washington, which had been accepted on the whole by the other provinces, was unpopular in Ontario, and our Government, and myself especially, was charged with having sacrificed its interests.   This question was the chief battle to be fought at the polls.

" Besides this, we were charged with having made an improvident arrangement with Nova Scotia, to the disadvantage of the tax-payers elsewhere, by the settlement which we made in 1868.   By this settlement, Nova Scotia, previously almost in a state of rebellion, was reconciled to the Union, and confederation made a success.   Still the cry was most successfully used in western Canada against us.   Added to this was the ever-popular appeal to the people against the increase of the burthens which would be imposed upon them by the construction of the Pacific Railway.

" As Your Excellency has perhaps had an opportunity of knowing, I had been for some time desirous of quitting official life, believing that I required, and had earned, a night of rest.

My colleagues, however, as one man, stated that they would not go into the contest without me, and I nerved myself for the struggle.

"From my point of view, I considered that on the result of the elections depended the continuance of Confederation. I may be wrong, but my opinion then was, and still is, that in the hands of the present Opposition, connected with and supported, as they are, by the 'alien,' 'annexation,' and 'independent' elements, Confederation would not last ten years.

"We had, amidst great difficulties, administered the affairs of Canada for five years, under the new constitution, with less friction than could have been anticipated. We had soothed provincial jealousies and ambitions, and conciliated the recalcitrant provinces, but still the embers of disunion were hot. I thought that with five years more over our heads we might safely consider that the gristle had hardened into bone, and the union been thoroughly cemented.

"When, therefore, Sir George Cartier and I parted at Ottawa, he to go to Montreal, and I to Toronto, I asked him to do what he could with our friends in his province in the way of getting us pecuniary subscriptions to our central fund at Toronto. We spoke of several parties in Montreal who would be likely, from party attachment, or from interest, or from other moving cause, to aid us, and Sir Hugh's name was, of course, mentioned, as being the richest man in Canada, and the one most interested in procuring the return of members in favour of the large, I may say, the Imperial policy which had characterized our administration. Aid had come to the fund from Montreal from several quarters, and I was not surprised to receive a communication from Sir Hugh Allan, that he would contribute twenty-five thousand dollars to the Ontario fund.

"As regards myself, I was made the medium through which the subscriptions were paid, but it might, had he so chosen, have been remitted through any other channel.

"I did not consider it at all an unusually large subscription from a man of his wealth. Others, with not a twentieth part of his means, subscribed from five to ten thousand dollars. I however, of course, expected that Sir Hugh would feel himself called upon to contribute to the Quebec fund.

" I may say here, that no portion of the election fund, whether subscribed by Sir Hugh Allan or any one else, was used in my own election. I paid all the expenses of that contest, which was a severe, and, for a small constituency, a costly one.

" I had forgotten to state, in the first part of my narrative, that it was not until the 26th July, 1872, when my own election was going on at Kingston, that I gave up the idea of effecting an amalgamation between the two companies before the conclusion of the election.

" On that day I saw Mr. Macpherson, and the consequence of our conversation was, that I sent to Sir George Cartier the following telegram :—

" ' Have seen Macpherson. He has no personal ambition, but cannot, in justice to Ontario, concede any preference to Quebec in the matter of the presidency, or in any other particular. He says the question about the presidency should be left to the Board. Under these circumstances I authorize you to assure Allan that the influence of the Government will be exercised to secure him the position of president, the other terms to be as agreed upon between Macpherson and Abbott, and the whole matter to be kept quiet until after the election, then the two gentlemen to meet the Privy Council at Ottawa and settle the terms of a provisional agreement. This is the only practical solution of the difficulty, and should be accepted at once by Allan. Answer.'

" On the 30th, I received a letter from Sir Hugh Allan, stating that he had, on that day, made an arrangement with Sir George Cartier respecting the position of his company with respect to the Pacific Railway, to the effect, among other things, that, if the attempts at amalgamation failed, the construction of the railway should be confided to the Canadian Pacific Railway Company, of which he was the head. He did not send me a copy of his arrangement with Sir George, but merely stated what he considered its purport.

" I at once saw that, if Sir George had entered into any such arrangement, he had made a grievous mistake, which the Government could not too soon repudiate. I immediately telegraphed him that I could not agree to any such arrangement,

and that I would go down to Montreal the following night
and see him on the subject.

"On receiving my message, Sir George communicated it to
Sir Hugh Allan, and it was then agreed that the arrangement
should be considered as waste paper, and that the whole matter
should stand over until after the elections, and be considered
as resting on the basis of my telegram of the 26th.

"I may say here, *par parenthèse*, that, on reference to the
arrangement which Sir George made, he did not profess to
bind the Government, but merely stated that he would use
his influence to have it carried out. He, of course, had no
power to make an arrangement on behalf of the Government,
not having been authorized to do so.

"It is too evident, however, from the evidence that has
come out before the Commissioners, that Sir Hugh Allan took
undue advantage of the failing health and waning mental
faculties of Sir George.

"After this, on securing my own election, I went to Toronto
for the purpose of aiding my friends. The contest over the
whole province, as was anticipated, proved to be severe
in the extreme, and we were getting the worst of it. Every
member of the Ontario Government went into the field, either
as a candidate or a political agent, and its whole power was
used to defeat my friends.

"As the Provincial Government has all the local and
county patronage of every kind, and the whole control of the
sale and disposal of the public lands, timber, and mines, you
may easily fancy the extent of the power they can exercise.
Every manufacturer of lumber who wished to get an area of
country for lumbering purposes, and every person having got,
or wishing to obtain, or retain, a mining license, was trans-
formed into an electioneering agent. I had, of course, cries
for help from all sections, and redoubled my exertions to
procure it from every available source.

"Among others, I wrote to Sir George Cartier to procure
from Sir Hugh Allan ten thousand dollars more, and again
to Mr. Abbott. In writing to Sir George, I was quite unaware
of the extent to which he had committed himself in Montreal.
His persistence in offering for East Montreal, against all advice,

was most distressing. It was known that, if elected at all, it must be after an enormously expensive contest, and I pressed him to take a rural constituency, where he would have been returned by acclamation.

"Not until after his death, and the evidence was produced, were any of his colleagues aware of his insane course. As I have already said, it showed too clearly that mind had broken down as well as body. Of course, I can only say this to you, as I would rather suffer any consequences than cast any reflections on his memory before the public, or say anything that would have even the appearance of an attempt to transfer any blame that may attach to these transactions to one who is no longer here to speak for himself.

"No member of the Government here knew or had any suspicion of the nature of the arrangement made between Sir George and Sir Hugh Allan, or of the papers signed by the former, until they were recently published. I certainly did not.

"I think I have given you a statement of all the facts connected with the raising of money for election expenses that particularly affect myself. The evidence before the Commission, which is very full and unreserved, tells the whole story.

"The Government have been subjected to an ordeal that no Government, that I am aware of, has ever before been exposed to. Their arrangements for the elections have been laid open by the deliberate theft of papers from Mr. Abbott, for which theft the thief has been paid by members of the Opposition in Parliament. I believe that, notwithstanding the publicity unwarrantably given to these transactions, no stain can rest upon the Government.

"Mr. McMullen, the agent of the American capitalists, who attempted to get possession of our railway and were frustrated in the attempt by the Government, has endeavoured to connect the loan of money by Sir Hugh Allan with the granting of the Pacific Railway Charter. This was done with the object, first, of revenging themselves on the Government for refusing to admit them to a share of the enterprise, and, in the second place, of killing the enterprise itself.

"The American Northern Pacific Railway, which has since come to grief with the fall of Jay Cooke and Co., dreaded nothing more than the successful commencement of our Canadian line, hence the deliberate attempt to destroy the line and the prestige of all connected with it.

"The advances made by Sir Hugh Allan, however, had no connection, expressed or implied, with the Pacific Railway charter. He subscribed to the fund, both in Ontario and Quebec, in the face of a positive intimation from the Government here, through me, that the road would not be given to his company, but only to an amalgamated company.

"There could be no necessity for the advance of a single sixpence by him in order to secure him an interest in that amalgamated company. The right of his company to be fully represented in it could not be resisted, and he, as the most prominent man of his company and province, would, as a matter of course, assume a powerful position on the amalgamated board. No Government could exclude him or his company from that position, and the Government informed him that he and his company would get that position, and would get no more.

"Sir Hugh Allan therefore knew, before he subscribed or paid any money, the extent of the interest which his company would have in the road. It would be neither more nor less than that agreed upon between Mr. Abbott on his behalf, and Mr. Macpherson as the representative of the other company.

"Sir Hugh Allan's position with regard to the Pacific Railway was, therefore, assured beyond a doubt, if the construction of the line went on at all. His danger was that, if the Opposition carried the country at the elections, they would reverse the whole railway policy of Canada. They had already declared against the immediate construction of that work in its entirety. They were using the cry against it vigorously at the polls, to defeat those men who, if elected, would uphold the railway policy of the Government, and, if the construction of the Pacific Railway were abandoned or even postponed, the detriment to Sir Hugh Allan's interest would have been enormous. The other lines of railway with which he had involved himself to a large amount, and which were to extend from the Eastern terminus of the Pacific Railway proper at Lake Nipissing, back of Toronto, to the Atlantic at Quebec, ran imminent risk of being also postponed. The local traffic of the country did not require the Grand Trunk Line and this interior line; but, if the Pacific Railway were once constructed, there would be ample work for both in the future, as well as for Sir Hugh's fleet of steamships.

"It was, therefore, of importance, to his interests and the undertaking with which he had so connected himself, that a Parliament favourable to such enterprises, and to the development of the country thereby, should be elected, and, as a man of business, he expended his money accordingly. And it suited the purposes of the Ministerial party to accept his subscription, as well as the subscriptions of others.

"The Conservative party in England does not repudiate the action of the brewers and distillers and the Association of Licensed Victuallers in electing candidates in their interests, and we did not repudiate or reject the influence of the railway interest. Our misfortune was that, by the base betrayal of these private communications, the names of certain members of the Government, including myself, were mixed up in the obtaining of these subscriptions. Had this betrayal not taken place, it would have been only known that Sir Hugh Allan, and the railways with which he had been connected, had taken a decided line in supporting one party in preference to another, by their influence and money.

"To sum up this matter shortly, I would repeat that Sir Hugh Allan was informed, before he subscribed a farthing, that his railway company would not get the privilege of building the railway. He was informed that that work would only be entrusted to an amalgamated company, under the terms of the Act passed by Parliament; that such amalgamation would be effected on terms fair to the provinces of Ontario and Quebec, as agreed upon between the representatives of the two rival companies; and that such amalgamation would only take place after the elections.

"When, in November last, all attempts at effecting an amalgamation failed in consequence of the position taken by the Ontario Company, the construction of the road might fairly have been given to Sir Hugh Allan's company, but the Government declined to do so.

" Under the powers vested in them by the Government Act, they issued a Royal charter in which they gave the preponderance of interest to the province of Ontario, according to population.   They gave a fair representation to every one of the other provinces, and, of the thirteen shareholders and directors of which the company was composed, only one was the nominee or the special choice of Sir Hugh Allan.   The others were selected without the slightest reference to him, some of them against his most strenuous opposition, and they included three of the incorporators of the Ontario Company, two of whom had been directors in that company.

" In that charter there were no advantages given, nor could they be given, by the Government.   Parliament had decided what the subsidy in money and land should be, and that was given and no more.   But the charter was carefully drawn with the one object of preventing, by any splitting up or transferring of stock, the clandestine admission of American capitalists as shareholders.   The Government did not even use the influence, which I had promised Sir Hugh, with the members of the board of the two companies, if amalgamation had taken place, in order to get for him the position of president.   As has been proved before the Commission, the directors, without any intimation of preference on the part of myself or any of my colleagues, selected Sir Hugh, from his wealth and business connection with kindred works, as their president.

" This has been a most unfortunate business for us, amounting to a calamity, but we must bear it, as best we may, believing and knowing that we made no unworthy barter, or barter of any kind, of the powers entrusted to us, for the sake of securing support at the elections.

" I know that Your Excellency will, under the circumstances, pardon me for this long story.

> " Believe me, my dear Lord Dufferin,
> > " Very faithfully yours,
> > > " JOHN A. MACDONALD.

" P.S.—It has been stated in the English press that I should not have mixed myself up in these money matters, but should have left it to our Carlton and Reform Clubs. This may be true, indeed is true, if such clubs existed; but, as a matter of fact, the leaders of political parties have always hitherto acted in such matters, and there can be no special blame attached to a leader for continuing the invariable practice on this occasion.

" J. A. M.D.

" His Excellency the Governor General, Quebec."

Sir John Macdonald's correspondence of this period abounds with confirmation of his statement that no bargain or agreement of any kind was made by him with Sir Hugh Allan in relation to the charter for the Canadian Pacific Railway. Thus, on the 17th of April, 1872, he writes to Sir John Rose :—

" The Pacific Railway occupies the attention of our capitalists at present almost to the exclusion of everything else. First there is the Hugh Allan Company, composed of Jay Cooke and Co., Scott of Philadelphia, and other Yankee millionaires ; second, the Montreal Company proper, consisting of Brydges, Reekie, and that set ; and third, the Ontario Company, headed by D. L. Macpherson.

" There will, I have no doubt, be a coalition between numbers two and three, and Allan will, I think, be obliged to abandon his Yankee confrères. If so, we shall have a strong company of Canadian capitalists who will undertake and finish the railway. We intend to be liberal both in money and lands, as it is of importance to settle that country at once."

And six months later (October 24th) :—

" I wrote you a long letter about railway matters, and I send you, confidentially, copies of the correspondence. If Cartier is in town give them to him, and say to him that I sent them to you instead of to him, as I thought it likely he would be off to Nice, or somewhere on the continent. These papers, with my letter of last mail, will post you exactly as to the present position of affairs. Council assembles to-day, and we shall take up the question and settle our policy. I fancy that it will result in our issuing a new charter to a new company, on the board of which will be represented all the provinces, thus :—The board to consist of thirteen, of which five will come from Ontario, four from Quebec, and one from each of the other provinces of Nova Scotia, New Brunswick, Manitoba, and British Columbia. The stock will be allotted in the same proportions: five-thirteenths to Ontario, four-thirteenths to Quebec, and so on."

On the 16th of December, he wrote to Sir Alexander Galt:—

" The Government had and have only one object, and that is to build the Pacific as speedily and on as reasonable terms as possible. I went to Toronto to see McPherson, and at one time thought the matter was arranged, but McP. finally took the position that Allan must be excluded from the presidency, as the president for the first year would settle the whole policy of the company. It was to no purpose that I argued that the P. was only one of a board, and that the board, if well selected, would settle the policy and force it on the P. If D. L. M. had only gone on the board he would have been V.P., equally potential with Allan, and would have been backed in all things reasonable by his co-directors. Just consider: with D. L. M. and four Ontario men; Collingwood Schreiber, a Toronto man (brother-in-law of Hon. George Allan), for Nova Scotia ; Burpee, the civil engineer, for New Brunswick ; Donald Smith, for Manitoba; and a B. Columbian,—what could Allan do in the way of selling the roadway to the Northern Pacific, or Jay Cooke and Co. ? The thing is preposterous !

" I was so anxious to include McP., that I stood alone in Council as to the exclusion of members of Parliament from the direction, lest I might affect his seat in the Senate. After he finally declined I gave up the point. Had he gone on the board, I assume, as a matter of course, they would have sent a sub-committee, of Allan, McP., and some one else, to England to arrange financial matters. Now we must make the best of things as they stand, but nothing has distressed me so much for a long time as McP.'s drawing back."

On the 4th of January, 1873, to Sir George Cartier :—

" With respect to the Pacific Railway, the matter stands thus : Macpherson and the Interoceanic Company have declined to amalgamate with the Pacific Railway Company. The Government, therefore, came to the conclusion that it would

not do to give the Canada Pacific Railway Company, headed
by Sir Hugh Allan, the contract, as it would have been a false
start, and would have united all Ontario against them. We
therefore decided to give the charter to a selected body of
capitalists, and have made considerable progress. I shall
enclose you a rough draft in galley of the proposed charter.

"We have decided that no members of Parliament shall be
on the board of directors, as first appointed. Ontario is to have
five members, and I have already selected Mr. MacInnes, a
wholesale merchant of Hamilton, whose wife is a daughter of
Sir John B. Robinson; John Walker of London, a rich man
and a friend of Carling's; and the partner of the Hon. Frank
Smith, Senator, Toronto. There are two vacancies to be filled
up, and I think it likely that Sandford Fleming will be one
of them.

"The Quebec men are not yet selected, but there will be no
difficulty about them. We propose meeting on the 14th instant
to settle the terms of the charter and get the machinery in
motion.

"As Donald A. Smith cannot be on the board, being an M.P.,
I think it would be well to put Sir Stafford Northcote on, if he
will act. I have asked Smith to write Northcote to that effect.
The New Brunswickers have selected Mr. Burpee, a civil
engineer, and brother of the member for St. John, as their
representative. Tupper is now at Halifax, and will select his
man for Nova Scotia. I scarcely know whom to choose for
British Columbia. Cornwall, as a Senator, is not eligible.
However, we will put on some man as a *locum tenens* for the
present."

A week after Mr. Huntingdon made his motion, Sir John
wrote to Sir George Cartier :—

"You will have seen by the papers that on Wednesday, the
2nd, Huntingdon rose in his place and made a statement, which
I send you. He had given us a verbal notice that he was
going to move as to the Canadian Pacific Railway, when we
went into ways and means, so our friends were prepared for
the vote.

"Having made his motion, he sat down without offering
a word of explanation. I immediately took advantage of his

blunder, and had the members called in and a vote taken, which resulted in a majority of 31 ; with three of our friends then in town accidentally absent, viz. Cluxton, Robillard and Blanchet.

" This vote was very satisfactory, but Council felt that we could not properly allow it to remain in that position. I accordingly, the very next day, gave notice that I would move for a committee. It was fortunate that we took that course, as we found great uneasiness among our friends who had voted with us. It looked so like stifling an inquiry that they were afraid of the consequences to themselves in their constituencies. I am satisfied that if the question had been brought up again on a specific motion it would have been carried. Our course, therefore, in spontaneously asking for the inquiry was fortunate in all respects. The committee has now been struck. It consists of Hillyard Cameron, McDonald of Pictou, Blanchet, Blake, and Dorion. This is a first-rate committee. McDonald of Pictou is as true as steel, and is, I think, the ablest man in the House of Commons. He has at once taken the very first rank and position in it. Huntingdon's motion is, I understand, founded altogether on letters written by Allan to McMullen of Chicago.

"The imprudence of Sir Hugh in this whole matter has almost amounted to insanity. His language has been as wild as his letters, and, between you and me, the examination must result greatly to his discredit. So far as the Government is concerned, I have no fear but that the report must be a satisfactory one. Allan and Abbott must both be here to give their testimony."

The Commission having finished its labours, which were wholly inquisitorial, Parliament was summoned for the 23rd October, to receive its report. An amendment to the address was immediately offered by Mr. Mackenzie, the leader of the Opposition, to the effect that, in view of the facts disclosed before the Commission, the Ministry had merited the "severe censure" of the House. The debate lasted a week, but before it was over numerous defections from the Government ranks showed that the Ministry was doomed. If anything could have saved it, it would have been the speech in which the Prime

Minister reviewed and replied to the charges which had been made against him. His effort on that occasion—one of the greatest of his life—was looked forward to with an interest which was only exceeded by the enthusiasm which it evoked. When, on the afternoon of Monday, the 3rd of November, he rose to address the House, every member was in his place, and the galleries were thronged with an expectant multitude, many of whom had come from a distance to hear the anxiously looked-for explanation of the leader of the Government. The Governor General, debarred by official etiquette from being present, was represented by Lady Dufferin, who remained to the end; and by her side, an equally interested listener, sat the present Prime Minister of England.* In eloquent and pathetic language Sir John Macdonald recounted his connection with the railway negotiations, and indignantly repudiated the charge that he had betrayed those interests which he had been commissioned to guard. Going over the ground at greater length than in his letter to the Governor General, he maintained that he had made no bargain with Sir Hugh Allan, and that Sir Hugh had received no special power, privilege, or advantage over the other members of the directorate. He spoke with great vigour for upwards of four hours, and concluded with this appeal to his countrymen, whom he had served so long.

" Sir, I commit myself, the Government commits itself, to the hands of this House, and far beyond the House, it commits itself to the country at large. We have faithfully done our duty. We have had party strife setting province against province; and more than all, we have had in the greatest province, the preponderating province of the Dominion, every prejudice and sectional feeling that could be arrayed against us. I have been the victim of that conduct to a great extent; but I have fought the battle of Confederation, the battle of Union, the battle of the Dominion of Canada. I throw myself upon this House; I throw myself upon this country ; I throw myself upon posterity ;

---

* Government House, Ottawa, November 1, 1873.

" DEAR SIR JOHN,—Pray excuse the liberty which your kindness encourages me to take. But I am leaving for Quebec to-day, having very little more time. But if I were perfectly certain that you were going to speak on Monday I would give up Quebec and stay to hear you ; and if you would therefore tell me if this be settled you would confer a favour on—Yours very truly, ROSEBERY."

and I believe, and I know, that, notwithstanding the many failings in my life, I shall have the voice of this country, and this House, rallying round me. And, sir, if I am mistaken in that, I can confidently appeal to a higher court—to the court of my own conscience, and to the court of posterity. I leave it to this House with every confidence. I am equal to either fortune. I can see past the decision of this House, either for or against me ; but whether it be for or against me, I know— and it is no vain boast for me to say so, for even my enemies will admit that I am no boaster—that there does not exist in this country a man who has given more of his time, more of his heart, more of his wealth, or more of his intellect and power, such as they may be, for the good of this Dominion of Canada."

For the first and last time of his life he failed—or perhaps I should not say he failed, as before he rose he must have felt that the judgment of the House was against him,—but then and then only was his supreme effort in vain. His majority, not large in April, had been steadily melting away. A sense of extreme uneasiness pervaded the Ministerial ranks, which was ominous for the Administration. There was a "sound of going on the tops of the mulberry trees," a feeling of impending change everywhere abroad. Apart from those, on the one hand, who were clamorous for his fall, and those, on the other, who were prepared to stick by their leader through thick and thin, there were some who, while ready to acknowledge that Sir John Macdonald personally was free from blame—that he had been drawn by circumstances beyond his control—that he was the victim of atrocious calumnies—that, in spite of Sir George Cartier's weakness, he had steadfastly protected the interests of Canada, both against American speculators and against the approaches of Sir Hugh Allan—that, although it had never entered into his thoughts to make a single illegitimate concession in consideration of the support and assistance he expected on other grounds to receive from Sir Hugh Allan— were impelled to the conclusion that a Government which had benefited politically by large sums of money derived from a person with whom it was negotiating on the part of the Dominion, could no longer command their confidence or support, and that for them the time had come to choose between their conscience and their party. He who had spent his life in reading the minds and hearts of politicians, was not blind to what was going on about him. He resolved to spare the Conservative party the injury that must result from open schism, and many old-time followers the pain which public abandonment of their leader must entail. On the day following the conclusion of his speech, and without waiting for the result of the vote of want of confidence, he placed his resignation in the hands of the Governor General, and on the same afternoon announced its acceptance to the expectant House.

A new administration was speedily formed under the leadership of Mr. Mackenzie. Parliament was prorogued, and dissolution immediately followed. In the ensuing elections the Liberal party swept the country from end to end. Their triumph was complete. The great obstacle to their success was removed. Overwhelmed in the ruin which had overtaken his party, he had fallen, like Lucifer, never to rise again. So said all his opponents,* and not a few who called themselves his friends. He himself said nothing.

After announcing the resignation of his Ministry, Sir John Macdonald moved the adjournment of the House. He then went over to his office, directed his secretaries to pack up his papers, drove home, went upstairs to his bedroom, and remarked quietly to Lady Macdonald, "Well, that's got along with."

---

* Not quite all. A prominent member of the Liberal party in the Senate thus addressed him two days after his resignation :—

Ottawa, November 7, 1873.

"DEAR SIR JOHN,—Being sure that your time and thoughts have been intensely preoccupied these last few days, I have refrained from seeking an opportunity of paying my respects to you in person. I should, however, feel ill at ease if I left Ottawa without finding some means of making known to you that charges, doubts, admissions notwithstanding, I entertain a confident expectation that you will continue to occupy a large, if not the largest, space in the public mind. I have pored not a little over some portions of our country's history, and I conclude therefrom, that a good wholesome appetite for power, and tenacity of office, have very generally characterized our most eminent men, who have not infrequently sustained their positions by recourse to means not altogether in conformity with the letter of the law, and I cannot for a moment doubt that your great services to the Dominion and to the Empire will live long after the details of the Pacific affair are buried in oblivion.

"With best wishes for your health and prosperity, I remain very faithfully yours, —ROBT. POORE HAYTHORNE."

" What do you mean ? " said she.   " Why, the Government has resigned," he replied, arraying himself in his dressing-gown and slippers, and picking up two or three books from a table close by.   " It's a relief to be out of it," he added, as he stretched himself on the bed, opened a volume and began to read, intimating that he did not wish to be disturbed.   That was all he said on the subject at the time, nor did he allude to it again. There were no bitter reflections upon those of his supporters who had failed him in the hour of need—no harsh words against those who had passed over to his foes, no repining at fortune. He knew that he had made the best fight possible.   The fortunes of war had gone against him, and he accepted defeat without a murmur.   And, indeed, this habit of mind was eminently characteristic of Sir John Macdonald throughout his career.   No matter what happened of a disagreeable nature he invariably would say, after the first momentary exclamation of surprise, regret, or it might be annoyance, " Well, it can't be helped," and would then dismiss the subject from his mind.

Shortly after the change Sir John removed to Toronto, to resume the practice of his profession, and to bide his time.   He had not long to wait.   Before two years had elapsed it began to be manifest that the closing words of his speech had found an echo in the hearts of the people of Canada.   He had been buried under the great inundation, but the wave which had overwhelmed him receded as quickly as it had risen, and when it again advanced he found himself borne forward to his old position at the head of affairs, by the potent forces of a national reaction.

CHAPTER XXIV.

THE RESTORATION.

1878.

IT is not proposed to follow, in these pages, Sir John Macdonald's
political career during the period which intervened between his
restoration to power in 1878, and his death in 1891. The
largeness of the subject, the nearness of the time, and the
presence amongst us of so many of the actors in those eventful
scenes, render any adequate performance of such a task impracticable just now. In the remaining chapters I shall, therefore, discarding chronology, content myself with indicating his
views on public questions not directly bearing on Canadian
politics, leaving to the future the record of his later and
more renowned triumphs.

Immediately after the resignation of the Ministry, Sir
John called a caucus of his followers, at which he urged upon
them the importance of losing no time in organizing as an
Opposition and formulating a plan of attack upon the Treasury
Benches. He told them, as leader of the party, the person
most attacked in the past, and most likely to be attacked in
the future, that it was a question for them to consider whether

they had not better choose another leader, a younger man, who had not been calumniated as he had been, adding that they should not allow any feelings of sympathy or of sentiment to interfere with the good of the country and of the party. One and all refused to fight under any other leader than their beloved chief. With much earnestness he besought them to think well of the suggestion of " an old man who had done his share of the fighting," and to weigh the whole matter carefully. With the object of giving them time for reflection, he adjourned the meeting until the next day, when he proposed to meet them and receive their answer. Punctually at the appointed hour he was in his place, to find himself alone. Not a single member of the party was anywhere to be seen. They would not, by their attendance, lend colour to the idea that they had even contemplated the possibility of a change of leader. Sir John had experienced many a triumph; he was destined to achieve many more, but at no time in his life, not on the ever-memorable 17th of September, 1878, not even when he was borne through the passes of the Rocky Mountains to the shores of the Pacific Ocean, over the railway which is, perhaps, the greatest monument of his courage and resolution, did he experience a prouder and more heartfelt satisfaction, than when he walked from the deserted committee-room to the House of Commons, there to receive from his devoted followers the assurances of their undiminished attachment, conveyed in ringing cheers which presaged his future triumph.

In the general election of 1874, the Conservative party, taken by surprise and weighted with all the disadvantageous circumstances which attend defeat, were well-nigh annihilated. Sir John Macdonald himself narrowly escaped defeat in his own constituency, was unseated on a petition, and re-elected by a majority even smaller than before. Out of 206 members of the House of Commons, the Conservatives did not number more than 45. The once great party had dwindled to a mere handful, to be pitied rather than feared. The Ministerial forces, rejoicing in their new-found strength, overflowed that portion of the chamber allotted to them, and, encroaching on the other side of the House, surrounded and almost engulfed the little band to the left of the Speaker. Nor was it only on the floor of Parliament that the outlook was dark. Like Frederick the Great at the beginning of the Seven Years' War, or Cortés in the valley of Otompan, wherever Sir John Macdonald looked he saw a hostile array drawn up against him. At Toronto, Quebec, Halifax, Fredericton, and Charlottetown, all the provincial Governments were active in their support of the federal administration, and animated with a common desire to crush him at the coming election. But his was not the heart to despond. He felt within himself the strength of his personality in the great province of Ontario. He knew that he had not deserved defeat in 1873, and his knowledge derived from long acquaintance with the people of his own province, told him that there were thousands who already repented of their rashness, and who impatiently awaited an opportunity of atoning for the past, by restoring him to his old position at the head of affairs. But he did not trust to sentiment alone. In the words of a distinguished French Canadian writer,* " he constructed with consummate skill the engine which destroyed the Mackenzie administration. From the very first he saw what a tactician could do with Protection, and, in so masterly a manner did he cover his troops with that rampart, that it was impossible for the Liberals to turn their flank."

During the sessions of 1874 and 1875, the Conservatives made little or no fight in Parliament, it being in accordance with Sir John Macdonald's tactics to conceal as far as possible the numerical weakness of his party, by avoiding divisions in the House. His leadership during those two years illustrates admirably his policy of playing the waiting game. He knew that no good could possibly result from publishing to the country every morning that his party numbered scarcely one-fourth of the House; so he was content to bide his time, assisting in the legislation, much of which had been framed by himself, and quietly awaiting an opportunity for striking a blow. In due time that opportunity arrived. In September, 1875, the appointment of Mr. Thomas Moss, M.P., to the Ontario Bench, created a vacancy in the representation of

* Hector Fabre.

West Toronto. Sir John felt that to carry this metropolitan constituency in the face of both the Ottawa and Ontario Governments would be the signal to the rest of the Dominion that the tide had turned. The task, however, was no easy one; few believed it possible, and it required all his persuasion to induce Mr. John Beverley Robinson to take the field in the Conservative interest. To the astonishment of the Ministry, Mr. Robinson was successful by a sweeping majority. His victory marks the beginning of that reaction which culminated on the 17th of September, three years later.

A few days after this triumph, Sir John attended a banquet given in Montreal to his friend, and afterwards his colleague, Mr. Thomas White. On that occasion he delivered an important speech, every line of which breathed war against the Administration. In the session of 1876 he announced in Parliament his scheme for improving the commercial condition of the country, and, in the following summer, expounded it to the people at a series of political picnics held throughout Ontario. These picnics proved immensely successful, and were repeated in 1877. In the session of 1878 he again pressed on Parliament the adoption of his policy of protection to native industries, and defined it in a carefully drawn amendment to a motion to go into supply.* His attitude towards that great question was briefly this : that, while the principle of free trade, viewed as an abstract proposition, was indisputably sound, its successful application in the concrete depended upon conditions which were not always present, and which certainly did not exist in Canada. It was, he contended, the duty of a statesman to deal with facts, not to speculate in theories, and to adopt such a policy as would

---

* " That this House is of opinion that the welfare of Canada requires the adoption of a National Policy, which, by a judicious readjustment of the Tariff, will benefit and foster the Agricultural, the Mining, the Manufacturing and other interests of the Dominion ; that such a policy will retain in Canada thousands of our fellow country- men now obliged to expatriate themselves in search of the employment denied them at home, will restore prosperity to our struggling industries, now so sadly depressed, will prevent Canada from being made a sacrifice market, will encourage and develop an active interprovincial trade, and moving (as it ought to do) in the direction of a reciprocity of Tariffs with our neighbours, so far as the varied interests of Canada may demand, will greatly tend to procure for this country, eventually, a reciprocity of Trade " (*Journals*, House of Commons, March 12, 1878, p. 78).

best meet the varying needs of the country. Free trade, in the absolute sense of the term—that is, the liberty of buying in the cheapest and selling in the dearest market—did not anywhere exist. The example of England was quoted, but England, while she had thrown open her ports to the world, found the markets of all other nations shut against her. Nor, supposing the anticipations of Bright and Cobden had been realized, and all Europe had imitated England's example, did it follow that a policy which suited an isolated country of limited area, dependent to a large extent upon the rest of the world for food, whose manufacturing interests had been created and fostered by centuries of protection, could be applied with advantage to the Dominion, whose geographical and economic conditions were widely different from those of the United Kingdom. Canada was a new and poor country, lying in close proximity to a great nation, whose markets were rigorously closed against her. Under a low tariff her struggling industries found it impossible to compete against the wealth, skill, and acquired capital invested in the great manufactories of the United States which had been built up by protection, and her skilled artisans and labourers were in consequence obliged to seek in a foreign country that employment which was denied them at home. Was there no remedy for this state of things? Sir John asked. Was Canada for ever to languish under a system which was steadily depleting her, merely that her rulers might continue faithful to the maxims of Cobden, every one of whose prophecies made with respect to the future of free-trade had been falsified by time? To do this, was, in his opinion, to degrade political economy to a superstition. He, for his part, was not prepared to make a fetish of free trade. Rather, he argued, did it become practical statesmen, charged with the responsibilities of government, to frame and carry out such a policy as would, by encouraging and developing our great natural resources, attract capital to the country, stimulate private enterprise, provide our people with employment at home, and so make Canada in fact, what she was already in name.

The Government of Mr. Mackenzie met this proposal with an emphatic negative. While admitting the serious character of the commercial depression then prevailing, they attributed its cause wholly to circumstances beyond their control, and denied the power of any government to remove it by legislation. They would have nothing to do with protection, which the Prime Minister ridiculed as an attempt to relieve distress by imposing additional taxation. He announced the resolve of his Government to adhere to a revenue tariff, and to trust to a natural revival of trade to restore prosperity to the country.

With the issue thus clearly joined, the two parties went to the polls. The result of the election was phenomenal. In the erstwhile Liberal province of Ontario, Sir John Macdonald captured no less than sixty-three seats out of eighty-eight. In Quebec the majority was equally decisive, and in the new Parliament, the leader of the little band of forty-five—"the old guard," as he used affectionately to call them—found himself supported by one hundred and forty-six members, out of a house of two hundred and six. This unparalleled revulsion of popular feeling surprised no one less than him to whose personal magnetism, apart altogether from questions of trade and tariffs, it was largely due. Yet it was not until the eve of the battle that Sir John could be prevailed upon to give his opinion as to the result. He had a rooted objection to counting upon the future, and especially to speculating upon the chances of an election contest. "An election is like a horse-race," he used to say, "in that you can tell more about it the next day." On this occasion, although he has told me he felt as sure as one could feel of anything that had not occurred, that the Mackenzie government was doomed, he maintained his habitual reserve far into the summer. Lady Macdonald has related that, during the eventful campaign of 1878, she could not obtain the slightest intimation of what he thought the issue of the fight would be. Towards the end of July it became absolutely necessary, for domestic reasons, that she should know whether they were to continue to occupy their Toronto house or not. Accordingly she brought the subject up, and, explaining the circumstances under which she desired to know, pressed him to give her some hint of what he thought was going to happen. Then for the first time he spoke. "If we do well, we shall have a majority of sixty ; if badly, thirty." He had eighty-six.

On his return to power Sir John Macdonald's first care was to bring into effect his "National Policy," in the framing of which he so thoroughly carried out his ante-election promises as to extort from Mr. Mackenzie, who all along professed himself as unable to believe that the Conservative leader really meant to introduce protection, the reluctant admission that in legislation he had "gone the whole hog." This paramount duty accomplished, he felt free to revert to his trans-continental railway policy, which he was more than ever determined to carry out. With the object, among others, of awakening interest at home on this subject, and his kindred policy of developing the North-West, he sailed for England in July, 1879.

There were few pleasures in Sir John's estimation comparable with a visit to England. The sea voyage, the rest and freedom from official worries, the change of air and scene, all contributed to render the trip agreeable. But what he enjoyed most of all was intercourse with Imperial statesmen. "I do not," he writes, "think there is anything in the world equal in real intellectual pleasure to meeting the public men of England. Their tone is so high and their mode of thinking so correct, that it really elevates one. When I read occasionally of the loss of the prestige and position of England, I am incredulous if only from the one fact that the statesmen of England are far superior to those of any other nation, east or west." *

Ten days after his arrival in London, Sir John received the Queen's commands to attend at Osborne for the purpose of being sworn a member of Her Majesty's Privy Council, to which he had been summoned seven years previously. The ceremony took place on Thursday, the 14th of August, 1879, in the presence of the Duke of Northumberland, the Duke of Richmond, the Lord Chancellor (Earl Cairns), and Mr. Home Secretary Cross. Immediately after taking the oaths, Sir John took his seat at the Board. Shortly afterwards, the Queen held a Council, before which he, not being a member of the Cabinet, withdrew, to resume his place a few moments later, when the Cabinet Council was over.

During this visit Sir John received much notice from

* To His Honour Judge Gowan, dated Ottawa, June 27, 1871.

leading men, among others from Lord Beaconsfield, Sir Michael
Hicks-Beach, Lord Carnarvon, Sir Stafford Northcote, and his
particular friend, the Right Honourable W. H. Smith.   Perhaps
I cannot better illustrate the attention paid him, than by
transcribing a page of his engagement-book.

"*Saturday, August* 16*th.*—Appointment with Sir Michael
Hicks-Beach at twelve o'clock.   Left for Highclere (Lord
Carnarvon's country seat), to spend Sunday.   Met at dinner
Lowe and wife, Cardinal Howard, Meade, of Colonial Office,
Sir Lintorn Simmons, etc.

"*Sunday,* 17*th.*—Rained all day.   Took a walk after
luncheon.   After dinner had a long conversation with Lord
Carnarvon and Cardinal Howard.

"*Monday,* 18*th.*—Returned from Highclere."

The remainder of the week was spent chiefly in receiving
callers and deputations on public business.

"*Saturday,* 23*rd.*—In the morning saw General Creagh
and Mr. Barron.   Evening, *Forget-me-not* at Lyceum with
Agnes (Lady Macdonald) and Clara.

"*Sunday,* 24*th.*—St. Paul's in the morning.   St. Alban's,
High Holborn, in the evening with Agnes, who also went to
Westminster Abbey, at 3 p.m."

Then follows another week of business interviews.

"*Monday and Tuesday, September* 1*st and* 2*nd.*—Hughenden.

"*Wednesday,* 3*rd.*—Saw Sir Michael Hicks-Beach at 12.30.
Dined with Sir Henry Tyler at Army and Navy Club.
Pleasant dinner.

"*Thursday, September* 4*th.*—Visited W. H. Smith at
Henley-on-Thames.   Spent Thursday from 11 a.m., till Friday
at 10.10 a.m.   Met Sir Houston Stewart, Vice-Admiral, and
Wm. Mackenzie Murray, etc.

"*Friday,* 5*th.*—Long conversation with Sir Michael Hicks-
Beach."

His previous acquaintance with Mr. Disraeli had been
confined to one or two interviews more or less formal, and
separated by considerable intervals of time.   It was, therefore,
with much satisfaction that, one day towards the end of August,
he received a cordial invitation from Lord Beaconsfield, to pay

him a visit at his country seat. On Monday, the 1st of September, he went down to Hughenden, dined with Lord Beaconsfield, the only other person present being Mr. James Daly, one of the latter's private secretaries, and stayed the night. After dinner, they spent a short time in the library, discussing among other things the classics, which subject was introduced by Lord Beaconsfield, who lightly descanted upon the great poets, orators, and philosophers of Athens and Rome.* In the course of the evening, his host asked Sir John if he smoked.

" No," was the reply.

" Perhaps you do not mind the smell of smoke ? " said Lord Beaconsfield.

" Not at all," answered Sir John.

" In that case," said his host, " we will adjourn to the smoking-room ; " adding, with that delicate consideration for those who served him, which was equally characteristic of his guest—for it was just what Sir John would have said—" I know Daly cannot get along without his cigar, and he wants to hear us talk."

The smoking-room was at the top of the house, and formed a sort of auxiliary library ; it was a large comfortable room, appropriately furnished, yet wearing, withal, a certain air of quaintness not ordinarily met with in an English house. Around the walls hung the portraits of the five Prime Ministers the county of Buckingham has produced,† which Lord Beaconsfield took occasion to point out to Sir John, remarking, as he did so, that he doubted whether there were three men in England who could give off-hand a list of the Prime Ministers since the accession of the House of Brunswick. Here the two statesmen held a long and interesting conversation, principally about Canada, its people, and its resources. That Sir John

---

* I observe that Sir William Fraser, in " Disraeli and His Day," p. 476, ridicules the statement by Sir Stafford Northcote (*vide* Lang's " Life of," vol. ii. p. 178), to the effect that Lord Beaconsfield was a classical scholar. Of course I am not qualified to express any opinion on the point, but this much I may say, that most certainly he introduced the subject during Sir John's visit to Hughenden. " We discussed the classics," were Sir John's exact words, and the impression conveyed by them at the time was, that Disraeli and he had just such a conversation as Sir Stafford Northcote relates took place on the occasion to which he has referred.

† Lord Shelburne, the two Grenvilles, the Duke of Portland, and himself.

made the most of his opportunity can be seen in the speech made by Lord Beaconsfield at Aylesbury a few days later, in which he extolled the "illimitable wilderness" of our great North-West, then awaiting cultivation and settlement.* They also, Sir John told me, related their several experiences in early political life; and Lord Beaconsfield added to the charm of the occasion by giving some interesting sketchy descriptions of remarkable characters of years gone by—Count D'Orsay among the number, whom he used to meet in the old days at Lady Blessington's.

"D'Orsay," said Lord Beaconsfield, in reply to a question of Sir John, "was a strikingly handsome man—as handsome as Saul."

"An ordinary Englishman," observed Sir John to me, "would have likened him to Apollo, but Disraeli had rather a way of putting forward his Jewish lineage. I recollect that, among other questions, he asked me how long I had been in public life. 'Thirty-five years,' I replied. 'Ah,' said he, 'I beat you; I have been forty years, as long as David reigned.'" †

In bidding his guest good night, Lord Beaconsfield said to him : "You have greatly interested me, both in yourself and in Canada. We are going into our elections shortly, but come back next year and I will do anything you ask me." Sir John returned next year; but, alas, for the instability of human greatness, the general election of 1880 had intervened, the Conservative Government was overthrown, and Mr. Gladstone

---

* "Let us look for a moment at the situation of Canada. The situation of Canada is most peculiar. Since the surrender of the Hudson's Bay Company, and the settlement of their affairs, the Dominion of Canada has become possessed of what I might almost describe as an illimitable wilderness, a wilderness of fertile land, not backwoods to be cleared, but treeless prairie land." (From a speech delivered by the Right Hon. the Earl of Beaconsfield, K.G., at Aylesbury, on the 18th of September, 1879.)

† Through the exceeding kindness of the Earl of Derby, I have had the advantage of Lord Beaconsfield's private secretary's recollections of this interview. Lord Rowton was not at Hughenden at the time, but I learn from him that whenever Lord Beaconsfield spoke of Sir John, especially after this visit, it was always of one whose abilities he recognized, and in whom he took much interest. Mr. Daly, as I have said, was present throughout Sir John's visit. By the favour of Lord Derby I sent my account to him for any observations that might occur to him, and he has replied that, in the main, it accords with his recollection of what took place.

ruled England.   Before Sir John's next visit, Lord Beaconsfield
was dead.

Sir John, who was much gratified by Lord Beaconsfield's
complimentary allusions at Aylesbury to Canada, thus expressed his acknowledgments.

" Stadacona Hall, Ottawa, October 7, 1879.

"DEAR LORD BEACONSFIELD,

"Canada has been in a state of pleasurable excitement ever since she received, by cable, the announcement that
you had made a speech at Aylesbury in which she was favourably spoken of.   Last mail brought us the full report, and your
speech has been published *in extenso* by our newspapers, and
eagerly read through the length and breadth of the land.   The
gratification of our people is extreme.   They say, truly, that
this is the first occasion on which a Prime Minister of England
has given prominence to Canada, her capabilities, and her
future—the first time that it has been proclaimed by such high
authority that England has an especial interest in Canada, can
look to her largest dependency for food supply, and become
independent of foreign nations.   The speech will be worth
much to Canada, and will send thousands of strong arms and
cheerful hearts to us, instead of adding to the strength of other,
and possibly hostile countries.

" This is ' Imperialism ' in its best aspect, and one might
well suppose that every Englishman would rejoice at the
prospect held out by it and you.   Yet I see that the Opposition
press in England are attacking the speech and impugning its
accuracy.   The attacks must fail, as the statements made by Your
Lordship are substantially correct, and will be fully sustained.
In one instance you actually understate the advantages held
out to the intending settler in Canada.   It is not required of
him to reduce his 160 acres of ' homestead ' or free-grant land
' to perfect cultivation ' within three years.   He is only required
to reside on it for the three years, to put up a habitable residence,
and to break up and cultivate such portion of the grant as shall
satisfy the Government agent that the occupant really means
to be a settler.

" There are one or two points of minor importance which

may, perhaps, bear correction. In speaking of wages Your
Lordship says, ' The rudest labourer will get 12*s.* a day, and
a skilled labourer 16*s.* or 18*s.*' Now, as a general rule, agricultural labourers are hired by the month, and not by the day,
and they are paid $12 to $16, or even $18 per month, with
board and lodging added. Except for a few days in harvest,
hiring by the day is not known, then the wages run from $1 to
$2 *per diem*, according to the state of the labour market, and
the skill of the labourer, board and lodging always added.
Again, you mentioned that there is an extensive emigration
from the Western States of the United States into ' the illimitable wilderness of Canada.' Now, there always has been, and
still is, an annual emigration from the older Atlantic States to
those of the Far West, but not, I think, as yet in any great
degree to the North-Western Territories of the Dominion.
There is already a considerable exodus from the United States
of Canadians who had left their own country and are now
returning sadder and wiser men. Some Americans have also
come to us, and, from the decided superiority of our country for
agricultural purposes, I anticipate, in the not distant future,
a large influx of Yankees—more, perhaps, than, from a political
point of view, is desirable. As yet, however, they have not
come in great numbers. From Western Canada, that is from
the Province of Ontario, there has been a very large emigration
of farmers to the Canadian Far West. They are selling their
cleared and improved farms at from $30 to $40 per acre,
and afford a great opportunity to English tenant farmers who
may shrink from encountering the hardships of the wilderness, of purchasing, at very low rates, beautiful farms in good
order.

"I am satisfied that Messrs. Pell and Read of the Royal
Commission, who are now on this continent, will more than
sustain your statements as to the agricultural capabilities of
Canada. You have also near you Lord Elphinstone, who
visited our North-West this year, and has become a large land-
holder there. He is, I believe, about to settle two of his sons
there. Pray pardon me for obtruding this long letter upon
you. Your kindness at Hughenden has emboldened me to do
so, and has at the same time increased, if possible, my earnest

wishes, as a life-long Conservative, for the permanence and success of your administration.

> " Believe me to be, dear Lord Beaconsfield,
> " Very faithfully yours,
> " JOHN A. MACDONALD."

I pass over his visits to England of 1880 and 1881, the former of which was devoted to the formation of the syndicate which undertook and constructed the Canadian Pacific Railway, and come to that of 1884, in some respects the culminating point in his career. Since his visit to Hughenden great changes had taken place in England, or rather in Downing Street, for ten years ago a change of government did not mean to the United Kingdom what it implies to-day ; but Sir John Macdonald found himself the object of as much attention under Liberal auspices as he experienced when his own political friends were at the head of affairs. He had not long arrived in London, and made himself comfortable at his old quarters, Batt's Hotel, Dover Street, Piccadilly, before he received the following gratifying intimation from the Prime Minister :—

> " 10, Downing Street, Whitehall,
> " November 15, 1884.
>
> " DEAR SIR J. MACDONALD,
>
>   " In acknowledgment of your long and distinguished services, Her Majesty graciously authorizes me to propose to you that you should receive the honour of a Grand Cross of the Bath.
>
> "Believe me to remain
> " Faithfully yours,
> "W. E. GLADSTONE."

To which Sir John replied :—

> " Batt's Hotel, Dover Street,
> "November 15, 1884.
>
> " DEAR MR. GLADSTONE,
>
>   " I have the honour to acknowledge the receipt of your note of to-day, informing me that the Queen has graciously authorized you to propose to me that I should receive the honour of a Grand Cross of the Bath.
>
>   " I gratefully accept this distinguished mark of Her Majesty's

favour, and I am especially gratified that this announcement should be made through you, and the honour conferred through your kind intervention.

> " Believe me to be, dear Mr. Gladstone,
> " Faithfully yours,
> " JOHN A. MACDONALD."

To those who may not be aware of the full import of this notification, I may say that no less an authority than Lord Beaconsfield has declared the Grand Cross of the Bath to be practically the highest meritorious distinction in the power of the Sovereign to bestow. In Sir John Macdonald's case, the honour was enhanced by the intimation that Her Majesty proposed to decorate him herself. A few days after the date of Mr. Gladstone's letter, he received the Royal commands to go to Windsor, on Tuesday the 25th of November, to dine and sleep at the Castle. The ceremony of investiture took place before dinner, in the presence of the Earl of Derby, Mr. Gladstone, Sir J. M'Neill, and some members of the Royal Family. As the guests stood awaiting Her Majesty's entrance, what thoughts may have passed through Sir John Macdonald's mind? Perhaps he recalled that November afternoon at Ottawa, when he confidently appealed to the future for that vindication which was denied him at the time. Perhaps he thought of the insolent prediction of his great rival, made twenty-six years before, that he was then about to retire from public life, a "thoroughly used-up character;" or it may be that his memory led him back to his early youth, to the day of his first visit to Windsor Castle, and to the description he wrote his mother "of the magnificence of the royalty of England." We can only conjecture. All he told me was, that before the ceremony he had a conversation with Mr. Gladstone, who was exceedingly cordial and pleasant, and that when he knelt before his Sovereign, Her Majesty was pleased to supplement the formal act of investiture with a few gracious words, expressive of the pleasure she felt in thus recognizing his loyal and faithful services to the Empire.

Sir John Macdonald spent the Sunday preceding his visit to the Queen as the guest of the Prince of Wales at Sandringham.

On Monday he was entertained at dinner by the Beaconsfield Club. On the day following his return to London from Windsor, he attended a banquet given at the Empire Club, where a brilliant company had assembled to do him honour. The chair was occupied by the Marquis of Lorne. Upwards of eighty noblemen and gentlemen were present, including the Duke of Sutherland, the Marquis of Salisbury, the Marquis of Normanby, the Earl of Kimberley, the Earl of Derby, the Earl of Carnarvon, the Viscount Bury, Sir Henry Holland, Sir Charles Tupper, Sir T. Brassey, Mr. W. H. Smith, and many other distinguished personages. Among the letters of apology was one from the Prince of Wales, expressing the great regret of His Royal Highness that he was not able to be present " to do honour to his old personal friend, Sir John Macdonald." The question of Imperial federation was at that time attracting a good deal of attention in England. It was known that Sir John had had the principal part in carrying out a scheme of colonial federation, which might prove the forerunner of the larger idea. Much interest, therefore, was felt in learning his views upon the great question of Imperial unity. As I propose in another chapter to devote a brief space to this subject, I shall content myself here with saying that his speech at this dinner conveyed the assurance that the people of Canada, both from a strong sentiment of loyalty as well as from a consideration of their political, moral, and material well-being, were fully resolved to maintain and strengthen by every available means the connection with the mother country.

I have not space to record all the kind and complimentary things said of him that night, whether by Lord Lorne, whose Prime Minister he had been, or, on behalf of the Conservatives, by Lord Salisbury, who had no better wish for Canada than that in her future " she may have many statesmen who will shed as much lustre on her history and confer as many benefits upon her people as Sir John Macdonald ; " or, on behalf of the Liberals, by the Earl of Kimberley, who said that " the whole company were met for the purpose of signifying in the person of Sir John Macdonald, an ardent desire for the unity of the whole Empire." * The gratification experienced by Sir John

* For the full account of this dinner and the reports of the speeches there

Macdonald at this spontaneous testimony of Imperial regard was naturally great, yet, keenly as he must have appreciated this splendid tribute to his political services, he was before the year closed to receive two demonstrations upon which he placed even a higher value than that of the Empire Club. For there he was comparatively a stranger. There he represented an idea, and he could not avoid the reflection that the honours of which he was the recipient were largely paid to the Prime Minister of Canada, to the foremost colonial statesman. But at home there awaited him the expression of a people's love for himself personally—not for the Prime Minister, or the Colonial statesman with Imperial ideas, but for their own "John A.," the fortieth anniversary of whose entrance into public life was celebrated at Montreal and Toronto in November with an enthusiasm that knew no bounds.

Sir John Macdonald paid his last visit to England in the autumn of 1885. He intended returning in 1886—among other reasons to receive the degree of LL.D. from the University of Cambridge *—but public business compelled him to change his plans. Had he lived, there is little doubt he would have gone in the summer of 1891.

It was during his stay in London in 1885 that Sir John suggested to Cardinal Manning, with whom he was on terms of personal friendship, the propriety of extending to Canada the honour of representation in the Sacred College. He pointed out that the occupant of the Archiepiscopal See of Quebec, the

delivered, see the *Times, Standard,* and other London papers of the 27th of November, 1884.

* "Christ's College Lodge, Cambridge, June 22, 1886.

"Sir,—I am directed by the Council of the Senate of this University to intimate to you their anxiety to offer to you the highest honour at their disposal—the Honorary Degree of Doctor of Laws.

"Should you be pleased to accept it they are anxious that you should receive it on July 9th, a day on which a large party organized by the Reception Committee of the Exhibition are expected to visit Cambridge.

"We consider that such action on your part would much enhance the interest of their visit, and would be gratifying to them, as it would be to us.

"An answer addressed to me at the Athenæum, Pall Mall, will find me there until Saturday.

"I have the honour to be, sir, your obedient faithful servant,
"C. A. Swainson, Vice Chancellor.

"The Right Hon. Sir John Macdonald, Premier of Canada."

cradle of Christianity on the continent of America, was, by reason of his distinguished name and social position, eminently fitted to adorn a dignity, for which Sir John doubted not he possessed higher qualifications. Three months after Sir John's return to Canada, he received this letter from Cardinal Manning:—

"Archbishop's House, Westminster, S.W., April 3, 1886.

"MY DEAR SIR JOHN MACDONALD,

"I have reason to hope that my letter to the Holy Father has not been without result, and that in the next Consistory you will find your wishes fulfilled. Let me thank you for giving me the opportunity of doing the least act in showing my veneration for the Church in Canada. . . .

"Believe me, my dear Sir John,

"Yours very truly,

"HENRY E. CARD. MANNING,

"Archbishop of Westminster."

At a Consistory held on the 7th of June, 1886, the Most Reverend Elzéar Alexandre Taschereau was created "Cardinal Priest of the Holy Roman Church."

CHAPTER XXV.

IMPERIAL FEDERATION AND HOME RULE.

SIR JOHN MACDONALD'S ATTITUDE IN REGARD TO IMPERIAL FEDERATION—
HIS ADVOCACY OF THE POLICY OF INTER-IMPERIAL TRADE—CORRE-
SPONDENCE WITH THE RIGHT HON. W. H. SMITH—DEFENCE—TRADE WITH
AUSTRALASIA—IMPORTANCE TO IMPERIAL UNITY OF THE CANADIAN
PACIFIC RAILWAY—HOME RULE : LETTERS TO LORD LISGAR AND THE
EARL OF CARNARVON ON THE SUBJECT OF—PROFESSOR GOLDWIN SMITH'S
CRITICISMS—ADDRESS BY CANADIAN HOUSE OF COMMONS ON THE IRISH
QUESTION CONSIDERED—SIR JOHN MACDONALD'S COURSE IN RELATION
THERETO.

To a colonial statesman of Sir John Macdonald's stamp, the
phrase "Imperial Federation" possessed an attractive sound.
With the general objects of that movement Sir John was in
full sympathy. On the occasion of the establishment of the
Imperial Federation League (November 18, 1884) in London,
he was present, and made a speech concurring in the views
there expressed by Lord Normanby and others, as to the desirableness of drawing more closely the bonds which united the
colonies with the mother country. At the banquet in his
honour a few days later, he adverted, as we have seen, to this
subject, and again expressed himself as favourable to the objects
of the league. At the same time he pointed out that the many
and great difficulties which stood in the way of Imperial
federation rendered any immediate attempt to lay down cast-
iron rules, or to submit to the colonies a cut-and-dried formula,
manifestly inexpedient. The problem presented by the league
could only be solved after much interchange of opinion between
Imperial and colonial statesmen. For this purpose time was
necessary. Sir John always declined to commit himself to any
of the theories advanced by certain of the more enthusiastic

members of the league, believing that none of them were
practicable.   During the last few years of his life, when asked
if he were an Imperial Federationist, he would reply somewhat
after this fashion : "That depends upon what you mean by
Imperial federation ? I am, of course, in favour of any feasible
scheme that will bring about a closer union between the various
portions of the Empire, but I have not yet seen any plan
worked out by which this can be done.   The proposal that
there should be a Parliamentary federation of the Empire I
regard as impracticable.   I greatly doubt whether England
would agree that the Parliament which has sat during so many
centuries at Westminster should be made subsidiary to a federal
legislature.   But, however that might be, I am quite sure that
Canada would never consent to be taxed by a central body
sitting at London, in which she would have practically no
voice; for her proportionate number of members in such an
assembly would amount to little more than an honorary representation.   That form of Imperial federation is an idle dream.
So also, in my judgment, is the proposal to establish a uniform
tariff throughout the Empire.   No colony would ever surrender
its right to control its fiscal policy."

But while Sir John Macdonald regarded both these schemes
as unworkable, he by no means despaired of the future of
Imperial federation.   Indeed, I may say that he looked upon it
as necessary to the continuance of the Empire's greatness, that
some form of co-operation—some common bond, other than their
common allegiance—should be established between the colonies,
uniting them with one another, and with the motherland.
That bond, in his opinion, should be one of material interest.
Parliamentary federation we could not have, but he saw no
insuperable difficulty in the way of a commercial union between
England and her great colonies.   A union for purposes of
defence and trade was, in his judgment, the true Imperial
policy.   Take, for example, the case of the Dominion.   Sir John
Macdonald believed that a mutually preferential commercial
arrangement between England and Canada under which a
small duty should be levied upon foreign corn coming into the
United Kingdom, and a similar advantage accorded to British
manufactures by Canada, would not raise the price of food in

England,* and would result in a large and permanent development of trade, both to the mother country and the colony.

In reply to the objection that this policy was at variance
with the deeply rooted attachment of Englishmen to the doctrine
of free-trade, he would answer that the time was rapidly
approaching when the power of that superstition would be
broken, and when Englishmen would awake to the supreme
folly of sacrificing their material interests to the worship of a
theory which was every day being disproved by the stern logic
of facts. Shortly before his death, Sir John Macdonald received
two remarkable indications of the change in public sentiment
at home, which he confidently predicted. In January, 1891,
Sir Gordon Sprigg, at that time Premier of Cape Colony,
delivered an address to the City of London branch of the
Imperial Federation League, in which he urged the adoption of
the Imperial trade policy advocated by Sir John Macdonald.
The next day's *Times* contained a leading article upon this
address, in which this significant passage occurs :—

"When, however, we come to deal with a commercial union, we tread
upon ground that has to be traversed with caution. Sir Gordon Sprigg tells
us that free-trade is not a fetish in the colonies, and that the theories of the
text-books are not allowed to stand in the way of any fiscal measure that
seems advantageous. As to the text-books, they are getting somewhat out-
worn even here. Our modern economists have so many qualifications to
make in the fine, square-cut doctrines of the older school, that the science is
rapidly becoming unrecognizable. There is still a considerable amount of
fetish worship, but the ideas upon which any commercial union must rest will
not in future incur the furious and unreasoning hostility that would have
greeted them twenty years ago. It is getting to be understood that free-
trade is made for man, not man for free-trade, and any changes that may
be proposed will have a better chance of being discussed upon their own
merits, rather than in the light of high and dry theory backed by outcries
about the thin end of the wedge. The British Empire is so large and so com-

---

* His view was that a duty of something like five shillings a quarter on foreign corn
would suffice to secure the English market to the colonies, and at the same time would
not affect the cost of bread. Sir Charles Tupper, in two able papers (*Nineteenth
Century* for October, 1891, and April, 1892), sets this forth with great clearness.
He shows from official reports that, in the years 1890 and 1891, when the price of corn
varied ten shillings and sixpence a quarter, the fluctuations had to reach practically
ten shillings a quarter before it made a halfpenny difference in the four-pound loaf.
In the latter article Sir Charles Tupper states that, during the Canadian elections of
1891, he had several conversations with Sir John Macdonald upon this subject of
"inter-imperial" trade, and that their views practically coincided.

pletely self-supporting, that it could very well afford, for the sake of a serious political gain, to surround itself with a moderate fence. There would, of course, be some economic disadvantage in a customs union, but if a larger political advantage could be gained, there is no sound reason that we know of why the transaction should not be regarded, like any other, in the light of expediency." *

A fortnight after these words were written the Canadian Parliament was dissolved. The general election which followed was on the question of commercial union with the United States, which Sir John Macdonald opposed. The polling took place on the 5th of March. On the 7th, the Right Honourable W. H. Smith, then First Lord of the Treasury, and leader of the House of Commons, wrote him :—

" [Private.]

" 3, Grosvenor Place, S.W., March 7, 1891.

"MY DEAR SIR JOHN,

" Let me congratulate you on success. It is not so big as I should have wished, but I am very glad indeed, for the sake of the old country, that you have won.

" It is disquieting to see that Ontario and Quebec have not given you a majority, but there, I suppose, the McKinley Tariff hits hard.

" What can we do? What course is open to us ? Retaliatory duties are, I fear, almost impossible for us here, as they could only be placed on bread stuffs, and our workmen are easily inflamed by a cry of dear food ; but what other method exists to preserve our own market and re-open yours ?

" Do not understand me as advocating such duties, but I am sensible of the extreme gravity of the situation, and of the future, and I want light.

" For the present your elections give us time to breathe and to think. Understand, I write for myself alone, and in strict confidence.

" Yours sincerely,

" W. H. SMITH."

This cry for light, coming from the leader of the Imperial House of Commons, was a distinct admission that free-trade was not all-in-all, and was so interpreted by Sir John Macdonald, who thus replied :—

" [Private.]

" Earnscliffe, Ottawa, April 8, 1891.

"MY DEAR MR. SMITH,

" Pardon me for not sooner answering your kind note of congratulation.

* *Times,* January 15, 1891.

"During the contest I forgot that I was an old man, and overworked myself. I am now only gathering myself together and working off arrears of correspondence.   *   *   *   *

"'How can we be aided by the mother country?' is the question of the day, and it is hard to answer.

"Nothing effectual can be done until after Lord Salisbury goes to the country. If he win—which Heaven grant—some Imperial policy can lbe framed and carried out. Meanwhile, manufacturers and their working people must, or rather should, be taught, that they can find friendly and expanding markets in the colonies, if they are treated in the same spirit. Take Canada, for instance : our tariff is a revenue tariff in substance, and averages 30 per cent., while the prohibitory tariff of the U.S. averages fully 60 per cent. Now, Canada has undertaken the development of her resources on so large a scale that she must have revenue, and from various causes can only look to customs and excise for it. While, therefore, she cannot promise a reduction of her customs duties, she will be quite ready to give British goods a preference of 5 or even 10 per cent. in our markets if our products receive a corresponding preference in England. The United States are the chief rivals of English manufacturers with us at present ; with such a differential scale of duties as I suggest, all that we do not make ourselves would be supplied by the mother country.

"I see that Mr. Cecil Rhodes is in favour of such a policy, and I have little doubt Australasia would adopt it.

"The Americans boast that such is the extent and diversity of their soil, and climate, and products, that they are independent of the rest of the world. But they cannot compare with the British Empire in those respects. It is a world in itself. But I must not weary you with my speculations.

"Again thanking you for your good wishes.

"Believe me

"Yours very sincerely,

"JOHN A. MACDONALD.*

"The Rt. Honble. W. H. Smith, M.P., etc."

---

* Had Sir John Macdonald lived eleven months longer, he would have received a still more significant indication of the fulfilment of his predictions that English states-men were fast coming to view this question in the light of practical experience. In

Sir John Macdonald had long favoured the idea of a preferential arrangement with the mother country. A few weeks before his death, he makes this clear, in a letter to a friend :—

"I agree with you that we should have a Reciprocity Treaty with England. Years ago,* I, with Sir Leonard Tilley and Sir Charles Tupper, made a proposition to that effect, while we were on a visit to London. The difficulty is that no English statesman has yet mustered courage to take up the question. Lord Salisbury will probably go to the country next summer, and, if successful, I shall renew the proposal. We can hope nothing from Gladstone, so we must watch events." †

With respect to the question of defence, Canada, under the administration of Sir John Macdonald, by the construction of an Imperial highway across the continent, and by the grant of

a speech delivered at Hastings, May 18, 1892, the Marquis of Salisbury, then Prime Minister of England, gave utterance to these words :—

"England only maintains the position which she occupies by the vast industries existing here, but a danger is growing up. Forty or fifty years ago everybody believed free-trade had conquered the world, and prophesied that every nation would follow the example of England. The results, however, are not yet realized. Despite the prophecies of the free-trade advocates, foreign nations are advocating protection. They are excluding us from their markets and are trying to kill our trade, and this state of things seems to grow worse. We live in an age of war tariffs. An important point is, that while nations are doing everything to obtain each other's commercial favour, none is anxious about the favour of Great Britain, because Great Britain has stripped herself of the armour and weapons with which the battle is to be fought. Now as to the attitude which we have taken. Regarding it as disloyalty to the glorious and sacred doctrines of free-trade to impose duties on anybody for the sake of anything we get, thereby may be noble, but it is not business like. On these terms you will and do get nothing. If you intend to hold your own in this conflict of tariffs you must be prepared to refuse nations which injure you access to your markets. We complain most of the United States, and it so happens that the United States mainly furnishes us with articles which are essential to the good of the people and with raw material which is necessary to our manufacturers. We cannot exclude either without serious injury to ourselves. I am not prepared, in order to punish other countries, to inflict dangerous wounds on ourselves. We must confine ourselves to those matters wherein we shall not suffer much whether importations continue or diminish. While we cannot raise the price of food and raw material, there is an enormous mass of imports, such as wine, spirits, silk, gloves and lace from countries beside the United States, which are merely luxuries, and of which a diminished consumption might be risked in order to secure access to the markets of our neighbours. I shall expect to be excommunicated for propounding such a doctrine, but I am bound to say that I think the free-traders have gone too far."

* In 1879.
† To J. S. Helmcken, Esq., M.D., dated Ottawa, March 30, 1891.

liberal subsidies to Atlantic and Pacific lines of steamships, has provided means of rapid communication between the centre and the extremities of the Empire, which must not only further the material development of each part, but also promote the security of the whole. She has thus shown in the most practical manner her willingness to co-operate in the Empire's defence, and given a pledge that her efforts in the future will not be less than they have been in the past.

In regard to the possibility of trade with Australia, Sir John was an enthusiast in his views. He firmly believed that the community of interests between the mother country and her great colonies, which he strove to promote, would surely be established, and that Canada, from her geographical position in relation to Great Britain, the East, and Australia, could not fail to reap untold benefits thereby. It was the fixity of this belief which enabled him to carry to completion, in the face of opposing forces of every kind, his project of uniting the Atlantic with the Pacific by a railway running exclusively through British territory. The Canadian Pacific Railway is now an accomplished fact, and no one who witnesses the desire of the public men of Canada and Australia for closer intercourse, can doubt that before many years the anticipations of its builder will be realized, and that Canada, as the essential link between England and her far distant colonies, will share in the prosperity and greatness which Sir John Macdonald hoped and believed would distinguish, for ages to come, the mighty Empire whose interests lay so near his heart.

Among the latest important utterances of Sir John Macdonald on the subject of British connection, I may refer to a speech delivered by him on the occasion of the public banquet of the Queen's University, Kingston, at which he reiterated and emphasized the conviction of a lifetime in these words:—

"I am satisfied that the vast majority of the people of Canada are in favour of the continuance and perpetuation of the connection between the Dominion and the mother country. There is nothing to gain and everything to lose by separation. I believe that if any party or person were to announce or declare such a thing, whether by annexation with the neighbouring

country, the great republic to the south of us, or by declaring for independence, I believe that the people of Canada
would say ' No.' We are content, we are prosperous, we have
prospered under the flag of England ; and I say that it would
be unwise, that we should be lunatics, to change the certain
present happiness for the uncertain chances of the future. I
always remember, when this occurs to me, the Italian epitaph :
' I was well, I would be better, and here I am.' We are well
we know, all are well, and I am satisfied that the majority of
the people of Canada are of the same opinion which I now
venture to express here. For the language which I heard this
morning, the language which I have heard this afternoon,
and the language which I have heard to-night show that, at
all events, all who are connected with the University of
Queen's are men in favour of the continuance of the connection
between the Dominion and Great Britain. I say that it would
bring ruin and misfortune, any separation from the United
Kingdom. I believe that is the feeling of the present Parliament of Canada, and I am certain that any party, or the
supposed party, making an appeal to the people of Canada, or
any persons attempting to form a party on the principle of
separation from England, no matter whether they should
propose to walk alone, or join another country, I believe that
the people of Canada would rise almost to a man and say, ' No,
we will do as our fathers have done. We are content, and our
children are content, to live under the flag of Great Britain.' "

Upon the burning question of Home Rule for Ireland, the
antithesis of the idea of Imperial unity, Sir John Macdonald's
views can be clearly outlined. It is scarcely necessary for
me to say, that, in relation to this, as to all other questions
of Imperial concern, he was a Unionist to the core, and,
as such, deprecated the policy of Mr. Gladstone, which he
regarded as fraught with danger to the security, if not the
existence of the United Kingdom. At the same time, it is
equally true that he entertained a sympathy for the Irish
race in their misfortunes, which centuries of misgovern-
ment had entailed. From the beginning of Mr. Butt's
agitation in 1870, he had given his attention to the problem
that their unsatisfactory political condition presented. While

in Washington, in 1871, he found leisure, among his pressing duties as High Commissioner, to elaborate a scheme for the local self-government of Ireland, which at that time might have gone far to satisfy the legitimate aspirations of its people.

Thus, in 1871, he wrote to Lord Lisgar :—

"As I have finished my treaty-making work, I propose to jot down, as suggested by Your Excellency, a summary of our conversation when I had the pleasure of visiting you at Spencer Wood in September last.

"Ireland is now demanding a home Parliament and home legislation, and, at the same time, it is evident that the Parliament of the United Kingdom is unable to do all the work that is thrown upon it. It is worth while, therefore, to consider whether the wishes of Ireland might not be gratified to a reasonable extent, and, at the same time, the British House of Commons be relieved of a portion of the work, the accumulation of which at present clogs and impedes Imperial legislation.

"The repeal of the Union and the restoration of the Irish Parliament, with all the powers that it enjoyed in 1800, is, it seems to me, entirely out of the question. With the feeling of hostility to everything English that now exists and will long continue in Ireland, it is certain that the Legislature of the latter would at once commence to undo everything that has been done by the united Parliament. Public men would vie with each other in expressions of enmity against England and the English, and that party would be the most popular which would adopt the most extreme course in thwarting the policy of Britain, both foreign and domestic.

"The establishment of a home Parliament with limited powers, such, for instance, as those conferred on the provincial legislatures of Canada, would, if possible, be still more objectionable. Great impatience at the restrictions would at once be displayed, and an agitation early commenced for their removal, reviving all the old reminiscences and struggles about Poyning's law and the commercial regulations of yore. Every attempt would be made to overstep their jurisdiction by Bills so ingeniously drawn as to leave a doubt whether they were *ultra vires* or not.

" We, as you know, have found great difficulty in keeping the subordinate legislatures in Canada from exceeding their powers, but our difficulty is as nothing when compared with the trouble that would be given to the Imperial Government by the Irish Legislature. What they could not do by Bill, they would endeavour to do by resolution, petition, address, remonstrance, etc., etc.

" Experience shows us what continued agitation will do as to Irish matters. In the long run the English people and Parliament will, from a mere sense of weariness, yield, as they have always done, to Irish turbulence, and then would come the severance from England.

" This severance would in such case be complete, for the sentiment of loyalty and of attachment to monarchical institutions seems altogether to have faded away in Ireland. The consequence would be a rampant democracy, such as we see at this moment dominating in Paris.

" How, then, can the proposed object be attained without danger to the Empire ? I think it can be done on the *divide et impera* principle. My plan is shortly this :—

" That the members from each of the four provinces of Ireland, who are elected to the Imperial Parliament, should form Grand Committees, to meet in their several provinces in annual sessions, say in November. In these committees all measures of a local and private nature should be initiated, and upon them should be conferred limited powers of direct taxation. These powers might be very limited at first, to be afterwards increased, as experience proved that it might be done with safety.

" In carrying the measures through these local bodies, all the forms and checks of the House of Commons should be observed and maintained, and the Bills, after third reading, returned to the clerk of the House of Commons, the only question to be raised there being whether the measures were *ultra vires* or not.

" I need not trouble you with any details as to the measures which might properly be entrusted to the local bodies, but reference might profitably be made to the division of powers between the local and general legislatures of Canada in that regard.

"While an Irish Legislature, even with limited powers, might be too strong to be kept in proper restraint, these four separate bodies could not become formidable. There would be little danger of their joining together in any concerted action.

"It would be well to reserve to the Imperial Government and Parliament authority to suspend the powers of any of the Grand Committees, in case of persistent abuse. This would operate as a check, and, if put in force against any one province, would be a significant and, I think, a sufficient warning to the others.

"In order to relieve the House of Commons effectually of the private and local legislation, which hampers it so much, and obstructs the progress of legislation in an Imperial sense, the same system might be adopted for England and Scotland. England might be divided into 'north' and 'south' of the Humber, or into as many sub-divisions as was thought expedient, and the ancient principality might have a little Parliament of its own, in the shape of a Grand Committee.

"The Scotch members manage Scottish affairs at present in a committee-room at Westminster. They, however, attend to all measures, whether of a public or private nature, affecting Scotland. This custom has, I suppose, originated in the pledge given in the Act of Union, that the laws of Scotland should not be altered except for the manifest advantage of the people of Scotland. Under this stipulation, no matter how important the alteration of a Scottish law may be to Imperial interests, yet, if it be not for the manifest advantage of Scotland, it cannot be altered without a breach of the spirit of the Union Act. It would, however, I suppose, gratify Edinburgh and the Scottish Lion if a Grand Committee, such as I have mentioned, with like powers, were to assemble there. The Scotch members could still attend to matters of a general nature as they do at present.

"If a general plan of this kind were adopted, the only measures of a private or local nature which would remain for the British Parliament to deal with would be those affecting more than one of the provinces. In Canada, for instance, when an Act of incorporation for a railway is wanted, application must be made to the Parliament of the Dominion, if such railway is to extend beyond the bounds of any one province. The Imperial Parliament would therefore have ample time to dispose of the great questions of general and Imperial interest, which are alone worthy of its attention.

"It may be said that this plan would entail a great amount of work on the members. I am satisfied that it will considerably diminish it.

"Your experience must have shown you how much time is wasted by the intermingling of private with public business, and how even a great measure is impeded in its progress by the necessity of adjourning over private Bill days.

"The provincial Assemblies having nothing but private business to do, would give the measures full consideration, and despatch them in half the time they would occupy if before the central Parliament; and, in the same way, the progress of legislation at Westminster, not being obstructed by discussions on petty matters, would be greatly accelerated.

"On the whole, it is pretty clear that no greater draft would be made on the members by this arrangement than at present, while they would be nearer home and more accessible to their constituents desiring to consult them on local matters.

"It would, I think, be a mistake to elect men to sit in these local Legislatures only. There is no necessity for it. The men so selected would be inferior in every way, and, being elected for local purposes, would represent only local interests and prejudices. Besides, they would be setting themselves up in opposition to the general Parliament, and would take pride in doing so. The members elected for the Imperial Parliament represent the people in every way as much as mere local representatives could do. They understand their interests as well, and any provincialism in their politics and undue subservience to local prejudice would be cured by their chief responsibility being as members of the Imperial Parliament.

"I would propose that after a local measure, reported by Grand Committee, has received one reading in the Commons, it should go to the Upper House. The House of Lords wants work, and the great functions of that august body as a regulator of the legislation of the country cannot be better exercised than in the supervision of this local legislation. The Lords would keep such legislation in some degree of harmony, and prevent eccentric attacks on the rights of property, which might be popular in some quarters or provinces.

"Such are the general outlines of my plan, which I send to Your Excellency for what they are worth." *

Fourteen years later he thus addressed Lord Carnarvon, at the time the newly appointed Lord Lieutenant of Ireland, on the same subject :—

"I have watched Your Excellency's progress with great interest, have wondered at your success, and still more at Lady Carnarvon's courage. May your course continue to have all the success it deserves. I presume that the subject of local and municipal government will greatly engage your attention. I do not fear giving the Irish people considerable powers of local self-government and taxation so much as many in England do. They are frightened by the conduct of the city and town corporations, and by the accounts of the abominable corruptions of New York and other cities in the United States.

"But in rural America, whether British or Republican, experience has, I think, shown that the Irish people can be trusted. The Celtic Irishman, like the French peasant, tho' not so steadily industrious as the Anglo-Saxon, is saving, economical, has few wants, likes to hoard his gains, and has a horror of taxation. He will vote for extravagant expenditure in cities, as, from the concentrated wealth there, the burden of taxation must fall chiefly on the rich, and the taxes are expended in city improvements, from which he gets much more as wages than he contributes as a tax-payer. The more money in the city purse, the more jobs for the working man. In the country it is quite different, and our experience in Canada is that the

---

* Dated May 11, 1871. The following day he wrote : "In my letter of yesterday I suggested that a Grand Committee should be appointed for each of the four provinces of Ireland. This may be considered too many, and if only two such committees were established they might not be too powerful for management. It might, perhaps, be more convenient that, while England should be divided into several provinces, the committees for those provinces should all sit at Westminster. So it might, perhaps, be with respect to Scotland, but I should think that the old national feeling would be gratified by seeing the ghost of a Parliament re-assemble at Edinburgh."

Irish farmer is as chary of voting for an increase of taxation for municipal or school purposes as his English or Scotch neighbour.   In fact, he is penurious to meanness.   He knows his vote for an increase is certain to take money out of his pocket, and that no portion of it will come directly back to him.   I have no doubt that the Americans have the same experience. It seems to me that if a measure could be framed for Ireland, by which the poorest cotter would be obliged to pay something for his hut, or his pig and his cow, and so that any increase voted by the municipal body would involve an addition to his rates, he would be slow to add to his own burdens for the sake of largely taxing the castle or the manor house.   He would, no doubt, like to have the pleasure of taxing his landlord to any extent, if he could do so without taxing himself.   If the normal rate, for instance, were a farthing on the pound, he would be slow to increase it to a ha'penny, if he has to pay the additional farthing ; but the municipal body should not be allowed to fix the values of property for taxation, or to grant exemptions, as they should be statutory.   The smallest hut should pay a fixed rate on the pound ; the house with two windows ; the house with two storeys, and so on, should do so too, and so with the acreage.   This was the old system in Upper Canada, and it worked well.   Now larger powers are given.   Values are assessed fairly, and the Irish have learned to be like other people.   But as a commencement in Ireland, it seems to me that our old system would be the safer.   All this may be very crude and inapplicable to Ireland, and prove my ignorance of its conditions.   However, I have thought that you would not dislike to know our experience as to the fitness of our Irish for self-government." *

Sir John Macdonald's course in relation to the addresses on the subject of Home Rule passed at various times by the House of Commons of which he was leader, has been criticized and misrepresented at home by Professor Goldwin Smith and others whom Mr. Goldwin Smith has misled.   It seems proper, therefore, that I should briefly narrate what actually took place in the Canadian Parliament in regard to this subject, and make

* To His Excellency the Earl of Carnarvon, dated Rivière du Loup, September 8, 1885.

clear Sir John Macdonald's share of responsibility in connection therewith.

On the 27th of February, 1888, the *Times* published a letter from Professor Goldwin Smith on "Canada and Commercial Union," in which this sentence occurs :—

"I have seen something of protectionist 'loyalty.' It was not from that quarter that, when we were struggling to prevent Canada from being used to abet the dismemberment of the United Kingdom, sympathy or assistance came. The political chief of this commercial interest it was who, to conciliate the Irish vote, set going a series of Home Rule resolutions in Canadian Legislatures. He was represented the other day, no doubt with the same object, by a member of his Cabinet at the Nationalist meeting of Sir Thomas Esmonde. In discerning who really love her, England is sometimes as blind as Lear."

Three times within recent years the House of Commons of Canada adopted addresses to Her Majesty on this subject. The first occasion was in 1882, when a series of resolutions were proposed by a private member, acting as spokesman of the Irish Home Rulers on both sides of the House. Sir John Macdonald was in nowise responsible for their introduction. Through his influence they were modified, and, as passed, the address was such as no Unionist could take exception to. The nature and extent of these modifications can best be judged by a comparison of the original resolutions and their final form, which I give, omitting the formal paragraphs.

RESOLUTIONS, 1882.

As originally proposed.

" We would most respectfully pray, may it please Your Majesty, that some such form of local self-government may be extended to Ireland, as is now enjoyed by the provinces comprising this Dominion of Canada, and under which Your Majesty's Canadian subjects have prospered exceedingly, so that Ireland may become a source of strength to Your Majesty's Empire, and that Your Majesty's Irish subjects at home and abroad may feel the

As acquiesced in by Sir John Macdonald.

" We desire respectfully to suggest to Your Majesty that Canada and its inhabitants have prospered exceedingly under a federal system, allowing to each province of the Dominion considerable powers of self-government, and would venture to express a hope that, if consistent with the integrity and well-being of the Empire, and if the rights and status of the minority are fully protected and same pride in the greatness of Your Majesty's Empire, the same veneration for the justice of Your Majesty's rule, and the same devotion to, and affection for, our common flag, which are now felt by all classes of Your Majesty's loyal subjects in this Dominion.

" We would further most respectfully pray that Your Majesty would be graciously pleased to take into Your Majesty's favourable consideration the cases of those persons who are now suffering imprisonment in Ireland, charged with political offences, with a view to extending to them Your Most Gracious Majesty's Royal clemency, so that, with their release, the inestimable blessings of civil liberty may be once more restored to all parts of Your Majesty's Empire."

secured,* some means may be found of meeting the expressed desire of so many of Your Irish subjects in that regard, so that Ireland may become a source of strength to Your Majesty's Empire, and that Your Majesty's Irish subjects at home and abroad may feel the same pride in the greatness of Your Majesty's Empire, the same veneration for the justice of Your Majesty's rule, and the same devotion to, and affection for, our common flag as are now felt by all classes of Your Majesty's loyal subjects in this Dominion.

" We would further express a hope that the time has come when Your Majesty's clemency may, without injury to the interests of the United Kingdom, be extended to those persons who are now imprisoned in Ireland charged with political offences only, and the inestimable blessing of personal liberty restored to them."

The only result produced by this address was a polite invitation to the House of Commons from Mr. Gladstone to mind its own business.†

* The *Journals of the House of Commons* read "sure means," and this rendering is to be found in *Hansard* and the *Votes and Proceedings*. The word "sure" is nevertheless a misprint. The original manuscript reads "some," and the following extract from a letter addressed, a few days after the adoption of the resolutions, by Sir John Macdonald to the Governor General makes it clear that this is the rendering he understood. The italics are his own.

" Your Excellency will see that the fifth paragraph, instead of praying for Home Rule unconditionally, now 'ventures to express a hope that, *if consistent with the integrity and well-being of the Empire,*' and if the *rights* and status of the *minority* are fully *protected* and *secured, some* means may be found of meeting the expressed desire of so many of Her Majesty's subjects in that regard." (From Sir John Macdonald to His Excellency the Marquis of Lorne, dated Ottawa, May 2, 1882.)

† The Colonial Secretary wrote : " Her Majesty will always gladly receive the advice of the Parliament of Canada on all matters relating to the Dominion, and the administration of its affairs ; but with respect to the questions referred to in the address, Her Majesty will, in accordance with the Constitution of this country, have regard to the advice of the Imperial Parliament and Ministers, to whom all matters relating to the affairs of the United Kingdom exclusively appertain." (Despatch from the Earl of Kimberley to the Marquis of Lorne, dated Downing Street, June 12, 1882.)

In 1886 the question was brought forward by Mr. Blake, who invited the House to "hail with joy" the Home Rule Bill of that year. Sir John Macdonald voted against Mr. Blake's resolutions, and caused to be carried an address reiterating in general terms the hope expressed in the resolutions of 1882. As before, I place this resolution and amendment in parallel columns.

RESOLUTIONS, 1886.

As proposed by Mr. Blake.

"That this House hails with joy the submission, by Her Majesty's Government, to the Parliament of the United Kingdom, of a measure recognizing the principle of local self-government for Ireland.

"And humbly to express to Her Majesty the earnest hope of this House, that the principle of the said measure may be affirmed, and that it may form the basis for such a settlement of this great question as shall conduce to the peace, happiness and prosperity of the Empire."

As acquiesced in by Sir John Macdonald.

"That this House, having reference to the tenor of the said answer,* does not deem it expedient again to address Her Majesty on the subject, but earnestly hopes that such a measure, or such measures, may be adopted by the Imperial Parliament as will, while preserving the integrity and well-being of the Empire and the rights and status of the minority, be satisfactory to the people of Ireland, and permanently remove the discontent so long unhappily prevailing in that country."

Once more, in 1887, the question came up in the form of resolutions condemnatory of what is called the "Coercion Bill." Sir John Macdonald voted against these resolutions, and in favour of an amendment, which I give below.

RESOLUTIONS, 1887.

As adopted by the House of Commons, Sir John Macdonald voting Nay.

"That this House has learned with profound regret of the introduction into the Imperial House of Commons of the Coercion Bill above mentioned, and earnestly hopes that a measure so subversive of the rights and liberties of Her Majesty's subjects in Ireland may not become law.

Proposed Amendment, acquiesced in by Sir John Macdonald.

"This House learns with regret that it is considered necessary to pass a coercive measure for Ireland, and it re-affirms its convictions as expressed in the Resolutions of 1882 and 1886, that a plan of local government for Ireland which would leave unimpaired the links connecting

* See note † on p. 229.

" That this House again expresses the hope that there may speedily be granted to Ireland a substantial measure of Home Rule, which, whilst satisfying the national aspirations of the people of Ireland for self-government, shall also be consistent with the integrity of the Empire as a whole."

Ireland with the British Empire and guard the rights of the minority, would be conducive to the prosperity of Ireland and the stability of the Empire."

Any one who takes the trouble to examine the qualified and guarded language of the resolutions to which Sir John is committed, cannot fail to perceive how little truth there is in Professor Goldwin Smith's insinuation that he compromised his loyalty in order to conciliate the Irish vote. It is surely not inconsistent with the most devoted loyalty to venture " a hope that, if consistent with the integrity and well-being of the Empire, and if the rights and status of the minority are fully protected and secured," *some* means may be found of meeting the wishes of the people of Ireland ; or to regret—not, as the original resolution proposed, the introduction of the Coercion Bill, but—the existence of the necessity that called for such a measure,—a very different matter. Such unexceptionable statements must surely command the assent of the staunchest Unionist. Indeed Professor Goldwin Smith himself makes this plain. Writing to the *Times*,* he says—

" Mr. Gladstone, in his pamphlet on the Irish Question, once more asserts that he has the British race in the Colonies on his side, and he exults in the belief that England, in upholding the Union, is deserted by all her children. Once more, so far as Canada is concerned, I traverse his assertion. A resolution in favour of his policy, moved in the Canadian Parliament by his friend Mr. Blake, was thrown out by an overwhelming majority, *and an amendment which any Unionist might have subscribed was carried in its room.*"

Even in their original form the addresses give no countenance to any disloyal or separatist feeling. On the contrary, they are profuse in their expressions of loyalty to the Queen and of the contentment of the Irish in the Dominion.

It is an undoubted fact that there exists in Canada a very general sympathy with the Home Rule cause. This is partly due to the favour with which the federal system is regarded amongst us, which finds expression in a laudable desire to

* September 1, 1886.

extend to others a share of the advantages we enjoy. Especially is this the case in Lower Canada, where the French Canadians, apart altogether from the merits of the question, are, in the abstract, Home Rulers almost to a man. The catch-words of "liberty," "freedom," "the right to manage our own affairs," "English dictation," and so forth, recall the struggles of their fathers for responsible Government, and, without stopping to reflect that there is no real analogy between Quebec and Ireland, they are led by sentimental considerations, highly creditable, no doubt, to their generous instincts, to sympathize with an agitation the nature of which many of them very imperfectly apprehend. In Ontario and the Maritime Provinces the Liberals as a rule are in accord with their party in the Imperial Parliament, while many Conservatives for the same reason are Unionists. But among those unfriendly to Home Rule are not a few whose opposition is not to the extending to Ireland of the principle of self-government, but to the influence of the Pope, who they firmly believe is personally conducting the Home Rule movement from the Vatican with the sinister design of subverting the liberties of the people of England. The number of Home Rulers in Ontario is large, but once convince the Orangemen that the grant of self-government to Ireland would not redound to the advantage of the Roman Catholic Church and it would be larger still. For one reason or another, therefore, I greatly doubt whether a motion condemnatory, let us say, of the principle of Mr. Gladstone's latest Home Rule Bill would obtain on its merits the support of one-third of the number of any legislature in Canada, nor do I believe that all the party pressure in the world could carry such a resolution through the House of Commons.

That Sir John Macdonald, in the face of such circumstances, should have been able on two occasions to eliminate what, from a Unionist point of view, are the objectionable features of the Home Rule resolutions we have been considering, and to reduce them to mere expressions of contingent hope, is at once evidence of his views upon the Irish question and of his rare skill in the management of the House of Commons.

CHAPTER XXVI.

GENERAL.

AMONG constitutional questions few possessed for Sir John Macdonald greater interest than the bicameral system. He frequently spoke of it as destined to be in the near future a practical issue of great importance. On more than one occasion he has been known to counsel young men to make a special study of the subject, adding that the time so employed would be well spent.

His view of the necessity for a second chamber may be expressed briefly by the story told of Washington, which Sir John was fond of relating. It is said that on his return from France Jefferson called Washington to account for having agreed to a second chamber.

"Of what use is the Senate?" he asked, as he stood before the fire with a cup of tea in his hand, pouring the tea into his saucer as he spoke.

"You have answered your own question," replied Washington.

"What do you mean?"

"Why did you pour that tea into your saucer?"

"To cool it," quoth Jefferson.

"Even so," said Washington, "the Senate is the saucer into which we pour legislation to cool."

This illustration, Sir John used to say, was perfect. Indeed

the all but unanimous opinion of Imperial statesmen,* coupled
with the fact that every British colony possessing responsible
government recognizes the utility of a second chamber,† was
to his mind a general admission of the necessity for an Upper
House, and limited useful discussion to the nature and constitution of that body.

Of that ancient and venerable assemblage, the House of
Peers, the oldest legislative body in the world to-day, he held
the opinion of the vast majority of educated Englishmen,
whether Conservative or Liberal, that it is one of the glories of
the Empire, and that any attack upon it is an attack upon
the constitution of which it is an integral part.   With Lord
Selborne,‡ he looked upon the House of Lords as " an institution
now unique in the civilized world; not unique because it is
out of date, but unique because it fills a place among our
institutions, the want of which is a deep misfortune to most
other countries.   To have an assembly which is to us a living
memory of all that is illustrious and great in the deeds and
lives of the greatest and most illustrious of our ancestors, an
assembly whose very constitution must and does stimulate to
public virtue those who have inherited the duties and the
names of those great men—an assembly which represents the
elements of permanence and stability in our institutions and
in our society—an assembly which is continually recruiting
itself from the people, and which always receives those recruits,
not as if it looked down upon them because they had not

---

* "The existence of a second chamber is confirmed by reason itself, because
tyranny may proceed from a body as well as from one man ; and it is a protection that
the ruling body should be divided into two branches, the emulation and even the
rivalry of which may prevent dangerous measures from being hurried through"
(Professor Bryce, *Hansard's Parliamentary Debates*, vol. cccxxxvi. p. 479, May 17,
1889).

Among the authorities collected by Sir John Macdonald on the question of an
Upper Chamber, and especially in regard to a second chamber in the colonies, I may
quote Thorold Rogers (in "Lords' Protests," vol. i. p. 27), Bonamy Price (in
Contemporary Review, vol. xxxviii. p. 947), Escott ("England and its People," vol.
ii. ch. 23), Sir David Wedderburn (in *Nineteenth Century*, July, 1881), Kebbel
(*Fortnightly Review*, May, 1882), and Fitzgerald (*Victoria Review*, October, 1882).

† Lord Kimberley, in a despatch dated February 2, 1882, to the Governor of
Natal (adverting to proposed reforms in that colony), observed: "There is at present
no instance of a single chamber with full parliamentary powers in a British colony
under responsible Government" (*Commons Papers*, 1882, C. 3174).

‡ Speech at Lord Mayor's Banquet, November 9, 1872.

hereditary distinction, but with cordial goodwill," such an Assembly he viewed as "a most valuable, a most priceless element in our institutions, and one that should always be valued and always be maintained by Englishmen."

We have already seen Sir John Macdonald's opinion of the constitution of the Canadian Senate, which was largely the work of his own hands. It is true that, at an early period of his career, he favoured an elective Upper House, but eight years' experience of this system was sufficient to change his views, and to convert him into a firm upholder of the nominative principle. Every year since Confederation strengthened the conviction of his matured judgment, and showed him more and more clearly the advantages of the nominative over the elective system. To his mind the chief among the objections to a Senate chosen by the popular vote, was the ever-present danger of its members claiming the right to deal with money Bills, and the consequent possibility of disputes with the House of Commons. The proposal that the provincial legislatures, whose members are elected for purely local purposes, should choose the senators to legislate on matters of general concern, was also objectionable, being opposed to the spirit of the constitution, which confined the local assemblies to a strictly limited sphere of action. He held that the system unanimously agreed to at the Quebec Conference had worked well, and should be undisturbed. A senatorship, in his opinion, was an important and dignified office, and a worthy object of ambition to any Canadian.

Among the useful attributes of the Senate is its jurisdiction in the matter of divorce. Speaking one day on this subject, Sir John observed that the late Lord Westbury had told him that, when he sat in the House of Commons, he had rather a stiff encounter with Mr. Gladstone on the establishment of a divorce court in England, against which Mr. Gladstone took strong grounds, "and Gladstone was right too," observed Sir John, "for of this I am convinced, that the establishment of the divorce court in England has been productive of much mischief. In former times, the procedure with respect to divorce was the same as in force in Canada to-day—that is, it could only be obtained from the Upper House of Parliament. In those days divorces were rare, expensive, and hard to get, and the morals of the community were spared the columns of scandal with which the English papers are occasionally filled. The only objection was on the ground of expense. It was urged that divorce was a luxury accessible only to the rich. The establishment of the divorce court in Canada would mean cheap and easy divorces, which would lead to great laxity in the marriage relation, and, by the publication of evidence in the press, would have an injurious effect on the morals of the community. They are beginning to see that now in the old country. I hope it may be long before we have anything of the kind in Canada."

Germane to the question we have been considering, is that of Imperial honours. Not only did Sir John Macdonald approve of the bestowal of these marks of distinction upon colonists, he did all that lay in his power to extend the practice, and to reduce it to a system. Writing to Lord Knutsford, in 1889, he says :—

"I can quite understand Her Majesty's desire to raise the degree of Knight Bachelor from the discredit into which it has in some degree fallen. One would like to see a Victorian knighthood as much esteemed as in the days of Queen Elizabeth. But it seems to me expedient that some liberal system should be worked out and put in practice with regard to the colonies. The idea of the mother country and her colonies being one great Empire seems more and more to be taking possession of the public mind, and colonists should be taught to look up to the Empress-Queen, as the *fons honoris.* The monarchical idea should be fostered in the colonies, accompanied by some gradation of classes. At present, with some few exceptions, Canadians are all on one democratic level, as in the neighbouring republic, and this fact, among others, is appealed to by the annexationists in Canada as proving that our national sympathies are with the Americans, or should be so."

As far back as 1873, Sir John Macdonald pressed on the Home Government the expediency of recognizing colonial merit by a more liberal distribution of Imperial honours. He was especially desirous that the Chief Justices of the several provinces of the Dominion should not be overlooked. In a letter addressed on the 15th of August of that year to the Governor General he discusses the constitution of the various provincial courts and the *personnel* of the judiciary, and concludes thus :—

"I see that all the Chief Justices in India are knighted, and I think it will be found that the same rule prevails in most of the colonies of the Empire. Surely the chief judges of the Supreme Courts of the Dominion, with its present population of four millions, should be placed on the same footing! Leaving out British Columbia, Manitoba, and Prince Edward Island for the present, as being too young or too small, the adoption of the rule will involve only eight knighthoods, or seven if the judge in equity in Nova Scotia be omitted, as not having the title of Chief Justice. Surely this number cannot be considered excessive. It should be remembered that these judges are not huddled together, and do not form members of one society. They are sprinkled over half a continent.

"I think that the adoption of this rule would give great satisfaction to the Bar of the Dominion, and as you have already learned, the Bar are really the aristocracy, the governing power in this country, as in the United States. I propose to carry out my promise to you ere long, and write you in full my imperfect ideas on the subject of the mode in which honours should be conferred in this country, and the extent to which the system may be advantageously carried out."

A few weeks after writing this letter, Sir John Macdonald went out of office, but in this, as in other matters, we see the steadfastness with which he advocated what he believed to be for the advantage of the Dominion. On his return to power in 1878, we find him again pressing this subject on the attention of Her Majesty's Government, in a memorandum addressed to Lord Lorne,* which goes at length into the history of the distribution of honours in Canada since 1841. The special object he had in view at this time was to acquaint His Excellency with the fact that, seven years previously, Lord Lisgar, then Governor General, had informed him that he had recommended Sir George Cartier, and Messrs. Tilley, Tupper, and Campbell, for K.C.M.G.'s, and that he had reason to believe his suggestion

* March 6, 1879.

would be acted upon. This information was communicated to those gentlemen at the time, but, before the necessary steps had been taken, changes in Canada and England prevented the carrying out of the recommendation. Less than three months after the receipt by Lord Lorne of this memorandum, Messrs. Campbell, Tilley, and Tupper received their stars.

In the mean time nothing had been done in regard to the judiciary. After waiting a few years, Sir John Macdonald again returned to the charge in a letter to Lord Lansdowne.

After pointing out that, prior to 1867, many Canadian Chief Justices had been honoured with knighthoods, and some of them with baronetcies, he continued :—

"The courts in the several provinces have not lost their importance, or the extent of their jurisdiction by the Union, and the population and wealth of these provinces have largely increased since that time, yet, with one exception, no rank has been conferred upon any Chief Justice since 1867. That exception is Sir Antoine Aimé Dorion, who was knighted on leaving political life in 1874, to accept the Chief Justiceship of the Queen's Bench in the province of Quebec; while the other Chief Justices in the Dominion, who were fully the equal of Sir Aimé Dorion, were unnoticed after years of judicial service. The opinion seems to prevail in England, that the provincial judges are of inferior status to that of the judges of the Supreme Court of Canada, a court only established a few years ago. Two judges of that court, Sir William Richards and Sir William Ritchie, were very properly knighted on appointment as Chief Justice. The court over which the latter presides is one of appellate jurisdiction from the different provincial tribunals, and has therefore a nominal superiority in rank, but the provincial Superior Courts are really more important, and their decisions are held in as great respect as those of the Dominion Court of Appeal. Now, it is a subject of common remark in Canada, that, while in most Crown colonies the Chief Justices have been honoured, the Bench of the great province of Ontario, with a population approaching that of Scotland, and soon to exceed it, has been altogether unnoticed. Since Confederation, two Chief Justices have been knighted in Newfoundland, and one of them made a K.C.M.G. Had that island joined the

Canadian Union, as was proposed in 1867, they would probably, like their brother judges, have been ignored. The only two judges of provincial courts now bearing titles are Sir Aimé Dorion, whom I have mentioned, and Sir Matthew Begbie, Chief Justice of British Columbia, who, though knighted since Confederation, holds his title apparently for services rendered while British Columbia was a Crown colony.

"I hope that Your Excellency will concur in the opinion that this apparent and noticeable neglect should not be allowed to continue, and I venture to suggest some rule for the distribution of titles among Canadian judges. I do not propose the adoption of the practice which obtains in England, of knighting all judges of the' Superior Courts, but I think that the rule might be established of knighting the Chief Justices of the Superior Courts of the four large provinces (Ontario, Quebec, Nova Scotia, and New Brunswick), on appointment to office." *

This representation was not without its effect, as the subsequent appointments of Chief Justices Meredith, Wilson, Galt, Allen, Johnson, and Lacoste show. In fact, Sir John Macdonald's suggestion has been adopted in its entirety, and it is now understood that the appointment of Chief Justices in the four larger provinces is always followed by the offer of knighthood.

Nor were Sir John Macdonald's efforts confined to procuring a due recognition of the higher judicial offices. He saw no reason why excellence in science, literature, or commercial pursuits should not receive the same distinction by the Crown in Canada as in England, and the honours conferred within the last ten years upon Professors Dawson, Wilson, and Dr. Grant, as well as upon Messrs. Donald A. Smith, Gzowski, and Hickson, attest the success which attended his efforts in this direction.

I trust that nothing I have said will lead any one to suppose that Sir John Macdonald desired anything like an indefinite

---

* "I have been long pressing Her Majesty's Government to lay down a rule that the Chief Justices of Ontario and Quebec should be knighted on appointment, as the Judges in England are. . . . The rank and status of a chief justice is much higher than that of a knight bachelor, and my reason for pressing the appointments was that it looked rather absurd to see the chief judge in every little Crown colony knighted, while not one in Ontario was so distinguished." (From Sir John Macdonald to C. J. Wilson, dated Ottawa, January 3, 1887.)

multiplication or indiscriminate grant of honours in this country. Nothing in his opinion would be more certain to defeat the object he had in view. His words on this point are very plain, and must commend themselves to all those who desire to see British institutions develop in this Dominion.*

The following letter, addressed by Sir John Macdonald to the Governor General on the subject of proposed changes in the table of precedence now in force in Canada, discloses his views on certain questions of interest in official circles :—

"Earnscliffe, Ottawa, April 15, 1886.

" Dear Lord Lansdowne,

"Sir Alexander Campbell has seen the members of Council about the question of precedence.

"They are all agreed that the Dominion has outgrown the position in which the General commanding at Halifax should represent Her Majesty in case of the Governor General's temporary absence, and unite in thinking that the Governor General should be empowered, in the event of leave of absence, to appoint, under his seal-at-arms, the Chief Justice or other judge of the Supreme Court as Administrator.

"It might also be provided that, in the event of the Governor General's sudden decease, the Chief Justice, if within the Dominion, or, in his absence, the senior judge, should assume the Administration until a successor is appointed.

"You will observe from the proposed table of precedence † that a change is made, giving to members of the Cabinet precedence over Lieutenant Governors of provinces. Personally, I have no opinion in the matter, and should be well satisfied to

---

* "In conclusion, I beg to say that I hope the practice of conferring honours will not degenerate into a matter of course, and a number of honours be bestowed upon each change of Ministers. In our new country, many men enter political life who, although good men in themselves and capable of administering public affairs, are, from want of early education and manner as well as of social position, not qualified for honorary distinction at the hands of the Sovereign. In such cases there is danger of a degree of ridicule attaching to the persons honoured, which may extend to the honour itself, and impair its value in public estimation ; and this danger will be increased when (as must not infrequently happen) the disadvantages of want of education and manner are shared by the wife with her husband." (From Sir John Macdonald to His Excellency the Governor General, dated Ottawa, March 6, 1879.)

† See Appendix XXVII., for this table, which was never authorized.

leave things as they are, giving the Lieutenant Governor the *pas.* My colleagues, however, are unanimous the other way.

"You will also observe that, by number 6 in the table, the Moderator of the Presbyterian Church in Canada, and the General Superintendent of the Methodist Church, are placed next after the Archbishops and Bishops. As we have no State Church in Canada, and every denomination stands on the same footing, this seems reasonable enough. I think I mentioned to Your Excellency the other day, that the head of the Methodist Conference in England is about to be presented at Court in his representative capacity next after the Bishops.

"I would draw Your Excellency's attention to the fact that the general officers commanding Her Majesty's regular forces and militia, and the admirals in the North Atlantic and Pacific stations are placed as number 8. Formerly the general officer commanding at Halifax stood next to the Governor General, as being the person who, in the latter's absence, would assume the office of Administrator. If the suggestion to appoint the Chief Justice Administrator is adopted, this would seem to be the proper position for the general and admirals.

"My colleagues are divided as to giving rank to ex-Lieutenant Governors of Provinces. I spoke to Your Excellency on this point a few days ago, when you did me the honour of coming to Earnscliffe. I do not see how ex-Lieutenant Governors of Provinces can get rank after their duties cease, when retired Viceroys and Governors General cease to have any rank as such at Court in England.

"With respect to the question raised by —— as to the comparative rank of the Lieutenant Governor of the Province of ——, and the officer commanding the troops and naval forces, that will depend upon the decision of Her Majesty's Government on the suggestions made by my colleagues.

"In regard to the precedence to be given to the new Cardinal, I presume the best way to settle it would be to give a Cardinal the same rank in Canada as would be accorded him in England. Cardinal Wiseman was, as Cardinal Manning is, an Archbishop, to which office ecclesiastical duties in England are attached. As such they have been accorded rank at Court, but I am inclined to think that neither Cardinal

Weld nor Cardinal Newman have had precedence given to them at Court *quâ cardinales*. They are princes of the Church of Rome, and stand in the same position, as regards precedence, as other foreign noblemen. However, there can be no harm in our giving to Cardinal Taschereau the same position as Cardinal Newman would have at the Court of St. James.

"I return to Your Excellency the draft despatch on this subject that you were good enough to send me.

"I observe that you express no opinion on these subjects, but Lord Granville, doubtless, would like to know what you think of them.

"My colleagues think that whatever position may be given to Lieutenant Governors of Provinces, the following words should be added: 'At Ottawa, and elsewhere out of their own provinces; but, within his own province, each to take precedence of every one, save the Governor General and the members of his Cabinet.'

"Believe me, dear Lord Lansdowne,

"Yours very faithfully,

"JOHN A. MACDONALD."

The office of Governor General—the outward and visible sign of British connection—was, in Sir John Macdonald's opinion, an institution of the highest importance, and one that could not be safeguarded with too great care. When, in 1888, the action of the Queensland Government, in attempting to obtain from the Imperial authorities a promise that the name of the proposed new Governor of that colony should be submitted to them before the selection was definitely decided on, raised the question of the appointment of Colonial Governors, Sir John, being invited to express his opinion, caused Her Majesty's Government to be informed by telegraph that the "Canadian Government consider the present system of appointing the Governor General perfectly satisfactory, and would greatly regret any change. Reference to Government here for nomination or approval would introduce a disturbing element, and might eventually lead to the election of Governor, a change to be deplored."

The present manner of appointment directly by the Crown,

gives to the colonies an executive head, entirely unconnected with local parties, and for that reason qualified to hold the balance between them. If the Governor General does anything unconstitutional, an appeal always lies from him to Her Majesty's Government, whose servant he is. The cost to Canada of the maintenance of the office Sir John considered as money well spent, and he deprecated the attempts made in Parliament from time to time to investigate too closely the expenditure under that head. I recollect, when some voluntary economy on the part of a former occupant of Rideau Hall was announced, Sir John's remark that, "though well meant, it was a mistake; for," said he, "the people of Canada like to see the dignity of the office fully maintained." Such, indeed, he considered the chief function of the Queen's representative in this country, for I need scarcely say that, in Sir John's opinion, the Governor General in all matters (save those of direct Imperial concern) should, equally with Her Majesty, be ready at all times to accept and act upon the advice of Ministers enjoying the confidence of the House of Commons.

Of his personal relations with the earlier Governors under whom he served I have already spoken, and my remarks are equally applicable to Lords Dufferin, Lorne, Lansdowne, and Stanley of Preston. No one who was much with Sir John could fail to mark the exquisite admixture of courtesy and deference which characterized his manner towards the Queen's representative, sometimes rather oddly contrasting with their respective years, or to observe the consideration and respect which the various Governors paid to the veteran statesman who had been chief adviser to them all.

Sir John's term of office under Lord Dufferin was comparatively short, yet it was of sufficient duration to convince him of the advantage to Canada of that nobleman's connection with the Dominion. When in Opposition, at the period immediately preceding the general election of 1878, he, feeling assured of his speedy restoration to power, wrote privately to Sir Stafford Northcote, then Chancellor of the Exchequer, suggesting the expediency, on public grounds, of Her Majesty's Government asking Lord Dufferin to retain his position as Governor General for two years longer. After recounting the reasons which prompted him in the interests of Canada to make this request, he goes on to say :—

"I can quite understand that a Conservative Government might want this important position for a political friend, and, as a Conservative, I should, in ordinary times, be glad to see one of the same political principles as myself governing us; but the expediency of setting aside this feeling just now is so obvious, that I venture to urge it seriously on your attention."

Circumstances prevented the fulfilment of Sir John's wishes with respect to Lord Dufferin, but, in his successor, Canada acquired another friend whose interest in her welfare did not cease with his term of office. Of Lord Lorne's relations with his Prime Minister I will only say that they were uniformly agreeable, and it was with sincere regret that, in the autumn of 1883, Sir John bade adieu to a Governor General who, during his whole term, had cordially co-operated with his Ministers in the administration of public affairs.

Of Lord Lansdowne, "the ablest Governor under whom I have served, with possibly the exception of Lord Lisgar," it is not necessary to say anything, for he himself tells us his experience of association with Sir John Macdonald in words as graceful as I doubt not they are sincere:—

"Government House, Ottawa, May 23, 1888.

"Dear Sir John,

"I am a bad hand at leave-taking, and my difficulty does not diminish when I feel deeply what I have to say. I do not, therefore, like to trust to this afternoon for an opportunity of saying good-bye to you, and of telling you how sorry I am to part with you, and how much I have appreciated your kindness and confidence. I have often made the reflection that the position of a Governor General in this country is one that might be very agreeable or almost unendurable, according as his relations with his Prime Minister were or were not friendly, frank, and characterized by complete trust on each side. When I look back to the last four or five years, I can see how large a portion of their happiness and comfort has been due to the fact that our relations could be described in these words.

"Nor am I using an idle phrase when I say it has been an advantage to me, not only in respect of the Government of Canada, to be in constant communication with one whose experience of the public affairs of the Empire has been as wide as yours.

"I will not ask you not to forget us, because I am quite sure you will remember us, and not unkindly. I wish you good-bye, and as much happiness as is compatible with a servitude from which your country will, I suspect, not allow you to emancipate yourself.

"I hope we may yet meet and talk over the past and the future of Canada; in the mean time, think of me as a friend who wishes to preserve your friendship, and is grateful for your kindness to him.

"I am, dear Sir John,

"Yours sincerely,

"L."

The illustrious nobleman who has recently gone from our midst left no written record of his feelings towards Sir John Macdonald, nor indeed is any necessary. Those of us who recall the early days of June, 1891, and who witnessed the personal solicitude of the Governor General for the dying statesman's condition; who beheld him, evening after evening, on the lawn at Earnscliffe in the attitude of anxious expectation —and during those days the eyes of all Canada were fixed on Earnscliffe; who saw him follow his Prime Minister to the grave, need not be told Lord Derby's opinion of—I might almost say affection for—Sir John Macdonald.

No Governor was so mindful of Sir John Macdonald's feeble health and advanced years as Lord Stanley, for to none were they so apparent. On this subject I will but say that the delicate personal consideration which he experienced at the hands of the late Governor General was peculiarly grateful to him. I trust I shall not greatly err, if I add that his appreciation of Lord Stanley included the gracious lady who, during the last years of his life, so admirably fulfilled the duties devolving upon the wife of the Governor General of Canada.*

While adhering to my original intention of leaving to the future the recital of Sir John Macdonald's later political achievements, I may be permitted to say a word on a subject which he considered of great importance, namely, the Franchise Act of 1885. Imperial Federation, no doubt, was desirable,

---

* When the appointment of Lord Stanley of Preston was announced, after expressing his satisfaction at the choice of Her Majesty, Sir John Macdonald added: "His wife is a charming person. I was at Knowsley Hall when Colonel Stanley (as he was then) and his bride arrived from their honey-moon, and I recollect very well Lord Derby's words in introducing me. "Allow me, Mr. Macdonald, to present to you Lady Constance Stanley—once Lord Clarendon's daughter and now mine."

but to consolidate the various Canadian provinces was, after all, his immediate concern, and to perfect the work of 1867, the great object of his life. So long as the Federal Parliament, the paramount authority, did not control the franchise by which its members were elected, Confederation was incomplete.

Immediately after the general election of 1882, Sir John applied himself to the preparation of a measure designed to remedy this defect. In conformity with his usual treatment of important questions, this Bill, though introduced in 1883 and again in 1884, was not passed until 1885, after a prolonged resistance on the part of the Opposition, to which Sir John thus alludes in a letter to Lord Carnarvon :—

> " Les Rochers, St. Patrick, Rivière du Loup,
> " September 8, 1885.
>
> " DEAR LORD CARNARVON,
>
> " I have been down here with my belongings for some weeks, trying to restore my exhausted energies after a six month session in which your Parnellite obstruction was outdone.
>
> " The chief subject of contest was a Franchise Bill for the Dominion; and as it is, in my opinion, the completion of the Federal Constitution which you had so great a hand in constructing, I am sure you will take an interest in knowing that that constitution has at last been perfected. *Ex necessitate,* the Act of 1867—your Act—provided that the provincial franchises, until altered by the Federal Parliament, should be used for Dominion representation. As they did not greatly differ, those franchises were allowed to continue until now. But the provinces had begun to tinker at their electoral franchises, and in some cases legislated with the direct object of affecting the returns of the Federal Parliament, so that the independence of that Parliament was threatened, to such a degree that it had to be dealt with.
>
> " Our Radicals, or Grits, as they are called, violently opposed the change, as they had got possession of several of the provincial Legislatures, and could alter the franchises in those provinces at will. For two months and a half they used every means of obstruction, but patience and firmness defeated

obstruction in the end. On one occasion the House sat from three o'clock p.m. on Thursday until Saturday night at twelve without adjournment.

"With the Canadian Pacific Railway finished and my Franchise Bill become law, I feel that I have done my work, and can sing my *Nunc dimittis.* Lady Macdonald joins me in kind regards to Lady Carnarvon and yourself.

"Believe me,

"Your Excellency's very faithful servant,

"JOHN A. MACDONALD."

The main principles underlying Sir John Macdonald's Franchise Act are (1) uniformity of the suffrage, and (2) the recognition of a property qualification as determining the right to vote. He desired uniformity because he believed that, in a young country like Canada, composed of divers elements, whatever assimilates the political conditions of the various provinces ought to be sought after and promoted.

The qualification, while fixed at a standard sufficiently low to admit large numbers of new voters, was intended to be a barrier against the domination of a mere mechanical majority. The idea that a man should vote simply because he breathed was ever repellant to Sir John Macdonald's conception of government. I have heard him express the opinion with much energy that no man who advocated universal suffrage had any right to call himself a Conservative. He favoured the extension to single women of the privilege of voting on the same terms as men,* his argument being that the exclusion of women otherwise duly qualified was at variance with the theory of a property qualification, and that any departure from this fundamental rule was fraught with danger to the stability of our institutions. Apart from this paramount reason he was

---

* "I believe that is coming as certainly as came the gradual enfranchisement of woman from being the slave of man until she attained her present position as almost the equal of man. I believe that time is coming, though perhaps we are not, any more than the United States and England, quite educated up to it. I believe the time will come, and I shall be very proud and very glad to see it, when the final step towards giving women full enfranchisement is carried in Canada" (Sir John Macdonald: speech on introduction of Franchise Bill, *Commons Debates,* 1885, p. 1134).

prepared to welcome the advent of a new and powerful conservative factor in politics, whose tendency he believed would be to strengthen the defences against the irruption of an unbridled democracy.

There remains but one question of practical politics in relation to which I propose to outline Sir John Macdonald's attitude. I refer to those issues of race and religion which periodically threaten the peace of Canada. It must be apparent to the most careless student of Sir John Macdonald's history, that, British and Protestant though he was, at no time in his career had he any sympathy with that fierce intolerance of everything French or Roman Catholic which at the present time is abroad in the province of Ontario. As far back as 1854, we find him counting on his " friendly relations with the French." In 1855 he introduced and carried a Bill in the interest of the separate schools, against the bitter opposition of George Brown. In 1863 he supported by speech and vote Mr. R. W. (now Senator) Scott's Act, establishing a system of separate schools. In 1867 he perpetuated this right to the Roman Catholics of Ontario, and at the same time provided the French Canadians with liberal guarantees for the security of their language, institutions, and laws. In 1870 he secured, or thought he had secured, like privileges to the Roman Catholics of Manitoba. We are not left in doubt as to his view of what was intended by the operation of the Manitoba Act. In the very beginning of the present agitation in that province, he thus addressed a member of the local Legislature, who had applied to him for counsel :—

" You ask me for advice as to the course you should take upon the vexed question of separate schools in your province. There is, it seems to me, but one course open to you. By the Manitoba Act, the provisions of the B.N.A. Act (sect. 93) respecting laws passed for the protection of minorities in educational matters are made applicable to Manitoba, and cannot be changed ; for, by the Imperial Act confirming the establishment of the new provinces, 34 & 35 Vict., c. 28, sect. 6, it is provided that it shall not be competent for the Parliament of Canada to alter the provisions of the Manitoba Act in so far as it relates to the province of Manitoba. Obviously, therefore, the separate school system in Manitoba is beyond the reach of the Legislature or of the Dominion Parliament."

It is true that the highest legal tribunal in the Empire has put a different interpretation on the Manitoba Act, but with the merits of this question we are in nowise concerned here. My object is merely to show what were the views of him who had by far the greatest share in the framing of this piece of legislation, as to its scope and effect.

On the kindred question of the dual language his opinions were equally decided and outspoken. He fully sympathized with the French Canadians in their natural attachment to their mother tongue, and in the summer immediately preceding his death, carefully noted and put by for use in the session of 1891, the following extract from a speech by Mr. Gladstone, which he observed expressed (*mutatis mutandis*) his own views on the proposal to abolish the official use of the French language in Manitoba.

"There appears to be a desire—I will not say the evidence is demonstrative, but, still, in the manner in which the question is brought forward, there seems to be a desire—to a great extent to substitute the British for the Italian language in Malta. Well, I am opposed to any such substitution. I think, and my mind goes back to the case of Wales, that there is nothing in the world that the Welsh would so vividly resent as any officious attempt to change the language of their country. And, gentlemen, they are perfectly right. The union between a nation and its language, the union between even a small people like Wales and its language, is a due and an affectionate union; it is bound up with all its traditions; and when we went into Malta we engaged to respect their traditions, and no attempt, no policy, I do not care where it began—I believe it began in some former time—but we have evidence before us now which induces me to say, that, in my opinion, the Maltese have been sacredly promised the preservation of their language and institutions, and are entitled to claim among the very first elements of that promise, that we shall pay due respect to the customs established among them and inherited from their forefathers, which are bound up with all their ideas, and which above all they wish to retain." *

In holding these views, Sir John Macdonald could not be charged with any antecedent prejudices in favour of the Roman Catholic religion or the French Canadian race; rather do I think that to the entire absence of prejudice in his large and liberal

* From speech of the Rt. Hon. W. E. Gladstone to the Wesleyans, reported in the *Weekly Times*, August 1, 1890.

mind is to be ascribed the cause which determined his political attitude on these questions. While, like Disraeli, he admired the ecclesiastical polity and admirable discipline of the Church of Rome, he had not, so far as I am aware, any sympathy with her theological system. Nor do I think that the stately forms of Roman Catholic worship appealed even to his senses. In fact, I have heard him say that he liked a religious service to be as simple as possible. I surmise, for I cannot speak from absolute knowledge, that, in common with many excellent Christians, he cared little for the principle of dogma in religion, or for the doctrine of a visible Church. We must, therefore, look elsewhere for the reasons which guided his course.

In my opinion (and it is all a matter of opinion) he sided with the Roman Catholics, in the beginning of his career, partly because he believed their claims were just, and partly because of the natural generosity of his nature, which prompted him to espouse the weaker side. The alliance once contracted eventually begot mutual obligations; for it must not be forgotten that, if Sir John Macdonald stood by the Roman Catholics, they stood by him. Indeed, for many years, as we have seen, he was sustained in power by the almost united support of Lower Canada. While thus united by the political traditions of many years to Lower Canada, whose inhabitants he viewed as a quiet, moral, law-abiding, tolerant people, Sir John Macdonald was by no means blind to the defects of the French character, chief among which he placed a predisposition to fall a prey to demagogues, and an extreme sensitiveness on matters affecting their race. I have heard him say too (though this can scarcely be called a defect), that a Frenchman, whether in France or in Canada, no matter what his intellectual calibre may be, finds great difficulty in really understanding the British constitution, for the reason that his mind is too logical to allow him to accept the paradoxes which abound therein. He illustrated his point by saying, that the French mind cannot conceive how it is that many prerogatives of the Crown exist only because they are never used, and that the moment they were exercised they would cease to be.

Of all the charges brought against Sir John Macdonald by his political opponents, that of corruption was perhaps the most common. It was not generally alleged that he actually used his position to enrich himself or the members of his own family, though such imputations occasionally were made. The standing charge, however, was that he never scrupled to reward his political friends in various illegitimate ways out of the public treasury, and that in this practice is to be found the secret of his long continuance in office. My experience during the last ten years warrants a different conclusion. I have observed that almost every political supporter lost to him during the decade was alienated by his refusal to be influenced in the execution of his high office by considerations of a political or a private nature. A notable instance of this has recently been furnished to the press, by a gentleman who considered himself aggrieved because Sir John would not give him, at a nominal price and without competition, a timber limit, which had previously been applied for. Many other instances of Sir John's resolve to protect the public interest could be cited.

For example, in 188-, tenders were invited for a large public work. When the time for awarding the contract approached, Sir John Macdonald was at Rivière du Loup. While there he received an urgent telegram, followed by a letter from an M.P., begging him to use his influence with the Minister of Public Works to extend the time for receiving tenders. To this correspondent Sir John thus replied :—

"I have yours of the 7th instant, and had previously got your telegram about extension of time for opening of tenders for——. Such an extension of time, at the request of intending contractors, would be unprecedented, and would give rise to all kinds of charges against the Public Works Department. The knowledge that such extension was given in any one case would have a disturbing effect on all future advertisements for tenders. There would be no end of applications on the part of friends (after having perhaps found out what the previous tenders amounted to) for further extension. We are always very glad to help our friends as far as we properly can, but we must consider the public interest first. This work had been advertised for tender for a month or more."

A few weeks before the general election of 1887, an active parliamentary supporter wrote him, advocating certain changes

in the public service in his constituency, which would involve
the superannuation of an employee. Sir John answered to the
effect that he did not see how this could be done. His correspondent replied with some warmth, that, if it were not done,
"we," meaning the Conservative party, "may as well put up
the shutters." This called forth a rejoinder from Sir John, very
nearly in these words. "You say that if —— is not super-
annuated, we may as well put up the shutters. Now, you know,
as well as I do, that —— is not a fit subject for superannuation.
To pension him at this time, on the eve of an election, would
be a job that I would rather smash twenty Governments than
sanction."

A few weeks later, he was in the thick of the election.
His own contest in Kingston was, as usual, a hard one.
One morning, in the month of January, a gentleman, reputed
very well off, called at Earnscliffe, and after transacting the
business that had brought him there, said, "Sir John, I know
you are having a hard time of it in Kingston. I know, too,
you are not over-well provided with this world's goods. I should
very much like to be allowed to give you a subscription towards
defraying your own election expenses." With that he put
down an envelope containing a considerable sum of money,
and took his leave before Sir John could say a word. I was
not in the room at the time, but during the day Sir John told
me of it, adding, "I know that —— is actuated by the best
of motives, and I would not hurt his feelings for the world;
nevertheless, in view of the fact that he is (or recently has
been) a Government contractor, it would not do for me to
touch a penny of this. I want you to take this package, seek
out ——, and return it to him with my thanks, explaining
why it is impossible for me to accept his kind aid." This
I did on the same day.

Some years before the date of which I have been speaking,
Sir John, during one summer, occupied the country house of
a friend who had relations with the Government. At the
end of the season he inquired as to the rent, and was informed
there was nothing to pay. This he would not hear of. It
was in vain that the owner represented that Sir John had
done him a service by occupying a house that otherwise would

have remained empty. He insisted upon paying full value for the use of the property, and, the owner remaining obdurate, he sent his cheque by post.

Similar examples of his scrupulous care in all matters affecting his relations with anybody who might, at any future time, ask a favour of him as head of the Government, could be multiplied indefinitely. In fact, some people might be disposed to think that he carried this caution to the verge of eccentricity.

When the city of Vancouver was in its infancy, or, rather, before there was any city there at all, Lady Macdonald one day expressed the wish to purchase two lots on what is now the town site, and asked Sir John's permission to do so.

Said she, " I don't want any money ; I have three or four hundred dollars of my own, and the Colonel " (her brother) " will give me three or four hundred more." .

" No, my dear," he replied, " you had better not ! "

" Why ? " said Lady Macdonald.

" Well, if you were to buy any lots out there, the first thing I should know would be that a post-office or a custom-house was put on them without my knowing anything about it, and I should have it thrown at me in Parliament that you had been paid for them ten cents more than they were worth."

So the lots were never bought.

It is, of course, inevitable that he who fills the office of Prime Minister should be a mark for calumny of every degree and kind. It is incident to the position, the penalty of greatness. Nevertheless, I am disposed to think that few men have been exposed to the bitterness of party rancour to the extent which it was Sir John Macdonald's fortune to experience at the hands of a portion of the Canadian press. I do not refer to any criticism, however violent or unjust, of his public acts, nor even to ungenerous allusions to his personal failings. I speak now of the malignant inventions deliberately set afloat with the express object of defaming his character and of causing pain to those who loved him. I will not dwell at any length on a topic at once so disagreeable and so humiliating to a Canadian, but it is necessary that I should give one or two instances of this shocking mode of warfare, against which the Conservative chieftain had to contend.

Sir John spent the summer of 1873 at Rivière du Loup with his family. It was the period of the "Pacific scandal," and, consequently, a time of unusual political excitement. On the afternoon of the 5th of August, Lady Macdonald received an ambiguously worded telegram of inquiry from a friend, as to the state of her husband's health. A few minutes later another came, followed by more of mysterious import, all hinting at something apparently too dreadful for expression. Lady Macdonald at once took them to Sir John, who equally with herself was at a loss to divine their meaning. Telegraphic inquiries soon brought the truth. The Montreal *Witness*, the day before, had published what purported to be telegraphic intelligence from Rivière du Loup, to the effect that Sir John Macdonald had attempted to commit suicide by jumping off the pier at that place.* On the following morning the Toronto *Globe* published the statement in the form of a special from Montreal, in which city, it was good enough to add, the rumour had caused a "very painful sensation." It was speedily shown that no such telegram had ever been sent from Rivière du Loup, or received at Montreal, and that the whole affair was deliberately manufactured to feed the excitement which the publication of the McMullen correspondence, a few days before, had produced.

The only notice Sir John took of this outrage was to despatch reassuring telegrams to his relatives and intimate friends, one of which read, "It is an infamous falsehood. I never was better in my life." As far as he personally was

---

* The following is the paragraph as it appeared in the *Witness* of the 4th of August, 1873. "SAD OF THE PREMIER.—A telegram was shown to several gentlemen in the city this forenoon anent the doings of Sir John A. Macdonald, at Rivière du Loup.] It stated that yesterday afternoon Sir John attempted to commit suicide by jumping from the wharf into the water. He was rescued, but now lies, it is asserted, in a precarious condition."

The *Globe's* report next day was substantially the same as the above. On the 6th it published, under the form of a correction, an insinuation that something had happened to the Premier, which his friends were endeavouring to hush up. The italics are mine. "The sensation concerning the Premier is rapidly dying out *under the influence of repeated assurances* that the rumour was without foundation" (*Globe*, August 6, 1873. Telegram from Montreal).

concerned, newspaper attacks, even of a nature so vile as this one, affected him but little. Indeed, he used to say they rather gratified his vanity than otherwise, reminding him, as they did, how, when a boy, he invariably found the best apples growing on a tree at whose foot lay the greatest number of sticks and stones. One can imagine, however, the pain these atrocious falsehoods must have inflicted upon the absent members of his family, as well as the shock to his wife and daughter by his side.

I pass over fourteen years, and come to the days immediately preceding the general election of 1887. Only those who have accompanied a Prime Minister through a general election can realize the demands that such an ordeal makes upon the resources of a party leader. During this particular campaign, Sir John worked harder than at any corresponding period, save only at the election of 1872. His correspondence was enormous, and its management severely taxed the energies of himself and three secretaries. After a hard day's work we had suspended operations for dinner, to resume our labours immediately afterwards, when the evening papers were brought in, among them the Toronto *Globe,** containing a long circumstantial account, headed "The Premier's Condition," of Sir John Macdonald's "mental collapse," accompanied with an editorial on the "strange, sad, and probably incredible story," which, while in part true, they "on the whole" declined to believe. The whole tone of the article conveyed the impression that their refusal to do so was merely an exercise of the charity which thinketh no evil at the expense of their judgment. Sir John, who was in excellent health at the time, read it all, smiled, and told us the story of his "suicide" in 1873.

* January 22nd.

CHAPTER XXVII.

LAST DAYS.

THE SUMMER OF 1890—VISIT TO PRINCE EDWARD ISLAND—TO HALIFAX AND
ST. JOHN—GENERAL ELECTION OF 1891—FAILING HEALTH—LAST ILL-
NESS—DEATH—UNIVERSAL MOURNING—THE QUEEN'S LETTER—STATE
FUNERAL—UNVEILING OF BUST IN ST. PAUL'S CATHEDRAL—LORD
ROSEBERY'S SPEECH—"SI MONUMENTUM REQUIRIS CIRCUMSPICE."

I HAVE now arrived at the last scene in the drama we have
been so long considering.

The summer of 1890 was a fine one, and Sir John Macdonald seemed greatly to enjoy his quiet retreat at Rivière du
Loup. In August he paid a short visit to Prince Edward
Island, where he had not been for twenty years. He returned
to Ottawa early in September, and towards the end of the month
left for Nova Scotia, on a short political tour. After two or
three days spent at Halifax, where he addressed a large audience
in the open air, he ran over to St. John, to see his old friend
Sir Leonard Tilley. While there, he held another meeting,
leaving for Ottawa early next morning, by special train over
the Canadian Pacific Railway's "short line." It was his first
trip over this route, and he appreciated the novelty, especially
the sight presented by the New England forests, then in the full
glow of their autumnal splendour. During the whole day we
had the train to ourselves. He spoke more than usual about
the future, and seemed full of vigour.

His good health continued throughout the autumn. I
seldom saw him better than in the months of October and
November. I recollect telling him so, and remember his
jaunty reply that he felt "tolerably well for an old chap."

On the 2nd of February, the day on which the report

As to myself — my course is clear — a British subject I was born — a British subject I will die. With my utmost effort — with my latest breath will I oppose the "Veiled Treason" which attempts by sordid means and mercenary proffers to lure our people from their allegiance — During my long public service of nearly half a century I have been true to my country and I can with a clear conscience appeal to the Electorate with equal confidence to the men who have trusted me in the past and to the Generation of the rising country with whom such its destinies for the future to give me their hand and there was but and countenance ~~content~~ ~~efforts~~ in this my last effort for the unity of the Empire, and the preservation of our commercial & political freedom.

FACSIMILE OF ORIGINAL DRAFT OF THE LAST ADDRESS OF SIR JOHN MACDONALD.

[Vol. II. p. 257.

advising the dissolution of Parliament was agreed to in Council, I drove home with him to dinner. He was full of energy, and was busy outlining his election address * until a late hour. It was then he talked over the plan of campaign, and told me he would direct the battle from Toronto, as he did not feel able to move about as much as in 1887. Circumstances prevented his leaving Ottawa as early as he wished, and it was not until Sunday night, the 15th of February, that he started for Toronto.

As I always feared would be the case, he was insensibly drawn into the conflict, and was unable to resist the urgent appeals to him from all parts of the province. On Tuesday, the 17th of February, he addressed a large political meeting in Toronto. On Wednesday he went to Hamilton and spoke, on Thursday to Strathroy. On Friday he was in London. On Saturday he spoke at Stratford, St. Mary's and Brampton, and returned to Toronto more fatigued, I thought, than on similar occasions in the past. On the next night he left Toronto for Kingston. The weather in the west had been mild, but it was bitterly cold in Kingston. To this sudden change of temperature I attribute the chill, from the effects of which he never fully recovered. On Monday he remained in bed. On Tuesday he came downstairs about noon, and met some political supporters from Napanee, who pressed him to run out there next day and hold a meeting. He was very loth to go, but finally consented; and, on Wednesday the 25th, he started on the fatal trip. The day was raw and bleak. On his arrival at Napanee he was driven in an open carriage to the town hall, where the arrangements for the meeting were very bad. The crowd was so dense that they invaded the platform from which he was speaking. I saw that he was warm and tired, and did my utmost to induce the local politicians to allow him to return to his car. Nothing, however, would satisfy them but his presence at another meeting in a different part of the town. The open carriage was again called into requisition, and he was driven through the town, where the performance was repeated. When he returned to the car there were several telegrams awaiting him. I went to his room to take his

* See Appendix XXVIII.

instructions, and found him lying across the bed, his face of an ashen grey. "I am exhausted," he said, and indeed he looked it.

On his return to Kingston he took to his bed, and remained there until we left for Ottawa. While in Kingston those about him had daily consultations with Doctor Sullivan, who was afraid of congestion of the lungs, and said that his heart's action was alarmingly weak. Immediately on his return to Ottawa (the morning of election day), Sir John went to bed. A special wire ran to Earnscliffe, and when evening drew on I took him up the news to his bed-room. With the intelligence of his own election, that of his son and some personal friends, he seemed gratified, but said little. About ten o'clock, that is when the result of the elections in not more than half the constituencies was known, and the fate of the Government still hung in the balance, he said, "I think that will do for to-night," turned over, and went to sleep. That, however, was nothing extraordinary, for, on the night of the general election of 1887, he remained in the library only until half-past nine o'clock, and the result was by no means assured when he rose, took his candle, said, "Good night, gentlemen," and retired.

He remained in bed, or indoors, a great part of the month of March, with an occasional run into town, and was very miserable throughout April and the beginning of May. It was after he began to go out that I first became seriously alarmed. He did not seem to gain strength, and complained again and again of feeling weak. His colour, too, was bad; that ashen hue of which I have spoken being often on his face, especially at the close of a long day's work.

On Tuesday, the 12th of May, I went over to his private rooms in the House of Commons as usual. About a quarter to four he came in, and went into the inner room, called me, and said that he was to meet his Excellency the Governor General with Sir John Thompson at four o'clock. I noticed at the time that there was something wrong with his speech. I had had no experience of paralysis, but I felt sure this was a premonition of something serious. I came back to tell him Sir John Thompson would be there very soon. He said, "He must come

at once, because he must speak to the Governor for me, as
I cannot talk. There is something the matter with my
speech."

When the interview was over, his Excellency and Sir John
Thompson spoke to me privately on the subject, and both
expressed their greatest concern, Lord Stanley saying he felt
sure there was cause for alarm, as he had seen similar symptoms
in the case of one who died of paralysis. After they left
Sir John came into the outer office and spoke to me. For the
first time in my life I noticed a trace of nervousness in his
manner. "I am afraid of paralysis," he said; "both my
parents died of it, and," he added slowly, "I seem to feel it
creeping over me." I at once called a cab, and there being
some delay, he and I walked down the Parliament grounds to
meet it. He was then better, and got into the cab without
difficulty. I begged him to let me drive home with him, but
he would not permit it, saying, "There is no necessity." He
added, "You must be careful not to mention this to Lady
Macdonald." There was a ball at Government House that
evening, on my way to which I called at Earnscliffe, and found
Sir John in bed reading. His speech was almost restored again,
and he had seen the doctor in the mean time. This attack
passed off, and on Saturday, the 16th, he gave a dinner, at
which he looked wretched, but on Monday morning he seemed
better, and all through the week was more like his old self.
On Saturday, the 23rd of May, he gave another dinner. On
the morning of that day he asked me to prepare a list for a
dinner on the 30th, which, alas! he was destined never to eat.
On looking over it, he said, "Thursday is a holiday, is it not?"
I answered that it was. "Well," said he, "I think we might
give a dinner on Thursday as well as on Saturday. However,
let that stand until Monday."

At dinner, on the 23rd, he was in capital spirits. When I
left him at 10 o'clock I thought he was almost himself again.
But on Monday morning I learned that he had been very
unwell all day Sunday. It appeared that, on Saturday night,
after his guests had gone, he threw himself into an easy-chair,
and the room being warm, a window was opened, and the
draught affected him. On Monday, Tuesday and Wednesday

he was weak and miserable, and those about him were much alarmed.

During the night between Wednesday and Thursday, about half-past two, he suddenly called out of his sleep to Lady Macdonald, who immediately went to him, and found that his left arm was partially paralyzed. · On Thursday morning he was better, and the paralysis seemed to be wearing away. He appeared to feel the gravity of the situation, for he insisted on signing a certain document connected with the disposition of his property. I asked him when he wished to sign it. He said, "Now, while there is time." Afterwards he saw Sir John Thompson, with whom he showed an inclination to discuss public business, a disposition which the Minister of Justice, in view of his serious condition, discouraged as far as possible.*

During the morning he instructed me to prepare for him two resolutions, of which he intended giving notice in the House of Commons; one respecting the North Shore bonds, and the other about what is known as the Carleton Branch of the Intercolonial Railway. He spoke several times during the day in regard to these matters, and was not satisfied until I had brought him one of the draft resolutions, and explained that in the absence of some necessary information I was unable to prepare the other one. All that day he was much interested in public affairs, and his mind was as bright and active as ever.

On Friday morning, the 29th of May, he was the same as on the previous day, having passed a good night. About eleven o'clock he inquired, as he had done a hundred times before during slight indispositions, what letters there were. I answered that there were not many, and few of any importance, and asked if I should bring them up. He replied with a slight gesture of

---

* Sir John Thompson, in speaking of this interview, has said, that at it, Sir John Macdonald's intellect was as acute and vigorous as on the first day he ever saw him.

The last piece of business he transacted was the granting of leave of absence to Mr. B. Davies, an official of the Prince Edward Island Railway. Mr. Davies is an old man, an offence towards which, as Sir John observed, he was very indulgent.

The last letter he signed was addressed to his friend Mr. E. W. Rathbun of Deseronto. That was on Wednesday. The last letter he dictated was to Senator Boulton, on Friday. I am not able to say with certainty what was the last letter he wrote with his own hand, but am inclined to think it was a note to Mr. Speaker White on Wednesday. He certainly wrote nothing more than his name after Wednesday.

impatience, "Yes, of course." I did not bring them all up, however, but only a few of minor importance, to which he dictated some replies. I observed that he soon got tired, and I left the room about twelve. Shortly afterwards Dr. Sullivan (his Kingston physician) saw him for a few minutes. About half-past two he sent for me about a trivial matter. When I left him he was reading the *North American Review,* and seemed easy in mind and body, so much so that the members of his family were encouraged to hope that the worst had passed. Indeed his composure might have deceived any one unversed in medical science. While, from his expression of the day before, " I will sign now while there is time," as well as from what I afterwards learned that the doctors had told him, there is little doubt that on that Friday afternoon Sir John fully realized the extreme gravity of his condition, yet neither by voice, look, nor manner did he manifest the slightest disquietude. The history of Sir John's last illness is in some respects an epitome of his life. As long as he could he strove against the sense of weariness that oppressed him, and when at length the inexorable laws of nature asserted their sway, he assumed that quiet dignity which ever marked his acceptance of the inevitable, and calmly awaited the last dread summons.

At half-past three his doctor called, and after spending a few minutes in the office, went upstairs. He sat down by the bedside, and put a few questions, which Sir John answered as usual. About four o'clock, while conversing quietly with Dr. Powell, he gently leaned his head back on the pillow, yawned once or twice, and became apparently unconscious. The doctor at once saw that he had received a second stroke, this time complete right hemiplegia. From that moment, he never spoke nor exhibited more than a sort of semi-consciousness. He remained in this condition for eight days, passing quietly away at a quarter-past ten, on the evening of Saturday the 6th of June. The moment of his death was peaceful in the extreme. In the afternoon the final change came. His respiration, which had previously been very rapid, now became abnormally slow, and gradually slower and slower, until it ceased altogether.

During his illness messages of inquiry from all parts of the

Empire rained down upon Earnscliffe. From far-off India came the sympathy of the Viceroy, addressed to Lady Macdonald, in the brief but expressive words, "I grieve for you and for Canada." The Queen's solicitude showed itself in daily inquiries of the Governor General. On hearing of the death of her faithful servant Her Majesty telegraphed:—

"I am deeply grieved at the news of the death of Sir John Macdonald. He will be a great loss to Canada and to his Sovereign. Pray express my deep sympathy with Lady Macdonald.

" VICTORIA R.I."

Her Royal Highness the Princess Louise, the Marquis of Lorne, the Right Honourable W. H. Smith, Sir Charles Tupper, Lord Mount Stephen, Sir Donald Smith, and other friends of the dead statesman at a distance testified to their grief. At home the demonstrations of regret were well-nigh universal. In addition to the individual sympathy of hundreds, nearly every public corporation in Canada placed on record, in the form of an address to Lady Macdonald, their sense of the loss sustained to the country by the death of the Prime Minister. When all was over, Her Majesty addressed the heart-broken widow in a letter full of gracious sympathy, which only one who had experienced the like affliction could feel.

" Windsor Castle, July 2, 1891.

" DEAR LADY MACDONALD,

" Though I have not the pleasure of knowing you personally, I am desirous of writing to express what I have already done, my deep sympathy with you in your present deep affliction for the loss of your dear distinguished husband.

" I wish also to say how truly and sincerely grateful I am for his devoted and faithful services, which he rendered for so many years to his Sovereign and this Dominion.

" It gives me much pleasure to mark my high sense of Sir John Macdonald's distinguished services by conferring on you a public mark of regard for yourself as well as for him.

" Your health has, I trust, not suffered from your long and anxious nursing.

" Believe me always

" Yours very sincerely,

" VICTORIA, R.I."

To which Lady Macdonald replied :—

         "Earnscliffe, Ottawa, July 27, 1891.

"MADAM,

  "I have received with the deepest emotion and with feelings of profound gratification the kind letter of sympathy with which Your Majesty has deigned to honour me on the sad occasion of my great loss and crushing sorrow.

  "The words of gracious acknowledgment in which Your Majesty is pleased to refer to my beloved husband's long and faithful services and devotion to Your Majesty's Throne and Person are indeed the richest earthly consolation I can ever know, and in gratefully receiving the high mark of favour by which Your Majesty has been pleased further to express this acknowledgment, I beg to convey my profound sense of Your Majesty's goodness to me and to him whose useful and unselfish life has now, in the providence and wisdom of God, been brought to a peaceful close.

  "With every assurance of renewed devotion and loyalty to Your Majesty and the Empire.

      "I have the honour to remain

        "Your Majesty's faithful humble servant,

           "AGNES MACDONALD."

A few days later it was officially announced that, in recognition of her husband's distinguished services to the Empire, Her Majesty had been pleased to grant to Lady Macdonald the dignity of a Peeress of the United Kingdom, with the title of Baroness Macdonald of Earnscliffe.

Parliament was sitting at the time of Sir John Macdonald's death. On Monday afternoon Sir Hector Langevin,[*] the senior member of the late Cabinet, formally communicated the melancholy news to the House of Commons, which at once ordered a State funeral, and adjourned for eight days to allow of a fitting expression of the national grief. On Tuesday and part of Wednesday the body lay in state in the Senate Chamber, where it was visited by thousands of high and low degree, who thronged to take a last look at the familiar face of the great leader. There, clad in the uniform of an Imperial Privy Councillor, and covered with the flag he had so long upheld, at his side the insignia of his orders, and on his breast a wreath of white roses, bearing the legend, "From

---

 * For Sir Hector Langevin's speech on this occasion, as well as the graceful and eloquent tribute of Mr. Laurier, the leader of the Opposition, see Appendices XXIX. and XXX.

Her Majesty Queen Victoria, in memory of Her faithful and de-voted servant," lay all that was mortal of Sir John Macdonald.

On Wednesday, after a stately and solemn pageant, the like of which had never before been witnessed in Canada, the remains of the deceased statesman were borne to Kingston, where, on Thursday, the 11th of June, they were laid in Cataraqui cemetery, near the grave of his mother, in con-formity with his expressed desire.* On the following day a memorial service, held in Westminster Abbey, gave those of his friends who were in London an opportunity of paying their tribute to the illustrious dead.

Seventeen months later, in the presence of a distinguished company, the present Prime Minister of England, then Secretary of State for Foreign Affairs, unveiled a bust, erected to the memory of Canada's great son, in the crypt of St. Paul's Cathedral. The bust, which is of white marble, stands in the south aisle of the crypt chapel, and represents Sir John Macdonald in the uniform of a Privy Councillor, with the star of a Grand Commander of the Bath on the breast, and the chain of that Order over the shoulders. On the pedestal is this inscription : " The Right Honourable Sir John Alexander Macdonald, P.C., G.C.B., D.C.L., for 19 years Premier of the Dominion of Canada. Born 1815, died 1891. 'A British subject I was born, a British subject I will die.' "

In the course of a brief address, Lord Rosebery said—

"We are gradually collecting within this cathedral the *Lares* and the *Penates*—the household gods—of our commonwealth. Up above there sleep Wellington and Nelson, those lords of war who preserved the Empire ; below here we have effigies of Dalley and Macdonald, who did so much to preserve it. We have not, indeed, their bodies. They rest more fitly in the regions where they lived and laboured ; but here to-day we consecrate their memory and their example. . We know nothing of party politics in Canada on this occasion. We

* " I desire that I shall be buried in the Kingston cemetery near the grave of my mother, as I promised her that I should be there buried." (Extract from Sir John Macdonald's will.)

The burial plot of the Macdonalds lies on the left hand side of the main road running through the Cataraqui cemetery. On the death of Miss Macdonald, in 1888, Sir John and Dr. Williamson had a conversation on the subject of a common monument, which was duly erected. Sir John's grave lies immediately to the left or west of this monument as one enters the gate of the plot, facing north. On the other side of the monument is the grave of Mrs. Williamson ; while to the left of Sir John's, the graves lie in the following order—sister, father and infant son, mother, wife.

recognize only this, that Sir John Macdonald had grasped the central idea, that the British Empire is the greatest secular agency for good now known to mankind; that that was the secret of his success, and that he determined to die under it, and strove that Canada should live under it. It is a custom, I have heard, in the German army that, when new colours are presented to a regiment, the German Emperor first, and then his princes and chiefs in their order, each drive a nail into the staff. I have sometimes been reminded of this practice in connection with the banner of our Empire. Elizabeth and her heroes first drove their nails in, and so onward through the expansive eighteenth century, when our flag flashed everywhere, down to our own times, when we have not quailed or shrunk. Yesterday it wrapped the corpse of Tennyson; to-day we drive one more nail in on behalf of Sir John Macdonald. This standard so richly studded imposes on us, the survivors, a solemn obligation. It would be nothing were it the mere symbol of violence and rapine, or even of conquest. It is what it is because it represents everywhere peace and civilization and commerce, the negation of narrowness, and the gospel of humanity. Let us then, to-day, by the shrine of this signal statesman, once more remember our responsibility, and renew the resolution that, come what may, we will not flinch or fail under it."

Among the many tributes to Sir John Macdonald's memory, I desire specially to refer to the following lines from the pen of Mr. Gustavus Wicksteed, between whom and Sir John there existed a warm friendship for upwards of fifty years. Mr. Wicksteed, who was born in 1799, is still hale, and looks forward to experience the unique distinction of having lived in three centuries.

> " ' *Quis desiderio sit pudor aut modus*
> *Tam cari capitis?*'—Hor., lib. i., *Carm.* 24.

> " In death's cold arms our country's father lies—
> When shall his equal glad her longing eyes?

> " By distance parted when her people were,
> Estranged and separate, scattered here and there,
> He, by a compact firm and wisely planned,
> Gave them for country all Canadian land.
> And stretched o'er mountain steep and prairie broad,
> For friendly intercourse, an iron road.

> " Long with consummate statesmanship he swayed
> The councils of the nation he had made,
> Contended for the right with tongue and pen,
> And won by kindly deeds the hearts of men;
> And old-time friends and old opponents vied
> In patriot sorrow when Macdonald died."

During Sir John Macdonald's last visit to Halifax, Professor Weldon, M.P., who was present and spoke at the public meeting addressed by the Prime Minister, uttered a remark which I have often recalled. In alluding to the central figure of the day's proceedings, he observed that, notwithstanding the demonstrations of welcome he had witnessed, people did not fully realize how great a man was in their midst. "In the time to come," he added, "when the things of to-day have assumed their true proportions, all men will recognize what Canada owes to Sir John Macdonald, and they will go about erecting statues to him in the market-places of the people."

It was fitting that, in the heart of the Empire he loved so well, the first memorial of Sir John Macdonald should have been raised. To Hamilton belongs the honour of being the first city in Canada to illustrate Professor Weldon's prophecy. There, a few months ago,* the successor of Sir John Macdonald, in the presence of assembled thousands, unveiled a statue to the memory of his late chief. Sir John Thompson's speech on that occasion, which was a noble and tender eulogy of his departed leader, will be found elsewhere.† It is a matter of regret that the limitations of this work prevent the insertion here of other speeches delivered on that occasion, and particularly of the tribute which Sir Oliver Mowat, a life-long political opponent, paid to the memory of one with whom, in youth, he had been closely associated.

Montreal, Toronto, and Kingston will soon share the distinction now possessed by Hamilton. A national monument is also in progress of erection at the capital, and, ere many years pass away, I doubt not that Professor Weldon's words will receive their literal fulfilment, that everywhere the people of Canada will raise statues to the memory of Sir John Macdonald, thus justifying, in a double sense, the application to him of the famous epitaph which his name must ever suggest in this Dominion, where those who "seek his monument" need only to "look around."

* November 1, 1893.   † See Appendix XXXI.

CHAPTER XXVIII.

PERSONAL CHARACTERISTICS.

SIR JOHN IN HIS OFFICE—HOME LIFE—AFFECTION FOR HIS DAUGHTER—
AMUSEMENTS—LITERARY TASTES—PARLIAMENTARY DINNERS—ANECDOTES
—BIRTHDAY OBSERVANCES—POETIC TRIBUTES—PHYSICAL COURAGE—
DEVOTION OF HIS FOLLOWERS—KINGSTON ASSOCIATIONS—RESEMBLANCE
TO LORD BEACONSFIELD—"OLD TO-MORROW"—"NO RESENTMENTS"—
PRIVATE SECRETARIES—SIR JOHN IN PARLIAMENT—HIS POLITICAL CON-
SISTENCY—GRAVER MOMENTS—RELIGIOUS FEELINGS—CONCLUSION.

WHEN first the announcement was made that these memoirs
were in contemplation, a hope was very generally expressed in
the Canadian press, that, while any record of Sir John Macdonald's career must necessarily be in great part devoted to
public affairs, they might disclose something of his personal
characteristics and of his private life ; that here and there
a glimpse might be afforded of the statesman abstracted from
the State. This natural desire I must now attempt to gratify,
though I have great doubts of my ability to meet it satisfactorily.
Indeed, were it not that his practice of transacting official
business under his own roof established a point of contact
between his public and domestic life, it would have been more
than difficult for one outside of his immediate family to know
anything of the private hours of a statesman, who allowed himself no relaxation from the daily task of administering the
affairs of the Dominion.

It is now many years since Sir John Macdonald found that
the interruptions at the Government Offices were such as to
render it impossible for him to do more than receive the constant stream of callers, who had, or who fancied they had,
business to transact with him. He was, therefore, compelled to
seclude himself many hours a day in his "workshop," as he

called it, at Earnscliffe, a snug retreat into which only his secretary could venture unannounced. There he descended every morning about half-past nine, to read and answer the pile of letters that awaited him. He attached great importance to the conduct of his correspondence, and made a point of answering all letters addressed to him as promptly as circumstances would permit. No correspondent was too humble or illiterate to receive a kind acknowledgment. Sir John wrote an easy flowing hand, and with the assistance of a secretary could despatch, in a quiet morning, an immense amount of correspondence. He preserved every letter written to him. To this rule there was no exception. He was not so careful to keep copies of the letters written by himself, though the omissions for the most part were confined to unimportant communications. In the matter of spelling he adhered closely to the British usage, and disliked excessively the utilitarian method of orthography in vogue in the United States. With the view of discouraging its spread in Canada, he caused a minute of Council to be passed, directing, that in all official publications, the English practice should be uniformly followed.* He sometimes dashed off important letters on the spur of the moment, but after writing them he would frequently let them lie for twenty-four hours, especially if they conveyed reproof, or contained unwelcome intelligence of any sort. Sometimes the delay caused him to modify his original words and occasionally to recall them. He was always particular about a correspondent's initials or titles. "There are few things," he used to say, "a man resents more than to receive a letter in which his name is misspelled," and he would take a good deal of trouble to avoid such a fault.

The callers at his house in the morning were, as a rule, confined to his colleagues, to whom he was always accessible, and to those who came by appointment, a large and constantly increasing number. Despite all the precautions that could be devised, his luncheon hour was often invaded to such an extent that he found himself obliged to resort to the French system of *déjeuner* at noon. This plan had its advantages, for while visitors might have no scruple in interfering with luncheon, the

* See Appendix XXXII.

sound of the breakfast gong seldom failed to dislodge the greatest bore. In order to add to the obligation of these *déjcuncrs*, Lady Macdonald frequently invited a few friends to breakfast, and thus contrived to secure to her husband a pleasant relaxation of an hour in the midst of his busy day.

'Sir John's appetite was small and easily satisfied. On rising he took a cup of tea in his bedroom. His *déjcuner* consisted of a minute portion of fish, game, or often a marrow bone, of which he was very fond; toast and butter without salt. Occasionally, when he saw anybody at breakfast with an appetite like his own, he would tell them of Lady Rose's remark to him on a like occasion, that "only innocent people ate breakfast."

He generally managed to devote at least two hours a day to his departmental duties. His afternoons were spent in Council, which generally rose in time for him to dine at half-past seven. The half-hour before dinner was given up to his invalid daughter, whom he loved with all the warmth of his affectionate nature. His first words on entering the house frequently were, "Where is my little girl?" He would sit down beside her, and talk over the events of the day. Such conversations, brimful as they were of light *badinage*, in which they both excelled, were delightful to listen to. Sometimes he joined in a game with her, or read to her some story in which she was interested. His dinner was simple in character, a single dish and a glass of claret often sufficing for his moderate wants. His leisure evenings were generally spent in the library, looking over the newspapers, or playing a game of "patience" of which he was very fond, and in the mysteries of which he was always ready to instruct any of his little daughter's friends who displayed curiosity to know what he was doing. Most of the time in which I knew him, he played "patience" several times a day. Often before going to Council, when his carriage was at the door, he would sit down at the table sacred to this amusement, and play a game, which he said had the same soothing effect upon him as a cigar upon a smoker. When he moved into summer quarters at the seaside, those whose duty it was to look after the arrangement of his temporary office always took care to provide a small table and a pack of cards for his exclusive use. I never knew him to play whist, or bezique, or any other game of cards save "patience." When invited to join in a rubber he always declined, saying that he was too old to learn. On one occasion he went further, and related to us a story of his experience at cards.

"In 1842, a lot of us sat down to play cards. There was John Cartwright, uncle of Sir Richard, M.P. for Lennox and Addington; Mackenzie Fraser; Yarker, the banker; Prior, a fellow in the Ordnance, and myself. We played loo, and I won everything. They then said that they must have their revenge. We played again, and I won. I am most unlucky, and this was a mere stroke of luck. I then said I will come back, but it must be for the last time, as I am leaving for England in a day or two. I came back and won the third time, nearly two thousand dollars in all, went home and had six months holiday on that money, and never played for money since."

What most impressed those who saw Sir John Macdonald at home, was the faculty he had of divesting himself of the cares of State. To watch him joining in a round game with a merry group of children, or sitting at the fireside chaffing with Lady Macdonald and his daughter, reading amusing paragraphs out of the newspapers, or descanting upon the topics of the day, one found it hard to realize that he was the same man who, a few hours before, had been harassed by the grave and perplexing problems which awaited him on the morrow. He retired early, but as a rule, not to sleep, for to the very last he was much given to reading in bed. But sleep came when courted, and, after a good night's rest, he was always ready to approach the questions which he had banished from his mind the evening before.

Sir John was an omnivorous reader: history, biography, travels, philosophy, in fact everything except perhaps natural science. If there was one class of literature he preferred, I think, it was political memoirs, one of his favourite books being Stanhope's "Life of Pitt." He also read constitutional works a good deal, and thought much of Bagehot, respecting whom he used to tell a story. On one of his visits to England he dined at the house of a gentleman whom he knew but slightly. Most of the company were entire strangers to him.

The conversation turned on constitutional history, and Sir John happened to remark that he thought Bagehot the best authority on the British constitution. "I am glad to hear you say that," said his left-hand neighbour, "for I am Mr. Bagehot."

Sir John read novels of all kinds, but latterly he used to say they had lost interest for him. He followed the magazines, in particular the *Nineteenth Century*, the *Contemporary*, the *Fortnightly*, the *Forum*, and the *North American Review*. He also regularly read the *Saturday Review*, the *Spectator*, the *St. James' Gazette* and the New York *Nation*, besides the leading Canadian papers.

Sir John was a prince of entertainers, and his parliamentary dinners were something to be remembered. It was his desire that every member of both Houses of Parliament who supported him should dine at Earnscliffe twice during the session. He never invited a member of the Opposition to dine with him during the session, for two reasons. In the first place, his majority was generally so large that it took him the whole session to entertain his supporters ; and, in the second place, he used to say that members of Parliament liked nothing so much as fighting their political battles over again round his table, recounting to him and to each other the stories of their political campaigns. Indulgence in general conversation of this sort in the presence of a single member of the Opposition would be at variance with the laws of hospitality, and Sir John's aim was that his dinners should be, not only the discharge of a social obligation, but a means of creating a feeling of good fellowship among his followers.

Mr. Hector Fabre, in the brilliant article from which I have already quoted, says :—

"Sir John Macdonald knows the House as each of us knows his office. He holds its every clue, big and little. The moment a new Parliament looms above the horizon he measures and gauges it, and quickly sees what he can make of it. He studies its face and analyzes it. He soon discovers those among the newly elected who are to be his constant adversaries, those whom he can use on occasion, and those in fine who will one day bow to his yoke. He is a keen judge of men, but more especially of members. He never confounds iron with steel, much less pure gold with base lead. He could after a first session mark with a red cross those who are never to be his, and with a blue those who would sooner or later belong to him. It is not that he is a sorcerer, but that he is deeply skilled in things Parliamentary. He knows the stuff of which each man is made : he knows how far it may be moulded so as to present a splendid courtier, or how far it will remain intractable in the hard granite of a Roman statue."

All this is most true, and, as regards the red and blue crosses, literally exact. At the beginning of a new Parliament he took the list of members, scored out the names of those he knew were none of his, ticked off his out-and-out supporters, and specially marked the few doubtful members. As time went on the attitude of the latter became defined, and more frequently than otherwise it happened that eventually the colour of their tick was blue. For social purposes these nondescripts were generally marked as Conservatives, and those whose privilege it has been frequently to have dined with Sir John Macdonald at his own table, will not think it an extravagant assumption to predicate that this circumstance may not have been altogether unconnected with their ultimate political course.

Sir John's reputation as a *raconteur* was widely established and justly deserved. He had an inexhaustible fund of anecdotes, which he was wont to draw on at his party dinners with marvellous effect. I shall relate only one which he generally kept for those of his friends who were rigid total abstainers.

Many years ago there resided in what is now the county of Elgin a gentleman of the name of Colonel Talbot, who belonged to the family of Lord Talbot de Malahide. Colonel Talbot had obtained from the Crown a large grant of land in the early days of the province, and had settled on it. He was a gentleman of the old school. One day Sir James Alexander, who was at the time engaged in collecting materials for a history of Canada, passed near by Port Talbot, and called on the Colonel, who received him hospitably, and pressed him to remain to dinner. Shortly after sitting down, the host turned to Sir James and said, "Do you drink sherry or claret ? " "Neither, thank you," replied Sir James. The Colonel looked keenly at his guest, but said nothing, evidently making up his mind that he had some reason for not taking wine at the moment. When the cloth was removed and the decanters were placed on the table, he said again to him, " What wine do you drink, Sir James ? " The latter replied, " Thank you, I never drink wine."

"The devil you don't," replied Colonel Talbot, reaching his hand for the bell-rope; "Order Sir James Alexander's horse," he said to the servant, and he then and there turned his guest out of his house.

I may mention here a good story, also of an after-dinner flavour, which was told of Sir John, not by him. Without vouching for its truth, I give it for what it is worth. It is related that, many years ago, Sir John was present at a public dinner, at which he was expected to deliver a rather important speech. In the conviviality of the occasion he forgot about the more serious part of the duty of the evening, and when at a late hour he rose, his speech was by no means so luminous or effective as it might have been. The reporter, knowing that it would not do to print his notes as they stood, called on Sir John next day, and told him that he was not quite sure of having secured an accurate report. Sir John received him kindly, and invited him to read over his notes. He had not got far when he interrupted him: "That is not what I said." There was a pause, and Sir John continued, "Let me repeat my remarks." He then walked up and down the room, and delivered a most impressive speech in the hearing of the delighted reporter, who took down every word as it fell from his lips. Having profusely thanked Sir John for his courtesy, he was taking his leave, when he was recalled to receive this admonition: "Young man, allow me to give you this word of advice. Never again attempt to report a public speaker when you are drunk."

Sir John Macdonald always observed his birthday, and liked others to remember it. On the 11th of January the mail bag was of portentous size, while all day the telegraph brought congratulations from far and wide. His last birthday was no exception to the rule. Among many congratulatory letters he received was one from an unknown little maiden, who wrote him a childish note to announce that her birthday was on the same day as his. She added a hope that he would not follow the "mean" example of a small boy of her acquaintance, who had not answered a letter she had written to him. To this youthful epistle Sir John replied :—

" Earnscliffe, Ottawa, January 6, 1891.

" MY DEAR LITTLE FRIEND,

" I am glad to get your letter, and to know that next Sunday you and I will be of the same age. I hope and believe, however, that you will see many more birthdays than I shall, and I trust that every birthday may find you strong in health, and prosperous, and happy.

" I think it was mean of that young fellow not to answer your letter. You see, I have been longer in the world than he, and know more than he does of what is due to young ladies.

" I send you a dollar note, with which pray buy some small keepsake to remember me by, and,

" Believe me yours sincerely,
" JOHN A. MACDONALD."

The Prime Minister's birthday afforded an opportunity to Canadian poets and poetesses, of which they never failed to take advantage. Astronomers tell us that our globe periodically passes through an enormous shoal of meteors, which it encounters only upon a particular day. It is true that occasional shooting stars rush through our atmosphere at other times, but the meteoric stream envelops us only on the 13th of November, three times in a century. This natural fact supplies an apt analogy to Sir John Macdonald's experience in the matter of poems, the only difference being, that the periodic time of the poems was once every twelve months instead of thirty-three years. It does not do to push similes of this sort too far; still, it is a fact that, like the meteors, the vast majority of the verses were inconsiderable objects. On the other hand, some were not wholly without merit. On the first day of his seventy-fourth year, he received a poetic tribute from his friend, Mr. Plumb, then Speaker of the Senate, from which I make a brief quotation.

" MY DEAR SIR JOHN,
      The years fly fast,
Each, seeming shorter than the last,
As swifter turns the spinsters' wheel
When shorter runs the thread they reel,

Or, as the shuttle quickest flies
When smallest is the woof it plies,
Till birthday upon birthday steals
Crowding upon each other's heels.
I try no longer to keep count,
Or reckon up the dire amount,
But, shirk or juggle as I may,
I cannot gain an hour's delay.
Yet there are some, the poet sings,
For whom the Gray-beard furls his wings,
And checks the sand grains in his glass,
And bids their stream more slowly pass.
And plainly, lapsing years disclose
That you're a favoured one of those.
Your wondrous vigour all admit,
And length of days add strength to it,
You lead by wise and gentle sway
While willing followers obey.

   *   *   *   *

Long may your honoured years increase,
Crowned with prosperity and peace.
With heartfelt joy this day we hail,
Best wishes speed by wire and rail,
While Britain's flag on sea and shore
Salutes our staunch old seventy-four."

Mr. Plumb's effort contributed to the periodic display. The following is from a stray visitant, which reached Sir John at the seaside in the summer of 1883, at a time when he was not so busy as usual. He read the poem from beginning to end, and handed it to Colonel Bernard with the remark that, "apart from their extravagant eulogy, these verses are not at all bad."

"*   *   *   *   *

In leafy pomp, long may the maple stand
Emblem of thee, as of thy cherished land.
With kingly port, amid its forest peers,
The lordly tree its lofty crest uprears.
Successive seasons vying homage pay,
And changing glories emulous display,
To crown its state and royally maintain
The spreading honours of its sylvan reign.
Its summer wreaths, gay with umbrageous bloom,
'Neath autumn's touch a richer tint assume.
Charmed at the view, the lingering sun delays
His wintry flight, and, mild in mellowing haze,

Bright o'er the shining splendour beams awhile
The soft effulgence of his farewell smile.
So thou, by grace of bounteous nature crowned
Leader of men, hast ready suffrage found.
The power, through force, that others lawless wield,
To thee, unsought, a willing people yield.
Thy rising fame, bright in its glowing prime,
Has brighter grown with lengthening lapse of time ;
Till now, when reached the autumn of thy days,
With brightest splendour full its glories blaze.

  *   *   *   *   *"

After breakfast Sir John usually drove to the Government offices. It is to these drives, always too short, that I am indebted for much of what I have been able to set down here respecting his private tastes, and opinions of men and things. Though sometimes so absorbed in thought that he would not utter a single word from the time he entered his carriage until he left it, he, as a rule, spoke more freely to me when walking or driving than at any other time. He was a keen observer of nature in all her moods, and noticed everybody and everything round him. I remember that he was ever on the alert to note the changes of the seasons, and particularly the first signs of spring. Those who have observed the softened look that marks a Canadian winter scene, just before positive evidences of the sun's growing power are apparent, can appreciate these lines of Coleridge which Sir John sometimes quoted on a bright winter's day towards the end of February, as he looked out over the glistening expanse of the frozen Ottawa to the Laurentian hills decked in their snowy mantle :—

 " And Winter, slumbering in the open air,
  Wears on his smiling face a dream of spring."

These drives recall another characteristic of Sir John Macdonald. I refer to his physical courage. Twice I have seen him threatened with danger from runaway horses, and on both occasions have marvelled at his coolness and self-possession. I have seen him, when seventy-one years of age, ride one hundred and fifty miles on the cow-catcher of the engine that carried him over the Rocky Mountains, and, when suspended nearly three hundred feet over a torrent, order the train to be stopped on the trestle, in order that he might enjoy the sublime prospect which that elevated position afforded.

When prudence demanded that a guard should be set over his house, he would give the necessary assent, from a sense of duty, but, so far as he personally was concerned, I do not think all the threats of violence he received in his life ever gave him a moment's concern, for his physical constitution was such that he did not know what fear was.

The devotion which Sir John Macdonald inspired was almost without parallel. There was nothing that his followers would not do or suffer for him, and this devotion extended through all ranks, and was strong among those who had never even seen him. I remember once being on an election tour with him and some of his Ministers. He was then travelling through Ontario, addressing large audiences several times a day. This was always a tax upon his strength, and occasionally it happened that, when he had spoken twice in a day, tired nature gave out. This occurred at a country town where he had been advertised to appear on a certain evening. Great preparations had been made to receive him, and, among other marks of distinction, a torchlight procession had been organized. From far and near the country people had come to do honour to the chieftain. As evening drew on, a large crowd gathered at the railway station. In due time it was announced that Sir John was too fatigued to appear, but that his colleagues would represent him. A murmur of disappointment succeeded this announcement. A moment afterwards I saw a stalwart farmer deliberately throw his lighted torch in the mud, exclaiming, in tones of bitter disappointment, "I have driven twenty-three miles to-day over bad roads to carry a torch for John A., and I'll be d——d if I carry it for any one else."

Among the residents of Kingston is a certain Mrs. ——, who is an ardent politician and worshipped Sir John. This worthy lady is not of a devotional turn of mind, and does not very often trouble the church. On one occasion, however, two or three years ago, she was present. The sermon was on the ingratitude of the Jews, and the way they treated the early Christians was commented upon. Mrs. —— listened attentively thereto. She was observed by many to be visibly affected by the recital. The clergyman thought that he had made an impression. Some days afterwards, he called upon his penitent, and, after a few commonplaces had passed between them, mentioned that he had noticed her presence in church the previous Sunday, and observed with satisfaction that his words had not been wholly ineffectual. The old lady, who above all things is honest, was unwilling to appear for a moment in a false light, and replied, " Oh, dear no, it was not that, but when you was talking it made me think how them d——d Grits do persecute John A."

Though Sir John Macdonald, while at the head of affairs, was obliged to reside at Ottawa, he always kept up as far as possible his connection with Kingston, which was closely associated with his whole life. After the death of their mother, Miss Macdonald went to live with her married sister, Mrs. Williamson, whose husband for many years was, and still is, a professor of Queen's University. Dr. Williamson owned a comfortable residence a little way out of town. This place, which is known as Heathfield, was formerly the property of Mrs. Mackenzie, the widow of George Mackenzie, with whom Sir John studied law. I have said that Miss Macdonald went to live with her sister, but this does not accurately describe the complicated family arrangement governing affairs at Heathfield, which, as nearly as I could master it, was as follows :—

Heathfield was owned by Dr. Williamson, who let it to Sir John as a home for his sister Louisa. Dr. Williamson and his wife boarded and lodged with Miss Macdonald. Miss Macdonald bought ten acres from the Doctor, a portion of which was devoted to the purposes of a kitchen garden. The Doctor had his own kitchen garden besides, out of which he partly supplied the household with vegetables, and regularly charged the establishment with everything thus furnished. When Sir John visited Heathfield, he, as the tenant in occupancy, sat at the head of the table, Miss Macdonald at the foot, and the Professor and his wife at each side—this in their own house.

The frequent allusions made by Sir John Macdonald, in his home letters, to "the Professor," is an indication of .the regard which he entertained for that remarkable man, who, in his ninetieth year, remains a marvel to all who enjoy the pleasure of his acquaintance. Dr. Williamson is a Presbyterian minister, and, as such, is versed in theology. He is, moreover, an excellent classical scholar, a botanist and geologist of no mean repute, while, I believe, astronomy and mathematics are his special studies. His retiring nature alone has prevented his great erudition from being more generally known. It is no exaggeration to say that this quiet, unassuming old gentleman, about whom the world knows little, is scarcely less eminent as a scholar than his illustrious brother-in-law was as a statesman.

Mrs. Williamson died in 1876. Miss Macdonald, between whom and Sir John existed a strong family likeness, survived her sister twelve years. She was a delightful old lady, with much of that fascination of manner which distinguished her brother. Though long an invalid, her cheerful and kindly disposition rendered her a universal favourite. Her death, in 1888, was a great grief to Sir John. Another resident of Kingston scarcely less dear to him than those whom I have mentioned, was his cousin Mrs. John Macpherson, the sister of his first wife, who, surrounded by her children and grandchildren, still enjoys a vigorous old age.

Sir John Macdonald's likeness to Lord Beaconsfield has often been remarked. It is commonly thought that this resemblance was merely physical or, rather, facial, but those who have known both statesmen intimately say, that it went further, and at times Sir John's manner and modes of expression reminded them more of Lord Beaconsfield than even his physical appearance, respecting which Sir Charles Dilke has observed :—

" The first time that I saw Sir John Macdonald was shortly after Lord Beaconsfield's death, and as the clock struck midnight. I was starting from Euston station, and there appeared at the step of the railway carriage, in Privy Councillor's uniform (the right to wear which is confined to so small a number of persons that one expects to know by sight those who wear it), a figure precisely similar to that of the late Conservative leader, and it required, indeed, a severe exercise of presence of mind to remember that there had been a City banquet from which the apparition must be coming, and rapidly to arrive by a process of exhaustion at the knowledge that this twin brother of that Lord Beaconsfield, whom shortly before I had seen in the sick room, which he was not to leave, must be the Prime Minister of Canada." *

Sir Charles Dilke goes on to say "that the main point of difference between Sir John Macdonald and Lord Beaconsfield is the contrast between the former's buoyancy and the latter's well-known sphinx-like attitude." Sir John's face was not so impassive as Lord Beaconsfield's, possessing as it did more of light and shade. At the same time, the natural expression of his countenance was grave, and no one could possibly look more like a sphinx when he chose.

Sir John had the reputation of being a procrastinator, and to this idea is due his sobriquet of "Old To-morrow," which *Punch* † so delicately and gracefully alluded to in these lines, published at the time of his death :—

> "Punch sympathizes with Canadian sorrow
> For him known lovingly as 'Old To-morrow.'
> Hail to 'the Chieftain'! He lies mute to-day,
> But fame still speaks for him and shall for aye.
> 'To-morrow—and to-morrow' Shakespeare sighs.
> So runs the round of time ; man lives and dies.
> But death comes not with mere surcease of breath
> To such as him. 'The road to dusty death'
> Not 'all his yesterdays' have lighted. Nay,
> Canada's 'Old To-morrow' lives to-day
> In unforgetting hearts, and nothing fears
> The long to-morrow of the coming years."

Like many another popular idea, this estimate, so far as it ascribed his habit of deliberation to a constitutional defect, was fallacious. Rather was it the outcome of his quality of caution, which regulated his life, and ever prompted him to weigh all the circumstances of a case before taking action thereon. This was illustrated in many ways ; for example, in his choice of colleagues, and in his administration of patronage. It is very easy for a Prime Minister to invite a man to enter his Cabinet, but it is very difficult to repair a hasty selection. It is equally easy to fill a vacant office, but the step once taken is practically irrevocable. It has often been remarked—by those who are not . Prime Ministers—that, by promptly filling vacancies as they occurred, he would have saved himself much trouble and

---

* "Problems of Greater Britain," p. 44.   † June 20, 1891.

annoyance arising from the difficulty of deciding between the merits and claims of numerous aspirants thereto. Such a course might have saved him embarrassment, but, in his opinion, delay was often advantageous to the State, and to the party interests he was commissioned to guard. He preferred, as a general rule, to "hasten slowly," to weigh well all the circumstances, to keep his hand free as long as possible, and to act only in the light of the fullest knowledge he could gather. Such a course, he has observed, often saved him from the disastrous consequences of hasty and ill-considered action. He was a firm believer in the efficacy of time as a solvent of many difficulties which beset his path, and his wisdom in this regard has time and again been exemplified.

In matters of departmental administration there may have been some colour for the charge of procrastination, but this was due, not to indolence, but to the impossibility, even by working twelve to fourteen hours a day, of finding adequate time to devote to their consideration.

Akin to this habit of caution was the patience to which he himself attributed no little of his success as a party leader.* In this particular is seen his power of will, for by nature Sir John Macdonald was inclined to be impatient, and even at times irritable, yet, in spite of this, he acquired a habit of self-control which formed one of the most remarkable traits in his character. He often quoted Pitt's saying, that "the first, second and third requisites of a Prime Minister are patience," and no statesman ever laid this truth more deeply to heart.

Another rule of conduct which Sir John Macdonald laid down for himself was that illustrated in the axiom, "A public man should have no resentments." "——," he said to me one day, "is governed entirely by his hates—a fatal mistake in one who aspires to success in politics." Naturally of strong likes and dislikes himself, there were many men in public life whom he regarded with feelings the reverse of cordial, but he never allowed any personal feeling to interfere with his public duty.

---

* "The great reason why I have always been able to beat Brown is that I have been able to look a little ahead, while he could on no occasion forego the temptation of a temporary triumph." (From Sir John Macdonald to M. C. Cameron, Esq., dated Ottawa, January 3, 1872.)

An apt illustration of this occurs to me. Under circumstances set forth elsewhere in this volume,* a coolness once existed between himself and Sir Alexander Galt, which culminated in 1876. One of his first acts, on returning to power in 1878, was to offer Sir Alexander Galt the position of High Commissioner for Canada in London. On learning this, an intimate friend expressed surprise that he should have done so. "Have you forgotten," said he, "Galt's treatment of you while you were in opposition?" "Forgotten it? no, I can never forget it; but Galt is the most available man for the position, and do you think that under such circumstances I should be justified in gratifying my private resentment (if I had any) at the public expense?"

I trust I shall not be considered as desirous of giving undue prominence to the office I once held, if I devote a brief space to those friends of Sir John Macdonald who in past years occupied towards him the confidential relation of private secretary.

Of the late Chief Justice Harrison, his first secretary, I know little, save that the friendship between him and his patron continued unbroken through Mr. Harrison's political and judicial career. More than thirty years after their official connection had terminated, when the Chief Justice had been long in his grave, Sir John's kindness was extended to those who had no claim whatever upon him, save that of close relationship to "my first secretary Harrison."

Sir John's next secretary was Colonel Bernard, afterwards his brother-in-law. His period of service was also before my time. I enjoyed the privilege of his friendship in later years, when, despite the fact of his being a confirmed invalid, his courtesy of manner and varied store of information rendered his companionship at once entertaining and instructive. He has lately followed his old chief, and in him we have lost the only person really qualified, by reason of long and intimate association with Sir John Macdonald, adequately to perform the duty that I am now attempting to discharge.

To Colonel Bernard succeeded Mr. Charles Drinkwater, at present the widely known secretary to the Canadian Pacific Railway Company. The years of his incumbency comprised

* See Appendix XXXIII.

the most active period of Sir John Macdonald's career, and the Macdonald archives from 1864 till 1873 furnish ample testimony to the assiduity shown by Mr. Drinkwater in the performance of his arduous duties. On the retirement of Sir John in 1873, Mr. Drinkwater re-entered the railway world in which he has been so successful.

On Sir John's restoration to power in 1878, Mr. Harry Kinloch became his private secretary. Ill health compelled Mr. Kinloch to retire after a short period of service. He was succeeded by Mr. Frederick White, the present Comptroller of the North-West Mounted Police, who served his chief for many years with a devotion rare even in a liegeman of Sir John Macdonald. Mr. White's nominal tenure of office was from 1880 till 1883, but for many years before and after that period Sir John Macdonald largely relied upon his invaluable assistance, which was always of " great use and comfort " to him.

Only those who have been Sir John Macdonald's secretaries can form any just estimate of the uniform thoughtfulness and consideration he manifested in his dealings with them, a consideration which extended to the trivial events of everyday life. It is true that he was exacting in his demands. He required all a man's time. The thought of holidays never entered his mind. But to those who caught his spirit and were willing to be on duty all the year round, no life could be more pleasant than constant association with a statesman who ever conveyed the impression to his secretary that he was a co-worker with him in a common cause, who rarely gave a direction unaccompanied by an explanation of the reasons for it, who courted suggestions of all kinds, and even invited criticism of his own work. " I want a memorandum on such a subject," he would say, explaining in a few words what was in his mind. " I wish you would try your hand at it." If the secretary expressed a doubt as to his ability, he would add, " Never mind what mess you make of it, the worst attempt will give me some useful idea. See what you can do."

This enviable position was attained only after much preliminary service, for Sir John Macdonald was naturally reserved, and was slow to give his confidence. " I do not want any one about me whom I cannot trust implicitly," he would say, which meant that the coming man had to undergo a long period of probation, during which interval he rarely came in contact with the chief, who recognized only his principal secretary. Yet, even to those in training, Sir John Macdonald's consideration extended itself. Perhaps a single illustration may not be beneath the dignity of this history. A few weeks before his last illness he sent for me. "I am going up to Toronto on Monday," he said. "I want you to come with me. See about the arrangements as usual." A few minutes later he rang. "By the way," he said, as I entered, "I don't think Mr. Beard" (his assistant secretary) "has ever had a trip anywhere with me." I replied that he had not. "Well," said Sir John, "if you don't mind, I think I'll take him up to Toronto with me. It will give the young man a change."

This consideration extended even to his servants, among whom was his faithful attendant Chilton. When Sir John left Ottawa for the country in 1885, he instructed Chilton, who lived in town, to bring his wife out to Earnscliffe to take charge of the place. Shortly after reaching Rivière du Loup the need of a messenger became apparent. I pointed this out to Sir John, who observed, "I think I'll send for Ben. The sea air will do the old man good" (he was twenty years younger than Sir John). So he instructed me to write Chilton to come down. After the letter had been addressed a thought struck him, and he added with his own hand a postscript to the effect that, as Mrs. Chilton would be alone at Earnscliffe, she was to invite her married son and his wife to take their father's place during his absence. These incidents may be trivial, some may regard them as out of place, but it seems to me they afford more clearly than a ream of State papers an insight into the character of Sir John Macdonald.

Though always effective in debate, Sir John Macdonald lacked many of the qualifications of an orator. His voice, while pleasant, was not strong, nor remarkably distinct; and a slightly hesitating manner, which disappeared under the influence of excitement, rather impeded the flow of his ideas. He rarely prepared his speeches, preferring the impromptu semi-conversational style of the English House of Commons, to the more studied methods to which we are accustomed. Yet, while he

could not be called a great speaker, there was no place in which
he showed to more advantage, or was more at home, than in
the House of Commons, where his lightest utterances always
commanded universal attention. The report that the "old man
was speaking" would always clear the lobbies and smoking-
rooms of the House at any hour of the day or night. Much of
this interest was no doubt due to his position, but more to his
unique personality. His style, like everything belonging to
him, was peculiarly his own. Mr. Fabre thus admirably
portrays his lighter moods :—

"An actor Sir John undoubtedly is. Graceful and pleasant in bearing,
quick and ready in word and action, he acts his speeches as much as he
delivers them; he acts with voice, head, and gesture. The inflections he
gives to his voice awaken his dormant energy: he warms to his work, the
hand ever in motion gives as it were a fresh impetus to every shaft as it falls
from his lips and imparts to it a twofold force of irony. Sir John is, indeed,
given to lashing himself, particularly in his opening sentences : but the process
seldom fails in its effect: his energies are aroused, the flame bursts and the
adversary is scorched. Sir John excels in reply ; he is, above all, brilliant in
retort. He is languid at times in stating his case, and rather gropes through
his opening sentences; but when he is stung in the fight, and has to give back
a blow, he is himself at once, and his keen incisive words, piercing the flesh like
a highly tempered blade, never fail to draw blood. Yet he is too clever and too
well versed in the knowledge of mankind to be cruel: his executions are always
amusing: they extort a smile even from his gloomiest victims themselves."

In the ordinary routine of debate he was clear and skilful in
argument, possessing in a high degree the faculty of com-
pression, of seizing the salient points of any argument in which
he was interested. His speeches seldom exceeded an hour in
length, and frequently occupied less time, forming a marked
contrast to the set orations of another distinguished Canadian,
who rarely spoke in Parliament without exhausting the whole
subject he rose to discuss, and who, by reason of his desire to
avail himself of everything that bore on his argument, frequently
succeeded in producing weariness rather than conviction in
minds less gifted than his own. Sir John, on the other hand,
was somewhat impatient of detail. He never wasted his
time looking up authorities or wading through official papers.
When he wished to speak on a subject calling for research, he
briefly indicated the line he proposed to take to some one to whom

he confided the task of getting up the facts. When these were marshalled in due order in the narrowest possible compass, he would devote a few moments to their assimilation, and then, often provided with nothing more than a few notes, generally on the back of an envelope (which he not infrequently contrived to mislay), he would deliver a short speech, presenting, despite the technical inaccuracies inseparable from extempore delivery, a luminous exposition of the whole subject. This was the nearest approach to preparation in which he indulged, save on rare instances, when the magnitude of the question demanded exhaustive treatment. Such, for example, was his speech on the Washington Treaty in 1872, when he spoke for six hours, or his speech in the following year on the Canadian Pacific scandal. His speeches on the National Policy in 1876 and 1879, and on the Canadian Pacific Railway in 1880, follow in importance. The after-dinner speech he himself liked best was that delivered in Montreal at the "White" Banquet in 1875.

Sir John's habitual demeanour in Parliament was marked by that old-fashioned courtesy now rapidly becoming a lost art. Though by nature somewhat hasty, he seldom suffered himself to be provoked. With one or two exceptions he was on friendly terms with those who most violently opposed him, and even to those with whom his personal relations were most frigid he was always ready to do justice. I cannot refrain from giving an illustration of this.

Some years ago, Sir John received a letter from no less a personage than Mr. Erastus Wiman, conveying to him the startling intimation that a dark plot was on foot to wrest Manitoba from the British Crown, by an armed insurrection, and among the promoters of this nefarious scheme were Mr. Edward Blake, then leading the Opposition, and Sir Richard Cartwright, his first lieutenant. To this preposterous invention Sir John replied :—

"[Private.]

"Rivière du Loup, September 11, 1884.

"MY DEAR MR. WIMAN,

"Thanks for yours of the 6th instant. I can quite understand ——'s mode of action. He goes to Washington and exaggerates the state of feeling in Manitoba. Most probably the gentlemen he sees receive him politely, and say they will be very glad if Canada can be induced to join the Union. With this statement he proceeds to Winnipeg, and pursues the same course of exaggeration. I don't believe a word of his statement about Mr. Blake and Sir Richard Cartwright. The latter has expressed his belief in the future independence of Canada, but that is all. Neither of them would countenance for a moment anything like a rising in arms. I shall look forward with interest to your promised communication after visiting Washington. I shall be at Ottawa after this week. I need not say how much obliged I am to you for the interest you take in this matter.

> " Believe me
> " Yours faithfully,
> " JOHN A. MACDONALD.

" Erastus Wiman, Esq., 314, Broadway, New York City."

When he had finished dictating this letter, which he did with perfect gravity, he smiled grimly, and said, " This is a new *rôle* for me, defending Blake and Cartwright." I asked him what motive Wiman could have had in writing such rubbish. "Oh," replied he, " he wants to ingratiate himself with me, and he thinks this statement, with which he has been stuffed, will be acceptable to me, because it reflects upon my opponents."

As a stump speaker Sir John was inimitable, and never failed to arouse the enthusiasm of the people, who loved his merry way of appealing for their support. Nothing can better illustrate his power in this direction than is afforded by the story of the Scotch farmer, a Radical of the straitest sect, who, at the close of a political meeting, in the earlier stages of which he had shown a disposition to interrupt the speaker, stole round, Nicodemus like, to the back of the stage, and hurriedly shook hands with Sir John, evidently desirous to escape the observation of his political friends.

A criticism of Sir John Macdonald, not infrequently heard, is, that he possessed no fixed convictions on public questions, but was ever ready to trim his sails to popular opinion, in short, that he was an opportunist. Indeed, this has been so often repeated that it has come to be looked upon almost as a truism by those who have never taken the trouble to inform themselves upon the point. Not many weeks ago I heard a gentleman, by no means ill-disposed towards the memory of the late Conservative leader, observe, that it was "well known" that, prior to 1878, Sir John Macdonald had always been a free-trader, and that he adopted protection solely for the reason that he believed it to be the most effective weapon that could be employed against the Mackenzie Administration.

I cannot help feeling that, however incomplete in other respects these memoirs may be, they furnish ample proof of the fallacy of this estimate of Sir John Macdonald's character. Let us begin with the question of protection. In order to determine whether Sir John's economic views remained uniform throughout his life, it is necessary to recall what they were at a given time, say in 1878. It is, no doubt, perfectly true that Sir John never considered protection, any more than free-trade, a dogma divinely revealed, applicable in all circumstances and under all conditions. To do so would, in his judgment, have been even more reprehensible than participation in the fetish worship practised by the devotees of Cobden. His attitude on this general question, as we have seen, was, to use the words employed by the *Times* in a moment of unwonted candour, that while free-trade is ideally the more excellent way, "free-trade was made for man, not man for free-trade, and that if it were to our advantage 'to surround ourselves with a moderate fence,' there was no sound reason . . . why the transaction should not be regarded in the light of expediency." So much for theory, now for the facts. What was Sir John Macdonald's course in relation to this question as regards Canada? We have more than once referred to the fact that, so long ago as 1846, in the course of his second session, he advocated, from his place in Parliament, protection to native industries.* In 1850 he belonged to an association one of whose chief aims was to promote a "commercial national policy."† In 1858 he was a member of an administration whose Finance Minister announced protection to native industries as the policy of the Government. In the general election of 1861 he, at various

* See *ante*, vol. i. p. 42.   † See *ante*, vol. i. p. 71.

times and places, explained and defended this policy.* Lastly, on the eve of the general election of 1872, seven years before the introduction of the National Policy, Sir John wrote :—

"At the hustings in Western Canada and in all the constituencies, except Toronto, the battle will be between free-trade and a national policy. The farmers are indignant at the Opposition having taken the duty off American cereals last session, and they all say, and say truly, that if I had been here, instead of at Washington, it would not have occurred. It is really astonishing, the feeling that has grown up in the West in favour of encouragement of home manufactures."†

It will be observed that these views of Sir John Macdonald, expressed in 1846, 1850, 1858, 1861, and 1872, are in close agreement with the position taken by him in regard to protection to native industries during the last fifteen years, and when it can be shown that the opinion held by a man at thirty-one, was his opinion at thirty-five, at forty-three, at forty-six, at fifty-seven, at sixty-four, and at seventy-six, it is, I think, not unreasonable to assume that he maintained it unchanged through life.

---

* See *ante*, vol. i. pp. 207–209.

In an address to the electors of the city of Kingston, dated June 10, 1861, he said, alluding to this subject: "We have, however, readjusted the tariff on imported articles, so as to secure sufficient revenue, and, at the same time, incidentally to encourage home manufactures. The success of our policy in this respect is already shown by the numerous manufactories of every description, which have sprung up in both sections of the province."

At Caledonia, in the course of the same campaign, he said: "Now, in making the readjustment of the tariff, we adopted this system : in the first place we took off the duties on the necessaries of life which the poor man uses, as much as possible ; in the second place, we increased those on articles of luxury which the rich man buys ; and, in the third, we raised the taxation of those goods which our own mechanics can manufacture, so as in a manner to give them incidental protection."

At St. Catharines he spoke thus: "It is said that we have increased the taxation of the country. Some of you will be surprised to hear that we have not raised the taxation higher than it was during the time of Mr. Hincks. We have, however, readjusted the tariff, reducing the duties on articles of necessity and raw materials, and increasing those on what is required for home manufacturing—this being a direct encouragement to our artisans and mechanics. It is as if formerly there had been half a dollar duty on a hat, and half a dollar on a silk neck-tie ; whereas now there are three-quarters of a dollar on a hat and one quarter on a silk neck-tie, thus protecting the maker of hats, which we can manufacture in this country, and letting the consumer have his silk neck-tie cheaper, which we cannot produce."

† To George Stephen, Esq., dated Ottawa, February 20, 1872.

So, also, with the question of education, to which I have already referred.*

As for his relations towards the French Canadians, it is superfluous to add a word to what I have said. For years and years he fought their battle against George Brown and the *Globe*, and to the very end of his life continued to be their friend. So also in regard to the acquisition of the North-West, the Intercolonial Railway, the Canadian Pacific Railway, and other large questions of the past forty years his policy was uniform throughout. There is just one exception to this general rule. It is true that in 1856 he favoured an elective Upper Chamber, while afterwards he upheld the nominative principle. On this subject the experience of eight years caused him to change his mind, and satisfied him that the plan of appointment by the Crown was preferable to the elective system. But in this change there is no reason to attribute motives of expediency; for it is a fact that, at the Quebec Conference, the members from all the provinces, save Prince Edward Island, were unanimous for a nominative Senate. That object would have been attained with equal certainty had he formed one of a minority in opposition to it.

Finally, let us take the paramount subject of British connection. At what period in Sir John Macdonald's life did his loyalty wane? Was it in 1837, when he carried his musket to uphold the Queen's authority? Was it in 1844, when he declared his resolve to resist, from whatever quarter it might come, any attempt to weaken Canada's union with the mother country? Was it in 1850, when he joined a society whose first object was declared to be the maintenance of British connection? Was it in 1858, when he resigned office as a protest against what he viewed as an indignity offered by the Opposition of that day to Her Majesty? Was it in 1867, when he expressed in the most solemn and emphatic manner, in the presence of the Queen herself, Canada's resolve to abide " under the sovereignty of your Majesty and your family for ever " ? Was it in 1879, when he was sworn of Her Majesty's Council as a recognition of his eminent services to the Empire? Lastly, was it in 1891, when he reiterated in the most formal and impressive

* See p. 218.

manner his resolve to die a British subject? Let those who are disposed to question the uniformity of his political conduct, trace his course in relation to the events which have engaged public attention in Canada during the last forty years, and, so far from attributing inconsistency to him, they will, I venture to think, unite in the opinion that the history of constitutional government discloses few examples of statesmen possessed of more settled convictions or greater constancy of purpose than animated Sir John Macdonald.

Sir John Macdonald was so philosophical, so given to accept things as they were, that he very rarely indulged in cynicism. For that reason the few occasions on which he did so are strongly marked in my recollection. To so great a mind the defects of constitutional government must have been no less apparent than its many and great advantages, yet I never heard him, even by implication, refer to them, except once. On the eve of the general election of 1887, the issue of which he thought more than doubtful, he observed to me with a touch of bitterness in his tone, "Here we are going to the country for its verdict upon our policy and general administration of the public affairs of Canada; yet we stand to be defeated, not by reason of anything we have done or left undone, but, in one province (Quebec), because in the ordinary course of justice a rebel * has suffered death for his crimes, and, in another (Ontario), because Lord Salisbury will not grant Home Rule to Ireland."

By the endeavour of certain extremists in Parliament to force the Government to disallow the Jesuits' Estates Act in 1889, those ministerial supporters who represented Ontario constituencies were placed in an extremely awkward position. A few days before the vote was taken, one of them · in a quandary came to confer with his leader on the subject. I happened to enter the room when the M.P. was leaving. As the door closed, Sir John said, "—— is a plucky fellow. He has already seen me about the vote on the Jesuits' Estates Act. He is naturally apprehensive of the consequences to him of sticking to the Government, yet he won't desert us. He has come in now to tell me that he was elected to support me, and

* Louis Riel.

he is going to do it, though he knows full well that in voting with the Government in this matter he is committing political suicide. It is examples of this sort that reconcile one to public life. And yet," he added, speaking with much emphasis, "you will find that, in less than a week, this man, who is deliberately sacrificing his political future rather than abandon his leader, will be stigmatized as a traitor." His name (why should I withhold it) is George Dickinson, ex-M.P. for Carleton, and he was only one of many who, on that occasion, risked their political lives for the sake of the "old man."

Sir John Macdonald seldom alluded to the past, but, walking through the Senate lobby on his way to the office in the House of Commons one day, he said, pointing with his cane to the various portraits of the ex-Speakers that adorn the walls: " Poor —— was a good fellow ; he was my colleague for many a day ; *dead, dead,*—nearly all gone. Why," exclaimed he, looking back, " whenever I come this way, I feel as if I were walking through a churchyard !"

He did not often speak of death. I remember, however, on one occasion, it was the evening of his sister Louisa's funeral, we were sitting by the fire together, that he told me this story, a slightly different version of which is to be found in Stanhope's " Conversations with the Duke of Wellington."

" There is somewhere in Europe a monastery, a rule of which is, that, when any member of the Order dies, his portrait is painted and hung up in a place specially devoted to that purpose. In the course of time a picture gallery of very considerable proportions grew up, the care of which devolved on a member of the society. One day this old monk remarked to some visitors to whom he was showing the pictures :—

" 'Do you know that when I look upon the years I have spent gazing on these unchanging faces before me, and when I reflect upon the number of my companions who have died and taken their places upon these walls, I feel sometimes as if, after all, they' (pointing to the pictures) ' were the realities, and we are the shadows !' "

About a month before Sir John's last illness, the conversation at the breakfast table one morning turned upon death. Said he, " I cannot conceive how any one could consent to live his life over again." Somebody said, " Should you like it ? " He said emphatically, " Certainly not." I did not quite catch his meaning, so I remarked, " With all your experience to guide you ? " " Ah," said he, " that is a different matter. I do not mean that at all. What I mean is, to begin and lead your past life all over again, exactly as it has been led."

Sir John Macdonald was a firm believer in the truths of Christianity. Although I never heard him discuss religious subjects, I have frequently remarked his reverential spirit as disclosed in little things. For example, in his letters, whenever he spoke of plans for the future he invariably qualified his statements by the letters "D.V.," and if they were accidentally omitted by his secretary he would add them with his own hand. Though, from the very nature of his duties, he was more than ordinarily absorbed in the cares of this world, he was regular in his attendance at divine service, and always found time personally to conduct family worship. He usually attended the Church of England with Lady Macdonald, but, as I have already had occasion to say, he cared little for external forms of worship, and was at all times ready to accept the ministrations of the Presbyterian and Methodist Churches. He was in full sympathy with the objects of the Salvation Army; for which organization he had always a kind word, and ofttimes something more.

Such, in brief, are a few of the notes which illustrate at once the strength and tenderness of Sir John Macdonald's character, a character not unmixed with the alloy of human weakness. No man was more deeply conscious of his own shortcomings. He sometimes alluded in his speeches to what he called his " manifold sins of omission and commission," and always with the plea that to him much should be forgiven by the people of Canada because he " loved much." This appeal was not made in vain. The very reflection that so great a man needed forgiveness at the hands of his fellow-men, the very acknowledgment that the leader, equally with his followers, was compassed with infirmity, enlarged the sympathy which he always inspired, and thus even in his weakness Sir John Macdonald was strong.

The Conservative chieftain was a great man, and, unlike

many who have made their mark, his was a complete and well-proportioned greatness. One knows not which most to admire, the amplitude of his intellect, his fertility of resource, the loftiness of his spirit, or the consummate foresight, tact, and patience which he displayed in his administration of the complex affairs of the Dominion. Yet, above and beyond all, there was one quality which must ever be regarded as his special characteristic, the chiefest of his gifts—his great power of sympathy. Whoever it was that first said Sir John Macdonald was "intensely human," struck the key-note of his character. He knew every chord of the human heart, he understood every passion that swayed man's nature. His intellectual gifts, joined to his rare talent for command, would no doubt have raised him to eminence, but it is to the indefinable faculty which he possessed of entering into the minds and hearts of others that I ascribe his long continuance in power. This quality, largely inborn, was assiduously cultivated. He never neglected an opportunity of adding to his knowledge of mankind or of profiting by it, and thus, by the constant habit of speaking kind words and of doing kind acts in his own inimitable way, he so grounded himself in the affections of a whole people as to enjoy, amid the unrest and change going on all round him, power almost interruptedly for well-nigh forty years.

My task is ended. I freely acknowledge that the relation in which I stood to Sir John Macdonald, and the sentiments of gratitude and affection which I cherish for his memory, render difficult the exercise of that impartiality at once so desirable and so rare in a political biography. However that may be, I have at least provided material for the use of future historians, who, enjoying the advantage of perspective and free from the disabilities under which I labour, will be able to form a more dispassionate estimate of his life and work.

As to the ultimate judgment of history upon Sir John Macdonald there is no room to doubt. The lapse of years bringing with it the fulfilment of that which the extraordinary elevation of his gifted mind enabled him to see from afar, cannot but add lustre to a name that will ever remain deeply graven in the hearts of the Canadian people, for whom no spot will retain more grateful or more abiding associations than the little hill outside the city of Kingston, where, under the waving pine trees, John Alexander Macdonald awaits the resurrection of the dead.

APPENDICES TO VOLUME II.

APPENDIX XVI. (See p. 20.)

(See p. 20.)

" [Private.]

" Ottawa, January 18, 1869.

"My dear Sir John Young,

"I feel it my duty to call your attention to a matter of great importance, on which I think it will be well that your Excellency should receive explicit instructions from Her Majesty's Government.

" Previous to the union of the provinces, the Governor of each province either assented to or withheld Her Majesty's assent to, or reserved for Her Majesty's assent, such Bills passed by the Legislature as he thought proper, and he was specially enjoined by the Royal instructions to reserve certain classes of Bills therein specified. The same practice is continued by the Union Act with respect to legislation of the Parliament of Canada.

" The Act provides that the Lieutenant Governor of each province may reserve Bills for the consideration of the Governor General, but there is no provision by which the latter is to take Her Majesty's pleasure on such legislation. The Royal instructions are also silent on this point.

"In the absence of instructions I presume that Your Excellency would exercise the powers of assent to, or reservation of Bills, under the advice of your Council.

" Now, although the powers of the provincial Legislatures are considerably more limited than those possessed by the same Legislatures before the Union, yet they have jurisdiction in very many cases to which the Royal instructions would seem to apply. I mean, that a provincial Legislature may pass a Bill under our present constitution which, if it were passed by the Parliament of the Dominion, would be reserved by you under such instructions.

"If you turn to the 7th paragraph of the instructions you will see that it is quite competent for a local Legislature to pass Bills coming within the 2nd, 5th, 6th, 7th, and 8th classes therein mentioned.

" Again, doubts have already arisen as to the respective jurisdictions of the local and general Legislatures.

" It is difficult to make the local Legislatures understand that their powers are not so great as they were before the Union, and there has already been shown a tendency to enlarge them, and, in case of doubt, to give themselves the benefit of the doubt, and construe their powers in the largest sense. In fact, the question that convulsed the United States and ended in the Civil War, commonly known as 'the States rights' question, has already made its appearance in Canada.

"There will be no difficulty in managing this question if some principle of action is laid down by the Colonial Office and steadily adhered to. You have, of course, a check on unconstitutional legislation by the use of the veto power vested in you by the Union Act; but you may have a body of advisers composed of 'States rights' men, who will look more to sectional than to general interests.

"The natural tendency of public men is in that direction. Each member of your Government holds his position from his supposed influence in his own province, and he will be disinclined to lessen that influence by acting for the Dominion and against his province should their interests come in conflict.

"This is more especially the case now, when the General Government is new, and the Dominion has no associations, political or historical, connected with it. We are all yet mere provincial politicians. By-and-by it is to be hoped that some of us may rise to the level of national statesmen.

"It would, under the circumstances, I think, be satisfactory to yourself to have specific instructions, in your capacity as an Imperial officer, as to your course :—

"1st. When an Act of a provincial Legislature relates to any of the classes or subjects mentioned in the 7th paragraph of the Royal instructions.

"2nd. When it is, in your opinion, unconstitutional or in excess of the power of the local body.

"In addressing this to Your Excellency I feel that I am, to some extent, travelling out of my beat; but my anxiety for the well-working of the new constitution, with the framing of which I had a good deal to do, will, I hope, be a sufficient excuse.

"Believe me, my dear Sir John Young,

"Faithfully yours,

"JOHN A. MACDONALD."

APPENDIX XVII. (See p. 36.)

(See p. 36.)

" [Private.]

" Government House, Halifax, Nova Scotia,
" September 15, 1868.

" MY DEAR SIR JOHN,

" I have begged Lord Monck to keep you *au courant* of all that has been going on here, by forwarding to you my letters to him, but I may as well, in case he (Lord Monck) has failed to do so, send you newspaper extracts which will explain everything concerned with a small affair I have had with my Atty. Genl. I hope you will agree with me in thinking that, constitutionally, I was justified in asking from him, as one of my Ministers, an explanation of words attributed to him in debate, while I have passed over endless rebellious speeches made by independent members in the H. of A. He backed out * * * * and a majority of the members of the Assembly passed a vote of censure upon me for having called the Atty. General to book, which I forced them to expunge, so now we have kissed and made friends again. I am nervous as to the speech I shall have to deliver on Friday next. I have written off a short one, but whether or not it will suit my advisers remains to be seen. You will see by the accompanying newspaper clipping that Howe, although walking within five minutes' walk of the H. of A., would not go, with his brother delegates, to receive the thanks of the House. I have not seen him lately, so I am at a loss to guess upon what grounds he absented himself so pointedly. I fear the people of the country are 'ahead' of our friend 'Joe,' and that he will have great difficulty in restraining them. Nothing can be more violent than the tone of all the members of the H. of A., including my own Council; and if the *Morning Chronicle* is to be allowed to continue to fulminate its treason throughout the land, I do not know how we are ever to get the country quiet. I send you one or two specimens. Pray give the accompanying letter to Lady Macdonald, and

" Believe me to be yours sincerely,
" HASTINGS DOYLE."

Sir John thus replied to General Doyle as to the constitutionality of the latter's course :—

" As regards the privileges of the Assembly you would, perhaps, have been technically more in the right had you, in your first communication, not referred to his reported language expressly as having been delivered in the House of Assembly.   This is, however, a mere verbal criticism, and does not really affect in substance the constitutionality of your course. Wilkins might perhaps have bothered you had he declined to enter into any discussion as to any speech delivered by him in Parliament, but his answer made you complete master of the position." *

* From Sir John Macdonald to His Excellency General Doyle, dated Ottawa, September 21, 1868.

"[Confidential.]

"Ottawa, September 4, 1868.

"MY DEAR HOWE,

"Since my return, I have been watching, with great interest, as you may suppose, the proceedings of your Legislature.

"Wilkins' resolutions are strong enough in all conscience, and there has apparently been a good deal of violent speaking, but, on the whole, the proceedings seem satisfactory enough.

"I am very glad that the Legislature has set to work to attend to the legislation actually required, and I hope there will be no revolutionary action before prorogation.

"In Canada here, I think the feeling of satisfaction is very general at the resolution to limit the attempts for repeal to legal and constitutional means, and I think, too, that there is a general desire to make things pleasant for Nova Scotia. We are to appoint the railway commissioners in the beginning of next week, as well as the chief engineer, and we intend to set to work vigorously on the construction of the line.

"This is one instance in which the unhappy state of affairs with you operates greatly to the disadvantage of Nova Scotia. We want a good man to represent her interests specially on the Board. We cannot appoint a Union man without giving offence to the majority in Nova Scotia, and an Anti won't take the office. I shall therefore appoint some subordinate officer of the Government to the situation *pro tem.*, in the hope that ere long things may be in such a position with you as to enable you to recommend a man to us.

"I do not believe that there is yet any truth in the rumours about reciprocity, but that question will be upon us before we know it. In such case, we depend on your going to Washington.

"Whenever you think it well for me to write you the letter that we discussed at Halifax, I shall be ready to do so, and it will have the concurrence of all my colleagues.

"I should like to hear from you as to the exact line that you would desire me to take; but I suppose that the matter had better stand over until after your prorogation.

" Would it not be well for you to press Annand to come up and discuss the financial question ?

" Believe me very faithfully yours,

" JOHN A. MACDONALD.

.. The Hon. Joseph Howe, Halifax, N.S."

" [Confidential.]

" Halifax, September 15, 1868.

" MY DEAR SIR JOHN,

" I was in the country when your letter of the 4th arrived, and did not get it till yesterday. In replying to it, I wish to define at the outset our relative positions, and the basis on which our correspondence, if any satisfactory result is to be attained, ought to proceed.

" So many absurd lies get into the newspapers in all the provinces that we cannot on these points be too explicit or candid with each other. If any good comes of our correspondence, it can only be by ultimately taking the population of British America into our confidence. Our oral communications, so far as they went while you were here, might have been published on the house-tops, and I shall write nothing to you which you are not at liberty to print whenever you choose, or to show to any of your friends in the mean time.

" Up to the period of your departure my public action was limited to these three points :—

" 1. That you and your friends should come and go in peace, and with the courtesies of war ;

" 2. That you should have a fair hearing, and be at liberty to submit, in writing, through any channel you chose to select, whatever you had to propose ; and,

" 3. That until all peaceful and loyal methods of dealing with the difficulties with which we were perplexed had been exhausted, it was wise to limit the agitation for repeal to legal and constitutional means.

" On your part it was assumed that, however the difficulties had arisen, you recognized the necessity for dealing with them in a just and generous spirit, and were prepared to make an effort to place the relations of the colonies on a footing of mutual confidence and co-operation.

" On one point we both agreed, that any attempt to break down the Opposition by mere patronage would be a failure, and that no public man in Nova Scotia, whose support would be worth having, could take office under the Dominion Government until he could bring with him the confidence and support of the province.

" It is perhaps to be regretted that you were not prepared to submit, in official form, the explanations and proposals made to the committee of the convention, because, in the absence of any definite propositions, matters have drifted for a month, until the excitement has increased, and the cry for repeal or annexation is heard all over the province.

" The visit of General Butler and his friends made for the purpose, scarcely disguised, of encouraging the annexation feeling, with offers of men and money, has added new complications, and we have just escaped collision between the Governor and the local Legislature, which, whatever the result of a dissolution might have been, would, had a rupture been forced, have increased the feeling of bitterness and exasperation.

" The danger is now over, the session will close in a few days, and, if anything is to be done, no time should be lost in making the effort.

" The first step should be for you to put in writing the substance of your oral statements to the committee. Let this be done without delay. I will then show the paper to a few friends, and perhaps give you our views in writing. Nothing may result from this negotiation, but, if it fails, and trouble comes after, we shall have the satisfaction of knowing that we have exhausted the sources of friendly negotiation, and, besides, Her Majesty's Government will then be able to discern in what we agree, and, should that point be arrived at, where our interests are irreconcilable.

" Pending this negotiation, it will be sound policy to make no appointments in or for Nova Scotia, because all selections hitherto have been made from the minority of the population, and those officers, with the unpopular persons crammed into the Senate, create feelings the very reverse of those you desire to cultivate. By this course you risk nothing, because, should we be compelled to resume our old attitudes a month or two hence, you will then have all the patronage to strengthen your Government in any way you please.

" I still adhere to my pledge to help you to get a reciprocity treaty. I have made no secret of your offer and its acceptance, and would probably act with the full concurrence of the merchants of Halifax.

" Butler's committee have, I think, endeavoured to spread the apprehension here, that no treaty can be got without annexation.

" Counter statements to those handed to you by Tims and the Accountant General have been made in our Legislature. The Committee of Public Accounts will report in a few days, and Annand will make a financial statement. I will endeavour to get the facts sifted out, so that we may arrive at definite data about which there can be no further dispute.

" In the mean time,
" Believe me yours truly,
" Joseph Howe."

" [Confidential.]

·· Ottawa, September 26, 1868.

" My dear Howe,

" I have yours of the 15th instant.

" Your suggestions as to the basis on which our correspondence should be carried on are quite satisfactory to me, and your statement as to the nature of our conversations at Halifax I accept as correct in every particular.

" The newspapers, both with us and in Nova Scotia, have been filled with all kinds of absurdities. I do not think that we should in the slightest degree regard them.

" It is unfortunate that the occurrences in the provincial Legislature have revived the feelings of irritation that I had hoped were beginning to subside. I always was apprehensive of this ; but you, as I understood, thought that, so soon as the resolutions protesting against the Duke of Buckingham's despatch were adopted, things would go on smoothly.

" I am afraid that Blanchard's forcing a discussion on Wilkins' resolutions was very injudicious, and fanned the flame. However, the House has now been prorogued, and I suppose will not re-assemble for eleven months or so. During that time moderate men have their opportunity, and will, I hope, embrace it.

" My three previous letters were written for the purpose of impressing upon you, as strongly as possible, my sense of the great injury caused to Nova Scotian interests by the present state of affairs, and it occurs to me that you can make great use of this argument with your friends.

" While Nova Scotia suffers, the Canadian Government also suffer. If we delay the filling up of important offices in Nova Scotia, we are charged with neglect of duty. If we appoint union men we are told that it is an insult to the majority of the people. If we offer to appoint one of the majority we are told that we are attempting to bribe him. This state of things surely should not last.

" You say that it is perhaps to be regretted that I was not prepared to submit, in an official form, the explanations and proposals made to the committee of the convention. I thought that this matter had been perfectly understood between us.

" You suggested my writing you a letter before I left Halifax, and said you would answer it in a month or so. I stated that if it was to be postponed so long, I might as well defer writing until the end of the month, or about the prorogation, and that I would then write with the concurrence of *all* my colleagues. This would, of course, give my statements more weight than if they came from myself alone.

" Our Council will re-assemble next Monday, and, after consulting with them, I shall write you in full. My letter will, however, be merely a repetition of the statements made before the committee, and, as the whole of the Provincial Ministry were present when the statements were made, it will give them no new information. It will, I hope, strengthen your hands.

" From all I can learn of matters in Nova Scotia, and I hear much from both sides, I am satisfied that you have only to declare your will that the present constitution should have a fair trial, and your will will be law. All your own friends, all the moderate Antis, and the whole union party will rally round you, and you must succeed.

" I have heard nothing further from Washington as to reciprocity, but I still hope that your services will be required before New Year.

                                " Believe me
                                        " Yours faithfully,
                                                "JOHN A. MACDONALD.

" The Hon. Joseph Howe, Halifax, N.S."

" [Confidential and separate.]

" Ottawa, November 4, 1868.

" My dear Howe,

" I duly received your letter in answer to mine of the 6th of October, and I have called Rose's attention to the question of Finance. He has been, for some time, busily engaged in an examination of the subject, and hopes in a few days to be in a position to communicate with you thereupon. Meanwhile, I desire to write you a letter for your own eye alone, which, after having read, you may put into the fire or return, as you please.

" Believing as I do, and as I think you do, that it is time to put an end to the present anomalous state of things, and that all further attempts on the English Parliament will be fruitless, I think that some decided line of policy should be taken in the interests of Nova Scotia, as well as of the Dominion.

" It is hopeless to expect any change of opinion in the present Provincial Government. They are a body of men who have risen to the surface only on the repeal cry, and their incapacity for administration is so well known, even to themselves, that they can hope to retain office only by a continuance of the agitation. It is quite evident that they are reckless of the effect on Nova Scotia, or the ruin to its interests, so long as they remain in power ; they would rather ' reign in hell than serve in heaven.' To wait, then, for any signs of conversion on their part is to be like the peasant in the fable, who sat by the river side until the river should pass by.

" I look upon you as the sole means, but the certain means, of arresting their downward course.

" Mirabeau would have arrested the French Revolution had he not prematurely died. You are the Nova Scotian Mirabeau, and judging, I am glad to say, by the state of your health when I last saw you, I do not think you will have your French prototype's untimely fate.

" What course is there open to you to attain this desirable result? My idea is this, that the financial question should be settled in a manner favourable to Nova Scotian interests, and that this once effected you should openly appeal, in the spirit of your late admirable letter, lately published, to the loyalty, moderation, and good sense of the whole people. You will have, of course, the extreme men, the political hacks, and those who have nothing to lose, to confront; but you will have all your own friends, political and personal, all men of property who desire the cessation of this ruinous agitation, and the whole union party at your back. You can get up an enthusiasm on your side if you please. The local Government will either be whipped in, or you can place them in such a position that, upon a dissolution and an appeal to the people, you can, with your united forces, secure, in the local Parliament, a majority who will give their confidence to Ministers in whom you confide.

" This, you will say, is a bold game, but, ' out of the nettle, danger, you will pluck the flower, safety.'

" If some such course as this is not adopted, how is it to be visible to the world that there is a reaction in Nova Scotia, even though it is well understood that such a reaction exists ? Your local Parliament will sit for three years yet. Its members are so deeply committed to the support of the present anti-confederate Government that they cannot well retrace their steps, and so the disease, which is now in its *acute* and therefore curable form, will become a chronic and inveterate sore. There is a glorious and patriotic game before you; let me urge you to play it.

" You have, by a life-long service of pecuniary disinterestedness, in the public cause, earned the right to rise far above the fear of an unworthy suspicion that you are actuated by mercenary motives. Let no fear of such an imputation deter you from this course.

" Pray pardon my writing so strongly to you, but the exigency of the case requires speedy and energetic action.

" It is to be regretted that Annand cannot, or, rather, will not come here. I did not much expect that he would, as it is his game to prevent all *rapproche-ment*. Anything that will quiet or diminish the anti-union feeling will weaken his hands and diminish his power. But if you ask him to come and he won't, and if a man like McLelan therefore will come, he (Annand) will be put in the wrong, and the prestige of having effected an advantageous settlement for Nova Scotia will transfer the game to your hands. It would do so more effectually if you would come accompanied by McLelan. This is, however, altogether for your consideration; meanwhile, I shall hurry Rose (who, however, needs no spur) as to the financial *resumé*.

" In your last telegram you say that another letter is on the way, which I shall look for with great interest.

" Believe me

" Yours sincerely,

" JOHN A. MACDONALD.

" The Hon. Joseph Howe, Halifax, Nova Scotia."

" [Confidential.]

" Halifax, November 16, 1868.

" MY DEAR SIR JOHN,

" I have been so much engaged, writing public letters and discussing the state of affairs with old friends, that I have not, until this forenoon, had half an hour to reply to your letter of the 4th instant. I assume that my public letters are reprinted in the Canadian papers, and that you see them all, but for fear that you should not, you will find one or two of the last enclosed. You will scarcely understand, however, how matters move here without running your eye over the " Anti " and other Halifax papers, which you can get from some of the printers with whom they are exchanged.

" On my return home, and long before I saw or had any communication with you, I had made up my mind that any further appeals to England were hopeless, unless we could revive the old idea of a union of the Maritime Provinces and go over with a scheme of Government in our hands. All the delegates shared this opinion. On my way out I saw Mr. Munn, a wealthy merchant of Newfoundland, who gave me no encouragement to expect aid from that island, and two friends who had been sent to New Brunswick and Charlottetown had brought back discouraging accounts from those provinces. Under these circumstances I took it for granted that we would all fall back upon the view that nothing more could be done in England. This opinion I expressed without any reserve : but delegations are pleasant things, and I soon found that some of my friends were not disinclined to have another, and that the local Government naturally felt that, so long as the cry for repeal could be kept up, they would have the protection of a powerful party to shield them from all criticism of the policy or acts of the Administration.

"Having the control of all the 'Anti' newspapers secured by a distribution of the public printing among them, this policy was soon indicated; and, before the convention met, the country were informed that the prospects of repeal were brightening, that a new Parliament and another delegation would work wonders, and that, if they did not, then a seizure of the revenue offices and annexation would settle the question.

"In accordance with this policy, from the moment it was known that the Canadian Ministers were coming down, to insult and bluff them off was part of the programme. My protest and expressed determination that they should be heard, and that any terms they might offer should be fairly considered, disturbed this policy, and at once all sorts of rumours were set in circulation, to which point was given in the subsidized press.

"When the convention broke up I took no further part in the movement, but, if asked, gave my opinions freely. Thinking to frighten and silence me, the repeal papers were set to work to praise me one day and threaten me the next. I took no notice of this sort of thing till everybody could see that the provocation had been ample, and then gave my views frankly to the country, with what effect it is perhaps too early yet to conjecture. I should have done this even if convinced that, at first, not a dozen persons were with me, because I should depend upon the sober second thought of my countrymen to come right at last and do me justice.

"But I should deceive myself, and you too, if I allowed you to suppose that I could lead them as I like. As a whole they are intelligent, keen politicians, and deeply feel what they regard as great wrongs. They have, besides, got the idea into their heads that your government is not to be trusted, and that you are a sort of wizard that, having already beguiled Brown McDougall, Tupper, etc., to destruction, is about to do the same kind of office to me. The independence of my position alone enables me to fight this battle, and I must hold it or be beaten. It is true that I might take office and carry my county with me, but I would not at present carry the country; and, from the first, I have always said that to do less would only be to make a wreck of myself, leaving all the work to be done over again.

"At present there is, in many quarters, hope from the new Parliament, but the widespread feeling in favour of annexation to the United States now complicates matters a great deal. You can have no idea how rapidly this feeling has developed. There are whole districts where the sentiment of loyalty is dead, where no 'enthusiasm' can be evoked by anybody.

"Mirabeau was an able man, but unprincipled and as ugly as the devil; and, besides, the French Court, having no sincere desire to make just concessions, was not worth saving. They played with a revolution, and lost time till it was too late to save the nation. You have lost some time. Had we been met at Ottawa last winter in the same spirit which you evince now, things might have taken a different turn. But the past is behind us, and cannot be recalled. Looking to the future, I must fight my battle here in my own way, and it will be sound policy for you to allay the discontent, so far as you honourably can, by the most liberal concessions that are compatible with justice to the other portions of the Dominion.

"I have not had time to give you my views on the constitutional aspects of the question, but will do so shortly. In the mean time, think whether our section of the Senate cannot be reconstructed or made elective. Fancy all the Senators from Ontario or Quebec taken from a minority of the people, and including the most unpopular men in the province! You could not reconcile your people to that state of things. Turn this over in your mind, and see if some remedy cannot be suggested.

"Rose writes in the best spirit, and I hope to have his report this week.

"If any answer is to come to the minute and resolutions, it should be here without delay. If the question is to be left to the decision of the new Cabinet, they should not hang fire, but decide promptly.

"A most distasteful appointment has just been made of a postmaster at Weymouth. Enclosed is an extract of a letter from Savary. Show it to Campbell, and ask him to direct Woodgate to be more careful in future.

"Pray present my compliments to Lady Macdonald, and,

"Believe me

"Sincerely yours,

"JOSEPH HOWE."

"[Confidential.]

"Ottawa, November 24, 1868.

"MY DEAR HOWE,

"Thanks for yours of the 16th.

"I wrote you on the 20th, urging again the expediency of your coming up. Meanwhile Rose has completed his memorandum on the financial position. We have now an interregnum. We have no Governor, and of the members of our Council some are in Europe, and some scattered over the Dominion. Rose is, therefore, unable to submit his minute to Council, and the document has, as yet, no official value.

"As you are naturally anxious, however, to see the mode in which the question presents itself to us, I send you, confidentially, a copy which has been furnished me by him. He desires that, until it receives the sanction of his colleagues, its examination may be confined to yourself, McLelan, and E. M. McDonald, and we shall be glad to have your remarks on it at your convenience. I may say, that I have gone over the matter carefully with Rose, and generally agree in his conclusions.

" I think a meeting had afterwards better be arranged at some point to be agreed on. This, as I have already stated, is the best place; as many propositions agreed upon, provisionally, between you and Rose, could at once be submitted for the consideration of the Government, and settled without delay or correspondence.

" I await your leisure for your remarks on the constitutional aspect of the question—there is no hurry as to them.

" With respect to the constitution of the Senate as to number, you are much better off than you would be as one of the United States. You have 12 out of 72, or one-sixth. In the United States you would have 2 in 74, or one thirty-seventh.

" You complain that the Senate is crammed with your opponents, but then you must remember that the Government could not well appoint Senators who were pledged to destroy the constitution under which they would have held their commissions. There will be little or no difficulty, however, on this head. Of the twelve you reckon Mr. Locke to be a friend, there is the vacancy caused by poor Weir's death, and I believe that two others are prepared to resign their positions in order to facilitate any arrangement with you.

" Believe me, in haste,
" Faithfully yours,
" JOHN A. MACDONALD.

" The Hon. Joseph Howe, Halifax.

" P.S.—Herewith you have Rose's report, and his letter to me enclosing it."

" [Confidential.]

" Halifax, December 4, 1868.

" MY DEAR SIR JOHN,
" Rose's report has been received. He will show you my note thereanent.

" Having brought out all the points that ought to be considered, I have laid down my pen, and shall let the fellows blaze away. My position is now understood. I am not responsible for deceiving the country with the repeal cry, nor for the waste of time and money in another delegation.

" If there are breaches of law or annexation movements, everybody now knows that I do not sanction them, and that they will, if tried, be contrary to my advice.

" The members of the local Government are, of course, very savage, and a great many of the more ardent repealers sympathize with them and not with me, but I have reason to believe that sound thinkers in all parts of the country are beginning to reflect, and that justice will be done to me by-and-bye.

" The responsibility rests on the locals to get repeal, and when they break down, as they must, my policy will be justified. If they then attempt violence, Doyle and they may settle the matter.

" I shall not, just now, trouble you with constitutional questions. You could not volunteer material changes, and if I wish to press any I can do this better perhaps in Parliament. The Senate, I fear, will be the *bête noire*.

" Disraeli having resigned, Gladstone will soon be in a position to declare his policy, and, whatever it is, he should declare it without reserve and without delay.

" Annand called a few of the repealers together a few nights ago. They declared that to send another delegation was the only thing that could be done, though but small hopes of success were entertained.

" What news has the Governor General? Is any answer to come to the Minute of Council?

" What of reciprocity? We may expect General Butler to take special charge of Nova Scotia when Congress meets.

" The skirmish between Blanchard and McDonald will do no harm.

"Believe me, my dear Sir John,
"Yours truly,
"JOSEPH HOWE."

" [Confidential.]

" Halifax, January 4, 1869.

" MY DEAR SIR JOHN,

" Your letter of the 23rd has come to hand. It is better that Rose should not come here, for the reasons you give. I have some engagements which will keep me in this province till the 12th, but, after that, as soon as may be, McLelan and I will go on to Portland, notifying Rose by telegraph of the exact time and our whereabouts. We shall not trouble you meanwhile with criticisms of the financial reports, but will be prepared to discuss the whole subject fairly with Rose when we meet.

" The ' victory ' is, I think, fairly on the cards, but the battle has been a hard one, and there is a good deal of sullen resistance yet to be overcome. I wrote more than I at first intended, but stopped when I had brought out and illustrated all the salient points of the argument.

" Enclosed you will find my latest deliverance, which nobody has attacked or replied to.

" It is now pretty clear to everybody that my opinions have never changed since I left England; that the quarrel with old friends was forced upon me by their own folly; that Gladstone's Cabinet has been composed, as I months ago predicted it would be, of determined supporters of the Act of Union; that a delegation would be a forlorn hope, sent to scale walls where no breach had been made, and that I will be no party to annexation intrigues or revolutionary movements.

" The newspapers are now quiet, and the locals sorely perplexed. They could get an answer from Bright or Gladstone in two days for £10, but no message has been sent, for the best of all reasons—they know what the answer must be. Doyle's despatch must soon bring one, which I agree with you in thinking will be 'prompt and decisive.' When it comes there will be a further falling off of rational and moderate men. Disraeli's sudden resignation was not expected. Annand's intention was, I assume, to slip away to England with his delegates, putting off the meeting of the House till midsummer; a pleasant trip and six months' exemption from responsibility of any kind would thus have been secured. The future was to have been left to the chapter of accidents. But the complexion of the Cabinet staggers some of his colleagues, who have discovered that no resolution sanctioning a delegation was passed in the convention or the Legislature. They will not now venture to send one till the answer comes to Doyle's despatch, when, if it is decisive, such a movement would be sheer folly. What will next be done it is vain to conjecture. They are then pledged to seize the revenue offices and inaugurate a revolution. Will they have courage to do either? We shall see. I presume they will call the House together before doing anything. A *general strike*, as suggested by me in August, is the only thing that is practical, but that involves sacrifices which I doubt if they are prepared to make.

"What you say about Newfoundland is confirmed by my own letters from the Island.

"Judge Bliss has resigned, or will resign within a few days. Legislation is required before a new judge can be appointed. Wilkins is hungry for the place, and Annand anxious to be rid of him. They will perfect the legislation if you will first promise W. the place. Do nothing of the kind. He is not fit for the Bench nor does he deserve promotion, but the longer the suspense lasts the greater fool he will make of himself. It is already beginning to be known what he is at. When the matter comes officially to your knowledge, take plenty of time to deliberate.

"As respects general patronage the time has come when some use can be made of it. Hitherto I have declined all applications to sign recommendations to the Dominion Government, giving as a reason to everybody that, as I was not a supporter of it, I had no right to ask favours or interfere with its patronage. Matters have so far changed that this reason can hardly now be given, and, besides, it is not wise to continue the system of giving all places to a minority of the population if better can be done. If you agree with me, it may be as well to direct the heads of departments to notify me when vacancies occur or new arrangements are to be made. If there are objections to this being done state them frankly. You can write me by Rose to Portland.

"Wishing Lady Macdonald and yourself many happy returns of the festive season,

"I am, my dear Sir John,

"Very truly yours,

"JOSEPH HOWE."

APPENDIX XIX. (See p. 62.)

" [Private.]

" Department of Justice, Ottawa, Canada,
" February 16, 1870.

" My DEAR LORD,

" Before you leave Ottawa on your mission of peace, I think it well to reduce to writing the substance of the conversation I had the honour to have with you this morning.

" I mark this letter 'private' in order that it may not be made a public document, to be called for by Parliament prematurely; but you are quite at liberty to use it in such a manner as you may think most advantageous.

" I hope that ere you arrive at Fort Garry, the insurgents, after the explanations that have been entered into by Messrs. Thibault, de Salaberry, and Smith, will have laid down their arms, and allowed Governor McTavish to resume the administration of public affairs. In such case, by the Act of the Imperial Parliament of last session, all the public functionaries will still remain in power, and the Council of Assiniboia will be restored to their former position.

" Will you be kind enough to make full explanation to the Council, on behalf of the Canadian Government, as to the feelings which animate, not only the Governor General, but the whole Government, with respect to the mode of dealing with the North-West. We have fully explained to you, and desire you to assure the Council authoritatively, that it is the intention of Canada to grant to the people of the North-West the same free institutions which they themselves enjoy.

" Had not these unfortunate events occurred, the Canadian Government had hoped, long ere this, to have received a report from the Council, through Mr. McDougall, as to the best means of speedily organizing the Government with representative institutions.

" I hope that they will be able immediately to take up that subject, and to consider and report without delay on the general policy that should immediately be adopted.

" It is obvious that the most inexpensive mode for the administration of affairs should at first be adopted. As the preliminary expense of organizing the Government, after union with Canada, must, in the first instance, be defrayed from the Canadian treasury, there will be a natural objection in the Canadian Parliament to a large expenditure.

" As it would be unwise to subject the Government of the Territory to a recurrence of the humiliation already suffered by Governor McTavish, you can inform him that, if he organizes a local police of twenty-five men or more, if absolutely necessary, that the expense will be defrayed by the Canadian Government.

" You will be good enough to endeavour to find out Monkman, the person to whom, through Colonel Dennis, Mr. McDougall gave instructions to communicate with the Salteaux Indians. He should be asked to surrender his letter, and informed that he ought not to proceed upon it. The Canadian Government will see that he is compensated for any expense that he has already incurred.

" In case a delegation is appointed to proceed to Ottawa, you can assure them that they will be kindly received, and their suggestions fully considered. Their expenses, coming here and returning, and whilst staying in Ottawa, will be defrayed by us.

" You are authorized to state that the two years during which the present tariff shall remain undisturbed, will commence from the 1st January, 1871, instead of last January as first proposed.

" Should the question arise as to the consumption of any stores or goods belonging to the Hudson's Bay Company by the insurgents, you are authorized to inform the leaders that, if the Company's government is restored, not only will there be a general amnesty granted, but, in case the Company should claim the payment for such stores, that the Canadian Government will stand between the insurgents and all harm.

" Wishing you a prosperous journey and happy results,

" I beg to remain, with great respect,

" Your very faithful servant,

" JOHN A. MACDONALD.

" To the Right Reverend the Bishop of St. Boniface, Fort Garry."

APPENDIX XX.   (See p. 71.)

EXTRACT FROM A LETTER WRITTEN BY SIR JOHN MACDONALD, ON THE SUBJECT OF HIS ACTION IN SELECTING SIR FRANCIS HINCKS FOR THE OFFICE OF FINANCE MINISTER, DATED NOVEMBER 17, 1869.

"IN the first place, I felt myself bound in honour to carry out the coalition principle, at all events for this Parliament. The Government went to the polls in 1867, as a coalition, and received a very considerable support from that section of the Reform party that adhered to Howland and McDougall. In fact, in the western part of Ontario, a good many of our Conservative friends were elected by Reform aid, and by the split in the Reform ranks which the coalition effected.

"Howland and McDougall having both left the Government, I looked around me for their successors. After the course taken in denunciation of the coalition by McKenzie and Blake, I could not ask them to join the Government.   They would have refused, and, even if they had assented, their appointment would have been a just cause of offence to my own friends and the friends of my colleagues now in the Government.   I would then have been obliged to have taken two persons of no mark or likelihood, bringing no strength, and who would have been completely read out of the Reform party as traitors, by the *Globe* and the *Globe's* influence.

"When Hincks arrived in Canada, I felt that he was just the man I wanted.   When he left in 1854 he was Prime Minister, the head of a Reform Government, and the leader of the Reform party ; and he had more supporters in the Parliament elected that year than any other man in Canada.   His defeat was owing to a junction of the Conservatives of Upper Canada (who were there in a miserable minority) with the seceded Grits headed by Malcolm Cameron, John Rolph, and George Brown, and the Rouges of Lower Canada.   On the fall of his Government, through his instrumentality the reins of power were put into Conservative hands in the person of Sir Allan MacNab, I acting as his lieutenant ; and from that time until the last election, if the Conservatives have in fact ruled the destinies of Canada, it was owing to that coalition.   During the remainder of his stay in Canada, that is for the whole of the first session after our coming into power, Hincks behaved with all loyalty to the Government, and gave us an unswerving support.   On his return to Canada, he has found that his old Reform friends are still true to him. They have hitherto been obliged to submit in silence, from sheer lack of pluck, to the misguidance of Brown. They now know that in Hincks they will have a leader who is not afraid of him or any other man living, and the strongest proof I can give you of their desire to sustain him is shown in the fact that four undoubted Liberals in the present House of Commons, who were frightened for their lives before, offered through me to resign their seats in favour of Hincks. I will give you their names when we meet. No one felt more convinced than did Brown of the great blow to him and to his section of the Reformers that Hincks' appointment would be. He became literally frantic, and raked up all the old stories against Hincks in the most blackguard style.

"Now, before Hincks left Canada, and after he had given up place and power, he did what every honest man would do under the circumstances, he challenged a Parliamentary inquiry as to the conduct of himself and his colleagues. If you look back to the journals of that time you will find that the committee was composed of men of intelligence and undoubted honour, with the exception of Brown himself: and that committee, after a careful and full investigation (during the course of which, by the way, Hincks was treated with a good deal of unfairness), he was cleared from all moral delinquency of every kind. That decision I felt then, and feel now, to have been a just one, and I would ask you what more could any man do under the circumstances than Hincks did at that time.

"A good deal has been said in the newspapers about my expression, now become historical, about being 'steeped to the lips in corruption.' These words of mine were not applied in any way to Hincks personally, but to his whole Administration, and they were based upon the charges strongly and circumstantially made by the *Globe* and the Grit press, on the authority of Malcolm Cameron and other men who had been in the Government of Baldwin and Hincks. Now, it is a fact that every one of Hincks' colleagues, excepting James Morris, subsequently became my colleagues, and were sustained by the Conservative party, and I see no reason why he himself should be considered as under a *taboo*. Since the action of the committee in 1854–55, I have never said one word against Sir Francis. I considered that he had received a full and impartial trial, and an honourable acquittal.

"That he will add strength to the Ministry I have no doubt. A sufficient proof of that is the accession of Aikins to the Government. He was a *Grit* of the most *Grittish* stamp, and was one of those who, beguiled by Brown, voted with us and against Hincks' Government in 1854. He has told me that he has regretted that vote ever since. Now Aikins declined last year to come into the Government with McDougall alone, as he did not think that he (McDougall) was of sufficient strength or ability to lead the Reform wing of the coalition. He says now that things are all altered, that he recognizes in Sir Francis a man under whom the Reformers can rally, and has come into the Government unreservedly and unconditionally.

"The adhesion of Aikins is of great strength to Hincks and to us. He is an Irish Protestant and the representative layman of the whole Wesleyan-Methodist community, who look up to him as their political leader. With him in the Cabinet, the friends of the Government may confidently rely on getting the Methodist support at the next general elections, which, as you know, is of no little consequence in anything like a close struggle of parties. Then, again, I think sure that Hincks' course on the banking and currency questions will meet with the approbation of Western Canada. While he sees much to admire in Rose's scheme, he is not committed at all to its details, and can modify the measure in such a way as to give the country the same amount of security, and, at the same time, not hamper the banking institutions.

"For the last twelve years the cry has been, however unjust, that our currency and banking, as well as our tariffs, have always been subject to Montreal influences, and been worked to Montreal advantage. This has grown into the public mind, and it has been said that no matter what party is in the result is the same. We had either Galt or Holton or Rose. And a general belief prevails that King's resignation of the active management of the Montreal Bank is only preparatory to his making a bold push as a political financier.

"Hincks has always been and is now quite unconnected with any Montreal interests, and stands quite independent of them ; and I feel confident that the result of his action on the question will be to secure the support of the western banking institutions, and, indeed, of the eastern ones as well, who object to the enormous power of the Montreal Bank.

"There are some Conservatives who are afraid that Hincks may perhaps play his own game to their injury as a political party. I have no fears of that kind. I know him well, and believe him to be as true as steel ; and, besides, his interests lie in quite another direction, as I will explain to you when we meet.

"I may mention that I have talked this matter over with Hillyard Cameron, and those other Conservative friends that I have had the opportunity of meeting, and they all agree as to the policy of my course. Cameron says that I was bound in honour to carry out the coalition frankly, and while, of course, he recognized some of the inconveniences connected with Hincks' long absence from the country and the revived charges against him, felt so strongly the importance of his success that he wrote, while here, a letter to Deacon of Renfrew, the county master of the Orange body there, entreating him to give his support to Hincks against Findlay. D. L. McPherson, Carling, and others are enthusiastic upon the point."

APPENDIX XXI. (See p. 98.)

"The Arlington, Washington, March 25, 1871.

" My Lord,

" Availing myself of your kind permission, I now desire to state in writing the reasons why I did not concur in the proposition made by Her Majesty's High Commissioners conceding to the Americans the right of fishing in the in-shore waters of Canada, for a term of years, in exchange for the admission of coal, salt, lumber, and fish, free of duty, into the United States.

" The right of Canada to exclude Americans from fishing in the waters within the limits of three marine miles of the coast of the Dominion is free from doubt, and not contested by the Government of the United States.

" In the despatch of the Right Honourable the Secretary of State for the Colonies to the Governor General of Canada, of the 16th of February last, it is stated that Her Majesty's Government are of opinion that such right ' is beyond dispute, and can only be ceded for an adequate consideration.'

" Now the admission of the articles above referred to into the American market free of duty, is not an adequate consideration, and I believe that view will be entertained by the Government and people of Canada.

" The duties on coal and salt are certain to be repealed at the next meeting of Congress in December, as is admitted by the United States High Commissioners, and the unpopularity of these taxes is such that there is no chance of their being re-imposed. Their repeal cannot, therefore, be taken into consideration as forming any portion of an equivalent.

" The compensation proposed is, therefore, practically reduced to free fish and lumber.

" The removal of the duties on these articles, although they may be of sufficient importance to allow them to be accepted as make-weights in addition to some other substantial equivalent, cannot be considered of themselves as in any degree an adequate consideration.

" The steadily increasing price of mackerel (the chief and most valuable portion of the inshore "catch" of fish) in the markets of the United States, which has risen within a few years from some six or nine dollars to twenty-eight dollars per barrel, shows that Canada has a certain market for her fish, and that the duty is in a great measure, if not entirely, paid by the consumers. The Americans will purchase our mackerel whatever the price may be.

" So with the article of lumber. The supply from their own forests is altogether inadequate to meet the American demand, and the chief, if not the only value of the concession would be, the admission of certain inferior qualities of lumber into the United States, which is of so little value that it will scarcely bear the cost of transportation free of duty.

" Canada, therefore, by the proposed arrangement will be called upon to cede the privilege of using her fisheries without anything like an adequate consideration, and I do not think she can properly be expected to make so great a sacrifice.

" As it appears that the United States Government will not return to the free-trade arrangements of the Treaty of 1854, some other equivalent must be sought.

" The only one that suggests itself to me is a substantial payment in money in addition to the admission of the four articles referred to, free of duty.

" I therefore deem it my duty to express again to Your Lordship my strong conviction that the proposed arrangement will not be accepted by Canada, and I may add that it would be difficult for me to justify or defend it in the Canadian Parliament.

" I have the honour to be

" Your Lordship's very obedient servant,

" JOHN A. MACDONALD.

" The Right Honourable the Earl de Grey and Ripon."

" Washington, March 27, 1871.

" *Memorandum.*

" On Saturday, March 25th, at 11 a.m., I placed in Lord de Grey's hand a copy of my telegram of the 22nd instant to the Canadian Government, and of their answers of the 24th. I then stated :—

" That the proprietary rights of Canada to the fisheries were indisputable and undisputed, and that Her Majesty's Government had promised the Government of the Dominion that they would only be ceded for an adequate consideration ;

" That I did not consider that the proposition which it had been determined, after lengthened discussions, and the rejection of several other proposals, to make to the American Commissioners, namely, to cede the right of fishing in our inshore waters for a term of years in exchange for the admission of coal, salt, lumber, and fish free of duty, would give Canada an adequate consideration ;

" That the duties on coal and salt were certain to be repealed at any rate, and that the proposed compensation was therefore practically reduced to free fish and lumber ;

" That if some other substantial equivalent were given, the removal of the duties on those articles might be accepted as make-weights, but could not be considered as of themselves a sufficient compensation ;

" That the Americans would purchase our mackerel (the most important portion of the catch of fish in our waters) whatever the price might be ;

" That the case was the same with regard to lumber—that the Americans have no sufficient home-supply and therefore must buy it from us, and that the chief value of the concession to us would be the admission of certain descriptions of lumber of such inferior quality as scarcely to bear the cost of transportation free of duty ;

" That I therefore wished to be understood as not concurring in the proposition ;

" That in my opinion its adoption would be extremely distasteful to the people of Canada, and that I doubted its acceptance by the Canadian Parliament.

"JOHN A. MACDONALD."

APPENDIX XXII.   (See p. 131).

(See p. 131).

"1311 K. Street, Washington, April 27, 1871.

" MY DEAR SIR JOHN,

"I observe in the telegram from Sir George Cartier, of which you sent me a copy yesterday, a passage to the following effect :—

"'The Queen's Government have formally pledged themselves that our fisheries should not be disposed of without our consent; to force us now into a disposal of them for a sum to be fixed by arbitration and free fish would be a breach of faith and an indignity never before offered to a great British possession.'

"It is difficult to read these words without supposing that they are intended to imply that H.M. Government contemplate the adoption of some course of proceeding which would be a breach of faith with Canada, and would offer an indignity to that portion of the Queen's dominions.

"I feel bound, therefore, to let you know without delay that I distinctly deny the justice of any such charge.

"The consent of Canada is, as you know, clearly reserved in the draft articles, and the Government at home has never contemplated for a moment the admission into any treaty of provisions affecting the proprietary rights of Canada without the insertion of such a reservation.

"Believe me, my dear Sir John, yours sincerely,

"DE GREY."

"The Arlington, Washington, April 28, 1871.

" MY DEAR LORD DE GREY,

"It is quite true, as you state in your note of yesterday, that the articles relating to the fisheries do not come into force until the necessary legislation has passed the Canadian Parliament, and that therefore, if unsatisfactory to Parliament, they will never take effect.

"In that sense, therefore, I am bound to say that, while I think the turn events have taken to be unfortunate, I consider that H.M. Government may fairly hold that it has substantially saved the rights of Canada by reserving to her the ultimate decision of the matter. The right thus reserved to Canada by the treaty, however, is merely one of veto.

"The terms of settlement have, in the first place, been made by instructions from H.M. Government, not only without the consent of Canada, but against her solemn protest. The proprietary rights of the Dominion in the fisheries being admitted, the Government of Canada evidently consider that their previous assent should have been obtained in the same manner as the sanction by the Cabinet at home of the terms of the Alabama and San Juan articles was asked for and received by your Lordship.

"If, therefore, under the present arrangement the Canadian Parliament should, from a regard to its own interests, decline to sanction the treaty, Canada would, as between herself and the mother country, be placed in the invidious position of apparently thwarting the policy of the latter; whilst, as between Canada and the United States, upon Canada also would be thrown the onus of publicly repudiating the terms which I have (although vainly) sought to assure the Imperial Government and my colleagues in this Commission would be distasteful to the Dominion, and meet, in all probability, with rejection by her Parliament.

"This divergence of opinion would be taken advantage of by the United States—England would be prevented from giving the same moral support to Canada in the assertion of her rights as she has hitherto done, and the American fishermen would be encouraged and incited to pay less regard than ever to the laws of the Dominion.

"On the other hand, the Canadian people would be taught to believe that England had made their interests a matter of secondary consideration. They would be especially told so by the American press, and I need scarcely point out to your Lordship how injuriously this belief might affect the relations now happily existing between Canada and the mother country.

"In connection with this subject I beg also to remind you that the original object of the Commission has been altogether ignored in the present negotiations.

"On the 27th of July last the Colonial Secretary informed the Governor General, by despatch, that Her Majesty's Government would, in compliance with the request of Canada, propose to the Government of the United States the appointment of a Commission to settle the questions which have been so long in dispute as to the geographical limits of the exclusive fishing rights of Canada under the Treaty of 1818. This promise was carried out by Sir Edward Thornton's first letter of the 26th of January last, in which he stated the desire of Her Majesty's Government that a friendly understanding should be come to between the two Governments as to the extent of the rights which belong to the citizens of the United States and Her Majesty's subjects respectively with reference to the fisheries. Now, the present temporary arrangement, even if it should take effect, does not do away with the expediency of settling this question. If unsettled, it would be revived in its most inconvenient form at the expiration of the term, and, besides, I do not see how the value of the Canadian fisheries can be accurately estimated by the proposed arbitrators until their extent is ascertained.

"Believe me, my dear Lord de Grey,

"Faithfully yours,

"JOHN A. MACDONALD."

APPENDIX XXIII.   (See p. 136.)

"[Private.]

"Her Majesty's High Commission,
"Washington, May 6, 1871.

"MY DEAR SIR JOHN,

"I have been thinking over the conversation which took place between us yesterday, and I am anxious to repeat to you the arguments which I then employed with a view to impress upon you the importance of your name being attached to the treaty, which we hope to sign on Monday next.

"It is not necessary for that purpose that I should enter into any consideration in detail of the merits of that treaty. I believe it to be one which, taken as a whole, and regarded as it ought to be, as a broad settlement of the many differences which have lately sprung up between Great Britain and the United States, is fair and honourable to all parties, and calculated to confer very important advantages upon our respective countries. I should doubtless have desired to see it differently framed, in some parts, but all negotiations, unless carried on under the shadow of a triumphant army, are necessarily compromises, and I am convinced that the arrangement to which we have come is the best that under the conditions of the problem before us we could have secured.

"Believing this, I am naturally most anxious not to run any risk of the treaty being rejected by the Senate, and I cannot doubt that the absence of your signature would lead to that result. It would be a very serious matter if the signature of any member of the Commission were wanting, but any of our names could, I think, be more safely spared than yours.

"It appears to me, therefore, that you would incur a responsibility of the gravest kind if you were to withhold your signature ; such a step, moreover, would not only be one involving in all probability consequences very greatly to be deprecated, but it would, as it seems to me, be inconsistent with your position as a member of the Joint High Commission. We of the English portion of the Commission are not separate members of a conference acting each by himself, but we are jointly the plenipotentiaries of our Sovereign, bound by the instructions which we receive from Her Majesty's Government, and directed now to sign this treaty.

"I hold, therefore, that it is our clear duty to sign; that we act under the orders of our Government, and that, in the position which we occupy, we should not be justified in disobeying those orders. I trust that, under these circumstances, you will see the great importance, and indeed, as I believe, the absolute necessity of your not separating yourself from your colleagues in the signature of the treaty, and

       " I remain, yours sincerely,

                     "DE GREY."

APPENDIX XXIV.   (See p. 151.)

"I do not desire to anticipate the full and ample discussion which Parliament will give to England's recent diplomatic efforts to buy her own peace at the sacrifice of our interests, or of that comedy of errors into which she has blundered; but this I may say, that the time is rapidly approaching when Canadians and Englishmen must have a clear and distinct understanding as to the hopes and obligations of the future. If Imperial policy is to cover the whole ground, upon the faith of which our forefathers settled and improved, then let that be understood, and we know what to do. But if 'shadows, clouds, and darkness' are to rest upon the future—if thirty millions of Britons are to hoard their 'rascal counters' within two small islands, gather round them the troops and war-ships of the Empire, and leave four millions of Britons to face forty millions, and to defend a frontier of three thousand miles, then let us know what they are at, and our future policy will be governed by that knowledge. No Cabinet has yet dared to shape this thought and give it utterance. Leading newspapers have told us that our presence within the Empire is a source of danger, and that the time for separation is approaching, if it has not already come. Noble Lords and erudite Commoners have sneeringly told us that we may go when we are inclined. As yet, neither the Crown, the Parliament, nor the people of England have deliberately avowed this policy of dismemberment, although the tendency of English thought and legislation daily deepens the conviction that the drift is all that way. We must wait, my young friends, for further developments, not without anxiety for the future, but with a firm reliance on the goodness of Providence, and on our own ability so to shape the policy of our country as to protect her by our wit, should Englishmen, unmindful of the past, repudiate their national obligations."

APPENDIX XXV. (See p. 156.)

Thus on the 9th of November, 1872, he writes :—

"I am happy to say that I continue to improve in my health. I am undergoing a daily medical treatment, and the milk diet. I read with great interest the correspondence about the Pacific Railway."

"*Nov.* 16*th.*—Many thanks for your kind letter. I shan't fail to give you every week news about my progress, and other matters going on here. About the tea and coffee matter, I had, yesterday, with Lord Kimberley a protracted discussion."

"*Nov.* 23*rd.*—I feel happy to tell you that Doctor Johnson says I continue to improve in health. Lord Kimberley sent for me on Thursday to talk over matters."

"*Nov.* 30*th.*—You will be pleased to hear I continue to progress with regard to the state of my health. However, I feel very tired in living a life of doing nothing."

"*Dec.* 5*th.*—I have again to tell you I continue to improve in my health. The fact is, I do everything possible to obtain my cure as soon as possible. I wish I was near you to assist you in all your troubles."

"*Dec.* 14*th.*—Have nothing new to report to you since my last, except that I continue to improve under the same milk diet and medical treatment. Tell me in your next when you expect to convene our Parliament. Will you be ready for the middle of February or the middle of March? If you call Parliament at this latter period, I hope I shall be well enough to return to Ottawa during the session, to be on the spot to assist you with all my might. The weather has been awful here since my arrival. I do not think I have been able to take a little walk more than ten times since my arrival. It rained or was cold nearly every day. I feel pretty well, but weak."

"*Dec.* 28*th.*—I continue on improving. I obey my doctor most loyally. I wish so much to be able to return to assist you."

"*Jan.* 11, 1873.—I continue to progress in my health. Many thanks for your kind letters. I feel pleased at what you say of my success."

"*Jan* 18*th.*—I saw Dr. Johnson yesterday. He continues to be satisfied with the progress I am making. If there is anything about which it might be useful I should speak to Lord Kimberley, let me know of it as soon as possible. I saw Lord Monck on Tuesday, etc."

"*Jan.* 25*th.*—I had a long interview on Thursday last with Lord Kimberley, etc."

" *Feb. 1st.*—Many thanks for your 'cable.' I am glad Parliament will only meet in March. I hope it will enable me to attend a portion of the session."

" *Feb. 15th.*—I have just had a long visit from Lord Lisgar. He is to write me a letter about what happened at the interview given to Father Ritehot, which I shall send you by next mail accompanied with a statement of mine. No promise was made of an amnesty. Always bear in mind that throughout we stated that the amnesty was not a question for us but for the Queen."

" *March 22nd.*—I am happy to tell you I continue to improve daily. Cauchon makes a great mistake in leaving us. I dine to-morrow with Lord Granville, and I am sure we will have a talk over Canadian matters."

" *March 29th.*—I still continue progressing, and I hope to be able to sail on the 20th or 25th of April. . . . . Lady Cartier and myself dined on Wednesday last with the Prince and Princess of Wales. Both were very gracious to me. The Prince asked me to go and see him to-morrow at three, to have ' a chat,' as he said, ' over Canada.' "

" *April 5th.*—Thanks for your 'cablegram' of day before yesterday, which I at once sent over to Rose. . . . Dr. Johnson says I am still improving, and if I continue to thus improve there will no impediment to my sailing for Canada in the beginning of May. I was gratified to hear him thus speaking. As I had been requested, I called to see the Prince of Wales on Sunday last. He received me very kindly and graciously. He inquired minutely about my health and Canadian matters. He takes great interest in our doings. He said he might again visit Canada. His five children were around him at the time of my visit. It was a pleasant sight to see him surrounded by his family."

" *April 19th.*—I saw Dr. Johnson yesterday, who says I have improved favourably, though I was kept back by a cold, which I caught during the Holy Week. I am getting rid of it pretty fast now."

" *April 22nd.*—I have not much to tell you to-day beyond the good news about myself, that I continue improving. I expect I shall be able to sail on the 8th of May."

" *April 26th.*—My health continues improving. I saw Dr. Johnson yesterday, who again told me I will be able to sail on the 15th of May, if the weather gets warmer."

" *May 3rd.*—I saw Dr. Johnson yesterday. I feel happy to tell you he finds I am continuing to improve. I thought of sailing on the 15th of this month, but I will delay my departure until the 22nd or 29th. I will attend with Lady Cartier and the girls a State concert at Buckingham Palace on the 14th inst."

" *May 10th.*—I saw Dr. Johnson yesterday. He is satisfied with the state of my health, though the cold weather we are still having here works against my progress. My kind regards to our colleagues and to Lady Macdonald and, my dear Macdonald,

" Believe me, as always,
" Your devoted colleague,
" GEO. ET. CARTIER."

" MY DEAR MACDONALD,

"I telegraphed you this morning the sad news of the death of our old friend and colleague, and, as I know you and his many friends would like to have such particulars as I can give of his last days, I now send them to you.

"Up to Tuesday last he appeared cheerful and well, but I had often remarked an increase in nervousness, and that lately he was more easily fatigued than usual. He was looking forward with great interest to sailing on the 29th, and to going back to Canada again. On Tuesday, however, he complained of a pain in his stomach, and feebleness, and something like inflammation of the bowels set in. Dr. Johnson told me that in such a disease it was impossible to say where inflammation might strike. He, however, partially rallied, and on Thursday last was pretty well again. I sat with him for some time on Saturday, when he was less well, and I observed a very great change in his appearance. He talked with his usual interest of all public affairs in Canada, and fully hoped to be well enough to leave on the 29th. My own fears, however, on leaving him on Saturday, were very great, and I thought of telegraphing to you, but felt that it could do no good. On Sunday I called, but did not see him, and yesterday morning I got a telegram from Lady Cartier saying he was worse. I immediately went to see him, and there was a consultation between Dr. Johnson and Sir Thomas Watson, for the result of which I waited. They told me the case was very grave indeed, but they did not anticipate any immediate danger, although they stated that the inflammatory symptoms were very alarming, and if they did not soon cease he had not strength to pull through. At this time his stomach was very much swollen and his mind wandering a little, and he was occasionally in very great pain. In all his wanderings his mind seemed to dwell on public affairs, and on going back to Canada. I left the house yesterday evening, intending to call again early this morning, but about seven o'clock I got a telegram announcing that he had breathed his last. I immediately went to Lady Cartier, who expressed a wish that his remains should be sent over to Canada as speedily as possible, which I understood to be in consonance with Cartier's own desire. I also made the necessary arrangements in accordance with her particular wish, with regard to having the body embalmed, and forwarded to Liverpool, whence it will go by the steamer on Thursday week. Lady Cartier and the daughters would prefer not going in the same steamer, and they will probably go either by the previous or succeeding ship.

"His servant Thomas has been most attached to him throughout, and done everything for him. I am sure it will be a satisfaction to you to know that everything that skill and care could do for him was done, but his feebleness was quite unable to cope with the phase which the disease assumed. The physicians did not last night anticipate so early a fatal termination, and had arranged for another consultation this morning. The service will be performed quietly and respectably in the course of a few days. Lady Cartier and her daughters are quite satisfied with all the arrangements and I will see that everything is done to relieve them from care and anxiety. They are much cut up with the suddenness of the event, although they were prepared since last Tuesday to expect that the worst might soon arrive.

"I will not say how deeply I personally feel the loss of so dear a friend and colleague, one with whom both our associations have been of so uniformly kind a character. It will be a long time before we look on his like again in Canada, and the country has to deplore the loss of a most devoted and efficient public servant. I need not write to you more in this way. I am quite sure that you and all his colleagues feel as deeply as I do the loss of our old friend.

" Believe me ever

" Yours sincerely,

" JOHN ROSE.

" Right Hon. Sir John A. Macdonald, K.C.B., Ottawa."

Hon. Mr. Huntingdon moved, " that Mr. Huntingdon, a member of this House, having stated in his place, that he is credibly informed and believes that he can establish by satisfactory evidence,—

" That in anticipation of the legislation of last session, as to the Pacific Railway, an agreement was made between Sir Hugh Allan, acting for himself, and certain other Canadian promoters, and G. W. McMullen, acting for certain United States capitalists, whereby the latter agreed to furnish all the funds necessary for the construction of the contemplated railway, and to give the former a certain percentage of interest, in consideration of their interest and position, the scheme agreed on being ostensibly that of a Canadian company with Sir Hugh Allan at its head,—

" That the Government were aware that negotiations were pending between these parties,—

" That subsequently, an understanding was come to between the Government and Sir Hugh Allan and Mr. Abbott, M.P., that Sir Hugh Allan and his friends should advance a large sum of money for the purpose of aiding the elections of Ministers and their supporters at the ensuing general election, and that he and his friends should receive the contract for the construction of the railway,—

" That accordingly Sir Hugh Allan did advance a large sum of money for the purpose mentioned, and, at the solicitation, and under the pressing instances of Ministers,—

" That part of the moneys, expended by Sir Hugh Allan in connection with the obtaining of the Act of Incorporation and Charter, were paid to him by the said United States capitalists under the agreement with him,—it is

" Ordered, that a committee of seven members be appointed to inquire into all the circumstances connected with the negotiations for the construction of the Pacific Railway, with the legislation of last session on the subject, and with the granting of the Charter to Sir Hugh Allan, and others; with power to send for persons, papers, and records; and with instructions to report in full the evidence taken before, and all proceedings of said committee."

APPENDIX XXVII.   (See p. 240.)

APPENDIX XXVII.   (See p. 240.)

PROPOSED TABLE OF PRECEDENCE.

1. The Governor General.

2. Members of the Cabinet, according to seniority.

3. The Lieutenant Governors of Provinces and of the North-West Territories, according to seniority.

4. Members of the Privy Council, not of the Cabinet, according to seniority.

5. Archbishops and Bishops, according to seniority.

6. The Moderator of the Presbyterian Church in Canada, and the General Superintendent of the Methodist Church in Canada, according to seniority.

7. The Chief Justice of the Supreme Court of Canada.

8. General Officers of Her Majesty's Army serving in the Dominion; the Officer commanding the Canadian Militia and Officers of the rank of Admiral in the Royal Navy serving on the British North American or on the Pacific stations.   The relative rank of such Officers to be determined by the Queen's Regulations.

9. The Speaker of the Senate.

10. The Speaker of the House of Commons.

11. The Chief Judges of the Courts of Law and Equity of the several Provinces, according to seniority.

12. Retired Lieutenant Governors of Provinces.

13. Members of the Senate.

14. Puisné Judges of the Supreme Court of Canada, according to seniority.

15. Puisné Judges of the Courts of Law and Equity of the several Provinces, according to seniority.

16. Members of the House of Commons.

17. Members of the Executive Councils, within their Provinces.

18. The Speakers of the Legislative Councils, within their Provinces.

19. The Speakers of the Legislative Assemblies, within their Provinces.

20. Members of the Legislative Councils, within their Provinces.

21. Members of the Legislative Assemblies, within their Provinces.

22. Retired Judges of whatever Courts, to take precedence next after the present Judges of their respective Courts.

TABLE OF TITLES.

As at present, save that a clause should be added giving the title of " Honourable " to the Speaker of the House of Commons for the time being.

Ottawa, December 21, 1885.

APPENDIX XXVIII. (See p. 257.)

(See p. 257.)

Sir John Macdonald's Last Address to the People of Canada.

" To the Electors of Canada.

" Gentlemen,

"The momentous questions now engaging public attention having, in the opinion of the Ministry, reached that stage when it is desirable that an opportunity should be given to the people of expressing, at the polls, their views thereon, the Governor General has been advised to terminate the existence of the present House of Commons, and to issue writs summoning a new Parliament. This advice His Excellency has seen fit to approve, and you, therefore, will be called upon within a short time to elect members to represent you in the great council of the nation. I shall be a candidate for the representation of my old constituency, the city of Kingston.

"In soliciting at your hands a renewal of the confidence which I have enjoyed, as a Minister of the Crown, for thirty years, it is, I think, convenient that I should take advantage of the occasion to define the attitude of the Government, in which I am First Minister, towards the leading political issues of the day.

"As in 1878, in 1882, and again in 1887, so in 1891, do questions relating to the trade and commerce of the country occupy a foremost place in the public mind. Our policy in respect thereto is to-day what it has been for the past thirteen years, and is directed by a firm determination to foster and develop the varied resources of the Dominion, by every means in our power, consistent with Canada's position as an integral portion of the British Empire. To that end we have laboured in the past, and we propose to continue in the work to which we have applied ourselves, of building up on this continent, under the flag of England, a great and powerful nation.

"When, in 1878, we were called upon to administer the affairs of the Dominion, Canada occupied a position in the eyes of the world very different from that which she enjoys to-day. At that time a profound depression hung like a pall over the whole country, from the Atlantic Ocean to the western limits of the province of Ontario, beyond which to the Rocky Mountains stretched a vast and almost unknown wilderness. Trade was depressed, manufactures languished, and, exposed to ruinous competition, Canadians were fast sinking into the position of being mere hewers of wood and drawers of water for the great nation dwelling to the south of us. We determined to change this unhappy state of things. We felt that Canada, with its agricultural resources, rich in its fisheries, timber, and mineral wealth, was worthy of a nobler position than that of being a slaughter market for the United States. We said to the Americans : ' We are perfectly willing to trade with you on equal terms. We are desirous of having a fair reciprocity treaty, but we will not consent to open our markets to you while yours remain closed to us.' So we inaugurated the National Policy. You all know what followed. Almost as if by magic, the whole face of the country underwent a change. Stagnation and apathy and gloom—ay, and want and misery too—gave place to activity and enterprise and prosperity. The miners of Nova Scotia took courage ; the manufacturing industries in our great centres revived and multiplied; the farmer found a market for his produce, the artisan and labourer employment at good wages, and all Canada rejoiced under the quickening impulse of a new-found life. The age of deficits was past, and an overflowing treasury gave to the Government the means of carrying forward those great works necessary to the realization of our purpose to make this country a homogeneous whole.

" To that end we undertook that stupendous work, the Canadian Pacific Railway. Undeterred by the pessimistic views of our opponents—nay, in spite of their strenuous, and even malignant opposition, we pushed forward that great enterprise through the wilds north of Lake Superior, across the western prairies, over the Rocky Mountains to the shores of the Pacific, with such inflexible resolution, that, in seven years after the assumption of office by the present Administration, the dream of our public men was an accomplished fact, and I myself experienced the proud satisfaction of looking back from the steps of my car upon the Rocky Mountains fringing the eastern sky. The Canadian Pacific Railway now extends from ocean to ocean, opening up and developing the country at a marvellous rate, and forming an Imperial highway to the east, over which the trade of the Indies is destined to reach the markets of Europe. We have subsidized steamship lines on both oceans—to Europe, China, Japan, Australia, and the West Indies. We have spent millions on the extension and improvement of our canal system. We have, by liberal grants of subsidies, promoted the building of railways, now become an absolute necessity, until the whole country is covered as with a network ; and we have done all this with such prudence and caution, that our credit in the money market of the world is higher to-day than it has ever been, and the rate of interest on our debt, which is a true measure of the public burdens, is less than it was when we took office in 1878.

" During all this time what has been the attitude of the Reform Party ? Vacillating in their policy and inconstancy itself as regards their leaders, they have, at least, been consistent in this particular, that they have uniformly opposed every measure which had for its object the development of our common country. The National Policy was a failure before it had been tried. Under it we could not possibly raise a revenue sufficient for the public require-ments. Time exposed that fallacy. Then we were to pay more for the home-manufactured article than we used to when we bought everything abroad. We were to be the prey of rings and monopolies, and the manufacturers were to extort their own prices. When these fears had been proved unfounded, we were assured that over-competition would inevitably prove the ruin of the manufacturing industries, and thus bring about a state of affairs worse than that which the National Policy had been designed to meet. It was the same with the Canadian Pacific Railway. The whole project, according to our opponents, was a chimera. The engineering difficulties were insuperable, the road, even if constructed, would never pay. Well, gentlemen, the project was feasible, the engineering difficulties were overcome, and the road does pay. Disappointed by the failure of all their predictions, and convinced that nothing is to be gained by further opposition on the old lines, the Reform Party has taken a new departure, and has announced its policy to be Unrestricted Reciprocity—that is (as defined by its author, Mr. Wiman, in the *North American Review* a few days ago), free-trade with the United States, and a common tariff with the United States against the rest of the world. The adoption of this policy would involve, among other grave evils, discrimination against the mother country. This fact is admitted by no less a personage than Sir Richard Cartwright, who, in his speech at Pembroke on October 21, 1890, is reported to have said: ' Some men, whose opinions I respect, entertain objections to this (Unrestricted Reciprocity) proposition. They argue, and argue with force, that it will be necessary for us, if we enter into such an arrangement, to admit the goods of the United States on more favourable terms than those of the mother country. Nor do I deny that that is an objection, and not a light one.'

"It would, in my opinion, inevitably result in the annexation of this Dominion to the United States. The advocates of Unrestricted Reciprocity on this side of the line deny that it would have such an effect, though its friends in the United States urge, as the chief reason for its adoption, that Unrestricted Reciprocity would be the first step in the direction of Political Union. There is, however, one obvious consequence of this scheme which nobody has the hardihood to dispute, and that is, that Unrestricted Reciprocity would necessitate the imposition of direct taxation amounting to not less than fourteen millions of dollars annually upon the people of this country. This fact is clearly set forth in a remarkable letter, addressed a few days ago by Mr. E. W. Thomson—a Radical and free-trader—to the Toronto *Globe*, on the staff of which paper he was lately an editorial writer, which the *Globe*, with characteristic unfairness, refused to publish, but which, nevertheless, reached the public through another source. Mr. Thomson points out, with great clearness, that the loss of customs revenue levied upon articles now entering this country from the United States, in the event of the adoption of the policy of Unrestricted Reciprocity, would amount to not less than seven millions of dollars annually. Moreover, this by no means represents the total loss to the revenue which the adoption of such a policy would entail. If American manufactures now compete favourably with British goods, despite an equal duty, what do you suppose would happen if the duty were removed from the American, and retained, or as is very probable, increased, on the British articles? Would not the inevitable result be a displacement of the duty-paying goods of the mother country by those of the United States? And this would mean an additional loss to the revenue of many millions more.

"Electors of Canada, I appeal to you to consider well the full meaning of this proposition. You—I speak now more particularly to the people of this province of Ontario—are already taxed directly for school purposes, for township purposes, for county purposes; while to the provincial Government there is expressly given by the constitution the right to impose direct taxation. This latter evil you have so far escaped, but as the material resources of the province diminish, as they are now diminishing, the local Government will be driven to supplement its revenue derived from fixed sources by a direct tax. And is not this enough, think you, without your being called on by a Dominion tax-gatherer, with a yearly demand of $15 a family, to meet the obligations of the central Government?

"Gentlemen, this is what Unrestricted Reciprocity involves. Do you like the prospect? This is what we are opposing, and what we ask you to condemn by your votes. Under our present system a man may largely determine the amount of his contributions to the Dominion exchequer. The amount of the tax is always in direct proportion to his means. If he is rich, and can afford to drink champagne, he has to pay a tax of $1.50 for every bottle he buys. If he be a poor man, he contents himself with a cup of tea, on which there is no duty. And so on all through the list. If he is able to afford all manner of luxuries, he pays a large sum into the coffers of the Government. If he is a man of moderate means, and able to enjoy an occasional luxury, he pays accordingly. If he is a poor man his contributions to the treasury are reduced to a minimum. With direct taxation, no matter what may be the pecuniary position of the taxpayer—times may be hard, crops may have failed, sickness or other calamity may have fallen on the family, still the inexorable tax-collector comes and exacts his tribute. Does not ours seem to be the more equitable plan? It is the one under which we have lived and thrived, and to which the Government I lead proposes to adhere.

"I have pointed out to you a few of the material objections to this scheme of Unrestricted Reciprocity, to which Mr. Laurier and Sir Richard Cartwright have committed the Liberal party, but they are not the only objections, nor in my opinion are they the most vital. For a century and a half this country has grown and flourished under the protecting aegis of the British Crown. The gallant race who first bore to our shores the blessings of civilization passed by an easy transition from French to English rule, and now form one of the most law-abiding portions of the community. These pioneers were speedily recruited by the advent of a loyal band of British subjects, who gave up everything that men most prize, and were content to begin life anew in the wilderness rather than forego allegiance to their Sovereign. To the descendants of these men, and of the multitude of Englishmen, Irishmen, and Scotchmen who emigrated to Canada, that they might build up new homes without ceasing to be British subjects—to you Canadians I appeal, and I ask you what have you to gain by surrendering that which your fathers held most dear? Under the broad folds of the Union Jack, we enjoy the most ample liberty to govern ourselves as we please, and at the same time we participate in the advantages which flow from association with the mightiest Empire the world has ever seen. Not only are we free to manage our domestic concerns, but, practically, we possess the privilege of making our own treaties with foreign countries, and, in our relations with the outside world, we enjoy the prestige inspired by a consciousness of the fact that behind us towers the majesty of England. The question which you will shortly be called upon to determine resolves itself into this; shall we endanger our possession of the great heritage bequeathed to us by our fathers, and submit ourselves to direct taxation for the privilege of having our tariff fixed at Washington, with a prospect of ultimately becoming a portion of the American Union? I commend these issues to your determination, and to the judgment of the whole people of Canada, with an unclouded confidence that you will proclaim to the world your resolve to show yourselves not unworthy of the proud distinction that you enjoy, of being numbered among the most dutiful and loyal subjects of our beloved Queen.

"As for myself, my course is clear. A British subject I was born—a British subject I will die. With my utmost effort, with my latest breath, will I oppose the ' veiled treason ' which attempts by sordid means and mercenary proffers to lure our people from their allegiance. During my long public service of nearly half a century, I have been true to my country and its best interests, and I appeal with equal confidence to the men who have trusted me in the past, and to the young hope of the country, with whom rests its destinies for the future, to give me their united and strenuous aid in this, my last effort, for the unity of the Empire and the preservation of our commercial and political freedom.

"I remain, gentlemen,
"Your faithful servant,
"JOHN A. MACDONALD.

" Earnscliffe, Ottawa, February 7, 1891."

APPENDIX XXIX. (See p. 263).

(See p. 263).

SPEECH DELIVERED BY SIR HECTOR LANGEVIN ON THE OCCASION OF THE ANNOUNCEMENT OF THE DEATH OF SIR JOHN MACDONALD TO THE HOUSE OF COMMONS, JUNE 8, 1891.

MR. SPEAKER; having to announce to the House the sad event that has been known for two days now, I was afraid I could not trust to my memory, and I, therefore, thought it desirable to place in writing what I wished to say. Accordingly, I will now read the observations I desire to offer. Mr. Speaker, as the oldest Privy Councillor it falls to my lot to announce to the House that our dear old chief, the First Minister of Canada, is no more. After a painful illness of two weeks, death put an end to his earthly career on Saturday evening last. To tell you, Mr. Speaker, my feelings under the circumstances is more than I can do. I feel that, by the death of Sir John A. Macdonald, Canada has lost its greatest statesman, a great patriot, a man of whom any country in the world would be justly proud. Her Gracious Majesty the Queen never had a more devoted and loyal subject than the grand old man, whose loss we all deplore and regret from the bottom of our hearts. For nearly fifty years he has directed the public affairs of this country. He was among the Fathers of Confederation the most prominent and distinguished. He put his whole soul into that great undertaking, knowing full well that the confederation of all the British North American provinces would give to our people a country and institutions to be proud of, and to the Empire not only a right arm, but a great and safe highway to her Indian and other possessions. He told me more than once how grateful he was to the people of Canada to have allowed him to have consolidated that great work. The fact is, his love for Canada was equal to that he had for his own mother country. Mr. Speaker, when the historians of Canada write the history of the last fifty years, they will have to write the life of Sir John A. Macdonald, and, in writing his life, they may not agree with all his public acts, but they cannot fail to say that he was a great man, a most distinguished statesman, and that his whole life was spent in the service of his country, dying in the midst of his official duty, not having had a day's rest before he passed to a better world. I need not express, Mr. Speaker, my own personal feelings. Having spent half of my life with him as his follower and as his friend, his departure is the same as if I lost half of my existence. I remember how devoted he was, not only to the old province of Canada, but how chivalrous he showed himself to the province of Quebec, and specially to my French Canadian countrymen. He had only to say a word, and, instead of being at the head of a small band of seventeen Upper Canada members, he would have had all the representatives of his province behind him. But, as he told me several times, he preferred to be just to his French compatriots and allies, and the result was that, when Confederation came, the province of Quebec had confidence in him, and on his death-bed our great chief could see that his just policy has secured peace and happiness to all. Mr. Speaker, I should have wished to continue to speak of our dear departed friend, and spoken to you about his goodness of heart, the witness of which I have been so often, but I feel that I must stop; my heart is full of tears. I cannot proceed further."

(See p. 263.)

SPEECH DELIVERED BY THE HON. MR. LAURIER, LEADER OF THE OPPOSITION
IN THE HOUSE OF COMMONS, ON THE OCCASION OF THE ANNOUNCEMENT
OF THE DEATH OF SIR JOHN MACDONALD, JUNE 8, 1891.

" MR. SPEAKER ; I fully realize the emotion which chokes the hon. gentleman.
His silence, under the circumstances, is far more eloquent than any human
language can be.   I fully appreciate the intensity of the grief which fills the
souls of all those who were the friends and followers of Sir John Macdonald,
at the loss of the great leader whose whole life has been so closely identified
with their party, a party upon which he has thrown such brilliancy and
lustre.   We on this side of the House, who were his opponents, who did not
believe in his policy, nor in his methods of government—we take our full
share of their grief—for the loss which they deplore to-day is far and away
beyond and above the ordinary compass of party range.   It is in every respect a
great national loss, for he is no more who was, in many respects, Canada's most
illustrious son, and in every sense Canada's foremost citizen and statesman.
At the period of life to which Sir John Macdonald had arrived, death, whenever it comes, cannot be said to come unexpectedly.   Some few months ago,
during the turmoil of the late election, when the country was made aware
that on a certain day the physical strength of the veteran Premier had not
been equal to his courage, and that his intense labour for the time being had
prostrated his singularly wiry frame, everybody, with the exception, perhaps,
of his buoyant self, was painfully anxious lest perhaps the angel of death had
touched him with his wing.   When, a few days ago, in the heat of an angry
discussion in this Parliament, news spread in this House that of a sudden his
condition had become alarming, the surging waves of angry discussion were
at once hushed, and every one, friend and foe, realized that this time for a
certainty the angel of death had appeared, and had crossed the threshold of
his home.   Thus we were not taken by surprise, and, although we were prepared
for the sad event, yet it is almost impossible to convince the unwilling mind
that it is true that Sir John Macdonald is no more, that the chair which we
now see empty shall remain for ever vacant, that the face so familiar in this
Parliament for the last forty years shall be seen no more, and that the voice
so well known shall be heard no more, whether in solemn debate or in
pleasant and mirthful tones.   In fact, the place of Sir John Macdonald in this
country was so large and so absorbing that it is almost impossible to conceive

that the political life of this country, the fate of this country, can continue without him. His loss overwhelms us. For my part, I say with all truth his loss overwhelms me, and it also overwhelms this Parliament, as if indeed one of the institutions of the land had given way. Sir John Macdonald now belongs to the ages, and it can be said with certainty, that the career which has just been closed is one of the most remarkable careers of this century. It would be premature at this time to attempt to fix or anticipate what will be the final judgment of history upon him ; but there were in his career and in his life features so prominent and so conspicuous, that already they shine with a glow which time cannot alter, which even now appear before the eye, such as they will appear to the end in history. I think it can be asserted that, for the supreme art of governing men, Sir John Macdonald was gifted as few men in any land or in any age were gifted—gifted with the most high of all qualities, qualities which would have made him famous wherever exercised, and which would have shone all the more conspicuously the larger the theatre. The fact that he could congregate together elements the most heterogeneous and blend them into one compact party, and to the end of his life keep them steadily under his hand, is perhaps altogether unprecedented. The fact that during all those years he retained unimpaired not only the confidence, but the devotion—the ardent devotion and affection of his party, is evidence that, besides those higher qualities of statesmanship to which we were the daily witnesses, he was also endowed with those inner, subtle, undefinable graces of soul which win and keep the hearts of men. As to his statesmanship, it is written in the history of Canada. It may be said without any exaggeration whatever, that the life of Sir John Macdonald, from the date he entered Parliament, is the history of Canada, for he was connected and associated with all the events, all the facts which brought Canada from the position it then occupied—the position of two small provinces, having nothing in common but their common allegiance, united by a bond of paper, and united by nothing else—to the present state of development which Canada has reached. Although my political views compel me to say that, in my judgment, his actions were not always the best that could have been taken in the interest of Canada, although my conscience compels me to say that of late he has imputed to his opponents motives which I must say in my heart he has misconceived, yet I am only too glad here to sink these differences, and to remember only the great services he has performed for our country—to remember that his actions always displayed great originality of view, unbounded fertility of resource, a high level of intellectual conception, and, above all, a far-reaching vision beyond the event of the day, and still higher, permeating the whole, a broad patriotism—a devotion to Canada's welfare, Canada's advancement, and Canada's glory. The life of a statesman is always an arduous one, and very often it is an ungrateful one. More often than otherwise his actions do not mature until he is in his grave. Not so, however, in the case of Sir John Macdonald. His career has been a singularly fortunate one. His reverses were few and of short duration. He was fond of power, and, in my judgment, if I may say so, that may be the turning-point of the judgment of history. He was fond of power, and he never made any secret of it. Many times we have heard him avow it on the floor of this Parliament, and his ambition in this respect was gratified as, perhaps, no other man's ambition ever was. In my judgment, even the career of William Pitt can hardly compare with that of Sir John Macdonald in this respect; for although William Pitt, moving in a higher sphere, had to deal with problems greater than our problems, yet I doubt if in the intricate management of a party William Pitt had to contend with difficulties equal to those that Sir John Macdonald had to contend with. In his death, too, he seems to have been singularly happy. Twenty years ago I was told, by one who at that time was a close personal and political friend of Sir John Macdonald, that in the intimacy of his domestic circle he was fond of repeating that his end would be as the end of Lord Chatham—that he would be carried away from the floor of Parliament to die. How true that vision into the future was we now know, for we saw him to the last with enfeebled health and declining strength struggling on the floor of Parliament until the hand of fate pinned him to his bed to die. And thus to die with his armour on was probably his ambition. Sir, death is the law, the supreme law. Although we see it every day in every form, although session after session we have seen it in this Parliament striking right and left without any discrimination as to age or station, yet the ever-recurring spectacle does not in any way remove the bitterness of the sting. Death always carries with it an incredible sense of pain; but the one thing sad in death is that which is involved in the word separation—separation from all we love in life. This is what makes death so poignant when it strikes a man of intellect in middle age. But when death is the natural termination of a full life, in which he who disappears has given the full measure of his capacity, has performed everything required from him, and more, the sadness of death is not for him who goes, but for those who loved him and remain. In this sense I am sure the Canadian people will extend unbounded sympathy to the friends of Sir John Macdonald—to his sorrowing children, and, above all, to the brave and noble woman, his companion in life and his chief helpmate. Thus, Mr. Speaker, one after another we see those who have been instrumental in bringing Canada to its present stage of development, removed from amongst us. To-day, we deplore the loss of him who, we all unite in saying, was the foremost Canadian of his time, and who filled the largest place in Canadian history. Only last week, was buried in the city of Montreal, another son of Canada, one who at one time had been a tower of strength to the Liberal party, one who will ever be remembered as one of the noblest, purest, and greatest characters that Canada has ever produced, Sir Antoine Aimé Dorion. Sir Antoine Aimé Dorion had not been in favour of Confederation. Not that he was opposed to the principle ; but he believed that the Union of these provinces, at that day, was premature. When, however, Confederation had become a fact, he gave the best of his mind and heart to make it a success. It may indeed happen, sir, that when the Canadian people see the ranks thus gradually reduced and thinned of those upon whom they have been in the habit of relying for guidance, that a feeling of apprehension will creep into the heart lest, perhaps, the institutions of Canada may be imperilled. Before the grave of him who, above all, was the father of Confederation, let not grief be barren grief; but let grief be coupled with the resolution, the determination that the work in which Liberals and Conservatives, in which Brown and Macdonald united, shall not perish, but that though united Canada may be deprived of the services of her greatest men, still Canada shall and will live."

APPENDIX XXXI. (See p. 266.)

(See p. 266.)

SPEECH DELIVERED BY THE RIGHT HONOURABLE SIR JOHN THOMPSON, K.C.M.G., PRIME MINISTER OF CANADA, ON THE OCCASION OF THE UNVEILING OF A STATUE TO SIR JOHN MACDONALD, AT HAMILTON, ONTARIO, ON THE 1ST OF NOVEMBER, 1893.

"I HAVE unveiled the image of one of the most illustrious men of our generation. I have spoken of this being the first statue erected to his honour in Canada, but before it had been erected his bust had been unveiled in the cathedral of St. Paul's in the heart of England, as the memorial of one whose services to the Empire deserved to be ranked with those of Wellington and Nelson. These 'lords of war,' as Lord Rosebery said, 'preserved the Empire.' Sir John Macdonald accomplished no less in his labours to consolidate that Empire. As time goes on other statues will be raised to his memory in various parts of Canada, and yet the grandest thing for his memory will be that his fame needs no monument to extend or to preserve it. At the time of his death it was poetically and truthfully said, 'His work—a nation—stands his monument.' Of no man of any period can it be more truly said that he was the father and founder of his country. After a lapse of some years, when political asperities have ceased to mar the true estimate of the man, this will no longer be a point on which Canadians shall differ. His life was one of incessant political warfare; much of it was passed in times when the bitterness of strife between public men was far greater than it is to-day, and yet, from the moment of his death, the leaders of the party to which he was opposed have spoken generously of his great public services, his great devotion to the interests of his country, and his wonderful hold on the affections of the people. One of those leaders I am glad to see here to-day—and I am sure it will be gratifying to him—at an age when long public life has brought its only sure gift, a crown of grey hairs, to lay a flower on the monument of the statesman who was his personal and professional friend, although for long years his political opponent. The history of Sir John Macdonald is the history of a long and successful struggle with the greatest difficulties which government in the colonies has presented during the past fifty years. Of these difficulties the statesmen of older countries have but a very faint idea. In Canada they seem to have been greater than anywhere else. His earlier life was passed in a province where the scope of political ambition was confined to that province. The difficulties of its government had been such that to make administration possible it had to be divided, then reunited, and seemed likely to be divided again. The vast country to the west of her borders was a region of romance and rare adventure. With the provinces to the east communication was so difficult that a letter took weeks to reach its destination. Practically they were as remote as Europe is from us to-day, but Sir John lived to see, as the fruits of work in which he took a leading part, nearly all British North America united under one system of government, and connected by railways and other means of communication unequalled in their completeness in any part of the world. He saw the vast regions of the North-West held as the great domain of Canada, and traversed by railways east and west, and north and south. In the province of Canada there were burning questions about which half the population had taken up arms against the other half, and were ready to do so again and again. Some of those questions—the clergy reserves, the seigniorial tenure, the educational policy—have passed out of politics into history; others of them, some of them arising from the rivalries of race, and some from proximity to the United States and from the conditions of business and of politics, there are still present with us, but in a modified form, and with prospects that they will disappear as our people become more numerous and our resources become developed. Great honour is due to those who in times past aided Sir John in the settlement of those questions, but his career seems to embrace all others, and his mind seems to have risen to each great struggle which came on in turn, and to have called to his aid the men who were needed to carry his projects to consummation. He was the master builder among the many who did noble work in the structure of the nation. But it is not my task to-day to give you a narrative of Sir John Macdonald's life, or even of the great events in which he took part. I have only time to recall some of these by name, and then to say a few words to you about the leading features of his personal character and career. This last seems to be the more pleasing, and is, perhaps, even the more necessary part of my duty. History will take good care to record those great events, but it may not preserve so faithfully as we could wish some of the features of Sir John's character which were best known to those who were close to him from day to day, for it is eminently true of him, as was said of a great British statesman, that 'he leaves not only the memory of great achievements, but also the tender traditions of personal affection and social charm.' In the first place, Sir John's love of Canada and his desire to serve her must be put far in the front of all his characteristics. His daily thought might be expressed in Webster's words : 'Let our object be our country, our whole country, and nothing but our country.' 'Nothing but our country' in the sense that Canada was to be first of all in every consideration of public policy or personal action. His true and deep Canadianism was the 'pillar of cloud by day, and the pillar of fire by night,' to the hundreds of thousands whom he led as no man could have led by a mere party banner. It has been well said that, as this patriotism was the mainspring of all his action, so it was the source of the wonderful command which he had over the masses of his countrymen. He came into public life a stripling, just when he was advancing on a professional career in which he might look forward to honour, ease, and wealth. He left that career at a summons which he considered the urgent call of duty. He supposed he was leaving it but for a very brief period—to meet a crisis which might be past in a year or two. I once had to consult him as to the propriety of one of our friends coming forward at an election when there was a prospect of his having to retire at the end of a single session. I asked him if he would approve of such a step, and his answer was: ' Yes, certainly. Those are the terms on which I came into public life.' Nearly fifty years went by, and the call of duty which summoned him in his youth was only superseded by the last summons that comes to man. In the next place, I must mention his wonderful devotion to the interests of the Empire. This has made him more than a Canadian statesman. It has placed him in the shrine of the Empire's heroes. When he died, the Queen knew that her wreath upon his coffin covered the breast of as faithful a servant of the Crown as ever lived within her realm of England. The thought of the unity of the Empire was bright within him when, as a youth, he carried his musket during the disturbance of 1837. It breathed in his first election address of 1844, in which he said : ' The prosperity of Canada depends upon its permanent connection with the mother country, and I shall resist to the utmost any attempt (from what-ever quarter it may come), which may tend to weaken that union.' It animated him to the close of his life ; for in the great political struggle which was the final one, he spoke of ' This, my last effort for the unity of the Empire and the preservation of our commercial and political freedom.' He endeavoured to stimulate the same feeling in other colonies, and to strengthen British connection in other parts of the Empire. The policy of uniting the provinces, of railway connection from ocean to ocean, and of steam communication on both oceans, with the mother country and with other possessions of the Crown, all went in this direction. Another feature of Sir John's character that we, who knew him best, will long delight to remember, was the great amiability and gentleness of his nature. His patience was most remarkable. We know how he was daily beset by cares and difficulties, and by the worries which unreasonableness and selfishness make some men inflict without necessity and without a thought. It sometimes seemed to us that kindness, humour, and forbearance were the only shields which he turned to such attacks. He made all possible allowance for those who tried his endurance, and, with rare magnanimity, waited, without resentment, for the second thought of those who judged his actions hastily, when a sharp reply would have been given by most men. All this in one who relished the fierce conflict of debate, who was accustomed to ask no quarter in a fight, and to deal hard blows at his adversary, helps greatly to account for his wonderful success in dominating his party, and in attaching it to himself as no party was ever attached to a leader before. Everywhere his supporters hesitated to disregard his slightest wish—not because they feared him, but because they loved him. It used to be a popular delusion that when he took a new colleague he required from him his resignation in advance. I soon found that when he took a new colleague, the new comer's relations to his chief were controlled by affection and not by command. In that tie he had all the control that he needed over those who served under him. Even if Sir John had not been a statesman of such a high order, his quality as a parliamentarian would have made him a great man. He was a parliamentarian in the true sense of the word—in the sense in which that word has been applied to some of the great men who have adorned the Parliament of Great Britain. He was a most vigorous and effective speaker. Naturally quick, clear, and intense, he was full of earnestness, which went farther to convince and persuade than eloquence generally does, and his tact and urbanity in debate and in the ' management ' of the House won for him day by day the admiration of his opponents and the unbounded confidence of his friends. How well these qualities served him can be appreciated only by those who reflect on the difficulties of parliamentary life in Canada, the difficulties arising from a tendency to split up into classes and sections in consequence of race feelings and of sectional interests. In his long parliamentary career how well justified are those words of his, uttered long before its close : ' I know that in the long career of political life I have made many mistakes, that the Government of which I am a member has, of course, made errors and been guilty of omission as well as commission; but I can honestly say that the desire was good and the motive good.'

" A false estimate of Sir John's character is formed by those who regard him as having been selfish, or even as having been actuated by mere love of power. It was truly said of him, by one who could well describe him, ' The people believed that Sir John sought the office of First Minister only that he might best minister to the country, and the people's judgment was right. It was not an office that a self-seeking man could have kept for a single session.' Sir John himself said, more than thirty years before his death, ' If a man desire peace and domestic happiness, he will find neither in performing the thankless task of a public officer.' Again, how memorable are those words, which he uttered later in a great crisis : ' I have fought the battle of Confederation, the battle of Union, the battle of the Dominion of Canada. I throw myself upon the House, I throw myself upon this country, I throw myself upon posterity, and I believe that, notwithstanding the many failings of my life, I shall have the voice of this country and this house rallying round me. And, sir, if I am mistaken in that, I can confidently appeal to a higher court—to the court of my own conscience and to the court of posterity. I leave it with this House with every confidence. I am equal to either fortune. I can see past the decision of this House, whether for or against me, but whether it be for or against me, I know, and it is no vain boast for me to say so, for even my enemies will admit that I am no boaster, that there does not exist in Canada a man who has given more of his time, more of his heart, more of his wealth, or more of his intellect and power, such as they may be, for the good of this Dominion of Canada.'

" We who know him well know that, for years before the end came, he longed for rest and retirement ere he should reach the close of his life. Day after day was filled by unceasing toil, unwearying watchfulness and painful labours at details. Night after night, when men in all other occupations were enjoying rest in their homes, he was at his work in the House of Commons, seldom leaving his place until early morning—often the last to leave, and often beginning a long and arduous effort after midnight. This was not selfishness in a man who had sacrificed wealth and honours that he might have earned, and the peace and happiness of domestic life, which he loved fully as well as any other, and for which his whole nature craved when he had reached the three score years and ten. It was not mere love of power which kept him to those daily and nightly tasks. It was devotion to a duty which became more pressing and unavoidable as years rolled by. He could be replaced when he was no more, but while his services could be had no man could replace him. On the first day when he was seized with his last illness he passed out of the House of Commons in the afternoon, and beckoned me to follow him. We went to his retiring-room, near the chamber, and, as he sank into a chair, he told me that he had been attacked by some affection of the throat. His condition was too plain to be mistaken, but I tried to cheer him by speaking of his need of rest, and of the desire of his colleagues that he should spare himself the toil of attending at each day's session. I shall never forget his words as he turned his pallid face to me and said, ' It is not that ; I am worn out.' He knew that the rest for which he had longed in vain had nearly come, but that he must meet it at the grave. No doubt he had a love of fame—' the sovereign passion of public men,'—but what public man, worthy of his calling, is without it ? In truth, unselfishness and devotion to duty are among Sir John's highest characteristics. He was ambitious in the best sense of the word. He was ambitious to infuse into the minds of his countrymen sentiments and ideas which were wider than the issues of party—ambitious to make Canada great—ambitious to silence the voice of faction and the noise of discord—ambitious to leave this country and the Empire better off for the toils and sacrifices of his life. Ladies and gentlemen, I have performed in the few minutes that were available to me, what I described at the beginning of my observations, as indeed a loving task—a loving task because we all loved, with all our hearts, the great man whose political fortunes we followed, whose political principles we believed, and whose statue stands unveiled before you to-day. But as I have spoken of this duty to you as a task of love, I must tell you that it is a task of sadness too, because in recalling him to memory the voice of affection stirs one's heart so deeply that remembrance of the past, with its personal feelings and personal affections, is almost too much for the man who has this duty to perform. But how much sadder is the task made when I recall that, though but a little over two years ago we laid his body in the tomb, this afternoon, in the city of Montreal, the grave lies open to receive his successor. When I remember that to-day we are unveiling the statue of one great public man, and at this time to-morrow we shall be laying another great public man—another great son of Canada—in his last resting-place upon this earth. The man who succeeded him was worthy to be his successor. Sir John Abbott's great qualities of brain and heart, his great qualities of statesmanship, his great abilities and great desire to serve this country will never be thoroughly understood by the Canadian people, because his career as First Minister was so short. But in remembering the services of the two, in remembering the great characteristics of the two, in remembering the great love for Canada, the great attachment to Canada, the great desire to serve Canada, of the two, and the great devotion to British connection of the two—I say it of the last as well as of the first, without fear of contradiction or carping—the great love of Canada and the great patriotism of these men, places upon us who have public duties to discharge, either in connection with the Ministry or as simple voters and electors in this country, a great responsibility which we ought to consider well this afternoon. The sight of that statue of the departed leader in your public place, and the memory of the man who succeeded him in public life as Premier of the Dominion of Canada—the memories of these, which will do honour to this country, I care not what political or personal failings they may have had, place upon us the responsibility of carrying on— you as electors, us as public men—the task which they laid before them, and in the execution of which they strove with the genius of master hands, guided by the inspiration of heaven which falls upon truly patriotic men. I thank you, citizens of Hamilton, for the noble work which you have done in erecting the first statue to Sir John Macdonald. Addressing this vast assemblage which is here to see that statue unveiled, I beseech you that you will learn by looking upon that figure the lessons which he whom it repre- sents desired that his countrymen should learn and should practise : devotion to the interests of Canada our country, and the determination that the banner of England shall continue to wave over this country as long as time shall last. How fortunate should we be, how fortunate would any man be, could he leave as his immediate successor did, 'not only the record of great achievements, but the traditions of personal affection, and of social charm.' Whether this may be our reward or not, let us steadfastly pursue in the future of this country the principles of the great men whom I have mentioned, and, in the words of Lord Rosebery, in unveiling the bust to the late Sir John Macdonald in the cathedral of St. Paul's : 'Once more remember our responsibility, and renew the resolution that, come what may, we will not flinch or fail under it.' "

APPENDIX XXXII.   (See p. 268.)

"THE undersigned, to whom was referred a communication from Doctor Hurlbert addressed to the Secretary of State on the subject of the spelling of certain English words, and also a letter from the Queen's printer in reference thereto, has the honour to report :—

"That, in his opinion, the only question with respect to the spelling of such words as 'honour,' 'favour,' 'labour,' 'honourable,' and the like is, what is the mode now accepted by the best authorities in England; it appears to him to be obvious that the same system should obtain in all portions of the British Empire.

"On a reference to the best dictionaries and encyclopædias now in use in England, it will be seen that these words are spelt with the 'u,' and that such forms as 'labor,' 'favor,' 'honor,' 'honorable,' etc., are apparently confined to the United States, with the exception of some few instances where they have been adopted in Canada.

"In consequence of this reference the undersigned has taken occasion to inquire into the mode of spelling these words in official and legislative use in England, and he has ascertained that the 'u' is in all such cases retained.

"The undersigned therefore recommends the issue of instructions to the effect that in all official documents, in the Canada *Gazette*, and in the Dominion Statutes, the English practice be uniformly followed.

"All of which is respectfully submitted.

"JOHN A. MACDONALD.

"Ottawa, May 30, 1890."

APPENDIX XXXIII.   (See p. 282.)

(See p. 282.)

"Montreal, Oct 13, 1876.

"MY DEAR BERNARD,

"I was very sorry to have missed you when in Toronto, but I only remained over for one day.

"I have no present intention of going to the West Indies. The fact is, I do not think the Government know what to do about the sugar duties, and it is idle to talk of negotiation without a fixed policy on this subject.

"I have some idea of going to England shortly, and should like much to go with you. I would in any case advise you not to put off sailing too long, or you may suffer from the cold at sea.

"I have thought for some time of writing you as a mutual friend to ascertain from Sir John the basis on which he would wish our future personal relations to stand. When in Toronto last June, I met him at Macpherson's, and he almost cut me. Of course I infer that the reference I felt obliged to make to his position in my letter to Mr. Ferrier must be the cause, and I have no hesitation in saying I am sincerely sorry, if I have wounded his feelings by the opinion I expressed on a purely public subject. He is, however, necessarily the only judge of how far my action justifies an attitude of personal estrangement, and if he considers that it does, I can only regretfully acquiesce. Will you kindly speak to him and learn his wishes? If he should unfortunately decide on the rupture of our former friendly relations, be good enough to say to him that, while I bow to his decision, it will in no respect impair or alter my own recollections of our past friendship, nor my wishes for his future welfare.

"Yours sincerely,

"A. T. GALT.

"Colonel Bernard."

"Toronto, October 23, 1876.

"MY DEAR BERNARD,

"As Sir Alexander Galt has written you with regard to the future personal relations between him and myself, I desire to state to him through you exactly how I feel in the matter. He rightly supposes that my coolness at Macpherson's was caused by the reference which he says he felt obliged to make to my position, in his letter to Mr. Ferrier. I did not then, and do not now, see that he was at all obliged by the circumstances to make any such offensive reference.

"He could have indicated his position with sufficient clearness without doing so, more especially as he had decided that that position should be one of inaction. This unnecessary attack (as I consider it) deeply pained me, coming as it did from one with whom I had so long acted and with whom I had so lately been in confidential correspondence. It aroused the unrestrained indignation of my friends, all of whom had been Sir Alexander's friends and supporters in days gone by, and some of them who had been behind the scenes reminded me that it was not thus that I had acted towards him. In 1864 I, with my colleagues, deliberately elected to fall with Sir Alexander on a motion specially directed against himself, when it was quite open to us to have taken the ground that the act complained of was the act of a former administration, for which the then existing Ministry could not constitutionally be held responsible. English precedents were placed in my hands establishing the sufficiency of that ground, and it was pressed upon me that it was unfair to those of the Government who had recently joined us to involve them in the acts of a former Cabinet. I put down, as my surviving colleagues can attest, any attempt to make Sir Alexander the scapegoat; and I took the first opportunity of preventing the point from being raised in Parliament, by declaring there that we were a band of brothers resolved to stand or fall together. Again, in 1865, I gained the undying hatred of George Brown, which has since been exhibited in every possible way, by sustaining Sir Alexander against him with respect to the Reciprocity negotiations at Washington. It had come to be a question which of the two should retire, and again I stood by Sir Alexander, when a contrary course would perhaps have smoothed my path in Ontario ever since.

"I must confess I was quite unprepared for the letter in question, and the more so that Sir A. had then recently both personally and by letter expressed to me his regret at the loss the Conservative party of Quebec had sustained of a leader by the death of poor Sir George Cartier.

"Now Cartier was the person with whom Sir Hugh Allan had primarily and principally to do, and was, to say the least of it, as liable to Sir Alexander's censure and to political ostracism as myself. I have heard Sir Alexander's attack on me truly described as 'spitting on Cartier's grave,' and I cannot help thinking that if he had been alive the attack on me would not have been written. But enough of this—*liberavi animam meam,*—and having done so, all I desire further to say is, that if Sir Alexander pleases we can meet in friendly intercourse and in society as before. The wound may be considered as healed over, but the scar will, I fear, remain for some time.

"Yours faithfully,
"JOHN A. MACDONALD.

"H. Bernard, Esqr."

"Montreal, October 31, 1876.

"MY DEAR BERNARD,

"I was again in Toronto when yours of 23rd was sent here, so did not get it in due course.

"I am deeply obliged by your having obtained from Sir John the frank statement of his views which you inclose. Though much pained by his reproaches, which I think are undeserved, still I feel that it would be unprofitable to discuss their propriety, and still more unsuited to my present object, to revert to matters in which I have, in the past, felt aggrieved myself. The only point on which I desire to say a few words is, on his assumption that I had, in a needless and uncalled for manner, made an attack upon him as a public man. The transaction which called forth my remarks was so essentially and fully a subject for discussion, that I cannot now see how reference to it could have been avoided, and, in saying what I did, I carefully made my observations apply solely to the political bearing of the matter. The only real point, therefore, is whether I might not simply have declined to become a candidate for West Montreal without referring to the position of the two contending political parties, and on this point I will say, in explanation, that I was urged by both sides, but principally by the Liberals, to come forward, and was led into a correspondence with Holton with reference to my determination not to be their candidate, which, coupled with what passed with the other side, made it necessary, in my own opinion, and that of my friends, to state explicitly the position I occupied towards both. So far from seeking to injure Sir John, I may say that I refused to come forward at the general election, when invited by at least two Conservative counties, because, had I then done so, I would necessarily have felt obliged to take ground calculated still further to add to his difficulties. My conscience fully acquits me of all intentional wrong towards him, and I feel quite sure that he cannot seriously blame me for holding and expressing opinions adverse to his public policy, when called upon as a public man myself to declare what I thought.

" With reference to that which Sir John says about Sir George Cartier I will only say, in brief, that it has always been a mystery to me, how either of them (knowing them as I did) ever got into the position they did.

" In conclusion, I will add, that I shall be heartily glad to meet Sir John on terms of friendly intercourse once more, and trust that the present soreness between us may disappear, under the influence of a wish, I hope, on both sides, that the past should be forgotten as well as forgiven.

" I sail for England with my daughter Amy, from New York, on the 11th, by the White Star Line. My business will first take me to Scotland for a few weeks, then I go to London, and I have a vague longing to come home by the West Indies. What say you ?

" I wish you could manage to sail with me on the 11th. It would be a real pleasure for me.

" Yours sincerely,

" A. T. GALT.

" Colonel Bernard."

INDEX.

PRINTED BY WILLIAM CLOWES AND SONS, LIMITED, LONDON AND BECCLES.

37, BEDFORD STREET, STRAND,
LONDON, W.C.

SELECTIONS FROM

MR. EDWARD ARNOLD'S LIST.

THE LIFE AND LETTERS OF MARIA EDGEWORTH.

Edited by AUGUSTUS J. C. HARE, Author of "Memorials of a Quiet Life,"
"The Story of Two Noble Lives," etc. Two vols., crown 8vo., cloth.
16s. net.

THE RECOLLECTIONS OF THE DEAN OF SALISBURY.

By the Very Rev. G. D. BOYLE, Dean of Salisbury. One vol., demy 8vo.,
cloth, 16s. With Photogravure Portrait.

ALPHONSE DAUDET.
A BIOGRAPHICAL AND CRITICAL STUDY.

By ROBERT H. SHERARD, Editor of "The Memoirs of Baron Meneval," etc.
One vol., demy 8vo., cloth, 15s.

SELECT ESSAYS OF SAINTE BEUVE,
CHIEFLY BEARING ON ENGLISH LITERATURE.

Translated by A. J. BUTLER, Translator of "The Memoirs of Baron Marbot,"
and late Fellow of Trinity College, Cambridge. One vol., 8vo., cloth, 5s. net.

WORKS BY THE DEAN OF ROCHESTER.
(THE VERY REV. S. REYNOLDS HOLE.)

MORE MEMORIES:

Being Thoughts upon England spoken in America.
By DEAN HOLE. One vol., demy 8vo., cloth. 16s.

The wide popularity of "The Memories of Dean Hole" ensures a cordial
welcome to this further volume of "Reminiscences," by the Dean of Rochester.
The Dean again has much that is instructive and amusing to say on many
subjects—on Art, on Sport, on Horticulture, and on matters Ecclesiastical.

A LITTLE TOUR IN IRELAND. By AN OXONIAN. With
nearly forty Illustrations by JOHN LEECH, including the famous steel
Frontispiece of the "Claddagh." Large imperial 16mo., handsomely bound,
gilt top, 10s. 6d.

**ADDRESSES TO WORKING MEN FROM PULPIT
AND PLATFORM.** One vol., crown 8vo., 6s.

THE MEMORIES OF DEAN HOLE. With the original
Illustrations from sketches by LEECH and THACKERAY. Twelfth Thousand.
One vol., crown 8vo., 6s.

A BOOK ABOUT THE GARDEN AND THE GARDENER.
With steel plate Frontispiece by JOHN LEECH. Second Edition, crown
8vo., 6s.

A BOOK ABOUT ROSES. Twentieth Thousand. Crown
8vo., cloth, 2s. 6d.

THE BRITISH MISSION TO UGANDA IN 1893.

By the late Sir GERALD PORTAL, K.C.M.G. Edited by RENNELL RODD, C.M.G. With an Introduction by the Right Hon. Lord CROMER. Illustrated from Photographs taken during the Expedition by Colonel RHODES, with a Portrait by the Marchioness of GRANBY. One vol., demy 8vo., cloth, One Guinea.

"The subject of Uganda has for the first time been made attractive to the general reader."— *Times.*

BY THE SAME AUTHOR.
MY MISSION TO ABYSSINIA.

By the late Sir GERALD H. PORTAL, C.B. With Map and Illustrations. Demy 8vo., 15s.

SEVENTY YEARS OF IRISH LIFE.

Being the Recollections of W. R. LE FANU. Third Edition, one vol., demy 8vo., 16s. With Portraits of the Author and J. SHERIDAN LE FANU.

"It will delight all readers—English and Scotch no less than Irish, Nationalists no less than Unionists, Roman Catholics no less than Orangemen."—*Times.*

Cheap Edition. Eighth Thousand.
RIDING RECOLLECTIONS AND TURF STORIES.

By HENRY CUSTANCE, Thrice Winner of the Derby. One vol., 8vo., cloth, 2s. 6d.

"An admirable sketch of turf history during a very interesting period, well and humorously written."—*Sporting Life.*

POPULAR EDITION.
With a Prefatory Chapter on Egypt in 1894 by the Author.
ENGLAND IN EGYPT.

By ALFRED MILNER, Formerly Under-Secretary for Finance in Egypt. Fifth Edition. Large crown 8vo., with Map, cloth, 7s. 6d.

"An admirable book which should be read by those who have at heart the honour of England." — *Times.*

"No journalist or public man ought to be permitted to write or speak about Egypt for the next five years unless he can solemnly declare that he had read it from cover to cover."—*Daily Chronicle.*

WILD FLOWERS IN ART AND NATURE.

By J. C. L. SPARKES, Principal of the National Art Training School, South Kensington, and F. W. BURBIDGE, Curator of the University Botanical Gardens, Dublin. With twenty-one beautiful Coloured Plates of Flowers from water-colours specially drawn for the work by Mr. H. G. MOON. In a handsome binding specially designed by Sir JOHN STIRLING MAXWELL, Bart. One vol., royal quarto, cloth, gilt edges, 21s. This splendid volume was issued in six parts during the year 1894.

COMMON-SENSE COOKERY

For English Households, based upon Modern English and Continental Principles, with Menus for Little Dinners worked out in Detail. By A. KENNEY HERBERT ("Wyvern"), Don of the Order of the Cordon-Rouge, and Author of "Fifty Breakfasts," etc. One vol., large crown 8vo., cloth, 7s. 6d.

BY THE SAME AUTHOR.
FIFTY BREAKFASTS.

Containing a great variety of new and simple Recipes for Breakfast Dishes. By Colonel KENNEY HERBERT ("Wyvern"), Author of "Culinary Jottings," etc. Small 8vo., cloth, 2s. 6d.

LONDON: EDWARD ARNOLD, 37, BEDFORD STREET, STRAND, W.C.
𝔓ublisher to the 𝔦ndia 𝔒ffice.

Mr. EDWARD ARNOLD'S

AUTUMN LIST OF

𝔑𝔢𝔴 *AND* 𝔉𝔬𝔯𝔱𝔥𝔠𝔬𝔪𝔦𝔫𝔤 𝔅𝔬𝔬𝔨𝔰

AND EDITIONS.

1894.

MEMOIR OF THE RIGHT HONOURABLE SIR JOHN ALEXANDER MACDONALD, G.C.B.,

First Prime Minister of the Dominion of Canada.

By JOSEPH POPE.

With an Introduction by the Baroness MACDONALD of Earnscliffe.

Two vols., demy 8vo., cloth, 32s.

With two Portraits of Sir JOHN A. MACDONALD.

These two volumes contain the authoritative record of Sir John Macdonald's life. Mr. Joseph Pope, the eminent Canadian barrister, who was present for the Dominion of Canada at the Behring Sea Arbitration, was for many years private secretary to, and an intimate friend of, Sir John Macdonald ; and it was in accordance with Sir John's own directions that Lady·Macdonald requested Mr. Pope to undertake the work of writing her husband's life, and put at his disposal a large collection of letters and papers which Sir John had carefully preserved. Mr. Pope has made free use of this correspondence, and some valuable appendices accompany each volume. A study of the life and policy of Sir John Macdonald, who for some forty years was the predominant influence in Colonial politics, and to whose genius the Dominion of Canada is in the main due, is essential to anyone who desires to be conversant with the affairs and history of Greater Britain, and these Memoirs—a faithful and authoritative record of the political and private life of the ' Colonial Beaconsfield '—may fairly claim to be the most important work on Colonial politics hitherto published.

LONDON :

EDWARD ARNOLD, 37 BEDFORD STREET, STRAND.

𝔓𝔲𝔟𝔩𝔦𝔰𝔥𝔢𝔯 𝔱𝔬 𝔱𝔥𝔢 𝔈𝔫𝔡𝔦𝔞 𝔒𝔣𝔣𝔦𝔠𝔢.

MEMOIR OF MARIA EDGEWORTH,

With a Selection from Her Letters by Mrs. Edgeworth.

Edited by AUGUSTUS J. C. HARE,

Author of ' Memorials of a Quiet Life,' ' The Story of Two Noble Lives,' ' Walks in Rome,' etc.

Two vols., crown 8vo., cloth, 16s. net.

This Memoir of Maria Edgeworth, by her step-mother, Mrs. Edgeworth, was privately printed in 1867, but is now published, by the kind permission of the Edgeworth family, for the first time. The letters of Maria Edgeworth, which form the greater part of this work, are full of literary and human interest, and many of them are of great historical value. The talented author of ' Belinda,' ' Castle Rackrent,' ' Moral Tales,' etc., was residing in Paris, 1802-3, during Buonaparte's consulship. In Paris, through her relationship with Abbé Edgeworth, Louis XVI.'s confessor, Maria Edgeworth came in contact with the most celebrated French people of the time, and gives in her letters a vivid description of their conversation and manners. Again in 1820 she stayed for some months in France, moving in the best society of the monarchy, and gives anecdotes of Necker, Madame de Staël, Madame Recamier, Dumont, Madame de Genlis, Duc de Broglie, and of other leading characters whom she met during her visit. Miss Edgeworth was intimate with most of the literary celebrities of the day in England. She visited, or received at Edgeworthstown, Sir Walter Scott, Lockhart, Sir James Macintosh, Lord Lansdowne, Lady Byron, Joanna Baillie, Hallam, Luttrell, Mrs. Barbauld, and her sketches of their conversation and life are bright and full of interest. The pictures of Irish life during the period have also their historical value ; she was at Edgeworthstown during the rising of '98, and had to fly with her father from the house. These volumes are edited by Mr. Augustus Hare, who also contributes a Preface to the work. While omitting any letters and other material of a personal nature which have ceased to be of interest, Mr. Hare has carefully preserved in these volumes all that is of value in the original Memoir.

THE RECOLLECTIONS OF THE DEAN OF SALISBURY.

By the Very Rev. G. D. BOYLE, Dean of Salisbury.

One vol., demy 8vo., cloth, 16s.

With Photogravure Portrait.

The Recollections of Dean Boyle cover a period of over sixty years. His father, who was Lord Justice General of Scotland, was an intimate friend of Sir Walter Scott and of the brilliant set of literary men who then resided in Edinburgh. In this volume many anecdotes are related of Sir Walter Scott and his friend Lockhart, Dr. Chalmers, Dean Ramsay, De Quincey, Professor Wilson, Jeffrey, with all of whom the Dean was brought in contact as a lad in Edinburgh. In England the talents of Dean Boyle soon brought him the notice and acquaintanceship of most of the more brilliant men of the last generation, and into close intimacy with Dean Stanley, Thackeray, and the best of his contemporaries. This volume will prove of interest not only to that wide class of general readers who like to learn at first hand the characteristics and conversation of the men whose names are familiar to them in politics and literature, but to those who value literary criticism, and the opinions of a man of talent and learning and close observation on the various social and ecclesiastical movements of the time.

LIFE OF ALPHONSE DAUDET.

By ROBERT H. SHERARD,

Editor of ' The Memoirs of Baron Meneval,' etc.

One vol., demy 8vo., cloth, 15s.

Mr. Sherard is fortunate in being well acquainted with M. Alphonse Daudet, the most popular of French novelists. A resident in Paris, a master of the French language, a friend of Alphonse Daudet, Mr. Sherard has every qualification to fulfil the task he has undertaken, to make English readers acquainted with the life and character of the brilliant author of 'Tartarin.'

MORE MEMORIES.

Being Thoughts upon England Spoken in America.

By DEAN HOLE.

One vol., demy 8vo , cloth, 16s.

The wide popularity of 'The Memories of Dean Hole' ensures a cordial welcome to this further volume of Reminiscences by the Dean of Rochester. The Dean again has much that is instructive and amusing to say on many subjects—on Art, on Sport, on Horticulture, and on matters Ecclesiastical. The material from which this book is formed has been collected by the Dean of Rochester for a series of Lectures in America in aid of the restoration of Rochester Cathedral, but every care has been taken that this shall not detract from the readable character of the book, in which Dean Hole treats, with the same light but pungent pen as before, of things grave and gay, past and present.

BY THE SAME AUTHOR.

A LITTLE TOUR IN IRELAND. By AN OXONIAN. With nearly forty Illustrations by JOHN LEECH, including the famous steel Frontispiece of the 'Claddagh.' Large imperial 16mo., handsomely bound, gilt top, 10s. 6d.

ADDRESSES TO WORKING MEN FROM PULPIT AND PLATFORM. One vol., crown 8vo., 6s.

Twelfth Thousand.

THE MEMORIES OF DEAN HOLE. With the original Illustrations from sketches by LEECH and THACKERAY. One vol., crown 8vo., 6s.

A BOOK ABOUT THE GARDEN AND THE GARDENER. With steel plate Frontispiece by JOHN LEECH. Second Edition, crown 8vo., 6s.

Twentieth Thousand.

A BOOK ABOUT ROSES. Crown 8vo., cloth, 2s. 6d.

COMMON-SENSE COOKERY

For English Households, Based upon Modern English and Continental Principles, with Menus for Little Dinners worked out in Detail.

By A. KENNEY HERBERT ('WYVERN'),

Don of the Order of the Cordon-Rouge, and Author of 'Fifty Breakfasts,' etc.

One vol., large crown 8vo., cloth, 7s. 6d.

Colonel Kenney Herbert, the Director of the Common-sense School of Cookery, has written in this volume a standard work on Cookery and the Management of the kitchen. The chapters of this book include 'To Housekeepers,' 'Kitchen Requisites,' 'The Menu,' 'On Roughing it,' etc., and chapters dealing with Soups, Sauces, Fish, Entrées, Braising and Roasting, Boiling, Vegetables, Game, Réchauffés, Fritters, Luncheons, Salads, Eggs, Macaroni and Rice, Toasts, Hors d'Œuvres and Savouries, Pastry, Pies, Curries. A complete and careful index concludes the volume.

BY THE SAME AUTHOR.

FIFTY BREAKFASTS. Containing a great variety of new and simple Recipes for Breakfast Dishes. By Colonel KENNEY HERBERT ('Wyvern'), Author of 'Culinary Jottings,' etc. Small 8vo., cloth, 2s. 6d.

'Colonel Herbert's book is one of the best of its kind, for it is thoroughly practical from beginning to end.'—*Speaker.*

'All who know the culinary works of "Wyvern" are aware that they combine a remarkable conviction and excellent taste with an exceptional practicalness and precision in detail. His "Fifty Breakfasts" will well sustain this reputation.'—*Saturday Review.*

'Distinctly it is a book to be read and studied.'—*Pall Mall Gazette.*

'Excellent from beginning to end, and should be in the hands of every cook in the kingdom.'—*The Hotel.*

SELECT ESSAYS OF SAINTE BEUVE,

Chiefly Bearing on English Literature.

Translated by A. J. BUTLER,

Translator of ' The Memoirs of Baron Marbot,' and late Fellow of Trinity College, Cambridge.

One vol., 8vo., cloth, 5s. net.

The literary criticisms of Sainte Beuve are acknowledged to be unequalled in delicacy and authority. The object of this volume is to collect the essays which bear upon English Literature, and also the references to English writers which are scattered through the works of Sainte Beuve. Mr. Butler's name is sufficient security that the translation is above reproach. The essay ' Qu'est-ce qu'un Classique ?' is included.

THE DRAUGHTS POCKET-MANUAL.

By J. GAVIN CUNNINGHAM,

Editor of ' Boy's ' " Chess and Draughts Corner," etc.

Small 8vo., cloth, 2s. 6d.

A complete handy guide to the rules and best methods of play for beginners and students. A large number of carefully selected games are given ; and the English, Italian, Spanish, Polish, and Turkish forms of the game of draughts are explained and illustrated.

A Companion Volume to the Chess Pocket-Manual.

A COMPANION VOLUME TO THE ABOVE.

THE CHESS POCKET-MANUAL. By G. H. D. GOSSIP,

Author of ' Theory of the Chess Openings,' etc. Small 8vo., cloth, 2s. 6d.

' Combines brevity with fulness perhaps more successfully than any similar work to be had.'—*Pall Mall Gazette.*

' Useful alike to the novice and the master.'—*World.*

' Well fitted to serve as a manual of reference.'—*Athenæum.*

' At a pinch it will tuck into the waistcoat pocket, and its information is neither too much nor too little to be mastered by anyone who lays himself out to be a good player.'—*Saturday Review.*

' The gambits and openings are very clearly put, and withal succinctly, but perhaps the best part of a really useful book is the pages devoted to ends of games.'—*Chronicle.*

THREE NEW STORIES OF ROMANCE AND ADVENTURE FOR BOYS.

A Romantic Tale of Crown and People.

THE DOUBLE EMPEROR.

A Story of a Vagabond Cunarder.

By W. LAIRD CLOWES,

Author of ' The Great Peril,' etc.

With Illustrations by FRED. T. JANE.

Handsomely bound. One vol., cloth, 8vo., 3s. 6d.

A Stirring Narrative of Strange Adventure.

SWALLOWED BY AN EARTHQUAKE.

By E. D. FAWCETT,

Author of ' Hartmann the Anarchist.'

With Illustrations by H. SEPPINGS WRIGHT.

Handsomely bound. One vol., cloth, 8vo., 3s. 6d.

An Exciting Story of Travel and Incident.

THE GOLDEN REEF.

A Story of the South Seas.

By MAURICE H. HERVEY,

Author of ' Dark Days in Chile.'

With numerous Illustrations. One vol., cloth, 8vo., 5s.

BAREROCK ; or, The Island of Pearls. A Book of Adventure for Boys. By HENRY NASH. With numerous full-page and other Illustrations by LANCELOT SPEED. Large crown 8vo., over 400 pages, handsomely bound, gilt edges, 5s.

'A book vastly to our taste—a book to charm all boys, and renew the boy in all who have ever been boys. There are all kinds of delights—a shipwreck, a desert island, a Crusoe-like life enjoyed by two boys, a "surprise party" of savages, and a wonderful coil of exciting incidents among West African blacks.'—*Saturday Review.*

WILD FLOWERS IN ART AND NATURE.

By J. C. L. SPARKES,

Principal of the National Art Training School, South Kensington, and

F. W. BURBIDGE,

Curator of the University Botanical Gardens, Dublin.

With 21 beautiful Coloured Plates of Flowers from water-colours specially drawn for the work by Mr. H. G. MOON.

In a handsome binding specially designed by Sir JOHN STIRLING MAXWELL, Bart.

One vol., royal quarto, cloth, gilt edges, One Guinea.

This splendid volume was issued in six parts during the year 1894. While the parts were being issued the following appreciative notices, among many others, appeared in the Press :

'The lithographic representations of these flowers (in Part I.) in colour are very successful, and the work promises to be an attractive as well as useful one.'—*Field*.

'Part II. of this handsome publication lies before us, and we have nothing for it but praise. The letterpress is excellent, and drawings, in colour, by H. G. Moon, are admirable, and, we rejoice to add, they are printed in England. We await future numbers of the series with interest. If they are as good as the last specimen, the volume, when completed, should be widely popular.' —*Black and White*.

'May be recommended to all who love flowers, and to all who love flower-painting. . . . The illustrations are really beautiful. They are of the natural size, excellently grouped, and the colour-printing—done, we are pleased to note, in England—is exceptionally good. There will be six parts, and we cannot doubt that they will command, as they certainly deserve, a very large sale.'— *Guardian*.

' A really delightful and instructive study of art and natural history combined. Nothing appears to have been spared that can contribute towards making this work as perfect as it is possible to make it. . . . The plates are justly described as a triumph of British colour-printing.'—*School Board Chronicle*.

' A happy combination of literary and artistic beauty of a very high order.'— *Schoolmaster*.

' A daintier present than this book when complete, at the moderate price of one guinea, comprising as it does science, poetry and art, it would be difficult to imagine.'—*Hearth and Home*.

' In point of technique, absolute faithfulness in drawing and colour-reproduction, these prints are the finest of the kind probably ever produced at the price.'—*Yorkshire Post*.

' To judge by the part before us, so artistic a volume on the subject has never appeared before.'—*Morning Post*.

WINE GLASSES AND GOBLETS

Of the Sixteenth, Seventeenth, and Eighteenth Centuries.

By ALBERT HARTSHORNE.

With many full-page Plates and smaller Illustrations.

This important work is in course of preparation, and will be largely illustrated with full-size plates and outline drawings, grouped and classified in such a manner that the owner of an antique glass or goblet will be able at once to ascertain its nationality and date.

DIANA'S LOOKING-GLASS, AND OTHER POEMS.

By CANON BELL, D.D.,

Rector of Cheltenham and Honorary Canon of Carlisle.

Crown 8vo., cloth, 5s. net.

BY THE SAME AUTHOR.

POEMS OLD AND NEW. Crown 8vo., cloth, 7s. 6d.

'Canon Bell's place among the poets will, we feel sure, be finally settled by this volume. In the amount of his workmanship, in the variety of it, and in the excellence of it, he makes a claim which will hardly be disputed for a place, not simply among occasional writers of poetry, but distinctly for a place among the poets.'—*The Record*.

THE NAME ABOVE EVERY NAME, and Other Sermons.
Crown 8vo.; cloth, 5s.

'A series of sermons which will prove a model of excellence in preaching.'—*The Rock*.

WINCHESTER COLLEGE, 1393—1893. Illustrated by
HERBERT MARSHALL. With Contributions in Prose and Verse by OLD WYKEHAMISTS. Demy 4to., cloth, 25s. net. A few copies of the first edition, limited to 1,000 copies, are still to be had.

'A noble volume, compiled by old Wykehamists, and illustrated by Herbert Marshall in commemoration of the 500th anniversary of the foundation of the oldest public school in England. Lord Selborne discourses eloquently on Wykeham's place in history. . . . "Wykeham's Conception of a Public School," by Dr. Fearon is most interesting : the Dean of Winchester writes of Wykeham's work in the cathedral; old traditions and customs are treated of by T. F. Kirby, the Rev. W. P. Smith, A. K. Cook, and others, while the Bishop of Salisbury contributes "Hymnus Wiccamicus," and the Bishop of Southwell, Canon Moberley and other writers supply appropriate poetry, all the verses being inspired with that intense love of his old public school which distinguishes a true Englishman.'—*Daily Telegraph*.

PLEASURABLE POULTRY KEEPING.

By EDWARD BROWN,

Lecturer to the County Councils of Northumberland, Cumberland, Hampshire, Kent, etc.

Fully Illustrated.   One vol., crown 8vo., cloth, 2s. 6d.

'This handbook is as useful as it is comprehensive.'—*Scotsman.*

'Mr. Brown has established for himself a unique position in regard to this subject, and what he has to say is not only sound counsel, but is presented in a very readable form.'—*Nottingham Daily Guardian.*

'May be commended as a safe and useful guide.'—*Leeds Mercury.*

BY THE SAME AUTHOR.

POULTRY KEEPING AS AN INDUSTRY FOR FARMERS

AND COTTAGERS. With fourteen full-page Plates by LUDLOW, and nearly fifty other Illustrations.   One vol., demy 4to., cloth, 6s.

INDUSTRIAL POULTRY KEEPING.   Paper boards, 1s.

A small handbook chiefly intended for cottagers and allotment holders.

FARM DAIRYING.

By JASPER A. STEPHENSON,

Director of Dairying to the Northumberland County Council, etc.

Fully Illustrated.   One vol., crown 8vo., cloth, 2s. 6d.

SUCCESSFUL BEE-KEEPING.

A Guide for Amateurs.

By CHARLES NETTLESHIP WHITE,

Lecturer to the County Councils of Huntingdon, Cambridgeshire, etc.

Fully Illustrated.   One vol., crown 8vo., cloth, 2s. 6d.

The Children's Favourite Series.

A charming Series of Juvenile Books, each plentifully illustrated, and written in simple language to please young readers. Special care is taken in the choice of thoroughly wholesome matter. Handsomely bound, and designed to form an attractive and entertaining Series of gift-books for presents and prizes.

PRICE TWO SHILLINGS EACH, OR GILT EDGED, HALF A CROWN.

'A charming set of books, which will rejoice the hearts of mothers, teachers, and children.'—*Child Life.*

'Prettily bound, well illustrated, edited with much good sense, and are admirable for presents.'—*Tablet.*

THREE NEW VOLUMES.

MY BOOK OF THE SEA.

A budget of Sea-Stories which have always a special fascination for the children of Britannia.

MY BOOK OF ADVENTURES.

A collection of exploits and adventures which have become famous all over the world.

MY BOOK OF TRAVEL-STORIES.

An outline of some of the most remarkable travels and explorations by great discoverers.

MY BOOK OF FAIRY TALES.

'For children of seven or eight there could not be a better fairy-book.'—*British Weekly.*

MY BOOK OF BIBLE STORIES.

'Written so that the youngest child can understand them.'—*Saturday Review.*

MY BOOK OF HISTORY TALES.

'A splendid introduction to English history.'—*Methodist Times.*

DEEDS OF GOLD.

'A first-rate book for lads and lassies is this. Children cannot but be better for reading such splendid examples of the performance of duty as those illustrated in this book.'—*Schoolmistress.*

MY BOOK OF FABLES.

A very good selection. The morals are rarely more than one line long, the type is large and clear, and the pictures are good.'—*Bookman.*

MY STORY-BOOK OF ANIMALS.

'This book will be found a favourite among the favourites.'—*The Lady.*

RHYMES FOR YOU AND ME.

It is sometimes thought that slovenly verse is good enough for children, so long as the sentiment and intention are right. The compiler of this volume does not think so; his choice is seldom at fault.'—*Spectator.*

WORKS OF FICTION.

THE MYSTERY OF THE RUE SOLY.

From the French of H. DE BALZAC, by Lady KNUTSFORD.

One vol., 8vo., cloth, 3s. 6d.

In her translation of this intensely exciting story of Balzac's, Lady Knutsford has endeavoured to preserve the style and character of the original, but, at the same time, has omitted or shortened several passages which have no direct bearing on the development of the tale, and would be now of little interest to English readers.

MISTHER O'RYAN.

An Incident in the History of a Nation.

By EDWARD McNULTY.

Small 8vo., elegantly bound, 3s. 6d.

'"Ould Paddy" and the "poor dark cratur" are as pathetic figures as any we have met with in recent romance, and would alone stamp their creator as a writer of real force and originality.'—*National Observer.*

'An extremely well-written satire of the possibilities of blarney and brag.'—*Pall Mall Gazette.*

'An Irish story of far more than ordinary ability.'—*Bookman.*

'A sad story, but full of racy Irish wit.'—*Church Times.*

'It is a book to circulate everywhere, a book which, by its pathos and its power, its simplicity and its vivid truth, will impress the mind as the logic and the reasoning of the statesman too rarely do.'—*Yorkshire Post.*

UNIFORM WITH THE ABOVE.

Sixteenth Thousand.

STEPHEN REMARX. The Story of a Venture in Ethics. By the Hon. and Rev. JAMES ADDERLEY, formerly Head of the Oxford House, and Christ Church Mission, Bethnal Green. Small 8vo., elegantly bound, 3s. 6d. Also in paper cover, 1s.

DAVE'S SWEETHEART.

By MARY GAUNT.

One vol., 8vo., cloth, 3s. 6d.

'It is interesting to watch the literature which is coming over to us from Australia, a portion of which is full of promise, but we may safely say that of all the novels that have been laid before readers in this country, "Dave's Sweetheart," in a literary point of view and as a finished production, takes a higher place than any that has yet appeared. From the opening scene to the closing page we have no hesitation in predicting that not a word will be skipped even by the most *blasé* of novel readers.'—*Spectator.*

'In every respect one of the most powerful and impressive novels of the year.'—*Daily Telegraph.*

'Essentially a strong book. The writer has a wonderfully clean way of describing the elemental facts of life, and lets her plummet line go down deep into the depths of the sea of human tears. The book is of interest down to the last line.'—*Tablet.*

'The narrative is throughout animated and rises occasionally to heights of great dramatic power, whilst the picture of life in the diggings is delineated in a way that compels admiration.'—*Weekly Sun.*

'The action is rapid and well developed, the incidents exciting, as becomes the nature of the subject, and the human interest unusually deep.'—*Morning Post.*

THIS TROUBLESOME WORLD. A Novel. By the Authors of 'The Medicine Lady,' 'Leaves from a Doctor's Diary,' etc. In three vols., crown 8vo., 31s. 6d.

THE TUTOR'S SECRET. (Le Secret du Précepteur.) Translated from the French of VICTOR CHERBULIEZ. One vol., crown 8vo., cloth, 6s.

HARTMANN THE ANARCHIST; or, The Doom of the Great City. By E. DOUGLAS FAWCETT. With sixteen full-page and numerous smaller Illustrations by F. T. JANE. One vol., crown 8vo., cloth, 3s. 6d.

LOVE-LETTERS OF A WORLDLY WOMAN. By Mrs. W. K. CLIFFORD, Author of 'Aunt Anne,' 'Mrs. Keith's Crime,' etc. One vol., crown 8vo., cloth, 2s. 6d.

THAT FIDDLER FELLOW : A Tale of St. Andrew's. By HORACE G. HUTCHINSON, Author of 'My Wife's Politics,' 'Golf,' 'Creatures of Circumstance,' etc. Crown 8vo., cloth, 2s. 6d.

TALES FROM HANS ANDERSEN.

(Second Series.)   With numerous Illustrations by E. A. LEMANN.

One vol., 4to., handsomely bound in cloth gilt, 7s. 6d.

The approval which met the first series of these Tales, illustrated by Miss E. A. Lemann, has encouraged the publisher to issue a second series, with numerous illustrations by the same talented artist.   This edition of 'Hans Andersen's Tales' is designed for the enjoyment of children and young people, and the illustrations are well qualified to appeal to their imagination.

Uniform with above.

TALES FROM HANS ANDERSEN.   (First Series.)   With nearly Forty original Illustrations by E. A. LEMANN.   One vol., 4to., handsomely bound in cloth gilt, 7s. 6d.

'Miss E. A. Lemann has entered into the spirit of these most delightful of fairy tales, and makes the book specially attractive by its dainty and descriptive illustrations.'—*Saturday Review.*

'An enchanting gift-book for young people.'—*Lady's Pictorial.*

'The prettiest and most fascinating gift-book for a child that could well be imagined.—*Educational Times.*

'A handsome prize and a welcome gift.'—*Church Times.*

BOOKS FOR THE YOUNG.

LAMB'S ADVENTURES OF ULYSSES.   With an Introduction by ANDREW LANG.   Third and Fourth Thousand.   Square 8vo., cloth, 1s. 6d.   Also the Prize Edition, gilt edges, 2s.

MEN OF MIGHT.   Studies of Great Characters.   By A. C. BENSON, M.A., and H. F. W. TATHAM, M.A., Assistant Masters at Eton College.   Crown 8vo., cloth, 3s. 6d.

THE BATTLES OF FREDERICK THE GREAT; Extracts from Carlyle's 'History of Frederick the Great.'   Edited by CYRIL RANSOME, M.A., Professor of History in the Yorkshire College, Leeds.   With a Map specially drawn for this work, Carlyle's original Battle-Plans, and Illustrations by ADOLPH MENZEL.   Cloth, imperial 16mo., 5s.

FRIENDS OF THE OLDEN TIME. By ALICE GARDNER,

Lecturer in History at Newnham College, Cambridge. Illustrated, square 8vo., 2s. 6d.

ETHICS FOR YOUNG PEOPLE. By C. C. EVERETT,

Professor of Theology in Harvard University. Crown 8vo., cloth, 2s. 6d. OUTLINE OF CONTENTS : Chaps. 1-10, Morality in General : Chaps. 11-20, Duties towards One's self ; Chaps. 21-29, Duties towards Others ; Chaps. 30-36, Helps and Hindrances.

THE CHILDREN'S DICKENS. DAVID COPPERFIELD

—THE OLD CURIOSITY SHOP—DOMBEY AND SON. Illustrated from the original plates, and abridged for the use of children by J. H. YOXALL. Square 8vo., cloth, 1s. 6d. each volume.

Also, specially bound for Prizes and Presents, with gilt edges, 2s. each.

TWILIGHT THOUGHTS—CLAUDE'S POPULAR FAIRY

STORIES. With a Preface by MATTHEW ARNOLD. Crown 8vo. cloth, 2s. 6d.

THE NINE WORLDS. Stories from Norse Mythology. By

MARY E. LITCHFIELD. Illustrated, crown 8vo., cloth, 3s.

GREAT PUBLIC SCHOOLS. ETON — HARROW — WIN-

CHESTER — RUGBY — WESTMINSTER — MARLBOROUGH — CHELTENHAM — HAILEYBURY — CLIFTON — CHARTERHOUSE. With nearly a hundred Illustrations by the best artists. One vol., large imperial 16mo., hand- somely bound, 6s. Among the contributors to this volume are Mr. Max- well Lyte, C.B. ; the Hon. Alfred Lyttleton, Dr. Montagu Butler, Mr. P. Thornton, M.P. ; Mr. Lees Knowles, M.P. ; his Honour Judge Thomas Hughes, Q.C. ; the Earl of Selborne, Mr. H. Lee Warner, Mr. G. R. Barker, Mr. A. G. Bradley, Mr. E. Scot Skirving, Rev. L. S. Milford, Mr. E. M. Oakley, Mr. Leonard Huxley, and Mr. Mowbray Morris.

L'AMARANTHE : Revue Littéraire, Artistique Illustrée.

Dédiée aux filles de France. A monthly Magazine containing original articles by the best French writers, specially intended for the perusal of young people. 1s. monthly ; annual subscription, including postage, 14s.

Cheap Edition. Eighth Thousand.

RIDING RECOLLECTIONS AND TURF STORIES.

By HENRY CUSTANCE, Thrice Winner of the Derby.

One vol., 8vo., cloth, 2s. 6d.

'An admirable sketch of turf history during a very interesting period, well and humorously written.'—*Sporting Life.*

VOLUMES OF REMINISCENCES.

SEVENTY YEARS OF IRISH LIFE. Being the Recol-
lections of W. R. LE FANU. Third Edition, one vol., demy 8vo., 16s. With Portraits of the Author and J. SHERIDAN LE FANU.

'It will delight all readers—English and Scotch no less than Irish, Nationalists no less than Unionists, Roman Catholics no less than Orangemen.'—*Times.*

RECOLLECTIONS OF LIFE AND WORK. Being the
Autobiography of LOUISA TWINING. One vol., 8vo., cloth, 15s. With Two Portraits of the Author.

'There is much to interest our readers in this autobiography. Miss Twining looks back over her work and the changes that have passed over society with the calm reflection won by long experience.'—*Guardian.*

ECHOES OF OLD COUNTY LIFE. Recollections of Sport,
Society, Politics, and Farming in the Good Old Times. By J. K. FOWLER, of Aylesbury. Second Edition, with numerous Illustrations, 8vo., 10s. 6d.

. Also a large-paper edition, of 200 copies only, 21s. net.

'A very entertaining volume of reminiscences, full of good stories.'—*Truth.*

THE MEMORIES OF DEAN HOLE. With the original
Illustrations from sketches by LEECH and THACKERAY. New Edition, twelfth thousand, one vol., crown 8vo., 6s.

'One of the most delightful collections of reminiscences that this generation has seen.' —*Daily Chronicle.*

STUDENT AND SINGER. The Reminiscences of CHARLES
SANTLEY. New Edition, crown 8vo., cloth, 6s.

'A treasury of delightful anecdote about artists, as well as of valuable pronouncements upon art.'—*Globe.*

THE BRITISH MISSION TO UGANDA IN 1893.

By the late Sir GERALD PORTAL, K.C.M.G.

Edited by RENNELL RODD, C.M.G.

With an Introduction by the Right Hon. Lord CROMER.

Illustrated from Photographs taken during the Expedition by Colonel RHODES, with a Portrait by the Marchioness of GRANBY.

One vol., demy 8vo., cloth, One Guinea.

'The subject of Uganda has for the first time been made attractive to the general reader.'—*Times.*

'In a word, his description of the expedition is one of the most deeply interesting records of East Africa ever written. The numerous illustrations in it are very well executed; and there is an excellent map of the route to, and the countries surrounding Uganda. No one who wants to understand the East African problem can afford to neglect this book.'—*Daily News.*

'For Mr. Rodd's memoir and editing there can wait nothing but the fullest gratitude. It is a valuable monograph of an expert on countries and questions vital to British interests. Even more, perhaps, than the dead diplomatist's official report, this book is at present our most valuable document for the decision of the problems of British East Africa.'—*Pall Mall Gazette.*

BY THE SAME AUTHOR.

MY MISSION TO ABYSSINIA. By the late Sir GERALD H. PORTAL, C.B. With Map and Illustrations. Demy 8vo., 15s.

WORKS BY RENNELL RODD, C.M.G.

POEMS IN MANY LANDS. Crown 8vo., cloth, 5s.

FEDA, with other Poems, chiefly Lyrical. With an Etching by HARPER PENNINGTON. Crown 8vo., cloth, 6s.

THE UNKNOWN MADONNA, and Other Poems. With a Frontispiece by W. B. RICHMOND, A.R.A. Crown 8vo., cloth, 5s.

THE VIOLET CROWN, AND SONGS OF ENGLAND. With a Frontispiece by the MARCHIONESS OF GRANBY. Crown 8vo., cloth, 5s.

THE CUSTOMS AND LORE OF MODERN GREECE. With seven full-page Illustrations by TRISTRAM ELLIS. 8vo., cloth, 8s. 6d.

POLAR GLEAMS.

An Account of a Voyage on the Yacht 'Blencathra.'

By HELEN PEEL.

With a Preface by the Marquess of DUFFERIN and AVA, and
Contributions by Captain JOSEPH WIGGINS and
FREDERICK G. JACKSON.

With Portrait and numerous Illustrations.

One vol., demy 8vo., 15s.

'As unaffected as it is entertaining.'—*Morning Post.*
'Lord Dufferin's preface is delightfully characteristic.'—*Daily Chronicle.*
'A most delightful volume.'—*Daily Telegraph.*
'Like a fresh breeze from the sea.'—*St. James's Gazette.*
'The story is told so gaily that we should have liked more of it.'—*Pall Mall Gazette.*

Volume X. of **THE ENGLISH ILLUSTRATED MAGAZINE.**
October, 1892—September, 1893. With nearly one thousand pages, and
one thousand Illustrations. Super-royal 8vo., handsomely bound, 8s.

Among the Contents of this Volume are two Complete short Novels by
BRET HARTE and ROBERT BUCHANAN. Also short Stories by GILBERT
PARKER; the Hon. EMILY LAWLESS;
Mrs. LYNN LYNTON; GEORGE GISSING; MARY GAUNT;
GRANT ALLEN, etc.

Among other Contributors to this Volume are: Rudyard Kipling; Henry
Irving; Hon. Robert Lyttelton; Norman Gale; Duchess of Rutland; His
Excellency Lord Houghton; Henry W. Lucy; Henry Holiday; Albert
Chevalier; Harry Quilter; George Augustus Sala; Marquis of Lorne, K.T.;
'A Son of the Marshes'; Mrs. Russell Barrington; Lord Ribblesdale; Hon.
and Rev. James Adderley, etc., etc.

Among the Artists who have contributed to this Volume are: Sir Frederick Leighton,
P.R.A.; G. F. Watts, R.A.; G. Bernard Partridge; Wyke Bayliss, P.S.B.A.; T. Hope
McLachlan; the late Vicat Cole, R.A.; the late Edwin Long, R.A.; G. W. Waterhouse,
A.R.A.; Walter Crane; W. Biscombe Gardner; H. Ryland, etc.

Hitherto unpublished writings by Charles Kingsley, John Ruskin, and Lord Macaulay
also appear in this volume.

PSYCHOLOGY FOR TEACHERS.

By Professor C. LLOYD MORGAN, F.G.S.,

Principal of University College, Bristol.

One vol., 8vo., cloth, 3s. 6d. net.

BY THE SAME AUTHOR.

ANIMAL LIFE AND INTELLIGENCE. With forty Illustrations and a photo-etched Frontispiece. Second Edition. Demy 8vo., cloth, 16s.

ANIMAL SKETCHES. With nearly forty Illustrations. New Edition, one vol., crown 8vo., cloth, 3s. 6d.

THE SPRINGS OF CONDUCT. Large crown 8vo., 3s. 6d.

THE JOURNAL OF MORPHOLOGY : A Journal of Animal Morphology, devoted principally to Embryological, Anatomical, and Histological subjects. Edited by C. O. WHITMAN, Professor of Biology in Clark University, U.S.A. Three numbers in a volume of 100 to 150 large 4to. pages, with numerous plates. Single numbers, 17s. 6d. ; subscription to the volume of three numbers, 45s. Volumes I. to IX. can now be obtained, and the first number of Volume X. is ready.

THE PHILOSOPHICAL REVIEW. Edited by J. G. SCHURMAN, Professor of Philosophy in Cornell University, U.S.A. Six Numbers a year. Single Numbers, 3s. 6d. ; Annual Subscription, 12s. 6d.

AMERICAN PHILOLOGICAL ASSOCIATION, TRANSACTIONS OF THE. Vols. I.—XXIV. Containing Papers by Specialists on Ancient and Modern Languages and Literature. The price of the volumes is 8s. 6d. each, except Volumes XV., XX., and XXIII., which are 12s. 6d. each. Volumes I. and II. are not sold separately. An Index of Authors and subjects to Vols. I.—XX. is issued, price 2s. 6d.

POPULAR EDITION.

With a Prefatory Chapter on Egypt in 1894 by the Author.

ENGLAND IN EGYPT.

By ALFRED MILNER,

Formerly Under-Secretary for Finance in Egypt.

Fifth Edition.   Large crown 8vo., with Map, cloth, 7s. 6d.

'An admirable book which should be read by those who have at heart the honour of England.'—*Times.*

'No journalist or public man ought to be permitted to write or speak about Egypt for the next five years unless he can solemnly declare that he had read it from cover to cover.'—*Daily Chronicle.*

THE POLITICAL VALUE OF HISTORY. By W. E. H.
LECKY, D.C.L., LL.D.   An Address delivered at the Midland Institute, reprinted with additions.   Crown 8vo., cloth, 2s. 6d.

THE CULTIVATION AND USE OF IMAGINATION. By
the Right Hon. GEORGE JOACHIM GOSCHEN.   Crown 8vo., cloth, 2s. 6d.

THE RIDDLE OF THE UNIVERSE. Being an Attempt
to determine the First Principles of Metaphysics considered as an Inquiry into the Conditions and Import of Consciousness. By EDWARD DOUGLAS FAWCETT.   One vol., demy 8vo., 14s.

LOTZE'S PHILOSOPHICAL OUTLINES. Dictated Portions
of the Latest Lectures (at Göttingen and Berlin) of Hermann Lotze. Translated and edited by GEORGE T. LADD, Professor of Philosophy in Yale College.   About 180 pages in each volume.   Crown 8vo., cloth, 4s. each.   Vol. I. Metaphysics.   Vol. II. Philosophy of Religion.   Vol. III. Practical Philosophy.   Vol. IV. Psychology.   Vol. V. Æsthetics. Vol. VI. Logic.

THE SOUL OF MAN. An Investigation of the Facts of
Physiological and Experimental Psychology.   By Dr. PAUL CARUS. With 150 illustrative cuts and diagrams.   Large crown 8vo., cloth, 12s. 6d.

HOMILIES OF SCIENCE. By Dr. PAUL CARUS, Editor of
The Open Court, Author of 'The Soul of Man.'   Large crown 8vo., cloth, 6s. 6d.

POLITICAL SCIENCE AND COMPARATIVE CONSTITU-
TIONAL LAW. By JOHN W. BURGESS, Ph.D., LL.D., Dean of the University Faculty of Political Science in Columbia College, U.S.A. In two volumes. Demy 8vo., cloth, 25s.

THE MARK IN EUROPE AND AMERICA. A Review of
the Discussion on Early Land Tenure. By ENOCH A. BRYAN, A.M., President of Vincennes University, Indiana. Crown 8vo., cloth, 4s. 6d.

HARVARD HISTORICAL MONOGRAPHS. Vol. I. The
Veto Power : Its Origin, Development, and Function in the Government of the United States. By EDWARD CAMPBELL MASON. Demy 8vo., paper, 5s. Vol. II. An Introduction to the Study of Federal Government. By ALBERT BUSHNELL HART, Ph.D. Demy 8vo., paper, 5s.

BETTERMENT. Being the Law of Special Assessment for
Benefits in America, with some observations on its adoption by the London County Council. By ARTHUR A. BAUMANN, B.A., Barrister-at-Law, formerly Member of Parliament for Peckham. Crown 8vo., cloth, 2s. 6d.

THE LAW RELATING TO SCHOOLMASTERS. A Manual
for the Use of Teachers, Parents, and Governors. By HENRY W. DISNEY, B.A., Barrister-at-Law of the Inner Temple. Crown 8vo., cloth, 2s. 6d.

SIX YEARS OF UNIONIST GOVERNMENT, 1886-1892.
By C. A. WHITMORE, M.P. Post 8vo., cloth, 2s. 6d.

'MODERN MEN' FROM THE 'NATIONAL OBSERVER.'
Literary Portraits of the most prominent men of the day. Two volumes Crown 8vo., paper, 1s. each.

A GENERAL ASTRONOMY. By CHARLES A. YOUNG, Pro-
fessor of Astronomy in the College of New Jersey, Associate of the Royal Astronomical Society, Author of *The Sun*, etc. In one vol., 550 pages, with 250 Illustrations, and supplemented with the necessary tables. Royal 8vo., half morocco, 12s. 6d.

PLANT ORGANIZATION. By R. H. WARD, Professor of
Botany in the Rensselaer Polytechnic Institute. 4to., flexible boards, 4s. This volume consists of a synoptical review of the general structure and morphology of plants, clearly drawn out according to biological principles, fully illustrated, and accompanied by a set of blank forms to be filled in as exercises by the pupils.

A HISTORICAL GEOGRAPHY. By the late Dr. MORRISON.
New edition, revised and largely rewritten by W. L. CARRIE, English Master at George Watson's College, Edinburgh. Crown 8vo., cloth, 3s. 6d.

A HISTORY OF ENGLISH METRE,
From the Earliest Times to the Present Day.
By Dr. JOHN LAWRENCE.
[In preparation.

No comprehensive view of this subject in English is at present in existence.

THE LIFE, ART, AND CHARACTERS OF SHAKESPEARE.
By HENRY N. HUDSON, LL.D., Editor of *The Harvard Shakespeare*, etc. 969 pages, in two vols., large crown 8vo., cloth, 21s.

THE HARVARD EDITION OF SHAKESPEARE'S COM-
PLETE WORKS. A fine Library Edition. By HENRY N. HUDSON, LL.D., Author of 'The Life, Art, and Characters of Shakespeare.' In twenty volumes, large crown 8vo., cloth, £6. Also in ten volumes, £5.

THE BEST ELIZABETHAN PLAYS. Edited, with an Intro-
duction, by WILLIAM R. THAYER. 612 pages, large crown 8vo., cloth, 7s. 6d.

THE DEFENSE OF POESY, otherwise known as AN
APOLOGY FOR POETRY. By Sir PHILIP SIDNEY. Edited by A. S. COOK, Professor of English Literature in Yale University. Crown 8vo., cloth, 4s. 6d.

Leigh Hunt's 'WHAT IS POETRY?' An Answer to the
Question, 'What is Poetry?' including Remarks on Versification. By LEIGH HUNT. Edited, with notes, by Professor A. S. COOK. Crown 8vo., cloth, 2s. 6d.

A DEFENCE OF POETRY. By PERCY BYSSHE SHELLEY.
Edited, with notes and introduction, by Professor A. S. COOK. Crown 8vo., cloth, 2s. 6d.

SELECTIONS IN ENGLISH PROSE FROM ELIZABETH
TO VICTORIA. Chosen and arranged by JAMES M. GARNETT, M.A., LL.D. 700 pages, large crown 8vo., cloth, 7s. 6d.

BEN JONSON'S TIMBER. Edited by Professor F. E.
SCHELLING. Crown 8vo., cloth, 4s.

THE PRACTICAL ELEMENTS OF RHETORIC. By JOHN
F. GENUNG, Ph.D., Professor of Rhetoric in Amherst College. Crown 8vo., cloth, 7s.

A HANDBOOK TO DANTE. By GIOVANNI A. SCARTAZZINI.
Translated from the Italian, with notes and additions, by THOMAS DAVIDSON, M.A. Crown 8vo., cloth, 6s.

DANTE'S ELEVEN LETTERS. Translated and Edited by
the late C. S. LATHAM. With a Preface by Professor CHARLES ELIOT NORTON. Crown 8vo., cloth, 6s.

SPANISH IDIOMS, WITH THEIR ENGLISH EQUIVA-
LENTS. Embracing nearly 10,000 phrases. By SARAH CARY BECKER and Señor FEDERICO MORA. 8vo., cloth, 10s.

THE INTERNATIONAL EDUCATION SERIES.

NEW VOLUMES.

THE EDUCATION OF THE GREEK PEOPLE.

By THOMAS DAVIDSON.

Crown 8vo., cloth.

A scholarly treatise, showing the influence of ancient Greek education on modern civilization.

SYSTEMATIC SCIENCE TEACHING.

By EDWARD G. HOWE.

Crown 8vo., cloth.

A practical work, illustrating modern laboratory methods of instruction in all branches of science.

EVOLUTION OF THE PUBLIC SCHOOL SYSTEM IN MASSACHUSETTS.

By GEORGE H. MARTIN.

Crown 8vo., cloth.

RECENT VOLUME.

THE INFANT MIND ; or, Mental Development in the Child. Translated from the German of W. PREYER, Professor of Physiology in the University of Jena. Crown 8vo., cloth, 4s. 6d.

' Noteworthy as being the first attempt made by a scientific man to initiate the average unscientific reader into the methods of psychological observation.'— *Educational Review.*

'The theoretical parts are reasonable and intelligible, and the practical suggestions are very good.'—*Pall Mall Gazette.*

'An excellent little work, which can be studied with advantage by mothers and all interested in the development of the young.'—*Leeds Mercury.*

ENGLISH EDUCATION IN THE ELEMENTARY AND SECONDARY SCHOOLS. By ISAAC SHARPLESS, LL.D., President of Haverford College, U.S.A. Crown 8vo., cloth, 4s. 6d.

EMILE ; or, A Treatise on Education. By JEAN JACQUES
ROUSSEAU. Translated and Edited by W. H. PAYNE, Ph.D., LL.D.,
President of the Peabody Normal College, U.S.A. Crown 8vo., cloth, 6s.

EDUCATION FROM A NATIONAL STANDPOINT. Translated from the French of ALFRED FOUILLÉE by W. J. GREENSTREET,
M.A., Head Master of the Marling School, Stroud. Crown 8vo., cloth,
7s. 6d.

THE MORAL INSTRUCTION OF CHILDREN. By FELIX
ADLER, President of the Ethical Society of New York. Crown 8vo.,
cloth, 6s.

THE PHILOSOPHY OF EDUCATION. By JOHANN KARL
ROSENKRANZ, Doctor of Theology and Professor of Philosophy at Königsberg. (Translated.) Crown 8vo., cloth, 6s.

A HISTORY OF EDUCATION. By Professor F. V. N.
PAINTER. Crown 8vo., 6s.

**THE VENTILATION AND WARMING OF SCHOOL
BUILDINGS.** With Plans and Diagrams. By GILBERT B. MORRISON.
Crown 8vo., 4s. 6d.

FROEBEL'S 'EDUCATION OF MAN.' Translated by
W. N. HAILMAN. Crown 8vo., 6s.

ELEMENTARY PSYCHOLOGY AND EDUCATION. By
Dr. J. BALDWIN. Illustrated, crown 8vo., 6s.

THE SENSES AND THE WILL. Forming Part I. of
'The Mind of the Child.' By W. PREYER, Professor of Physiology in the
University of Jena. (Translated.) Crown 8vo., 6s.

THE DEVELOPMENT OF THE INTELLECT. Forming
Part II. of 'The Mind of the Child.' By Professor W. PREYER. (Translated.) Crown 8vo., 6s.

HOW TO STUDY GEOGRAPHY. By FRANCIS W. PARKER.
Crown 8vo., 6s.

A HISTORY OF EDUCATION IN THE UNITED STATES.
By RICHARD A. BOONE, Professor of Pedagogy in Indiana University.
Crown 8vo., 6s.

EUROPEAN SCHOOLS ; or, What I Saw in the Schools of
Germany, France, Austria, and Switzerland. By L. R. KLEMM, Ph.D.
With numerous Illustrations. Crown 8vo., 8s. 6d.

PRACTICAL HINTS FOR TEACHERS. By GEORGE
HOWLAND, Superintendent of the Chicago Schools. Crown 8vo., 4s. 6d.

SCHOOL SUPERVISION. By J. L. PICKARD. 4s. 6d.

HIGHER EDUCATION OF WOMEN IN EUROPE.
By HELENE LANGE. 4s. 6d.

HERBART'S TEXT-BOOK IN PSYCHOLOGY. By M. K.
SMITH. 4s. 6d.

PSYCHOLOGY APPLIED TO THE ART OF TEACHING.
By Dr. J. BALDWIN. 6s.

A NEW SCHOOL HISTORY OF ENGLAND.

By C. W. OMAN, M.A.,

All Souls' College, Oxford, Author of ' Warwick the King-maker,' etc.

A History of England, from the Earliest Times to the Present Day. Fully furnished with Maps, Plans of the Principal Battle-fields, and Genealogical Tables.

Crown 8vo., cloth.

Mr. Oman's object has been to tell the story of the English nation as a whole ; he has avoided, of set purpose, the method of dealing with any portion of it apart from the rest, in the dry isolation of a separate section, and has grappled with the more difficult task of blending the various elements—political, religious, economic, etc.—that make up English history, into a single perspicuous and consecutive narrative. Mr. Oman's familiarity with the principles and details of warfare in all ages is well-known, and his accounts of campaigns and battles are none the less interesting because they are intelligible. Most schoolboys are attracted to history by its dramatic and personal side ; Mr. Oman's treatment of it appeals to this sentiment, while at the same time he introduces his readers, almost without their knowing it, to the important matters which lie behind.

ARNOLD'S SCHOOL SHAKESPEARE.

General Editor : J. CHURTON COLLINS, M.A. Assisted by special editors in the preparation of the different plays.

Crown 8vo., each Play One Shilling net.

MACBETH. By R. F. CHOLMELEY, M.A., Assistant Master at St. Paul's School.

MIDSUMMER NIGHT'S DREAM. By R. BRIMLEY JOHNSON, Editor of Jane Austen's Novels, etc.

HENRY V. By J. H. F. PEILE, M.A., Headmaster of Bury St. Edmund's School, late Assistant Master at St. Paul's School.

KING LEAR. By the Rev. D. C. TOVEY, M.A., late Assistant Master at Eton College.

THE MERCHANT OF VENICE. By C. H. GIBSON, M.A., Assistant Master at Merchant Taylor's School.

HAMLET. By W. HALL GRIFFIN, Professor of English Literature at Queen's College, London.

THE TEMPEST. By E. L. VAUGHAN, M.A., Assistant Master at Eton College.

RICHARD II. By R. BRIMLEY JOHNSON.

KING HORN.

Edited, with Introduction, Text, Notes, and Glossary, by
JOSEPH HALL, M.A.
Headmaster of the Hulme Grammar School, Manchester.

[In preparation.

THE LIBRARY OF ANGLO-SAXON POETRY.

CYNEWULF'S PHŒNIX. (*New Volume.*) Edited, with Introduction, Text, and Critical Notes, by Professor W. S. CURRELL, Ph.D., of Davidson College, N.C.

BEOWULF, AND THE FIGHT AT FINNSBURH. Edited, with Text and Glossary, by JAMES A. HARRISON and ROBERT SHARP. Third Edition, revised. Crown 8vo., cloth, 6s.

CÆDMON'S EXODUS AND DANIEL. Edited, with Introduction, Text, and Glossary, by THEODORE W. HUNT, Professor of Rhetoric and English Language in Princeton College. Revised Edition. Crown 8vo., cloth, 3s. 6d.

CYNEWULF'S ELENE. Edited with Introduction, Text, Notes, and Glossary, by CHARLES W. KENT, Professor of English in the University of Tennessee. Crown 8vo., cloth, 3s. 6d.

ANDREAS : A LEGEND OF ST. ANDREW. Edited, with Introduction, Text, and Critical Notes, by W. M. BASKERVILLE, Ph.D., (Lips.), Professor of English Language and Literature in the Vanderbilt University. 1s. 6d.

ELENE ; AND OTHER ANGLO-SAXON POEMS. Translated into English by JAMES M. GARNETT, M.A., LL.D., Professor of the English Language and Literature in the University of Virginia. 4to., cloth, 5s.

ORIENTAL LITERATURE.

OMARAH'S HISTORY OF YAMAN. The Arabic Text, edited, with a translation, by HENRY CASSELS KAY, Member of the Royal Asiatic Society. Demy 8vo., cloth, 17s. 6d. net.

LANMAN'S SANSKRIT READER. New Edition, with Vocabulary and Notes. By CHARLES ROCKWELL LANMAN, Professor of Sanskrit in Harvard College. For use in colleges and for private study. Royal 8vo., cloth, 10s. 6d. For the convenience of those who possess the old edition, the Notes are also issued separately. 5s.

HARVARD ORIENTAL SERIES. Edited, with the co-operation of various Scholars, by CHARLES ROCKWELL LANMAN, Professor of Sanskrit in the Harvard University. Vol. I.—The Jâtaka-Mâlâ ; or, Bodhisattvâvadâna-Mâlâ. By ARYA-CÛRA. Edited by Dr. HENDRIK KERN, Professor in the University of Leyden, with Preface, Text, and Various Readings. Royal 8vo., cloth, 6s. net.

Vol. II.—Kapila's Aphorisms of the Sâmkhya Philosophy, with the commentary of Vijñâna-bhiksu. Edited in the original Sanskrit by RICHARD GARBE, Professor in the University of Königsberg. [*In the press.*

A SANSKRIT PRIMER. Based on the *Leitfaden für den Elementarcursus des Sanskrit* of Professor Georg Bühler of Vienna. With Exercises and Vocabularies by EDWARD DELAVAN PERRY, Ph.D., of Columbia College, New York. 8vo., cloth, 8s.

THE RIGVEDA. The oldest literature of the Indians. By ADOLF KAEGI, Professor in the University of Zürich. Authorised translation by R. ARROWSMITH, Ph.D. 8vo., cloth, 7s. 6d.

PUBLICATIONS OF THE INDIA OFFICE AND OF THE GOVERNMENT OF INDIA.

Mr. EDWARD ARNOLD, having been appointed Publisher to the Secretary of State for India in Council, has now on sale the above publications at 37 Bedford Street, Strand, and is prepared to supply full information concerning them on application.

INDIAN GOVERNMENT MAPS.

Any of the Maps in this magnificent series can now be obtained at the shortest notice from Mr. EDWARD ARNOLD, Publisher to the India Office.

ENGLISH CLASSICS FOR THE YOUNG.

Published in America by Messrs. GINN AND CO.

ROBINSON CRUSOE. Edited by W. H. Lambert. Cloth, 2s.

ARABIAN NIGHTS (Selections). Illustrated. Boards, 2s. 6d. ; cloth, 3s.

GULLIVER'S TRAVELS. Boards, 2s. ; cloth, 2s. 6d.

VICAR OF WAKEFIELD. Boards, 2s. ; cloth, 2s. 6d.

RASSELAS, PRINCE OF ABYSSINIA. Boards, 2s. ; cloth, 2s. 6d.

LAMB'S TALES FROM SHAKESPEARE. Boards, 2s. 6d. ; cloth, 3s.

SCOTT'S TALES OF A GRANDFATHER. Boards, 2s. 6d. ; cloth, 3s.

PLUTARCH'S LIVES (Selections). Boards, 2s. 6d. ; cloth, 3s.

IRVING'S SKETCH BOOK (Selections). Boards, 2s. ; cloth, 2s. 6d.

BENJAMIN FRANKLIN'S AUTOBIOGRAPHY. Boards, 2s. 6d. ; cloth, 3s.

THE PILGRIM'S PROGRESS (Selections). Boards, 2s. ; cloth, 2s. 6d.

OLD MORTALITY. Boards, 3s. 6d. ; cloth, 4s.

IRVING'S ALHAMBRA. Boards, 2s. 6d. ; cloth, 3s.

Miss Charlotte M. Yonge, Author of ' The Heir of Redclyffe,' etc., has written Introductions to the following volumes in this series :

QUENTIN DURWARD. Boards, 2s. 6d. ; cloth, 3s.

THE TALISMAN. Boards, 3s. ; cloth, 3s. 6d.

ROB ROY. Boards, 3s. 6d. ; cloth, 4s.

GUY MANNERING. Boards, 3s. 6d. ; cloth, 4s.

IVANHOE. Boards, 3s. 6d. ; cloth, 4s.

THE NATIONAL REVIEW.

The leading Political Review.

Price 2s. 6d. monthly.

Among a few of the important articles which have appeared during 1894 are the following : *January.* 'W. H. Smith as a Colleague,' by Lord Ashbourne ; 'The Garden that I Love,' by Alfred Austin ; and articles by T. Mackay, Lady Frances Balfour, Mrs. Asquith, etc.—*February.* 'The Life of Arthur Stanley,' by Sir Mountstuart Grant-Duff, G.C.S.I.; 'Edward Stanhope,' by the Hon. St. John Brodrick, M.P.; and articles by Hugh Bell, E. J. Cook, etc.—*March.* 'Luxury,' by Leslie Stephen ; 'The Referendum,' by Prof. A. V. Dicey, Hon. George Curzon, M.P., Earl Grey, K.G. ; A Family Budget by a Family Man ; and articles by H. D. Traill, Miss Taylor, Lord Stanley of Alderley, etc.—*April.* 'Foresight and Patience,' a poem, by George Meredith ; 'The Art of Reading Books,' by the Rev. J. E. C. Welldon; 'The Matabele War,' by F. C. Selous ; and articles by Lord Lilford, T. W. Russell, M.P., George Gissing, etc.—*May.* 'The Home Rule Campaign,' by the Right Hon. J. Chamberlain, M.P. ; 'The Duties of Authors,' by Leslie Stephen ; 'Another Family Budget'; 'Eton Cricket,' by the Hon. R. H. Lyttelton ; and articles by H. O. Arnold-Forster, M.P., Sir Herbert Maxwell, Bart., M.P., etc.—*June.* 'The Attack on the Church,' by Sir Richard Webster,' Q.C., M.P. ; 'Ocean Highways,' by the Right Hon. Lord George Hamilton, M.P.; 'The Great Conspiracy,' by the Rev. Athelstan Riley ; 'Developments of Tennis,' by J. M. Heathcote.—*July.* 'The Colonies and Maritime Defence,' by the Imperial Federation Committee ; 'An Irish Landlord's Budget '; 'Harrow Cricket,' by Spencer W. Gore ; and articles by J. L. Mahon, Sir David Barbour, K.C.S.I., etc.—*August.* 'Lords and Commons,' by H. D. Traill ; 'Human Evolution,' by Francis Galton, F.R.S., and Benjamin Kidd ; 'Sleeplessness,' by A. Symons Eccles, M.B. ; and articles by T. W. Russell, M.P. ; A. C. Benson, the Author of 'A Study in Colour,' etc., etc.

THE FORUM.

The famous American Review.

1s. 3d. monthly ; annual subscription, post free, 15s.

Index to Authors.

www.ingramcontent.com/pod-product-compliance
Lightning Source LLC
Chambersburg PA
CBHW030818110726
47900CB00006B/1659